Shadows of Change

Zora Stone

Print ISBN: 978-1-971405-00-1

Published by Smut by Design

www.zorastone.com

To Chloe & Chase. This is proof you can do anything you put your mind to.

CONTENTS

TRIGGER WARNINGS

Shadows of Change contains elements that may disturb some readers. Please be aware of the following:

Heat Level: Medium

- Slow burn romance, sexual tension and chemistry

- Kissing and moderate sensual content

- No explicit sexual content (yet)

Violence/Action:

- Magical combat and battles

- Minor injuries and blood

- Fantasy violence

- Non-graphic descriptions of past trauma

Emotional Themes:

- Loss of parents (backstory)

- Abandonment and trust issues

- Betrayal

- Processing grief

- Self-doubt and anxiety

Relationships:

- Polyamorous elements and multiple love interests

- Complex relationship dynamics

- Found family

- Strong friendships

General Content:

- Mild language

- References to alcohol

- Fantasy magic and supernatural elements

- Academic rivalry and bullying

Shadows of Change balances darker themes with hope, humor and healing. While it touches on serious subjects, it maintains an overall tone of empowerment and growth.

Questions? Contact me at ZoraStone.com

PROLOGUE

Kaia, Age Six

Golden light dances through Mama's wings, and I want to catch it in my hands, hold it forever. That's what happiness looks like—Mama's wings in sunlight, Papa's laugh rumbling through the meadow, and the soul-wisps spinning their silver stories around us. Our sanctuary feels like one big hug, warm and safe and perfect.

"Take that, evil creature!" I slash my wooden sword through the air, almost tripping over my own feet. A soul echo—that's what Mama calls them—twirls around my blade like a friend wanting to play. They're everywhere in our sanctuary, the spirits of Valkyries past, watching over us. Sometimes, when I can't sleep, they sing songs with no words, and I pretend they're all my aunts and grandmas keeping me safe.

Mama stands at the edge of the meadow, her wings shimmering like starlight caught in rain. The purple stone at her throat—the Heart of Eternity—pulses softly, matching the rhythm of the wards that protect our home. She always touches it when she thinks I'm not looking, like she's making sure it's still there.

"Careful, little warrior." Papa catches me before I can tumble into the flowers, his hands warm and strong. He smells like sunshine and metal, like the sword that hangs at his side. "Even the fiercest Valkyries must learn balance first."

"But I am fierce!" I swing my sword again, and the soul-wisps dance with me, weaving patterns that sparkle in the evening light. "See? The ancestors think so too!"

Mama's smile wavers—proud but worried. "They watch over you, little one. The souls of our sisters have guarded us since the beginning, before Alekir's betrayal changed everything."

"Who's Alekir?" I ask, but the question dies in my throat as something changes.

The soul-wisps flutter nervously, drawing closer to the ground. Mama's hand drifts to the Heart of Eternity, like she always does when something's wrong. The golden wards protecting our home flicker, just for a moment.

"Idris." Mama's voice sounds strange, tight in a way I've never heard. "Get her inside. Now."

But it's too late.

The wards shatter like golden glass, and darkness floods through—horrible, twisting shapes like skeletons made of smoke. Their eyes burn with hungry emptiness, and the air turns cold where they pass.

"Nightwraiths," Papa whispers, drawing his light-blade. "Solveig, he's actually done it. Alekir's turned them all."

Everything explodes into chaos. Mama's wings blaze brighter than I've ever seen, like she's pulled down stars to fight with. The Heart of Eternity burns violet against her throat. Papa's sword cuts rivers of light through the darkness, but more Nightwraiths pour through with every slice.

Other Valkyries soar from our home to help, their wings painting the sky in streams of color. But one by one, they fall. The soul-wisps try to shield them, to shield me, but the Nightwraiths devour them like smoke swallowing light.

I hide behind a fallen pillar, tears burning my eyes as I watch my home crumble. "Mama!" I scream as a Nightwraith's claws catch her wing. Silver blood rains down like falling tears.

Mama looks at me, and something in her face breaks. She tears the Heart of Eternity from her throat, the chain snapping with a sound like crying bells.

"Idris, cover me!" Her voice cracks. "The temporal wards—they're our only chance!"

Papa appears in a flash of light, his blade cutting through three Nightwraiths at once. "The time magic is unstable—"

"It's the only way." Mama presses the necklace into my hands. It burns hot, like holding a piece of the sun. "My brave one." Mama's hands tremble as she presses the necklace into mine. Her tears fall like stars, turning to light before they hit the ground, and each one feels like goodbye.

"You carry our light," she whispers, and her voice breaks in a way that makes my chest hurt. "You carry all our love, all our hope." She touches my cheek one last time, and her hand feels like home. "Remember that you were so, so loved, my darling. Remember that you were our greatest joy."

The necklace glows against my palm, matching my heartbeat as Mama's hands dance through the air. She whispers words that make my ears ring and the world wobble sideways.

"No!" I try to grab her, but reality stretches like taffy around me. Everything feels wrong, like I'm being pulled through water that's too thick. "Mama, please!"

"Live," she whispers as the world warps and twists. "Live for us, my darling. Find your way back when it's safe."

The last thing I see is Mama and Papa standing together against the darkness, glowing like the last stars in the universe as the Nightwraiths close in. Papa's sword flashes once more, a desperate arc of light. The Heart's violet glow flares in my palm, and everything goes dark.

***

I fall through endless nothing. My head feels stuffed with cotton, memories slipping away like water through my fingers. I try to picture Mama's face, but it's already going blurry. Something about light and a stone and—no, I can't remember. All that's left is an empty ache where the memories should be.

When I open my eyes, I'm under a strange tree in a forest I don't know. The necklace is warm in my hand, but its light has dimmed to a soft glow. The shadows here move differently than the soul-wisps did—deeper, stranger, but somehow familiar.

I curl under the strange tree, holding the necklace so tight it hurts. Everything feels wrong—the air, the ground, even the shadows that move like spilled ink around me. I try to remember Mama's face, but it's like trying to hold onto a dream. The harder I reach for the memory, the faster it fades, until all that's left is the feeling of missing something so big it has its own heartbeat.

The shadows whisper around me, not like the soul-wisps that sang lullabies, but like something wild learning to be gentle. They try to touch me, to make me feel better, but they don't know how. They're clumsy and strange and somehow that makes me cry harder—because they're trying so hard to help, and I'm so, so alone.

Then one shadow moves differently. I watch through tears as it takes shape: first four tiny paws, then ears that twitch with curiosity, finally a tail that curls like a question mark. A baby panther with eyes exactly like mine, glowing soft purple in the dark. He pads closer with such care, like he's afraid I'll break.

"Who..." My voice catches on a sob. Everything else is floating away, but this moment feels solid. Real. "Who are you?"

The shadow-cat pushes his head under my hand and starts to purr. The sound vibrates through me, steady as a heartbeat, strong as a promise. *I'll protect you*, he seems to say. *You're not alone anymore*. Never again.

I know three things with absolute certainty: something precious and beautiful is missing, leaving a hole big enough to swallow my heart; I'm lost in a place where nothing feels right; and this shadow-cat will never, ever leave me.

Chapter 1
KAIA

Present, Age Twenty-three

The shadows are restless today, coiling around my ankles like anxious cats as I weave between the cramped tables of Joey's All-Night Café. My regulars don't know it, but this greasy spoon is protected by the world's most dramatic security system. Three plates of congealed eggs balance on my arm while my shadows flick at napkins and nudge at coffee cups, determined to make my job harder than it already is.

Joey hired me two years ago after Mouse caught a rat in the kitchen. 'A cat with actual work ethic,' he'd said, not realizing Mouse was anything more than a stray who'd followed me in. The health inspector wasn't thrilled, but Joey insisted Mouse was part of the 'authentic diner experience.'

The rat never came back.

"Order up for table six!" Joey bellows from the kitchen. His voice bounces off the grease-stained walls, mixing with the clatter of silverware and the death rattle of the ancient coffee maker.

I bite back both a sigh and the urge to scold my shadows out loud. Normal people don't talk to their shadows. Normal people don't have shadows that move independently at all. But I gave up on normal somewhere between losing my parents and gaining a collection of clingy darkness that refuses to behave.

The morning rush hits like a tidal wave. The door chimes every few minutes, bringing in the usual mix of bleary-eyed office workers and construction crews fresh off the night shift. Their shadows—the ordinary, well-behaved kind—stretch across the checkered linoleum. Mine twitch with interest, teasing and blending with others, though no one ever notices the way their darkness subtly stirs when mine touches it.

"Can I get a refill, sweetheart?" A middle-aged man waves his empty mug at me. His suit's seen better decades, his tie boasts an impressive collection of coffee stains, and his smile has all the warmth of week-old toast.

"Coming right up." I paste on my best customer service smile—the one that says both I totally don't hate this job and please tip well enough that I can make rent this month.

Sixteen years in this world, and I still don't fit. Not in the noisy diner where the coffee machine screams like banshees, not in the city that smells like hot asphalt and desperation. And definitely not among these humans who can't see the shadows clinging to my heels like lost puppies.

As I pour his coffee, my shadows dart beneath his chair, making him shiver. He glances around, confused, and I mentally beg them to behave. They retreat, but I can feel their sulky presence like a toddler denied their favorite toy.

"Thanks, hon," he mutters, shaking off the odd moment. I move on to the next table, a group of construction workers debating the finer points of last night's game.

"Kaia, more coffee here!" one of them says, tapping his empty cup. I grab the pot and top off their mugs, catching snippets of their banter. As I turn away, one shadow snakes out to nudge a dollar bill off the table. I grab it mid-air and slap it back down before anyone notices. Not helpful, I think toward them, but they just flutter smugly around my ankles.

Mouse watches from his perch on the windowsill, violet eyes tracking my movement across the diner. To most, Mouse is just a black cat—when they notice him at all. The regulars have gotten used to him, though a few still mutter about health codes. But I know better. He's been my constant companion since the night everything changed, though those memories are as hazy as his current form suggests.

The weight of the amethyst necklace against my collarbone reminds me of those gaps in my memory. It's the only thing I have left from before Mouse and I woke up alone in a world that made no sense. Sometimes I catch my reflection in the diner's chrome surfaces, and the stone seems to shimmer faintly, like it holds secrets I can't access. Its presence is a constant reminder of what I've lost—and what I don't understand.

"Kaia!" Joey's voice snaps me back to reality. "Table three's been waiting five minutes for their check!"

I scramble to print out their bill, but my shadows get there first, sliding the receipt book from the counter into my hands. "Thanks," I mutter under my breath, then catch myself. Great. Now I'm thanking them.

The morning drags on in a blur of coffee refills and forced smiles. A kid in a booth by the window drops his syrup-covered fork, and my shadows dart out, catching it before it hits the ground. His mother blinks in confusion when I hand it back, probably wondering how I moved so fast. If she notices the flicker of movement around her son's feet, she doesn't mention it.

At one point, they even smooth the edge of a wobbling table as I pass by. The couple seated there exchange baffled glances, and I make a show of adjusting the napkin dispenser to cover for them. Shadows with an odd streak of helpfulness—who knew?

These small slips are happening more often lately. The shadows are bolder and harder to control. Even Mouse seems on edge, his ears constantly swiveling toward the door like he's waiting for something. Or someone.

Finally, mercifully, my shift ends. I hang up my apron, counting the meager tips in my pocket. Another day, another barely-enough paycheck. The necklace feels heavier than usual, and my shadows twist around my wrists like bracelets made of smoke.

"See you tomorrow, Kaia," Joey calls as I head for the door. "Try not to be late this time."

I wave without turning around, more than ready to get out of here. My shadows curl closer in their version of a hug like they somehow know just how I'm feeling. Mouse hops down from his window and pads along beside me, his tail held high like he's proud of surviving another shift without causing chaos.

That makes one of us.

My shadows stretch along the pavement, restless and alive. Mouse's fur bristles slightly, and he keeps pace with me instead of running ahead like usual. A sense of unease settles in my stomach, as dark and heavy as the shadows themselves.

Sometimes I really wish he could talk. It would make life so much easier.

The neighborhood is quiet, just the opposite of me. A cool breeze brushes my cheek, carrying a faint smell of rain. For a moment, it's like I'm back on the streets, huddling under a tattered blanket after being kicked out for the first time...

Even as a kid, my shadows made noise—not the kind you hear, but the kind you feel. The kind that makes people shiver and cross the street when they see you coming without really knowing why.

I learned to shrink, to make myself smaller, but the shadows? They never got the memo. One night, when I was about seven, my foster brother screamed when he saw something move. Not that he could see my shadows, but he could definitely see his stuffy inching toward the edge of his bed. I froze, unsure what to do. I hadn't moved it, but my shadows had—and it terrified me just as much as him.

His mother came running in, and I'll never forget the way her face twisted in fear as she listened to her son. As he convinced her wasn't making it up. I didn't understand at the time what I'd done wrong.

Then came the anger.

"You're cursed," she hissed, pointing to the door like she couldn't stand to be near me. "Get out!"

So I did. It was the first of many nights I spent on the streets.

I spent the next ten years bouncing between homes, each one more eager than the last to be rid of the weird girl with the "overactive imagination." No one ever saw the shadows directly—just their effects. A book sliding off a shelf. A door closing without wind. Little things that added up to too much strange.

Foster families had tried to help, but what could they do with a cursed girl? My shadows didn't care about boundaries. They slithered into bedrooms at night, knocking over picture frames and spilling secrets. I learned quickly: keep my head down, say nothing, trust no one.

The memory fades, Mouse nuzzling my ankle, a quiet reminder that he's here. But even he doesn't know the whole truth—the screams I still hear in my dreams, the isolation that comes with being different. The shadows aren't my enemies, but they aren't my friends either. They were just... there. And now, with the necklace growing heavier and the shadows growing bolder, I can't shake the feeling that my past is catching up to me.

My pity part is cut short by a sharper awareness of the present. My necklace presses against my chest, and my shadows writhe with a tension that wasn't there before slowly curling around my legs as though they'll shield me.

Something's wrong.

Chapter 2
KAIA

The walk home is quiet—too quiet. The morning bustle of the city seems muted as if the world is holding its breath. An unnatural chill creeps into the air, making my skin prickle beneath my coffee-stained uniform. My shadows twitch and writhe around my feet, their usual playful shenanigans replaced by something more urgent. Mouse's fur bristles as he continues to pad beside me, and a low growl rumbles again from his tiny chest.

That's when I hear it—a sound like dying leaves scraping across pavement, but wrong somehow. Distorted. The shadows around me seem to move with warning, and something tugs at the edges of my memory—a half-forgotten nightmare stirring awake.

I turn slowly, my heart hammering against my ribs.

The creature towers over me, its form flickering like a bad TV signal. It looks almost human, but stretched wrong, its too-long limbs ending in gleaming claws. Empty sockets fix on mine, and when it opens its mouth, the sound that comes out is like glass grinding on bone.

"The Heart calls," it rasps, reaching for me with those twisted fingers. The words sound wrong in its mouth, as if it's forgotten how to speak properly. "She lives... she lives..."

The jewel around my neck glows brighter than I've ever seen. My shadows surge forward instinctively, forming a barrier between us. Mouse—my quiet, unassuming Mouse—launches himself between us with a snarl that sounds impossibly deep for his size. His violet eyes blaze with an intensity I've never seen before, and for a moment, I swear there's something more to him—something bigger, more ancient. I wish I could say I had anything to do with their actions, but I can barely think straight.

"Stay back," I say, backing away slowly. My voice sounds steady despite the fear clawing at my throat. But the thing moves like smoke, too fast, too fluid. Something about the way it moves, the way its voice scratches at my mind, feels horribly familiar. But the memory stays maddeningly out of reach, like a nightmare I can't wake from.

It lunges, its claws tearing through my shadows like mist. I stumble backward, my carefully constructed normal life crumbling as quickly as my shadows reform. They lash out wildly, more defensive than coordinated, while Mouse weaves between my feet, his fur standing on end, that unnaturally fierce growl still rumbling from his tiny form.

"The Heart remembers," it hisses, its voice scratching at my mind like fingernails on glass. "The blood remembers..."

My hand flies to the amethyst necklace I've worn for as long as I can remember. It throbs warmly against my skin, and for a moment, I swear I hear whispers—see fragments of a memory just out of reach. A woman's voice, golden light, the beat of wings... The images slip away like water through my fingers, leaving only an ache of loss I can't explain.

The creature strikes again, and this time my shadows aren't fast enough. Pain blazes across my arm as its claws catch me, the touch sending ice through my veins. I cry out, more in shock than pain, and my shadows respond explosively. They surge outward in jagged spikes, forcing the creature back. The necklace throbs against my collarbone, its usual comforting warmth now a fierce heat.

A silver light flares bright, forcing the creature back into the shadows. The same light washes over me, healing the claw marks on my arm as if they never existed. When the glow dims, a man stands where the darkness had been, his staff still humming with residual energy. His dark robes ripple without wind, and his eyes fix on me with unsettling intensity.

"H—How?" I stammer trying to keep my voice level. I hate looking weak and something tells me this man is the last person I want to look weak in front of.

"That," he says calmly, as the creature retreats into the shadows, "was a Nightwraith. And that was not your victory. Merely survival."

"A what?" I demand, trying to keep my voice steady despite the way my hands shake. The word feels familiar, though I know I've never heard it before. It echoes in my mind like a half-remembered lullaby.

My shadows coil defensively around my legs as Mouse shrinks back to his normal size, though he continues to growl softly, ears down and eyes trained on the man. The stranger studies me like I'm a particularly interesting science experiment, his gaze lingering on the shadows that refuse to stay still.

"Who are you?" I ask, lifting my chin despite the tremor in my voice. "What was that thing?"

"Professor Thorne." He lowers his staff but doesn't extinguish its light. The runes cast eerie patterns across his sharp features. "And that was a Nightwraith—drawn to your power like a moth to flame. You can't hide forever, Kaia. The shadows around you grow stronger each day, and you barely maintain control."

I stiffen, my heart skipping a beat. "How do you know my name?"

His smile is sharp and knowing, reminding me uncomfortably of a predator sizing up its prey. "I know many things. Including the fact that you need proper training before your power destroys you—or worse, draws something far more dangerous than a lone Nightwraith."

"I don't need anything," I snap, but my shadows betray me, rippling with interest at his words. They stretch toward him like curious cats, ignoring my mental attempts to pull them back. "I'm handling it fine."

"Are you?" He arches an eyebrow. "Then perhaps you'd care to explain why your shadows are currently trying to read my magical signature without your permission?"

I glance down, mortified to find he's right. My shadows have stretched toward him, probing curiously at his robes like children reaching for something shiny. I yank them back, and they retreat sulkily, curling around my ankles in a way that feels distinctly unrepentant.

"Arcanum Academy," he says, pulling a card from his robes with an elegant flourish. "Where people like you learn to master their gifts, not just survive them. The choice is yours, but make it quickly." His eyes narrow, and the temperature seems to drop. "Time grows short, and the shadows are calling."

He turns to leave, then pauses, his lips curving into a knowing smirk. "Oh, and Kaia? Next time, try not to let your shadows steal from customers. The man in the suit is missing his wallet."

My shadows squirm guiltily as I find said wallet tucked into my pocket, right next to my measly tips from the morning shift. By the time I look up, Thorne has vanished, leaving only his card and the lingering scent of magic in the air—something ancient and electric that puts me on edge.

Mouse headbutts my leg, and my shadows curl around me like a protective cloak. They feel different now—more alert, more alive. As if Thorne's presence has awakened something in them.

Or in me.

I stare at the card in my hand, feeling the weight of choice pressing down on me.

My normal life is already in ruins. The words Arcanum Academy hang in the air, heavy with promise and threat. A place to learn control—but at what cost? I've fought so hard to build a life, even if it was a fragile illusion and a crap one at that. Can I really let it all go for this?I trudge toward my apartment, my mind reeling from the encounter. Mouse trots beside me, occasionally swatting at my restless shadows as they dance around us, clearly still keyed up from the fight.

"So," I say to no one in particular, "just a typical Tuesday morning. Get up, serve questionable eggs to cranky customers, nearly die at the claws of a nightmarish shadow creature. You know, the usual."

My sarcasm falls flat even to my own ears. The truth is, I'm shaken. That thing—the Nightwraith—felt familiar in a way that makes my skin crawl. Like a half-remembered nightmare or a song you can't quite place. Its words echo in my head: "The Heart calls... she lives..."

I absently touch the amethyst necklace, feeling its comforting warmth against my skin. It's always been there, as much a part of me as my own heartbeat. But now, for the first time, I wonder if there's more to it than just sentimental value. The way it had pulsed during the fight, and those fleeting images...

"What do you think, Mouse? Should we pack our bags for Shadow University?" I glance down at my feline companion. He gives me a look that somehow manages to convey both *"obviously"* and *"took you long enough"* in equal measure.

I sigh dramatically. "Fine, but if this turns out to be some elaborate prank, I'm blaming you."

As we round the corner to my apartment building, my shadows suddenly go haywire. They shoot out in all directions, wrapping around lamp posts and scaling walls like demented, incorporeal squirrels. A nearby jogger yelps as a tendril of darkness trips him, sending him sprawling onto the cracked sidewalk.

"Sorry!" I call out, frantically trying to reel my shadows back in. They resist like stubborn toddlers refusing bedtime. "Uh... I mean, are you okay?" I pause awkwardly as he glares at me. "Yeah, you're fine, okay good!"

The jogger picks himself up, brushing gravel from his knees and muttering about "kids these days" as he limps away. Mouse watches him go, tail twitching with what looks suspiciously like amusement.

I groan, burying my face in my hands. "This is exactly what I'm talking about," I tell Mouse as we climb the creaky stairs to my tiny apartment. My shadows trail behind us, leaving smoky swirls in the air that fade like morning mist. "I can't keep going like this. One of these days, my shadows are going to decide to play jump rope with a bus or something, and then where will we be?"

Mouse meows in what I choose to interpret as agreement, though he seems more interested in weaving between my legs, nearly tripping me on the landing.

Inside my apartment—all one hundred and fifty square feet of it—I flop dramatically onto my bed, staring up at the water-stained ceiling. "Okay, let's think about this logically," I say to Mouse, who's curled up on my pillow looking supremely unimpressed. "Pro: I might learn to stop my shadows from acting like caffeinated toddlers on a sugar rush. Con: I'll be surrounded by magical prodigies who probably learned to levitate their rattles before they could walk."

My shadows swirl restlessly, forming shapes that look suspiciously like schoolbooks and graduation caps. One even manages a pretty decent impression of what I assume is supposed to be a wizard's robe, complete with a pointy hat.

Traitors.

"Alright, alright," I mutter, swatting at the shadow display. "I get it. You want to go to magic school and become the next Harry Potter. But have you considered the very real possibility that I'll end up being the magical equivalent of the kid who eats paste?"

Mouse gives me a look that clearly says, *"You already eat paste, what's the difference?"* before starting to groom his paw with exaggerated indifference.

I stick my tongue out at him. Real mature, I know.

But as I lie there, I can't shake the memory of the Nightwraith, its twisted form reaching for me with those impossibly long claws. The way my shadows had lashed out, more panic than purpose. And then there was Thorne, with his knowing smirk and his talk of my power growing stronger. The amethyst at my throat pulses gently, as if reminding me it has secrets of its own.

"I'm probably going to regret this, Mouse," I mutter. He purrs encouragingly, and my shadows ripple with what feels suspiciously like excitement. They swirl around my feet in patterns that look almost like dancing. "Looks like we're going back to school."

I fish Thorne's card out of my pocket, eyeing it warily as if it might bite. The elegant script shimmers slightly in the dim light:

"Professor Rylan Thorne, Arcanum Academy - Where Shadows Meet Light."

Pretentious much?

With a deep breath that's equal parts resignation and "what the hell am I doing," I dial the number. My shadows cluster around the phone, as if they too want to hear what happens next.

It rings once. Twice. On the third ring, I'm seriously considering hanging up and pretending this whole day was just a weird dream brought on by too much diner coffee and those questionable eggs I sampled during my break.

"Ah, Kaia," Thorne's smooth voice answers, sounding entirely too smug. "I've been expecting your call."

Of course he has. Because apparently, I wasn't just joining a magic school, I was diving headfirst into every fantasy novel cliché imaginable. Next thing you know, he'll be telling me I'm the chosen one.

"Yeah, well," I say, trying to sound nonchalant and probably failing miserably, "turns out my social calendar was looking a bit sparse. Thought I might pencil in 'learn not to accidentally destroy the world with my freaky shadow powers' between 'laundry day' and 'existential crisis.'"

There's a pause, and for a moment I worry I've offended him. Then I hear a low chuckle. "Your humor will serve you well at Arcanum, Kaia. It's not an easy path you're choosing."

"Who said anything about choosing?" I retort. "This is clearly a last resort. My shadows are—" I freeze mid-sentence, the words dying in my throat as something finally clicks. Something that should have registered immediately but got lost in the chaos of nearly dying and being recruited for magic school.

He saw my shadows. Not just saw them—he knew what they were doing. He saw them steal the wallet, saw them trying to read his magical signature. No one sees my shadows. Ever. Even Joey, who's known me for years, only notices when people suddenly shiver or things mysteriously fall off shelves.

"How..." I start, then clear my throat and try again. "How exactly can you see my shadows?"

Another pause, longer this time. When Thorne speaks again, the amusement in his voice has been replaced by something darker, more calculating. "There are more people in this world who can see what you are than you realize, Kaia. I'll see you tomorrow morning. Pack light—shadows prefer to travel unburdened."

The line goes dead before I can sputter out a response. Mouse chirps questioningly as I stare at my phone. My shadows writhe uneasily, coiling closer like they're seeking comfort. I get the distinct impression they know something I don't.

"Well," I mutter, watching as they form abstract patterns of worry on my wall, "that wasn't ominous at all."

"Oh, and guys?" I say, glancing around at my naughty shadows, "no more stealing." They droop dramatically, like scolded children, but I catch one not looking the least bit phased by my words.

Figures.

Chapter 3
PROFESSOR THORNE

I watch Kaia's retreating form from the shadows, noting how her darkness trails after her like loyal pets. The Nightwraith's attack went exactly as planned—though its fascination with the Heart of Eternity was unexpected. Her shadows didn't just defend—they anticipated. They lashed out like living things, each strike guided by an intelligence that shouldn't exist. And that panther construct... its eyes held an awareness that no mere shadow should possess.

Fascinating.

That particular detail will require a report to Alekir.

As if I have nothing better to do.

My fingers trace the runes on my staff, still warm from the blast that drove the creature away. The timing had to be perfect. Too soon, and she wouldn't have felt truly threatened. Too late, and we might have lost our most valuable prospect in decades. Now, though, she's seen what's hunting her. Now she knows she needs protection.

I pull out my communication crystal, watching it swirl with stored magic as I review the recordings of her fight. Such raw, untamed power. Her shadows don't just react—they anticipate, forming barriers and weapons with an intelligence I've never seen before. Most inquisitive is that shadow-panther. Its violet eyes hold too much awareness for a mere construct.

A few humans pass by, giving me a wide birth, deterred by the shadow magic that surrounds me, if they even notice at all.

The crystal warms in my palm, signaling an incoming call. Earlier than expected. Interesting.

"Ah, Kaia," I answer, masking my satisfaction at hearing her uneven breathing. "I've been expecting your call."

"Yeah, well, turns out my social calendar was looking a bit sparse. Thought I might pencil in 'learn not to accidentally destroy the world with my freaky shadow powers' between 'laundry day' and 'existential crisis.'"

Her attempt at bravado would be amusing if it weren't so useful. Every crack in her voice, every pause between words, reveals another vulnerability to exploit.

I allow myself a small chuckle. Her humor is a mask for fear—useful information. "Your humor will serve you well at Arcanum, Kaia. It's not an easy path you're choosing."

"Who said anything about choosing?" she retorts. "This is clearly a last resort. My shadows are—" She stops abruptly, and I can practically hear the realization dawning. "How exactly can you see my shadows?"

Finally. The right question. I let the silence stretch, her unease growing with every second as a smile creeps across my face. "There are more people in this world who can see what you are than you realize, Kaia. I'll see you tomorrow morning. Pack light—shadows prefer to travel unburdened."

I end the connection, pulling out my other crystal—the one keyed to Alekir's frequency. This developmental phase requires a delicate touch. Alekir demands progress, but rushing her could jeopardize everything—and I'm not interested in his wrath. Push too hard, and she'll retreat further into herself. Not hard enough, and those shadows might actually succeed in protecting her.

***

The next morning is gloomy, perfect for viewing the gothic architecture of the academy for the first time. I arrive in my rune-carved carriage in front of an apartment building that can only be described as derelict. How anyone can actually live in this filth is beyond me. Yet Kaia stands on the curb with a single bag, her shadows more agitated than ever. That silly cat winds around her ankles, violet eyes fixed on me with unsettling intensity.

As I step out of the carriage in from of her, I notice just how sunk in her cheeks are, and the dark circles under her eyes. This may be easier than I thought.

"Your chariot awaits," I say dryly, noting how she flinches when I raise my hand to motion toward the open door. "Unless you've reconsidered?"

Her chin lifts defiantly. "Little late for second thoughts, isn't it?"

"It's never too late to choose a simpler path." I gesture to her rundown apartment building. "The café would surely take you back. Though I doubt they offer much protection against Nightwraiths."

Her shadows twist tighter around her legs as she visibly rejects the idea. "Just... tell me one thing. Why me? Really?"

I study her for a moment, choosing my words carefully. "Because power like yours doesn't appear by accident. You're a threat, Kaia, whether you realize it or not. And threats always attract predators."

It's not technically a lie. The best manipulations never are.

She climbs into the carriage, Mouse jumping up beside her. As we pull away from her old life, I observe her in the golden morning light. The Heart of Eternity glows faintly at her throat, and her shadows dance across the carriage's enchanted interior, investigating every rune and sigil.

"The academy will be... challenging," I say, watching her reaction carefully. "Not everyone appreciates the gifts of shadow magic. Some fear it. Others will seek to use it for their own ends."

"Is that what you're doing?" she asks sharply.

Clever girl.

I smile. "I'm offering you knowledge. What you do with it is entirely your choice."

Another half-truth. But she doesn't need to know that yet. She doesn't need to know about Alekir's plans, or the true purpose of the Heart of Eternity. She certainly doesn't need to know about the Valkyries.

All she needs to know is that she's special. Powerful. And completely out of her depth.

The rest will come in time. And once *he* arrives we'll have no reason not to move forward for Alekir as quickly as possible.

As the spires of Arcanum Academy pierce the morning mist ahead of us, I allow myself a moment of quiet satisfaction. The pieces are falling into place, and not even Kaia's shadows can warn her of what's to come.

Chapter 4
FINN

I'm perfectly balanced on the edge of the academy's western tower—which, let's be honest, is basically the most comfortable seat on campus. Alenya keeps telling me it's "completely inappropriate behavior for a mage," but really, what does she know about gargoyle seating ergonomics? If the architects didn't want people sitting here, they wouldn't have made them so inviting.

Besides, where else would I get a view like this?

My gaze sweeps over the forest-lined road winding up to the academy, and I spot it: Thorne's obnoxiously fancy carriage, rolling up like it owns the place. Normally, I'd find a snack or a nap more appealing than watching one of his dramatic recruit parades, but this time, something's... different.

Shadows.

Not just boring, stick-to-your-heels shadows, either. Not even your typical magical ones. These things move like they've got a pulse, darting and weaving behind the carriage like hyper puppies who can't decide where they're supposed to be.

I sit up straighter, my curiosity hooked.

"Interesting," I murmur, leaning forward. "What are you bringing me today, Thorne?"

The carriage stops at the front entrance directly below where my gargoyle friend and I are sitting. The door swings open, and I see her.

Oh.

My balance shifts dangerously as my breath catches. I barely manage to stop myself from tumbling off my stone buddy entirely.

She steps out of the carriage like she owns it—lean muscle, all fluid motion and sharp edges. Her skin's so pale it catches the morning light which doesn't really exist, but she's practically glowing, and her hair looks like it's permanently wind-swept, in a way that should be impossible after a carriage ride. But it's her eyes that lock me in place.

Violet. Deep, sharp, and way too guarded for someone her age. There's something wild behind them, too—a spark, like a hidden fire she's carefully controlling.

And then I realize the shadows are hers.

Oh, hell.

They're alive in a way I've never seen before, curling and twisting around her legs with minds of their own. One of them, a bigger one that looks like it runs the show, is actively herding the smaller ones away from Thorne's boots.

A born leader, that one.

I can't help the grin tugging at my face.

"Look at you, shadow mom," I murmur, watching as her chaotic shadows move around her. They make her look like she's at the center of a wild, beautiful dance only she knows the steps to. My heart does this stupid little flip thing, and I roll my eyes at myself.

This is not fair.

I'm about to dismiss it as no big deal—just another recruit (yeah right)—but then a sleek black panther hops out of the carriage after her. Not a real panther, obviously. Its body shifts like liquid smoke, violet eyes glowing as it scans the grounds. When it looks up at me, I swear it rolls its eyes.

"What's your problem?" I mutter.

The panther ignores me.

Rude.

Now, I should probably go down there and introduce myself like a normal person. You know, on the ground, through the door, like a perfectly respectable mage.

But where's the fun in that?

Instead, I let myself fall forward off the tower.

Halfway down, her shadows surge up like a tidal wave, and for a second, I think she's going to obliterate me.

"Whoa, whoa, easy there," I call, catching myself on a ripple of chaos magic before I hit the ground. I float the last few feet, landing lightly in front of her.

Show-off? Me?

Always.

Her shadows pull back, swirling protectively around her feet, but I'm too busy trying to keep my grin in check. Up close, she's even more striking, all sharp edges and tightly reined-in power.

And boy what power she has. If I can feel it now, just imagine if she lets go. I mean, I'd like to be there when it happens for sure. And I mean that in only the best possible way. A shiver zips down my spine at the thought.

"Hi there!" I say, shoving my hands in my pockets like I didn't just dramatically fall out of the sky or think some rather delicious thoughts. "I'm Finn. Welcome to Hogwarts for problem children. You must be the new shadow girl everyone's been whispering about."

She blinks at me, her gaze darting between me and the tower. "Did you just... jump off a fucking building?"

"More like a controlled fall. With style." I wink, but she's still staring at me like I might be insane.

Fair.

Before she can say anything else, I crouch down to get a closer look at her shadows. They flinch back for half a second, then one of the smaller ones wriggles forward, sniffing at my boot like it's inquisitive as the big one tries to pull it back.

"And who are these lovely void creatures?" I ask, smirking. "The big guy here's got CEO energy. Definitely a 'Bob from accounting' vibe, if Bob was made of living darkness."

The big shadow seems to straighten, and I almost laugh.

Bob it is.

"Bob?" the girl asks, her voice flat but with a hint of something—curiosity? Amusement?

"Yeah, look at him!" I gesture. "He's clearly running this operation." I glance at the smaller shadow investigating my boot. "And this one? Definitely a Finnick. Trouble written all over him."

Her lips twitch like she's trying not to smile, and I take that as a win.

Thorne clears his throat behind us, and I reluctantly stand.

"If you're quite finished, Mr. Veylan," he says in that clipped tone that makes everything sound like a scolding, "Miss Draven has an orientation to attend."

"Orientation?" I make a face. "Boring. I could give you the real tour. Best hiding spots, where the kitchen imps stash the good snacks, which professors you can prank without getting expelled..."

Her lips twitch again, and her shadows wriggle like they're excited. Even Bob looks like he's considering my offer.

"Mr. Veylan," Thorne snaps, his patience clearly running thin.

"Fine, fine," I say, backing away with my hands raised. I turn to her one last time, smirking. "But seriously. When you're done with Thorne's snooze-fest, come find me. The shadows will know."

Bob straightens again, and I wink at him.

"Keep them in line, big guy."

As I walk away, I hear her ask, "Is he always like that?"

"Mr. Veylan," Thorne replies dryly, "is a perfect example of why chaos magic is strictly regulated."

I grin to myself, already making mental notes.

Bob needs his own spreadsheet. For organizational purposes, of course.

Chapter 5
KAIA

The hall smells faintly of old parchment and ozone, the kind of scent that clings to places steeped in magic. Students' voices bounce off the high ceilings, and the light filtering through enchanted windows shifts like a kaleidoscope. Shadows twist uneasily around my legs, brushing against the marble floor like restless waves. Four massive banners dominate the walls, each representing a faction: Light's radiant sunburst on white, Shadow's crescent moon wrapped in darkness, Elements' intertwined elemental symbols, and Sorcery's tome surrounded by glowing runes. The banners seem alive with magic—Light's cloth shimmers with inner radiance, Shadow's ripples like liquid night, Elements' symbols pulse with raw power, and Sorcery's runes shift and change as I watch.

Mouse stays perched on my shoulder, his glowing violet eyes scanning the crowd. The energy in the air is overwhelming—too many people, too many bright lights and flashes of magic sparking in the corners of my vision.

It reminds me of the diner only everyone here is dressed much nicer, the air isn't filled with the aroma of greasy food and day old coffee, and my shadows aren't trying to actively steal from anyone for once.

At the front of the hall stands Professor Thorne, flanked by a handful of other professors who exude an air of power. Their robes shimmer with faintly glowing runes, and I can feel the magic thrumming around them like a low hum. Thorne's presence dominates, his sharp gaze scanning the students with calculated precision. Even without speaking, he holds the room in thrall.

The Light students cluster near the center of the room, glowing with quiet confidence, while the shadow mages stick to the edges, their gazes wary. Element users move between them easily, their energy crackling like a barely restrained storm.

I slide into a seat near the edge of the hall, preferring the illusion of escape. A group of older students sit nearby, their whispers just loud enough to overhear.

"You know Thorne's been here forever, right?" one of them says, a tall girl with fire-red hair. "My brother said he's been a professor since before the last Headmaster. People say he's got connections with... darker elements."

The others snicker, but one boy leans forward. "My dad told me he's worked with Alekir before. That's why he gets away with so much."

"Alekir?" the fire-haired girl rolls her eyes. "That's a bedtime story for toddlers. No one even knows if he's real."

"Well, I heard he's the one who pushed to keep Shadow and Chaos together," another girl says, her tone dripping with disdain. "Probably so he can keep an eye on them. Everyone knows shadow mages are just one step away from losing control."

The group mutters in agreement, and my jaw tightens. My shadows ripple with unease, but I force myself to stay still. Mouse nuzzles against my neck, pulling me back to reality as a sharp crack echoes through the hall. Thorne's staff strikes the stone floor, and silence falls like a dropped curtain.

The air itself feels charged with different types of magic—sharp sparks of elemental power, the warm glow of light magic, the subtle whispers of sorcery, and underneath it all, the cool ripple of shadow magic that makes my own shadows stir restlessly.

The shadows of other students stretch normally across the floor, but mine... mine seem to reach for something. They're drawn to Thorne in a way that makes my skin crawl, though I can't explain why. Mouse's claws prick my shoulder in warning.

"Welcome, initiates." His voice is a velvet blade, smooth but cutting. "You have come to Arcanum Academy not because you are ordinary, but because you are extraordinary—and dangerous. This is a place to hone your gifts, to learn discipline, and to discover where you belong in the world." His gaze sweeps the room, lingering briefly on me. "You will find no mercy for carelessness here. Strength will be forged in hardship, and only the worthy will endure."

Beside him, a professor steps forward—a stout man with a wide grin and glowing symbols etched across his skin. His voice is warm, in stark contrast to Thorne's. "I am Professor Hartley, Head of the Faction of Elements. You'll be learning much about the factions during your time here, so I'll give you the short version. Each of you will be evaluated and placed based on your core magic affinity."

A murmur ripples through the crowd, but Hartley continues, unfazed. "The four primary factions are Light, Shadow, Elements, and Sorcery. There are smaller divisions within these, but we'll get to those later. Placement isn't negotiable; the academy's system is—thorough." His grin sharpens slightly. "But I'll tell you this: no faction is inherently superior. They are all dangerous, and they are all essential."

The students themselves seem to advertise their affiliations. Light faction students practically glow, their uniforms trimmed in gold. Element users carry the scent of their power—ozone, earth, burning wood. Sorcery students' robes flutter with half-formed spells. And the shadow users... they try to blend in, but I notice how the darkness clings to them differently, how they instinctively seek the edges of the crowd.

The redhead snickers. "Shadow? What a joke. The losers' faction." A ripple of muffled laughter follows, and my shadows twist tighter around my legs. Mouse's tail flicks irritably, mirroring my own tension."

Thorne's voice cuts back in. "You will find your affinities tested in the coming weeks. Placement is determined by potential and discipline, not your desires." His gaze flicks toward a group of students who look like they've stepped out of a royal portrait, their shimmering uniforms denoting the Faction of Light. "Some of you will be disappointed. Adapt."

A soft voice interrupts, drawing the room's attention. "And some of you might surprise yourselves."

The speaker steps forward. She is tall and elegant, with silver-streaked black hair always pulled into a loose braid. Her dark, flowing robes seem to shimmer with hidden runes. Her eyes have an unusual silvery hue, suggesting a deep connection to shadow magic. A master of Soulbinding and Shadow Magic, Lira is one of the few who might understand my potential—and my struggles.

"I am Professor Lira," she says, her voice a calming counterpoint to Thorne's sharp edges. "I oversee Chaos and Shadow magic disciplines. This academy is more than a place of discipline. It is a sanctuary for those who would otherwise be misunderstood. Remember that your potential is not defined by the opinions of others but by your willingness to embrace who you are."

Her gaze lands on me for a heartbeat, warm and steady, before moving on.

The shift in energy is palpable, and even my shadows seem to calm under her soothing presence.

The difference between her and Thorne is like night and day—literally, as her shadow magic feels like a cool stream compared to his razor-sharp presence. Her voice feels like a balm against my raw nerves, and even my shadows respond, their restless twisting giving way to smooth, flowing movements. For the first time since I arrived, I feel... seen

Hartley's jovial tone returns. "In addition to your factions, you'll have access to a handbook—a guide to everything from rules and schedules to which parts of the academy you should absolutely avoid. Speaking of which, don't wander into the Deep Archives unless you've got a death wish." He chuckles, but the warning feels real enough.

"Finally," another professor speaks up, her voice crisp and clipped. She's tall and severe, with silver hair pulled into a tight braid. "I am Professor Kaleth, Head of Sorcery. You will respect the rules of this institution or face expulsion. Magic is a privilege, not a right."

My attention drifts as the professors continue their introductions, outlining the academy's purpose: to create balance in a world where magic often tips the scales toward chaos. They mention that the academy exists alongside human society—hidden in plain sight. Most humans have no idea magic exists, and the academy's protective wards keep it that way. The idea is unsettling. I grew up surrounded by people who didn't know my kind existed, and now I'm here—among others like me, but still isolated by secrets.

I find myself wondering about the years I lost—the gap between my childhood and the person I am now. My memories are fragments, sharp-edged and painful to touch. What would my parents think if they could see me here?

"You."

The sharp voice snaps me back. Thorne's eyes are on me, cold and assessing. I sit up straighter, my heart pounding.

"What do you think is the purpose of Arcanum Academy?" he asks.

My throat dries and Mouse quietly growls in my ear, his claws pricking my shoulder again in warning. My shadows go still, like they're holding their breath with me. "To... control magic?" I hazard knowing it's not the full answer.

Thorne's expression doesn't change, but something flickers in his eyes. "Control is a means, not an end. The academy exists to ensure magic serves its purpose—to protect, to heal, to create. When magic is wielded without purpose, it destroys. Remember that." His gaze lingers, heavy with unspoken meaning, like a warning meant just for me

As the orientation concludes, students begin to file out. I catch snippets of conversation—excited chatter, nervous whispers, and a few glances cast in my direction.

A light faction student bumps my shoulder, her magic sending a jolt through my shadows. She mumbles an apology, but I catch her quick step backward when she looks at me. My shadows want to reach for her, to show her what real magic feels like, but I hold them back. First day isn't the time to start a faction war.

Mouse's tail swishes irritably, and I resist the urge to glare at the students whispering about me. I focus on the faint hum of my necklace against my skin.

The glow is muted now, but its presence is a constant reminder of the power—and the danger—I carry. As I sit there, waiting for the other students to file out, I catch Thorne watching me again, his expression unreadable. But it's Lira's knowing smile that makes me wonder: just how much do they really know about what I am?

Chapter 6
KAIA

The hall empties slowly, echoes of excited chatter fading as students file out. I stay rooted to my seat, my shadows coiling anxiously around my ankles like restless snakes. Mouse, perched protectively on the bench beside me now, watches the retreating crowd with suspicious violet eyes.

"Overwhelming, isn't it?"

The voice is calm, almost musical. I look up and promptly forget how to breathe. Standing before me is a man who seems plucked from a classical painting—tall and lean, with light blonde hair that falls in soft waves past elegant cheekbones. His icy blue eyes hold a depth that could drown the unwary, and his relaxed posture hints at power beneath the surface, like a still ocean concealing its true strength

I swallow hard, my gaze inadvertently trailing down his form. His white t-shirt clings to his chest like a second skin, the fabric stretched taut over well-defined pectorals. Even through the material, I can trace the lines of his abs, each muscle clearly etched. The shirt rides up slightly as he shifts his weight, revealing a tantalizing sliver of pale skin above his waistband.

My eyes continue their journey downward, taking in how his light wash jeans hug his hips and thighs. They're worn in all the right places, softened by use but still managing to accentuate every curve and plane of his lower body. The denim clings to his long legs before tapering slightly at the ankles, where they meet a pair of well-worn leather boots.

Calm down Kaia, now is definitely not the time.

I realize I've been staring for far too long and force my gaze back up to his face, heat rising in my cheeks. His lips quirk in a knowing half-smile, amusement dancing in those impossibly blue eyes. My shadows writhe with embarrassment, and I resist the urge to let them engulf me completely.

"I'm Aspen," he says, his voice as smooth and intoxicating as honey. "And you must be Kaia. I've heard quite a bit about you already."

I try to formulate a response, but my tongue feels leaden in my mouth. Mouse, sensing my discomfort, presses closer to my side. His fur bristles slightly, a low growl rumbling in his chest.

"Anyway," he says, extending a hand. His voice maintains that same soothing quality, like waves lapping at a shore. "Professor Thorne asked me to help you get settled."

I hesitate before taking his hand, hyper-aware of how his cool fingers wrap around mine with gentle confidence. His grip is firm but not over-whelming. My shadows brush against his wrist, a light, curious touch that makes him shiver. His eyes flick to where they lingered for just a moment, but he doesn't pull away. Instead, his fingers tighten slightly, like he's holding onto a secret.

"I don't need a babysitter," I manage, grateful my voice remains steady as I pull my hand from his reluctantly. Which doesn't make any sense.

"Good, because I'm terrible with children." His grin sharpens, flashing just enough charm to be disarming. "Think of me more as... a very knowl-edgeable tour guide who happens to know which corridors won't try to eat you."

"The corridors what?"

"That was a joke. Mostly." He gestures toward the door, his expression warming. "Shall we? The Shadow Wing is across the academy, and you'll probably want to get settled."

I force myself to move, trying not to trip over my increasingly agitated shadows. Aspen points out landmarks as we walk—the library's ancient spires reaching toward perpetually stormy skies, the elemental gardens where plants hum with visible magical energy, the training grounds where students practice combat magic in specially warded arenas. He speaks with quiet authority, his commentary precise but engaging. Against my better judgment, I find myself relaxing slightly, though my heart refuses to slow its frantic pace.

We turn a corner into a corridor where the air feels heavier, the shadows thickening like mist around us. The magic here hums low, almost like a growl, and I'm so distracted by the way the darkness seems to pulse with life that I walk straight into what feels like a wall of heated muscle.

"Watch where you're—"

The deep voice cuts off, sharp and startled. My shadows flare defensively, curling into a dark shield as I step back. The warmth of whoever—or whatever—I walked into lingers uncomfortably close.

Golden eyes glare down at me from a face that should come with a warning label. It's like someone took Aspen and made him bigger, angrier, and somehow even more devastating to look at. Where Aspen is lean grace, this man is raw power incarnate. He towers at least 6'5", all broad shoulders and defined muscle, with sun-kissed skin that practically radiates heat. His dark blonde hair is tied back messily, with rebellious strands framing a face that belongs in epic tales of war gods and heroes. Battle scars trace patterns across his forearms, and beneath his shirt, a fiery rune glows like a caged ember.

Oh no.

He's hot. Literally and figuratively.

"Torric," Aspen says, his voice taking on a sharp edge beneath its usual smoothness. "This is Kaia. She's joining the Faction of Shadow." There's a warning in his tone that suggests this isn't the first time he's had to manage his twin's intensity.

"Great. Another stray." Torric crosses his arms, which only emphasizes his warrior's build. His piercing gaze sweeps over me like he's assessing an opponent. "Just what we need."

My shadows bristle, coiling tighter as Mouse lets out a low growl. "Sorry to disappoint," I snap, unable to stop myself. "I'll try to get lost somewhere more convenient next time."

Something flickers in Torric's eyes—amusement? Interest? It vanishes quickly beneath his scowl, but I caught it.

"The Shadow Wing isn't a sanctuary for every wayward magic user who—"

"That's enough, brother," Aspen cuts in, his calm voice suddenly sharp as ice. "Unless you'd like to explain to Professor Thorne why you're harassing his newest recruit?"

Even Torric, who looks like he could punch through a mountain for fun, seems to reconsider at Thorne's name. He steps back, though his molten gold eyes remain locked on mine with an intensity that sends shivers down my spine.

"Just stay out of my way," he mutters, his voice a low rumble that I feel more than hear, "and we won't have a problem."

"Perfect." I can't help but snark back.

His eyes narrow at my word but he stalks past us, radiating heat and barely contained power. I try not to watch him go. I fail spectacularly.

Aspen waits until Torric's heavy footsteps fade before turning to me with a knowing smile. "Don't mind him. He's all fire and no filter. He doesn't trust easily, but once he does, he's fiercely loyal. Just... try not to take his attitude personally. He's like that with everyone at first."

"Sounds like I'd just miss his delightful personality then," I mutter, forcing sarcasm to mask how flustered I feel. My shadows swirl agitatedly, betraying my attempt at nonchalance.

Aspen chuckles, his eyes crinkling at the corners. "Give it time. We're here, by the way."

I look up, grateful for the distraction, and find we've stopped before an ancient wooden door carved with intricate shadow runes. The door seems to drink in the surrounding light, and my shadows reach for it instinctively, like they've found a long-lost friend.

"Home sweet home," Aspen says, stepping aside. "At least for now. Your room is on the third floor, but first—" He pushes the door open, revealing a space that makes me stop dead in my tracks.

The Shadow Wing's common room is massive, with soaring vaulted ceilings and walls draped in deep purples and silvers that shimmer in the light of shadow-flame sconces. Plush armchairs and low tables scatter throughout, their surfaces covered in forgotten books, magical artifacts, and the occasional abandoned teacup. The room feels alive—shadows coil and shift along the walls as though welcoming newcomers, and the very air hums with ancient magic.

My shadows dart across the floor and walls, merging seamlessly with the ancient darkness as though testing its boundaries—or greeting an old friend. Mouse leaps gracefully from my shoulder to claim a particularly comfortable-looking armchair, his violet eyes scanning our surroundings with careful attention.

Aspen watches me with that same calm, assessing expression, hands tucked casually in his pockets. "Torric and I are one floor up," he says, breaking the moment. "Along with Finn and a few others that aren't here often. Malrik's quarters are... somewhere. He tends to move around."

"How mysterious," I murmur, letting my fingers brush against the cool stone wall. The shadows here feel different—older, more aware somehow, like they've been waiting for someone who could truly see them.

"Wait, Finn, as in the Chaos guy?" I ask genuinely curious.

Not that I'm thinking about him or anything.

Aspen's lips quirk up in a half-smile, but it fades as he studies me more closely. "That's the one." He pauses, "Are you alright? It's been quite a day."

I open my mouth to deflect with something sarcastic, but the words stick in my throat. Maybe it's the genuine concern in his eyes, or the way he hasn't pushed me to talk about things I'm not ready to share. Whatever the reason, I find myself admitting, "I don't know what I'm doing here."

His expression softens, and for a moment, I think he might reach out to touch my shoulder. Instead, he gestures to a nearby chair, his water rune catching the light. "None of us did, at first," he says gently. "Want to talk about it? I make a decent listener, and I promise not to tell Torric about any of it."

The joke startles a laugh from me, and some of the tension I've been carrying since arriving finally eases. My shadows settle into more relaxed patterns, curling lazily around my ankles instead of coiling like springs ready to snap.

I sink into the plush armchair, exhaling slowly as the cushions seem to mold around me. My shadows stretch out lazily again, exploring the nooks and crannies of this new space with growing confidence.

Aspen takes the seat across from me, his movements fluid and graceful and it makes me wonder how he handles himself in other ways. I mentally roll my eyes at myself and tell my libido to calm the hell down. The flickering light from the shadow-sconces plays across his features, highlighting the sharp angles of his face and the gentle curve of his lips. We sit in companionable silence, broken only by the soft crackle of magical energy in the air.

Suddenly, Aspen's eyes flick to a darkened corner of the room. His lips quirk up in a knowing smile. "Want to come out and say hello?" he calls out, voice tinged with amusement. "Or are we sticking to shadows today, Malrik?"

My heart leaps into my throat. I whip around, scanning the shadows, but see nothing. My own shadows bristle protectively, finally sensing something—or someone—watching.

Took you long enough.

Chapter 7
KAIA

For a heartbeat, nothing happens. Then, like ink bleeding through parchment, a figure materializes from the darkness.

If Aspen is the calm before the storm and Torric is the raging inferno, then Malrik is the seductive whisper of danger in the dark. He steps forward with predatory grace, all lean muscle and coiled power beneath perfectly tailored clothes. His jet-black hair is artfully styled, a stark contrast to his porcelain skin that seems to shimmer with an otherworldly light. But it's his eyes that capture me—silver-gray and piercing, like he can see straight through to all the secrets I've tried so desperately to keep hidden.

Those eyes lock onto mine, and the intensity in them makes my stomach do things I'm not ready to think about. "My apologies," he says, his voice a low, silky purr that sends shivers down my spine. "I didn't mean to intrude. I was merely... curious about our new arrival."

While I'm fixated on this man, I swear I hear Aspen chuckle.

He moves closer, and I catch his scent—dark spices and sweet shadows, an intoxicating combination that makes me want to lean in despite myself. My shadows stretch toward him like curious children, brushing against his sleeve before recoiling as though unsure. His silver-gray eyes narrow slightly, and I swear I see a flicker of recognition—or hunger. But it's gone before I can be sure.

Malrik's eyes widen fractionally, a flicker of genuine surprise crossing his face before it's replaced by a slow, dangerous smile. "Fascinating," he murmurs, voice dropping lower. "What exactly are you?"

My heart races as his intense gaze pins me in place. The question hangs in the air, loaded with curiosity and something darker, more hungry. I swallow hard, forcing myself to meet those mesmerizing eyes.

"I'm Kaia," I manage, hating how breathless I sound. "Just... Kaia."

Malrik's smile curves wider, equal parts alluring and predatory. "Oh, I very much doubt there's anything 'just' about you, Kaia."

He moves closer, and my shadows reach out again, brushing against him like curious cats. If he notices, he gives no sign, continuing to study me with that unnerving intensity.

"Your magic then," he prods, clearly not letting it go. "What is it exactly?"

When I don't answer, his grin sharpens, a dangerous glint appearing in his eyes. "Perhaps I could help you unravel that mystery. Shadow magic is... something of a specialty of mine."

He reaches out, fingertips ghosting over my cheek. His touch is cool, almost ethereal, and my breath catches. For a moment, the rest of the world fades away—there's only Malrik, his mesmerizing presence, and the dangerous dance we seem to be locked in.

"Tell me, Kaia," he purrs, leaning close enough that I feel his cool breath on my skin. "What do you desire most? Power? Knowledge? Or perhaps... something more?"

My heart pounds so loudly I'm sure he can hear it. I open my mouth to respond, though I have no idea what I'm going to say, when—

The door slams open with a resounding bang, shattering the moment like glass.

"Looking for me, Trouble?" a bright, mischievous voice calls out. "Or did you get lost in the broody boy's eyes?"

I jerk back, blinking rapidly as reality crashes back in. Malrik straightens, his expression smoothing into a mask of cool indifference. Only then do I remember Aspen's presence, guilt washing over me as I catch his raised eyebrow.

Finn practically bounces into the room, all barely contained energy and chaos. He's shorter than the others but still athletic, with wild auburn hair and the most troublemaking green eyes I've ever seen. Freckles dust his nose, and his grin is wide and infectious as he surveys the scene before him.

"Finn Veylan, just in case you forgot," he announces with an exaggerated bow. "Resident chaos-bringer and rescuer of damsels in distress. Though you don't seem very distressed. Disappointed?"

Aspen chuckles from his seat, shaking his head. "Finn, you're early."

"Or you're all late, depending on perspective," Finn replies with a wink before turning his attention back to me. "And you, Kaia—didn't I tell you we'd be friends? Look at you, already getting the grand tour of broody boys central. Lucky girl."

I can't help but snort, though it comes out more like a strangled laugh. "I'm starting to think 'broody boys central' is an understatement."

Finn's grin widens as he claims the armchair Mouse had been investigating. Mouse yowls indignantly, darting back to my shoulder to curl up in a huffy ball.

"Did you see that?!" Finn exclaims, pointing at Mouse. "Even your shadow-cat has attitude. I love it. We're going to get along famously, you and I."

"Glad I pass your rigorous approval process," I deadpan, though I feel my lips twitching upward. There's something disarming about Finn's energy, like he refuses to take anything—including himself—too seriously.

Malrik, however, doesn't share my amusement. He watches Finn with the barest furrow in his brow, silver eyes narrowed as though Finn is a puzzle he can't quite solve.

"Do you ever enter a room quietly?" Malrik asks, his tone sharp but tinged with something that sounds almost like fascination.

"Where's the fun in that?" Finn shoots back without missing a beat. He turns to me, eyes twinkling. "You don't mind, do you, Trouble?"

"Trouble?" I echo, raising an eyebrow.

"That's you," he declares confidently, leaning forward like we're sharing secrets. "Kaia, bringer of chaos, breaker of broody hearts, and newest member of our merry band of misfits."

I open my mouth to argue, but Aspen beats me to it. "You've known her less than a day, Finn. Maybe let her settle in before assigning nicknames?"

Finn waves dismissively. "Nicknames are a sign of affection. Right, Trouble?"

I shake my head, fighting a smile. "You're impossible."

"See? We're already bonding." He winks, sprawling in his chair with the kind of casual confidence only he could pull off.

Aspen sighs, though I catch his faint smile. "This is Finn Veylan, as he so thoroughly announced. You'll likely see more of him than you'd prefer, but he does grow on you."

"Like mold," Malrik mutters, though there's no real bite to it. He moves toward the door, his earlier intensity fading as he retreats back into the shadows. "Enjoy your stay, Kaia. Something tells me you'll be... interesting." With that, he's gone, leaving behind only a trace of his spicy-sweet scent and an unsettling flutter in my stomach.

"Don't worry about him," Finn says cheerfully, as if Malrik's ominous exit is perfectly normal. "He's always that dramatic. You'll get used to it."

I glance at Aspen, who nods. "Malrik has his reasons, but he's not as unapproachable as he seems. Give it time."

"Time," I repeat, exhaling slowly. "Right." *Seems to be a theme around here.* Time to process the fact that I've apparently entered the realm of gorgeous-but-confusing men who all seem to know more about me than I do."

Finn grins, unfazed. "Welcome to the Shadow Wing, Trouble. You'll fit right in."

Aspen rises gracefully, gesturing toward the grand staircase at the far end of the room. "Come on, Kaia. I'll show you to your room before Finn decides to make you his official audience or claim you as his roommate."

"Hey! Maybe she wants a roommate." Finn protests, but stays sprawled in his chair, giving me an exaggerated salute. "Later, Trouble. Try not to miss me too much."

As I follow Aspen up the staircase, my shadows flit around us, eagerly exploring every shadowed corner and alcove. The energy here feels different—darker, yes, but also warmer, like the shadows themselves are alive and watching with careful interest.

"Why does this place feel so strange?" I ask, glancing down as one of my shadows stretches curiously toward a particularly ornate banister carving.

Aspen looks back at me, his expression thoughtful. "The Shadow Wing responds differently to everyone. Maybe it just... recognizes something in you."

"Different," I echo, testing the word. "Is that what we're calling it?"

He pauses on the landing, turning to face me fully. "Sometimes being different is exactly what's needed. I'm sure you'll understand soon enough."

Before I can press him further, we stop before another door. This one is smaller than the entrance but just as intricately carved, its runes pulsing faintly in the dim light.

"This is you," Aspen says, stepping aside.

I hesitate, my hand hovering over the doorknob. Part of me wonders if it might explode when touched—given everything else today, it wouldn't be the strangest thing. But when I finally gather my courage, the knob turns easily, revealing a cozy space that makes my breath catch.

The walls are painted a deep gray that feels more like an embrace than an absence of light. A plush bed draped in silvery blankets sits against one wall, while a sturdy desk occupies the opposite corner, already stacked with leather-bound books I definitely didn't bring. The shadows in the room react immediately to my presence, swirling around my wrists like affectionate cats welcoming me home.

Mouse leaps from my shoulder to investigate the bed, sniffing the pillows before settling in with an approving chirp. "Well," I murmur, stepping inside. "It's not terrible."

Aspen's soft chuckle follows me. "High praise indeed. Get some rest, Kaia. Tomorrow will be... eventful."

I don't bother asking what he means by that. Somehow, I already know I'm not ready.

Aspen's lips quirk in a faint smile, but his gaze lingers on me for a moment longer than feels casual.

Once he's gone, I shut the door quietly look around the room trying to take it all in. This is nothing like my apartment. A humorless laugh escapes me. Nothing is quite like that shithole, but this? this is too much. I'm kind of afraid to touch anything because I definitely can't afford to replace it.

The shadows in the room seem to welcome me, swirling around like they already know I belong here. But do I? The cozy space feels like a stranger's home, too perfect, too much. Nothing like the life I left behind.

I don't belong here.

I sigh, and curl up on the extremely comfortable bed, finally letting exhaustion wash over me. My shadows drape around me like a protective cocoon while Mouse purrs steadily by my feet. The events of the last twenty-four hours swirl through my mind—not just the parade of impossibly attractive men, but everything else too. The lingering question of why I'm really here. The overwhelming sense that I'm completely out of my depth. The growing certainty that I'm not going to survive whatever comes next.

But between my shadows' gentle presence and Mouse's soothing purr, sleep claims me before I can spiral too far into doubt. My last coherent thought is a half-formed prayer that tomorrow might make more sense than today.

I really should have known better.

Chapter 8
KAIA

The morning chimes echoing through Arcanum's halls feel more like a death knell than a wake-up call. I groan, pulling my pillow over my head as my shadows flicker restlessly around the edges of my bed. Mouse, sprawled across my feet, lets out a small chirp that somehow manages to sound judgmental.

"I know, I know. First day. Have to get up." I sit up, watching my shadows twist anxiously around my ankles. "Any chance you guys could behave today?"

A tendril of shadow flicks a textbook off the desk in response.

"Right. Stupid question."

I drag myself out of bed, the cool stone floor sending a shiver up my spine. The uniform hanging in my closet seems to mock me with its crisp lines and perfect creases. I pull it on, grimacing at the stiff fabric but at least happy with the color choice. Black is definitely my color.

As I fasten the last button, my shadows dart around the room, tugging at loose threads and ruffling papers. "Seriously, guys?" I mutter, trying to smooth my uniform back down. "We talked about this. Best behavior, remember?"

A tendril of shadow curls around my wrist, almost apologetic. I sigh, grabbing my bag and heading for the door. "Come on, Mouse. Let's go face the music."

With the chaos of everything yesterday, I'm not surprised that the stairway down to the common room takes my breath away. It really is stunning in its textures and the movement of light and shadow make it feel alive.

I finally reach the common room, my stomach growling because I definitely missed dinner. But more pressing than food is figuring out where I'm supposed to go. I spot Torric hunched over a piece of paper at the table, his brow furrowed in concentration.

"Hey," I say, approaching cautiously. "Is that your schedule?"

Torric grunts, not looking up. He jerks his head towards the counter, where I see a stack of similar papers.

I roll my eyes. "You know, a simple 'yes' would have sufficed. Or maybe even pointing? I hear that's all the rage in polite conversation these days."

He finally looks up, his golden eyes narrowing. "I answered your question."

"Yeah, with all the charm of a grumpy troll," I snap, stomping over to grab my own schedule. I try to play it off with the joke, but the frustration bubbling under the surface has other plans. My shadows flare before I can stop them, darkening the space around us. Torric's brow seems to furrow in confusion.

Great. First day, and I'm already living up to my reputation as the weird girl. I take a deep breath, trying to rein in my temper and my powers. "Look, we're stuck here together. The least we could do is try to be civil."

Torric's expression softens slightly. "You're right. I'm... not great with mornings. Or people. Or mornings with people."

The change in his expression catches me off guard. I wasn't expecting him to back down, but I'll take the win and despite myself, I feel a smile tugging at my lips. "Well, that makes two of us. Truce?"

He nods, the ghost of a smile on his face. "Truce."

I glance down at my own schedule, groaning. "Now, any idea where Rune Methodology is?"

"Yeah, you can follow me," Torric says, gathering his things. He hesitates for a moment before adding, "Just... try not to let your shadow cat eat anyone on the way."

Mister grump has jokes this morning. Great. My shadows twist around my legs as we walk, flicking curiously at the edges of the corridor like they're mapping the way.

The Sorcery Wing's classroom is a circular chamber filled with workstations, each bearing an array of crystals, runes, and what looks suspiciously like scorch marks. I slip into an empty seat near the back, trying to ignore the way conversations halt as I pass. My shadows, agitated by my nerves, keep tugging at the hem of my robes.

"Is this seat taken?"

I look up to find a girl with lavender hair and an eclectic collection of crystals dangling from her ears grinning down at me. Without waiting for an answer, she plops down beside me, her various bangles creating a symphony of chimes.

"I'm Seren. And you're the new shadow mage everyone's talking about." Her smile grows wider. "Nice to meet someone else who doesn't fit the mold around here."

Before I can respond, Professor Idorath sweeps into the room, his pristine white robes a stark contrast to the chaos of his workspace. "Today, we begin with basic rune activation. Remember—precision is everything. One wrong stroke and—" He pauses for dramatic effect. "Well, let's just say the last student who made that mistake still hasn't regrown their eyebrows."

Seren leans over to whisper, "He's exaggerating. It was just one eyebrow."

Despite myself, I feel a smile tugging at my lips.

The task seems simple enough: inscribe a basic illumination rune and channel enough magic through it to create light. I stare at my parchment, trying to steady my hand as my shadows swirl around my fingers, making the simple lines wobble.

"Careful with the angle," Seren murmurs, her own rune glowing with a soft purple light. "Too sharp and it'll—"

My rune sparks violently, sending my inkwell flying. It would have splattered across three different students if my shadows hadn't instinctively caught it—only to drop it directly onto my own notes instead.

"Well," Seren says brightly, watching ink drip onto the floor, "at least you have good reflexes?"

"Miss Draven." Professor Idorath's voice cuts through the snickers. "Perhaps you'd care to explain how you managed to turn a simple illumination rune into what appears to be an ink fountain?"

My face burns. "I just—the angle was wrong, and then—"

"And then chaos ensued?" His eyebrow arches. "Shocking."

More laughter ripples through the class. My shadows twist tighter, and I can feel them plotting revenge. Please don't, I think desperately. Not now.

But it's too late. The shadows dart out, invisible to everyone else, and suddenly every inkwell in the room tips over simultaneously. Screams and curses fill the air as students scramble to save their notes.

"How did you—" Professor Idorath splutters, his own robes now sporting several ink stains.

"Not just one eyebrow this time," Seren whispers, barely containing her laughter as she helps me gather my things. "Come on, let's get out of here before he remembers he can give detention."

In the hallway, I wait for the judgment, the fear, the inevitable distancing that always comes when my magic acts up. Instead, Seren links our arms together, still grinning.

"That," she declares, "was the most entertaining first class I've ever had. Usually we just blow things up or turn something the wrong color. But you?" She gestures at the chaos we've left behind. "You have style."

"I have no control is what I have," I mutter, but I can't help smiling back.

"Control's overrated. Trust me, half the stuff I enchant ends up singing opera or developing a personality." Seren pulls out her schedule. "Please tell me you have combat training next. I want to see what other havoc you can cause."

For the first time since arriving at Arcanum, I feel something loosen in my chest. My shadows settle slightly, curling around my feet like content cats.

I laugh. "Let's go. Probably shouldn't keep the chaos waiting."

Chapter 9
KAIA

Combat training is held in an open courtyard ringed with ancient stone pillars. Faint runes radiate along their surfaces, creating barriers to contain stray magic. Aspen is already there when I arrive, his lean form casually propped against one of the pillars.

"Who is that?" Seren whispers, eyebrows waggling as she openly admires him.

"Just Aspen," I reply, finally meeting his eyes and catching the knowing smirk playing across his lips. He definitely heard her.

"Ready to learn some actual shadow manipulation?" he asks, pushing off from the pillar with fluid grace.

Before I can answer, a wave of heat announces Torric's arrival.

"Wait, there's two of them?" Seren's excited whisper carries, making Aspen choke back a laugh.

Torric strides in like he owns the place, already rolling up his sleeves. "Finally. Someone new to throw around."

"Try it," I mutter, my shadows coiling defensively.

Seren squeezes my arm. "Have fun!" she grins before darting off to her training group.

"Aw, look at them," comes Finn's voice from above. I look up to find him perched impossibly on top of one of the pillars, grinning down at us. "Your shadows are like tiny drunk octopi and I love them."

I blink at him, confusion warring with surprise at his comment, but before I can ask what he means, Torric interrupts.

"Can we focus?" he growls, though I catch the slight twitch of his lips. "Some of us are trying to train here."

Aspen steps forward, ever the mediator. "Kaia, let's start with something basic. Shadow magic isn't unlike water—it needs to flow naturally, not be forced."

He demonstrates, creating a smooth arc of water that catches the light beautifully. I try to mimic the motion with darkness, but my attempt sputters and breaks apart. My personal shadows twitch anxiously, making it harder to concentrate.

"No, no, no," Torric cuts in. "You're thinking too much. Magic is about instinct." He summons a flame to his palm. "Feel it, don't overthink it."

"Really helpful," I snap as my shadow construct dissipates. "Any other vague advice you want to share?"

"Oh! Oh!" Finn waves his hand enthusiastically. "I have some advice—your little friends are about to cause chaos."

I glance down to see my shadows reaching mischievously for Aspen's water flask. I quickly pull my focus back, trying to ignore Finn's knowing grin. "Sorry, I'm just having trouble concentrating."

Aspen's expression softens. "The magic will come. You just need to find your center."

"That's the problem," Torric says, running a hand through his hair in frustration. "You're fighting your instincts instead of working with them. Watch." He drops into a fighting stance. "Try to defend yourself."

"Wait, what—"

He launches forward, flame wreathing his fist. This time, instead of my personal shadows reacting, I manage to pull darkness from the air itself, forming a visible black barrier. The fire crashes against it with a hiss.

"See?" Torric's grin is wild and bright. "When you stop overthinking, you know exactly what to do."

"Great," I pant, letting the construct dissolve. "So I just need to be attacked to use magic properly. Really sustainable training method there."

"I mean, I volunteer to keep attacking you," Torric offers with a wink that makes my stomach flutter traitorously.

"Or," Aspen cuts in smoothly, "we could try something less likely to end in injury."

Finn, now sprawled on the ground, flashes a grin as chaotic as his commentary. "Let them fight. Ten coins on Kaia dumping him in the fountain."

I groan, fighting the smile threatening to form. "Don't encourage any-one," I mutter, though my shadows ripple eagerly, feeding off the energy of the moment.

Out of the corner of my eye, I catch Aspen watching me, his expression unreadable. For a split second, it feels like he sees something in me that I don't understand. It's unsettling—but I don't have time to dwell on it, not with Torric about to charge again.

"Let's take five," Aspen says, tossing me a water bottle. "Before Torric actually does burn something down."

I catch it gratefully, but before I can drink, one of my shadows knocks it sideways, spilling water down my shirt.

"Hey!" I sputter, glaring at the invisible culprit. "What was that for?"

"That one's definitely Patricia," Finn announces, materializing beside me with his usual impossible grace. "She's got attitude."

I stare at him. "You're... naming my shadows?" Then it hits me again. "You can actually see them?"

"Obviously." He points at my largest shadow, currently trying to look dignified. "That's Bob. Very serious fellow. Takes his job very seriously." The shadow actually straightens up at this, and I swear it preens.

"You can't just—" I start, but Finn's already pointing at another one.

"And that troublemaker over there? That's clearly Finnick."

"Finnick?" I repeat incredulously.

"Named after yours truly," Finn says with a dramatic bow. "A true agent of chaos."

As if to prove his point, Finnick tries to trip Torric, who stumbles and swears.

"Stop naming the shadows," I hiss, though I notice Bob is now actually responding when Finn addresses him. "They're not pets!"

"Tell that to Bob," Finn grins. "He's already practicing his guard dog routine."

Indeed, Bob has positioned himself between me and where Malrik lurks in the distance, looking distinctly protective. I hadn't even noticed when the brooding man arrived.

"And that overachiever?" Finn grins, pointing at the shadow looping endlessly around my ankles. "As I said, definitely a Patricia. Type A vibes, for sure."

Patricia bristles, clearly offended by the nickname, while Bob gives an approving nod like he'd been waiting for a second-in-command.

I drop my head into my hands with a groan. "This isn't happening."

"I still can't believe you can see them," I say, watching Finn interact with my shadows like it's the most natural thing in the world. Bob hovers near him attentively while Finnick seems determined to live up to his namesake by creating as much chaos as possible.

"Are you kidding? They're the best entertainment I've had in years." Finn stands beside me, grinning as Patricia attempts what looks suspiciously like an interpretive dance. "Pretty sure they've been trying to get my attention since day one."

I think back to the times my shadows have acted up around him, how they seem to perform specifically for his amusement. They've never responded to anyone else like this. It's like they know something I don't, and the way Finn interacts with them—like it's the most natural thing in the world—makes me question everything I thought I knew about them. "Is that why you're always..." I wave my hand vaguely, "...like this?"

"Like what?" His innocent expression isn't fooling anyone, especially not when Finnick chooses that moment to try stealing Torric's water bottle.

"Hey!" Torric snaps as the bottle mysteriously tips over. "What the—"

"Gravitational anomaly," Finn says seriously. "Very common in these parts. Right, Bob?"

Bob, to my eternal mortification, actually nods.

My gaze drifts to where Malrik still lurks in the shadows, his silver eyes unreadable. Something about his presence makes my shadows stir restlessly, though whether in warning or recognition, I can't tell.

"Don't mind mister brooding, dark and handsome," Finn says, following my gaze. "He's allergic to fun. Unlike Patricia here, who clearly has excellent taste in entertainment."

Patricia preens, and I have to bite back a laugh.

"You're going to make them impossible to deal with, you know that?" I mutter, though my shadows ripple with something dangerously close to pride. Finn just grins.

"Trouble, they were impossible long before I got here. I just gave them permission to own it."

Chapter 10
ASPEN

There's something about the way Kaia moves that I can't look away from—like she's not just learning magic but remembering it. Maybe it's the fierce determination in her violet eyes, or how her wild blonde hair catches the morning light as she dodges. Or maybe it's the way the shadows in the space respond to her, protecting her with an instinctive grace that makes my breath catch.

I force myself to focus on the training aspect, not on how my heart races when she smiles. I'm supposed to be teaching her, not getting lost in the way she makes the darkness bend to her will. But gods, it's mesmerizing. Her progress defies everything I know about magical development, and I find myself watching her hands, her form, the fluid way she transitions between defense and attack.

The air ripples with heat as Torric's fireball surges forward, the crackling flames casting flickering shadows against the courtyard's ancient pillars. Kaia's barrier hisses as it absorbs the attack, the sound sharp and satisfying. Every movement she makes feels both unpracticed and impossibly natural, like she's rediscovering something buried deep within her bones.

"Again," Torric growls, eyes blazing. He launches another fireball, larger this time. I tense, ready to intervene—not just because it's my job, but because something in me needs to keep her safe. But Kaia's ready. Her shadow magic surges upward, forming a shield that not only blocks the attack but seems to absorb it, growing stronger.

Her instincts are remarkable. Most students take months to develop this level of reactive control. Yet here she is, first day of training, already adapting and improvising like she was born to do it. I find myself studying her form, telling myself it's purely professional interest that makes me notice how the academy uniform hugs her curves, how her eyes flash with determination, how her smile grows wider with each successful block.

Torric takes it as a challenge, naturally. His next attack comes faster, hotter, a barrage of flame that would overwhelm most seasoned fighters. I step forward to call him off, my protective instincts flaring, but Kaia laughs—actually laughs—a sound of pure exhilaration that sends an unexpected shiver down my spine as her shadow magic whirls around her protectively.

"Is that all you've got?" she taunts, and I catch Torric's surprised expression before it splits into a fierce grin. My brother's always been drawn to power, and Kaia radiates it like a storm waiting to break.

I should stop this. It's beyond the scope of a normal training session. But I can't deny the raw potential unfolding before me, or how she commands the shadows with innate grace. She moves as if her body remembers skills her mind has forgotten. And more than that, I can't deny how watching her ignites something in me—a need to understand her, to protect her, to...

I cut that thought off quickly. She's my responsibility. Nothing more.

I might not be a professor, but Torric and I both know enough, and the school faculty are well acquainted with our father that they have us training students when professors are unavailable.

A flicker of movement catches my eye. Malrik lurks at the edge of the courtyard, half-hidden in shadow. He stands motionless, his silver eyes fixed on Kaia as they follow her every move with calculating intensity. What game is he playing? More importantly, why does his obvious interest make something twist uncomfortably in my chest?

"Torric," I call out, finally intervening as I see him gathering an alarming amount of fire. "That's enough. Let's give Kaia a break before you burn down half the academy."

My brother shoots me an annoyed look, but I can see the flush of exertion on his cheeks and the slight tremor in his hands. He's pushed himself harder than intended, caught up in the thrill of a worthy opponent. I can't blame him—there's something magnetic about Kaia, something that draws you in despite your best intentions.

I need to be careful. Whatever this pull is, whatever makes my heart race when she smiles or my magic respond to hers, I can't act on it. But as I watch her catch her breath while she banters with Finn, I know I'm already in trouble.

Chapter 11
TORRIC

I watch as the last of the students file out, my gaze lingering on Kaia's retreating form. She's talking animatedly with Finn, who's still gesturing at empty air and making her laugh. The sound hits me in an unexpected place—a mixture of admiration and something else I'm not about to examine too closely.

"Well," I say, turning to Aspen, "that was... unexpected."

My brother nods, his blue eyes thoughtful as ever. "She's a natural. I've never seen anyone pick up shadow manipulation so quickly."

"It's not just quick," I mutter, running a hand through my sweat-dampened hair. The memory of our sparring match still burns fresh in my mind—the way she'd met each of my attacks with an almost primal grace. "It's like she's been doing this her whole life. Did you see how the shadow magic responded to her? Even when she wasn't trying?"

Aspen's brow furrows. "I saw. It's as if the shadow itself is drawn to her. Or..."

"Or as if there's more to her magic than we can see," I finish, watching Finn dodge another invisible attack. "Speaking of which, what's his deal anyway? He's acting weirder than usual."

"Naming shadows that aren't there?" Aspen raises an eyebrow. "That's strange even for Finn."

"And we're not the only ones who've noticed," Aspen says quietly, nodding towards the edge of the courtyard.

I follow his gaze to where Malrik lurks in the shadows, his silver eyes cold and calculating, but there's something else—something almost protective—that makes my fire magic stir uneasily beneath my skin. He's never shown this much interest in a new student before. Or anyone for that matter.

"Great," I mutter. "Because this wasn't complicated enough already."

"When is it ever simple with us?" Aspen's lips twitch into a half-smile, but his eyes remain serious. "Something tells me this is just the beginning."

The words settle heavily in the air between us. I think of the way she'd moved during our match—fluid and powerful, responding with an intensity that matched my own. Her eyes had been alight with a wild joy that made my heart stutter in my chest. The memory of her power calls to something deep within me, an energy I don't fully understand but have always struggled to control.

And I swear those beautiful lavender eyes of hers can see right through me. She probably knows all of my weaknesses without even trying.

"We should keep an eye on her," I say, aiming for casual and probably missing by a mile. "Make sure she doesn't accidentally level the place while she's figuring out her powers."

Aspen gives me a knowing look that makes me want to singe his perfectly styled hair. "Just keep an eye on her, hm?"

I feel heat rising to my cheeks that has nothing to do with my fire magic. "You know what I mean."

"I do," he says softly. "And I agree. But Torric..." He pauses, choosing his words with typical careful precision. "Be careful. I think there's more going on here than we understand."

We start cleaning up the training area in companionable silence, but my mind keeps circling back to the sparring match. Her power doesn't just match mine—it challenges it, makes it flare hotter, brighter. And maybe that's what scares me most.

For a moment, the shadows seem to deepen, and out of that darkness, a shape emerges—a panther cub, its violet eyes gleaming with an intelligence that felt far too knowing. But when I blink, it's gone, leaving me to wonder if Finn's shadow-seeing madness is catching.

"Get some rest," Aspen says, clapping me on the shoulder. "Something tells me we're going to need it."

I nod as I gather my things, but I know sleep won't come easily tonight. Not with the memory of Kaia's fierce smile burning bright in my mind.

Chapter 12
KAIA

I wake to a cold bed and honestly the bedroom feels wrong without Mouse's warmth at my feet. I stare at the ceiling, my shadows curling restlessly around my ankles as I recall last night's conversation with the House Master.

"Familiars are not permitted in dormitories," he'd explained with rehearsed patience, his tone suggesting he'd had this conversation too many times before. "The academy has designated grounds for such companions."

I'd tried to explain that Mouse wasn't exactly a familiar, but the words had stuck in my throat. How could I describe what Mouse was when I barely understood it myself? My necklace seems to vibrate faintly against my chest, almost in sympathy.

My shadows twist tighter, agitated without Mouse's calming presence. One tendril reaches toward the window, as if searching, while another lashes out at my bedpost.

"I know," I mutter. "I miss him too."

I dress quickly, at least there's not much to think about with uniforms, and make my way downstairs. It's oddly quiet so I grab a granola bar from the box on the counter and make my way outside.

The morning air bites cold as I make my way across the grounds, I spot Mouse lounging atop a stone wall, looking entirely unbothered by his new sleeping arrangements. His violet eyes gleam with something like amusement.

"Well, at least one of us slept well," I grumble, as I make my way to him, trying to ignore how my shadows perk up at Mouse's presence.

"So the rumors are true. The Shadow Faction's newest recruit comes with her own pet monster."

I turn to find a girl watching me, her white uniform gleaming impossibly bright in the morning sun. Everything about her radiates perfection, from her platinum blonde hair to her imperious stance. The gold insignia of the Faction of Light catches the light at her throat, momentarily blinding me.

Mouse, oddly, just stretches lazily atop his wall, looking almost smug. His tail swishes once, deliberately, and for just a moment, her confidence falters, her gaze flickering uneasily to Mouse before she recovers, her perfect posture snapping back like a shield.

"He's not a monster," I say, bristling at both the accusation and the girl's tone. My shadows ripple beneath my feet, responding to my irritation. "And you are...?"

"Alenya Virath." She says it like I should recognize the name, like it should mean something profound. When I don't react, her perfect brows arch slightly. "Top student of the Faction of Light. Though I suppose those in the shadows don't keep track of such things."

I remember Finn's warning about her from yesterday. *Watch out for Alenya, he'd said. She makes the sun look harsh.* Now I understand what he meant.

"A pleasure," I say, not meaning it. "I'd introduce myself, but apparently rumors have done that for me."

Alenya's lips curve into something too sharp to be a smile. "Indeed. The shadow girl with her shadow beast. How... fitting." She sweeps past me, but I catch her casting a curious glance back at Mouse. For just a moment, I see something like fear flicker across her impeccable features.

Oh, joy. My first mean girl encounter. Because that's exactly what I needed to complete my "overwhelmed new student" bingo card. What's next, a pop quiz on advanced shadow manipulation? A surprise physical fitness test where we have to outrun rabid hellhounds?

I watch Alenya's retreating form, her white uniform practically glowing in the morning light. Seriously, does she have some kind of personal radiance spell? It's like staring directly into the sun, if the sun wore designer boots and had a superiority complex.

"Well, Mouse," I mutter, my shadows curling around him protectively, "looks like we've made a new friend. Think she'll braid our hair at the next slumber party?"

Mouse just blinks at me, looking far too amused for my liking.

Traitor.

I'm about to continue my semi-internal rant when a familiar presence falls into step beside me. Malrik. Because of course he'd show up now, when I'm already off-kilter and probably have spectacular bedhead. My shadows flutter nervously, and I swear they're trying to smooth my hair.

He doesn't say anything, but the way his silver eyes flicker between me and Mouse feels... deliberate. Like he's piecing together a puzzle. The silence stretches, and I'm torn between breaking it with some witty quip (that I'd definitely botch) or maintaining this weird, oddly comfortable quiet.

That's when I notice Mouse. The little shadow-beast is now weaving between Malrik's legs as we walk, his form seeming to blur slightly at the edges. And I swear, I absolutely swear, I catch the hint of a smirk playing at the corner of Malrik's mouth.

"Traitor," I mutter again, this time aimed at both of them.

Malrik's eyebrow quirks. "Talking to yourself already, Kaia? I thought that was at least a second-week-of-classes kind of breakdown."

"Oh no," I say, unable to keep the sarcasm from my voice, "I've got an accelerated program. Gotta stay ahead of the curve, you know. Next week I'll be wearing my uniform inside out and answering to the name 'Shadowqueen69.'"

His low chuckle sends an unexpected shiver down my spine. Damn it. My shadows react to my flustered state, curling closer to my feet as if trying to ground me.

"I look forward to it," he says, and I can't tell if he's mocking me or... flirting? No, definitely mocking. Probably.

We're nearing the classroom now, and I feel a spike of anxiety. What fresh hell awaits me today? Will Alenya be there, ready with more backhanded compliments? Will my shadows decide to misbehave spectacularly?

Mouse chooses that moment to abandon Malrik and twine around my ankles. The contact instantly soothes some of my frayed nerves, and I feel my shadows settling into a more manageable pattern.

"Thanks," I whisper to him.

Malrik glances down, that ghost of a smirk still playing on his lips. "Seems your 'shadow beast' has good instincts."

I narrow my eyes at him, catching something in his tone. "What's that supposed to mean?"

He shrugs, all innocence, but there's something knowing in his silver eyes. "Just an observation."

Before I can press him further, we enter the classroom. Professor Lira is already there, her silver hair gleaming in the light streaming through the tall windows. Her eyes lock onto me, then flick to Mouse at my feet, and I swear I see recognition there.

"Ah, Ms. Draven," she says, a hint of amusement in her voice. "I see you've brought a guest."

I brace myself for another lecture about rules and proper familiar etiquette, but Lira just smiles. "Some guardians can't be constrained by our rules, can they?"

I blink, caught off guard by her casual acceptance. "I... guess not?"

"Take your seats," Lira says to the class. "I'm Professor Aevorin, but you can all call me Lira or Professor Lira if you must. Today, we'll be discussing the finer points of shadow manipulation."

As I slide into my chair, I notice Alenya watching me from across the room. Her impeccable features are marred by a slight frown as she glances between me and Mouse. Throughout the lesson, Mouse appears periodically at different windows, somehow moving impossibly fast between vantage points. I try to focus on Lira's words about shadow theory, but I keep getting distracted by Alenya's increasingly bewildered looks.

Finally, as we're practicing a particularly tricky bit of shadow weaving, Alenya comes over to me. "Does your shadow cat actually teleport, or am I hallucinating?"

I'm so shocked by the genuine curiosity in her voice that I almost lose control of the shadow tendril I'm manipulating. "Uh... I'm not entirely sure," I admit, watching as my shadows twist into abstract patterns.

Alenya's brow furrows, and for a moment, I see past her perfect facade to the sharp mind beneath. "Interesting," she murmurs, more to herself than to me.

As class ends, Professor Lira calls me over. "Ms. Draven, a word?"

I approach her desk, anxiety bubbling in my stomach. My shadows twist closer, ready to defend or flee. But Lira's smile is kind as she says, "Your... companion is welcome in my future classes. Some rules exist to be bent, especially when ancient magic is involved."

I blink at Professor Lira, my mind struggling to process her words. "Ancient magic?" I repeat, feeling like I've missed a crucial piece of information.

Lira's silver eyes twinkle with something deeper than mere amusement. "Indeed. Your shadow guardian is... unique, to say the least. I suspect there's more to him than meets the eye."

As if on cue, Mouse slinks over to Lira's desk and, to my utter astonishment, curls up at her feet like he belongs there. The professor doesn't even flinch, just reaches down to scratch behind Mouse's ears. My shadows flutter with confusion.

"I... I don't understand," I stammer, watching Mouse purr contentedly. "He's never done that with anyone but me."

Lira's smile softens. "Mouse recognizes a kindred spirit, I think. Now, I imagine you have questions. This is a safe space to ask them, Kaia."

The weight of everything I don't know suddenly crashes down on me. Where do I even start? I take a deep breath, trying to organize my thoughts as my shadows swirl anxiously.

"My shadows," I begin hesitantly, watching as they respond to my voice. "They're not... normal, are they? Even for the Shadow Faction?"

Lira nods, her expression thoughtful. "Your instincts serve you well. Your shadows are indeed unique. They're more... alive, for lack of a better term. Most shadow mages manipulate existing darkness, which you have the ability to do as well. But yours? Yours seem to have a will of their own."

Alive. The word clings to me, heavy and strange. My shadows aren't just magic—they're something more, something I clearly don't understand. And Mouse... a guardian? The implications made my head spin. I shiver, remembering all the times my shadows have acted without my conscious direction. "Is that... dangerous?"

"Power always carries risk," Lira says carefully. "But it's not inherently dangerous. It's a gift, Kaia. One that, with proper training, could make you extraordinarily powerful."

I bite my lip, torn between excitement and fear. "And Mouse? What is he, really?"

Lira's gaze drops to the purring shadow-beast at her feet. "A manifestation of your power, I believe. A guardian born from your shadows, shaped by your subconscious needs and desires." She pauses, then adds softly, "And perhaps... a link to your past."

My mind reels with the implications. My amethyst necklace seems to heat more against my skin, and my shadows writhe with renewed energy.

I nod, not trusting myself to speak.

"We'll talk again." Lira says, giving me a reassuring smile as she returns to the book on her desk. As I turn to leave, Mouse materializes at my side, falling into step beside me like a shadow given form.

"Well," I mutter to him as we exit into the hallway, my shadows trailing behind us like a cloak, "that was... unexpected."

Mouse just blinks up at me, his violet eyes swirling with secrets that only deepen the questions already crowding my mind.

Chapter 13
KAIA

As I step into the hallway, my mind still reeling from Lira's revelations, I nearly collide with a wall of muscle. A wall of muscle that smells like an ocean breeze and sunlight, if that makes any sense. My shadows flutter in surprise, curling briefly around strong legs before I can pull them back. Hands brace my shoulders with a gentleness I don't think I've ever felt before.

I look up (and up) to find Aspen's ice-blue eyes twinkling down at me. His presence is like a cool balm after the intensity of my conversation with Lira, and I feel some of the tension leave my shoulders.

"I really need to stop doing that." The exasperation in my voice has no bite. Aspen's brows furrow, and before I can stop myself, I add, "Literally running into hot guys."

Seriously, Kaia? That's what you're going with?

He chuckles, the sound warming something in my chest. "Lost in thought?"

"You could say that," I manage, trying to ignore the way my heart does a little flip when he smiles, and the loss as he pulls his hands from my shoulders. My shadows jump, almost as if they're laughing at me. "Just had an... interesting chat with Professor Lira."

Aspen's eyebrow quirks. "Interesting, huh? That's Lira-speak for 'mind-blowing and probably terrifying,' isn't it?"

I can't help but laugh. "Got it in one. How'd you know?"

He grins, falling into step beside me as we start walking. "Let's just say I've had my fair share of 'interesting' chats with her. So, where are you headed next?"

"Thorne's class," I say, then groan. "Please tell me it's not another three-hour endurance test."

Aspen's laugh is rich and warm. "Nah, today's all theory, probably. Though with Thorne, that might be even more painful." He pauses, then adds casually, "I've got him next too. Mind if I walk with you?"

"Oh, um, sure," I stammer, caught off guard by the offer. Is he just being nice? Or...? No, don't be ridiculous, Kaia.

We walk in companionable silence for a moment, and I can't help but notice how Aspen seems to part the crowd effortlessly. Students move out of his way without him even trying, like he has some kind of invisible forcefield. Must be nice.

"So," Aspen says, breaking the silence. "How are you settling in? Besides the 'interesting' chats and endurance tests, I mean."

I consider the question, absently watching Mouse weave between our legs as we walk. For some reason I feel like I can actually talk to Aspen. I have no idea why, but he makes me want me to pull down the walls I've built up so high over the years. My shadows trail behind us like a living cape, occasionally reaching out to brush against passing students who get too close. "It's... a lot," I admit. "Everything here is so different from what I'm used to. The magic, the people, the sheer scale of it all. Sometimes I feel like I'm drowning in possibility."

Aspen nods, his expression softening. "I get that. It can be overwhelming, especially when you're still figuring out your place in it all."

"Exactly!" I exclaim, relieved that someone understands. "And don't even get me started on the whole faction rivalry thing. I swear, if one more person from Light gives me the stink-eye..."

Aspen winces sympathetically. "Ah, you've met Alenya, haven't you?"

I'm about to answer as we enter the underground training area, and my jaw drops to the floor. The space is vast, cathedral-like, with black marble pillars rising into shadows above us. Glowing runes run along the walls in mesmerizing patterns, and the air thrums with contained power.

Aspen smirks beside me. "It's something, isn't it?"

"You're not kidding." His chuckle calms me as we move deeper into the vast space.

Mouse tries to follow me in, but Thorne appears in front of us, his presence filling the space like a physical force. "No familiars in the combat arena." His tone brooks no argument. "Safety protocols."

I glance at Mouse, remembering Lira's words about ancient magic and guardians. But before I can explain, Thorne adds, "Even exceptional ones, Ms. Draven."

Mouse's violet eyes narrow, but he retreats, his form melting into the shadows near the doorway. I swear I catch Thorne watching with unusual interest, his dark eyes gleaming with something that makes my shadows curl defensively.

Asshole.

Chapter 14
Kaia

The arena is arranged in a semicircle, with students positioned at intervals marked by glowing runes. Black marble pillars rise around us this time, their surfaces carved with ancient symbols that seem to writhe in the flickering light. My shadows reach out curiously toward the nearest rune, only to recoil as if stung.

"Combat magic requires precision," Thorne announces, his voice echoing off the stone. "Shadow manipulation in battle can mean the difference between life and death. There is no room for... improvisation."

His gaze settles on me as he says the last word, and I feel my shadows bristle, one tendril slinking toward him before I can rein it in. Through the high windows, I glimpse Mouse's form darting past, checking on me. His violet eyes gleam with concern.

"Today, we'll practice offensive constructs," Thorne continues. "Watch carefully."

He raises one hand, and shadows coalesce into a perfect blade, its edge sharp enough to slice through the demonstration dummy without touching it. The control is impressive, but something about it feels wrong - too rigid, too forced. My own shadows shrink away from his demonstration, as if sensing something unnatural in his technique.

"Ms. Draven." Thorne's voice snaps me back to attention. "Demonstrate."

"I'm good." I manage, because no way do I want to do this.

He sneers, "It wasn't a request." Irritation visible on his face.

I reluctantly step forward, uncomfortably aware of everyone watching. My shadows swirl around my feet, agitated by the pressure. I try to shape my shadow magic as Thorne did, but it resists, wanting to move in its own way. The jewel around my neck seems to glow, its rhythm slightly erratic.

Control," Thorne snaps, like the word itself is a weapon. My jaw tightens, but I feel the cracks forming—his disdain hitting where I'm already weak. My shadows twist tighter, confused by my anger, or maybe reflecting it. I can't even tell anymore.

Thorne steps closer, adjusting my stance with precise movements that make my shadows recoil. "Again. Power without control is chaos, and chaos has no place in combat."

"I beg to differ!" I hear Finn yell from somewhere behind me. The snickers that follow will only encourage him.

I try again, focusing on pulling shadow magic from the darkness around me rather than using my personal shadows, which are still writhing unhappily at my feet. This time, the construct holds its shape better, though it's not nearly as precise as Thorne's.

"Better," he says, but his eyes are fixed on my personal shadows with an intensity that makes my skin crawl. "Though you have... additional resources at your disposal. Consider using them."

"Raw talent is rare," Thorne continues, pitching his voice so only I can hear. "But without proper guidance, it can be... dangerous. Both to yourself and others."

Something in his tone makes me think he's not just talking about standard shadow magic anymore. I force myself to meet his gaze, though my shadows quiver with unease. "I'm learning control."

"Are you?" His eyes flick meaningfully to where one of my shadows has started creeping toward him again. I hadn't even noticed. "Perhaps you could benefit from some additional instruction. Private lessons, to help you... focus your gifts."

Before I can respond, I feel a steadying presence beside me. Aspen. The air around him seems cooler, calming. "Professor," he says smoothly, "should we practice the defensive formations next?"

Thorne's expression shifts, becoming more distant. "Indeed. Everyone pair up. Ms. Draven, work with Mr. Agere. His control might prove... instructive."

As we move into position, Aspen murmurs, "You okay?"

I nod, though my shadows are still agitated. "Yeah. Thanks."

"The key," Aspen says as we square off, "is to work with the magic, not against it." His voice is calm, steadying. "Shadow magic responds to intention as much as will."

Easy for him to say. His shadow construct flows like water, forming a perfect shield. Mine still feels raw, unfinished, like trying to sculpt with smoke.

"Intention, not force," he reminds me gently.

"How do you even know all this?" I ask because seriously Aspen is like a professor with how much he knows.

His eyes darken "My father taught Torric and I everything long before we should have known." He pauses, "Abilities are supposed to manifest and become stronger with age, but it can be forced." I notice his eyes flick to his water ruin and I have so many questions. But I don't press, not with the topic dulling the light in his blue eyes.

I take a breath, trying to focus. This time, instead of forcing the shadow magic into shape, I let myself feel the darkness around us. It's different from my personal shadows - cooler, less alive, but still responsive. My necklace warms slightly against my skin, as if encouraging this approach.

"Hey," Aspen says softly, stepping closer. "You're thinking too hard. Let it flow naturally."

He reaches out, his hand hovering just above my arm. I can feel the warmth radiating from his skin, and my shadows respond, reaching out to brush against him. The contact sends a jolt through me, and suddenly my magic snaps into focus.

The shadows coalesce into a perfect replica of Aspen's blade, its edge gleaming wickedly in the low light of the arena. My personal shadows dance with excitement, and I feel a surge of pride mingled with surprise.

"Whoa," I breathe, staring at the construct in amazement.

Aspen grins, looking impressed. "See? You've got this."

"Adequate," Thorne's voice cuts through our moment of triumph. He's been circling the room, but seems to hover near our station more than others. "Though unconventional. Mr. Agere, demonstrate the standard form again."

I catch the slight tightening around Aspen's eyes, though his voice remains perfectly respectful. "Of course, Professor."

As Aspen demonstrates, I notice something odd. While everyone else's shadow constructs are uniform - precise, rigid things - his have a subtle fluidity to them, like he's adapted the standard forms to work better with his natural magic. My shadows reach out curiously, drawn to the grace of his movements.

"Your turn, Ms. Draven," Thorne commands.

My construct wavers as his attention fixes on me again. Through the window, Mouse is a dark blur of motion, and my personal shadows twist anxiously around my feet.

"Focus," Thorne snaps. "Control your... distractions."

Something in his tone makes my shadows bristle. The construct I'm trying to form suddenly warps, sprouting jagged edges before dissolving completely. The ambient shadows in the room seem to pulse in response to my agitation.

"I see we have much to work on," Thorne says silkily. "Perhaps those private lessons would be beneficial after all."

"I-" I begin, but he's already moving away, calling the class to attention for the next exercise.

Aspen catches my eye, his expression concerned. "You don't have to accept, you know."

"What?"

"The private lessons. Thorne offers them sometimes, not always for the reasons he says. Just... be sure it's what you want."

Before I can ask what he means, Thorne's voice rings out again. "Next, we'll practice offensive applications. Everyone find a new partner."

My shadows curl uneasily as I watch Aspen move away. Why do I get the feeling this is going to be a very long class?

I'm still trying to process Aspen's warning when a familiar drawling voice cuts through my thoughts.

"Partner up with me, shadow girl?" Finn materializes beside me, grinning like this is all terribly amusing. "Promise I'll go easy on you."

My shadows perk up at his presence, and I swear one of them actually waves. *Traitors.*

"Remind me again why I'd want you to go easy on me?" I ask, but I'm already moving into position across from him. My shadows trail after me like eager puppies.

Finn's grin widens. "Because otherwise I might have to actually try, and then where would we be?"

Before I can retort, Thorne's voice cuts through the chatter. "Begin. Remember - precision. Control. No... improvisations."

That last word is definitely aimed at Finn, who responds with an impossibly innocent expression that wouldn't fool a blind troll. My shadows quiver with what feels suspiciously like suppressed laughter.

We square off. Finn's shadow construct forms with surprising grace - all flowing lines and deadly edges.

Show-off.

"Come on, Trouble," he taunts playfully. "Show me what you've got."

I reach for the shadow magic again, trying to remember how it felt with Aspen. My personal shadows are practically bouncing with excitement, making it hard to concentrate on forming a proper construct.

"Focus, Ms. Draven," Thorne calls out. He's watching us intently, his dark eyes narrowed. "Control those... distractions."

Something in his tone makes my shadows bristle again. The construct I'm trying to form wavers, then suddenly snaps into perfect clarity - a wickedly sharp blade that would make Thorne proud.

Except...

"Um, Kaia?" Finn's voice is filled with barely suppressed laughter. "Your shadows are giving you a standing ovation."

I glance down to see my personal shadows doing exactly that - complete with tiny clapping motions and what appears to be an enthusiastic wave. Mortified, I try to rein them in, but they seem determined to express their appreciation for my success.

Thorne's expression could curdle milk. "Ms. Draven. A word after class."

Finn winces sympathetically. "Sorry about that. Though you have to admit, they've got great comedic timing."

I'm about to respond when Mouse appears at one of the high windows, his violet eyes fixed on something - or someone - behind me. I turn to find Malrik watching our practice session, his expression unreadable. His silver eyes seem to track the movement of my shadows, but that's impossible. Right?

Great. Just great. Because this day needed more complications.

"Again," Thorne commands, and I force myself to focus on the shadow magic, trying to ignore my personal shadows' continuing performance art.

As the other students file out after class, I stay behind, my heart hammering against my ribs. Finn squeezes my shoulder as he passes. "Want me to wait?"

I shake my head, though I appreciate the offer. "I'll be fine."

"If you're sure..." He hesitates, then adds quietly, "Find me after?"

I manage a nod, and he reluctantly leaves, though not before casting one last concerned look over his shoulder. My shadows reach after him briefly before curling back around my feet.

My personal shadows curl closer as Thorne approaches, their usual playfulness replaced by something almost protective. Through the window,

Mouse has gone completely still, watching with an intensity that makes me nervous.

"Ms. Draven." Thorne's voice is silk over steel. "Your raw talent is... remarkable. But your lack of discipline is becoming a problem."

I straighten my spine, trying to dismiss feeling like a child under his gaze. "I told you, I'm learning control."

"Are you?" His eyes fix on my shadows. "Because what I witnessed today was not control. It was chaos. And chaos..." He steps closer, his presence overwhelming, "chaos gets people killed."

"I wouldn't-" I start to protest, but he cuts me off.

"You don't know what you would or wouldn't do, because you don't understand your own power." His tone softens slightly. "That's why you need guidance. Proper guidance."

My shadows twist uneasily. "Professor Lira-"

"Professor Aevorin," he interrupts smoothly, "is an excellent teacher of theory. But combat magic requires a firmer hand." He pauses, studying me. "I could help you master this power. Private lessons, twice a week. We'll start with the basics of control."

Everything in me wants to refuse, but I remember how my shadows reacted during class, how easily they got away from me. What if he's right? What if I really am dangerous?

"I..." I hesitate, and his eyes gleam with something like triumph but it's quickly hidden behind his typically stoic mask.

"Think about it," he says. "But don't take too long. Power like yours," his voice low and deliberate, "has a way of drawing attention. Untrained magic invites... complications. Ones you may not be ready to face alone."

As if to prove his point, one of my shadows lashes out, curling aggressively toward him before I can stop it. Thorne doesn't flinch, just raises an eyebrow. "Predictable," Thorne murmurs, his gaze flicking to my shadows. "Chaos always seeks control, whether it knows it or not."

He turns away, dismissing me but not before I catch the smirk playing on his lips. "Let me know your decision by tomorrow."

I practically flee the arena, my shadows swirling agitatedly around me. Mouse materializes at my side the moment I clear the doorway, pressing against my legs in silent comfort.

"There you are!" Finn's voice makes me jump. He's lounging against the wall, clearly having ignored my dismissal. "That bad, huh?"

"I don't want to talk about it," I mutter, but I'm pathetically grateful he waited. My shadows stretch toward him, seeking comfort. I don't want him to notice my hands trembling in a way I can't control. That isn't me, that isn't how I work and I'm not about to start now. I steel my resolve in hopes of making it through the rest of the day.

"Fair enough." He falls into step beside me. "Want to grab food instead? I hear they're serving mystery meat in the dining hall. Ten gold says it's actually transmuted troll toes."

Despite everything, I feel my lips twitch. "You're disgusting."

"You love it." He grins, then sobers slightly. "Seriously though, you okay?"

I think about Thorne's words, about control and chaos and power that needs containing. About private lessons and firm hands and proper guidance. The amethyst thrums against my skin, as if trying to tell me something.

"I don't know," I admit quietly.

Mouse bumps my hand with his head, and my shadows curl around us both like a protective cocoon. At least I'm not facing this alone.

"Screw it," I mutter suddenly. "Mouse, you're staying in my room tonight. House rules be damned."

Finn's grin widens. "Now that's the chaos I like to see."

Chapter 15
KAIA

The summons arrives at breakfast, tucked neatly beside my plate like some kind of smug afterthought. I barely have time to grab my granola bar before Finn snatches it up, his grin all mischief as he reads aloud in an exaggerated, overly proper tone.

"Shadow Faction," he announces, ignoring my glare. "You are hereby required to attend a meeting with Professor Thorne in the combat arena at precisely eleven o'clock. Attendance is mandatory."

"Sounds ominous," I mutter, snatching the note back before he can add anything more. My shadows coil protectively around the parchment like they can shield me from whatever unpleasantness Thorne has in store.

"Mandatory Thorne time?" Finn grins. "Count me out. Or better yet, can I bring popcorn?"

Aspen looks up from his tea, his calm presence cutting through Finn's antics. "It's probably nothing. Orientation-related, most likely. It's pretty common."

"Orientation with Thorne?" Torric scoffs from across the table. "That sounds more like a prelude to torture."

Malrik doesn't say anything, but his silence speaks louder than Finn's theatrics or Torric's cynicism. His silver eyes flicker with something that makes my shadows curl tighter, and the knot in my stomach twists a little more. He gives me an almost imperceptible nod, his silver eyes glinting with something unreadable. Does he sense it too—the way Aspen's words don't quite match the tension in his tone?

Now, as I descend the winding stone staircase toward the combat arena, I can't shake the growing sense of dread. My shadows trail after me, their tendrils darting nervously at my feet. Bob insists on scouting ahead, while Patricia sticks close, probably taking mental notes. And Finnick is doing some type of dance? They're more jittery than usual, which does nothing to calm my nerves.

"So, Shadow Faction," Finn says, watching Bob investigate a particularly suspicious-looking step. "I hear they throw the best parties. What do you think?"

I roll my eyes, even as Finnick attempts to trip him. "Sure, if you want to party with brooding emos who think they're too cool for school."

"Sounds perfect," Finn quips with a wink that I definitely don't find charming. He gracefully sidesteps Finnick's attempt at sabotage when he tries and fails to trip him, which only encourages the shadow's antics.

"I have no interest in throwing a party," I complain, even though I know he's just trying to distract me.

Aspen's steady presence anchors me, his calm energy a contrast to my jittery nerves. He must see it all on my face though, because he leans in closer, heat radiating from him. "Don't worry," he says softly. "We'll face whatever it is together."

Before I can respond, Torric's voice booms off the stone walls, making my shadows jump.

"They use these meetings to weed out the weak," he says with a predatory grin. "Make the newbies fight to the death."

My stomach drops. "Tell me you're joking." Bob immediately puffs up while Patricia frantically starts cataloging escape routes.

I glance at Malrik, hoping for reassurance, but he's unnervingly quiet, silver eyes distant. My shadows reach toward him before I can stop them, and I swear his lips twitch in response.

Mouse prowls beside us as we reach the underground training area. The shadows here feel alive, pulsing with barely contained energy that makes my skin tingle.

That's when I spot Alenya, glaring at us disdainfully like we're something nasty she stepped in. Bob immediately starts making rude gestures that I'm glad only Finn can see.

"Well, well," she drawls. "If it isn't the misfit squad. You should stick to the shadows where you belong—out of sight."

The barb stings. My shadows quiver, but Malrik steps forward, looming over Alenya with dangerous grace.

"Watch that forked tongue," he says, voice low. The shadows around him seem to deepen. "Unless you'd like me to remove it."

Alenya's perfect mask cracks for a split second as her gaze flicks between Malrik and me. She recovers quickly, but I catch the unease in her eyes before she stalks away. I'm caught between feeling touched by his defense and unnerved by the casual threat.

"Geez, Mal," Finn whispers while Finnick makes exaggerated swooning motions. "Remind me never to piss you off."

As more students file in, Bob takes up a protective stance, Patricia organizes the other shadows into formation, and Finnick practices dramatic death scenes. At least someone's enjoying themselves.

The voices die down as Professor Thorne strides to the center, his dark robes billowing. His sharp gray gaze scans the room, lingering on me a heartbeat too long. My shadows twist closer.

"Welcome, first-years," his smooth voice carries effortlessly. "Today marks the beginning of a hallowed Arcanum tradition—the Dignus Trials."

A collective intake of breath ripples through the crowd. Even Finn is uncharacteristically silent. Bob abandons his stance to peer intently at Thorne while Patricia vibrates with the need to document every word.

Thorne's lips curl into a smile that doesn't reach his eyes. "These trials separate the exceptional from the adequate. In a few weeks, you face your first lone trial—a test of individual prowess and magical mastery."

My stomach flips. A few weeks? I can barely control my shadows on a good day. Finnick, sensing my distress, attempts a cartwheel that only makes me more nervous.

"Following that," Thorne continues, "you will undergo team trials within your factions. Your success—or failure—determines your standing here." His gaze fixes on me again, though I don't think anyone else notices. "Some of you may require... additional guidance to reach your full potential."

I glance at my group—Aspen's jaw is set with determination; Torric looks ready to either be sick or punch something; Malrik's face is unreadable, but tension radiates from him like heat.

"Remember," Thorne's gaze sweeps over us, "at Arcanum, mediocrity is not an option. The trials will test not just your magical ability, but your very essence."

As the crowd disperses, murmuring anxiously, I remain rooted. The weight of Thorne's words crashes over me like a tidal wave. My shadows mirror my anxiety, writhing restlessly around my feet while Mouse presses against my leg, a solid warmth against the cold dread settling in my stomach.

How can I possibly measure up?

As we file out of the combat arena, my mind whirls like a tempest. The Dignus Trials. The words echo in my head, each repetition amplifying the dread that's settled deep in my bones. My shadows writhe anxiously, their usually playful movements now frantic and erratic. Bob keeps darting ahead, then rushing back as if he can't decide whether to scout or protect. Patricia's busy muttering to herself, probably compiling lists of every magical skill I need to master in the next few weeks. And Finnick? He's alternating between dramatic fainting spells and what I can only describe as shadow push-ups.

I hang back as the others start up the winding staircase, my gaze drawn to Torric's broad shoulders. Unlike the rest of us, he and Aspen hadn't seemed shocked by Thorne's announcement. Curious and desperate for any insight, I fall into step beside him.

"Hey," I say, trying to keep my voice casual. "Can I ask you something?"

Torric grunts, which I take as assent. Up close, I can see the tension in his jaw, the way his golden eyes flicker with something that looks suspiciously like concern.

"You didn't look surprised," I press on. "About the trials, I mean. Did you... know about them?"

He's quiet for a long moment, and I start to think he's going to ignore me. But then he sighs, running a hand through his wild mane of hair. "Yeah," he admits gruffly. "I knew."

"How?" I ask, my curiosity piqued. I would have asked Aspen, but something he'd said earlier about their father had made me hesitate. "I mean, everyone else looked like Thorne had just announced we were going to be fed to dragons or something."

A wry smile tugs at Torric's lips. "Dragon-feeding is next semester," he quips, but there's no real humor in his voice.

We reach a landing, and Torric pauses, leaning against the cool stone wall. The torchlight casts flickering shadows across his face, making him look older, more serious than I've ever seen him.

"Our father," he begins, his voice low, "he's... well, he's friends with Thorne. Has been for as long as I can remember."

I blink, surprised. "Your dad is friends with that... that..."

"Pompous, terrifying asshole?" Torric supplies helpfully.

I can't help but laugh, some of the tension easing from my shoulders. "Yeah, that."

Torric nods, his expression growing somber again. "Aspen and I, we've been training for these trials our entire lives. Father made sure of it."

The weight of his words hits me like a physical blow. My shadows curl protectively around my ankles, sensing my distress. "Your entire lives?" I repeat, my voice barely above a whisper.

Torric's golden eyes meet mine, a storm of emotions swirling in their depths. He nods slowly, his voice dropping even lower. "Typically, magic manifests around twelve or thirteen, when puberty hits. It's this whole big thing – a coming of age moment, you know?"

I nod, even though it's not the same as what happened to me. I've always had my magic and my shadows, as far back as I can remember.

"But for us," Torric continues, his voice tight, "it was different. On our fifth birthday, our father..." He pauses, his fists clenching at his sides. "He forced these runes on us."

My eyes widen in shock, and I instinctively reach out to touch the fiery wolf emblazoned on his chest. Torric flinches slightly but doesn't pull away. Under my fingertips, I can feel a faint pulse of magic, wild and barely contained. It doesn't escape me how he shivers at my touch.

"Forced?" I whisper, horrified. "But how? Why?"

Torric's laugh is bitter, devoid of any real humor. "To give us an edge. To make us stronger, faster, more powerful than our peers. The runes aren't natural, Kaia. They're..." He struggles for a moment, searching for the right word. "They're cheating, essentially."

My shadows writhe in agitation, picking up on my distress. Bob puffs up indignantly, while Patricia seems to be furiously taking mental notes. Finnick, in a rare moment of seriousness, wraps a comforting tendril around my wrist.

"But that's not the worst part," Torric continues, his voice barely above a whisper. The torchlight flickers, casting deep shadows across his face, making him look haunted. "When we hit puberty, when our natural magic should have manifested... nothing happened."

The ache in my chest grows for this man. What he and Aspen must have endured. "You mean..."

He nods grimly. "The runes interfered with our natural magical development. Aspen and I, we should have had powerful shadow magic, like you. But because of what our father did..." His voice trails off, thick with emotion.

The torchlight flickers, casting restless shadows across Torric's face. His fists clench at his sides, and I can hear the strain in his voice as if the words themselves are painful to say.

The corridor suddenly feels too small, too confining. My heart aches for Torric, for Aspen, for the choices that were stolen from them before they were old enough to understand. My shadows stretch out, instinctively seeking to comfort, to protect.

I thought about the way my shadows seemed to have a life of their own, how they sometimes acted without my permission. Would I feel the same loss as Torric if someone had tried to cage them?

"That's why," Torric says, his eyes fixed on my writhing shadows with a mix of longing and resignation, "that's why I sometimes come across as... well, an ass. Especially about magic. It's not that I don't respect what you can do, Kaia. It's just..."

"You're mourning what you lost," I finish softly, understanding dawning.

He nods, a vulnerability in his eyes that I've never seen before. He takes a deep breath, his mask slipping back into place before he turns abruptly, leaving me there alone.

A tear escapes for those poor boys and what was done to them. I brush the tear away, trying to steel myself. Torric had been forced to fight with borrowed power, but my magic is my own—wild, unpredictable, and untamed. How can I possibly shape it into something worthy of the trials?

Chapter 16
KAIA

We've all made our way back to the Shadow Faction, and I've been staring out the window in the common room for longer than I'd like to admit.

"Hey, you okay there, Trouble?"

Finn's voice interrupts my spiraling thoughts. His arm slides around my shoulders, and I find myself leaning into him despite my best efforts to maintain some dignity. Even my shadows settle at his touch, though Bob seems determined to pat my head consolingly—which feels exactly like being brushed by a concerned cobweb.

"I'm fine," I lie, my voice brittle. "Just peachy. You know, if peaches were rotten and filled with maggots of self-doubt."

"Well, that's a delightfully gross metaphor." Finn squeezes my shoulder. "But seriously, Kaia, you've got this. We've all got this." He pauses, watching as Finnick attempts what appears to be a motivational shadow-dance. "And hey, at least your personal cheerleading squad seems confident."

I want to believe him. But as I look out at the academy grounds I can't help but feel overwhelmed.

I'm never going to be enough.

Finn's arms move, tightening around my waist as he shifts, settling behind me, his chin resting on my shoulder, and I can't help but place my hands over his where they rest on my stomach. The warmth of his body seeps into me, chasing away some of the chill that's settled in my bones.

I'm not used to touch, to this closeness, but with Finn it seems natural. It fills me with a warmth that's unfamiliar but welcome.

Outside, the academy grounds stretch before us, bathed in the soft glow of twilight. The ancient trees sway gently, their leaves shimmering with an otherworldly iridescence. In the distance, the spires of the Observatory pierce the darkening sky, their crystalline surfaces catching the last rays of sunlight and refracting them in a dazzling display of color.

"You know," Finn murmurs, his breath tickling my ear, "I think we could all use a bit of practice. What do you say we round up the gang and have ourselves a little shadow-slinging session?"

I consider his offer, watching as a group of students from the Light Faction glide by on shimmering discs of pure radiance. Their laughter carries on the evening breeze, a sense of longing for freedom like that washes over me.

"Yeah," I finally agree, my voice barely above a whisper. "That might be good."

As I lean back against Finn, I become acutely aware of a certain... firmness pressing against me. Heat rushes to my cheeks as I realize the effect our closeness is having on him. Part of me wants to tease him about it, but I'm too emotionally drained to summon my usual snark.

Instead, I turn in his arms, meeting his gaze. His green eyes are dark with a mix of desire and concern, and for a moment, I let myself get lost in them. It's easier than facing the doubts that threaten to consume me.

"Alright, let's do this," I say, injecting a confidence into my voice that I don't quite feel. "But if Bob tries to give anyone a shadow wedgie again, I'm calling it quits."

Finn's laugh rumbles through his chest, and I can't help but smile in response. As we step away from the window, my shadows swirl around us, seeming to pulse with renewed energy.

We reach the combat arena—other students already practicing spells, and huddled in strategic discussions—I can't shake the feeling that I'm drowning in expectations. Thorne's offer of private lessons echoes in my mind, tempting and terrifying. Patricia's frantic shadow-scribbling of what look like evacuation plans isn't helping my anxiety.

Mouse growls softly at my feet, probably unimpressed with my escape fantasy. Leaving would mean giving up the first place I've ever felt like I might belong. Even my shadows have found their niche, with Bob playing sergeant to the smaller wisps.

"Finn?"

"Yeah?"

"Promise me something?"

He grins at me, wrapping his arm over my shoulders again, green eyes twinkling. "Anything for you, Trouble. Except maybe my last cookie. A man's got to have limits." He shrugs. "But honestly, I'd probably give you that too."

I take a moment, needing to push back that hint of vulnerability in his tone.

"Promise me that when I inevitably crash and burn in these trials, you'll at least make my eulogy funny?"

His arm tightens, and for a moment, his usual playfulness vanishes. "Not happening, Kaia. Because you're not going to crash and burn. You're going to shine so fucking bright you'll put the Light Faction to shame. And we'll be right there with you, every step of the way."

As if to prove his point, he releases me and our little band of misfits materializes around us. Aspen, all grace and careful control. Torric, barely contained power and intensity. Malrik, quiet danger that makes my shadows quiver. And Finn...

Well, Finn is currently trying to juggle fireballs.

"Finn!" I yelp as flame whizzes past my ear. My shadows scatter in all directions, except for Finnick, who seems far too interested in the potential for chaos. "What in the name of all that's unholy are you doing?"

"Livening things up! Come on, Trouble, where's your sense of adventure?"

"Probably hiding with my sense of self-preservation," I mutter, but I'm fighting a smile. The familiar chaos is oddly comforting, even as Bob tries to herd the other shadows away from Finn's impromptu fire show.

That's when everything goes wrong.

Chapter 17
KAIA

One of Finn's fireballs spirals wild, hurtling straight for Aspen. I react on instinct, shadows erupting from my fingertips in a protective surge. But I've misjudged, overcompensated, and suddenly my power is everywhere, writhing with a life of its own. The air thickens as my shadows burst free, their movement erratic and wild, pulling at the edges of my control. A deep hum vibrates in my chest—a warning or an echo, I can't tell. Something doesn't feel right but I can't stop to think about it. Even Bob loses his usual composure, dissolving into the maelstrom. The shadows writhe and stretch, snaking toward the edges of the arena like living tendrils of ink. I hear startled gasps, the scrape of boots as students step back, but the shadows are too fast, too chaotic. The air is heavy, like trying to breathe through damp wool, and the deep hum in my chest grows louder, more insistent.

"I can't—I can't control it!" The words tear from my throat as Patricia's frantic attempts to catalog the chaos only make it worse. Mouse growls, hackles raised at the surge of power.

And then a figure steps between me and the spreading darkness. His hands move in an intricate pattern, and I feel my magic respond, settling back into my skin. My shadows retreat reluctantly, though they keep their distance from him—even Bob hanging back with unusual wariness.

"Breathe," he says, voice low and steady. "You're safe."

I stare up at him, heart pounding for reasons that have everything and nothing to do with fear. The way he moves, the quiet confidence in his stance—it's both attractive and slightly unnerving. "Who... who are you?"

His storm-gray eyes lock onto mine, and for a moment, I forget how to breathe. He's devastatingly handsome, with high cheekbones and a jawline that could cut glass. His dark hair falls in artful disarray, as if he just ran his fingers through it, and I have to resist the urge to do the same.

"Darian Luthar," he says, his voice a low, velvety purr that sends shivers down my spine. "I'm new to Arcanum."

I can't help but notice him—there's something almost too deliberate in the way he moves, like every step is part of a game I don't understand. He's tall, easily over six feet, with broad shoulders tapering to a lean waist. His black shirt clings to his muscular frame in all the right places, hinting at the strength beneath. Everything about him screams danger and mystery, from the way he holds himself—coiled tension, like a predator ready to strike—to the knowing smirk playing at the corners of his full lips.

Those lips... I shouldn't be staring at them, but I can't help myself. They look soft, inviting, and I find myself wondering what they'd feel like against mine. Heat floods my cheeks at the thought, and I force my gaze back to his eyes.

Big mistake. His gaze is intense, almost hypnotic, and I feel like I'm drowning in those stormy depths. There's something familiar about them, something that tugs at the edges of my memory, but I can't quite place it. It's maddening and intoxicating all at once.

"I... um... thanks," I stammer, cursing my sudden inability to form coherent sentences. "For the help, I mean. With the shadows."

Darian's smirk widens into a full-blown smile, and oh gods, it's unfair how attractive it makes him. "Happy to assist," he says, and even his voice is sexy—deep and rich, with a hint of an accent I can't quite place. "You've got quite the power there."

I should be focusing on his words, on the fact that he somehow managed to control my out-of-control shadows when even I couldn't. But all I can think about is the way his presence seems to fill the entire arena, drawing me in like a moth to flame. There's an aura of power around him, dark and alluring. My shadows curl away from him, an unease moving through them that I can't understand.

"Yeah, well," I manage, trying to summon some of my usual snark, "I like to keep things interesting."

He chuckles, the sound sending warmth pooling in my belly. "I can see that." His gaze sweeps over me, lingering in a way that makes my skin tingle.

He smiles, and it's like watching a storm break. "And you must be the infamous Kaia Draven."

"Infamous?" I manage to squeak, trying to ignore how my shadows seem to be huddling behind me. "I prefer 'misunderstood,' thank you very much."

"My apologies." His laugh does funny things to my insides, even as Mouse's low growl vibrates against my leg. "Allow me to rephrase. You're the intriguingly misunderstood Kaia Draven, whose reputation precedes her."

Before I can formulate a response that doesn't make me sound completely brain-dead, Finn materializes at my side. My shadows immediately perk up, Finnick doing what appears to be a victory dance.

"Careful there, new guy." Finn's tone is light, but there's an edge I've never heard before. "Our Kaia's got enough admirers without adding to the fan club."

I elbow him in the ribs, willing my face not to burst into flames. "I am not—that's not—" Patricia seems to be taking detailed notes on my eloquent response while Bob hovers protectively nearby.

"You wound me, Trouble!" Finn clutches his chest. "And here I thought we had something special."

I roll my eyes, but I'm grateful for his familiar banter. It helps ground me, even as I find my gaze drawn back to Darian's enigmatic smile. There's something magnetic about him, despite the way my shadows shrink from his presence.

Or maybe because of it.

"Well, I look forward to seeing what other... surprises you have in store, Kaia Draven."

The way he says my name, like he's savoring each syllable, does funny things to my insides.

The temperature around me seems to plummet as Malrik materializes on my other side. He doesn't seem happy about Darian's presence if the scowl on his face is anything to go by.

My shadows, caught between retreating from Darian and reaching for Malrik, create an awkward dance that would be comical if I wasn't so confused by the tension crackling through the air. Bob keeps his distance, his usually solid form wisping nervously, while Patricia hovers indecisively. It's Finnick who darts closest, curious despite the rising tension.

And Finn—he keeps his arm firmly around me, holding me against him like he's afraid I'll run off with Darian the moment he lets go.

What have I gotten myself into?

Somewhere in the chaos, Bob attempts to organize an emergency shadow meeting. I pretend not to notice when Finnick starts taking bets.

Chapter 18
MALRIK

I watch the scene unfold before me, my jaw clenching as this... Darian... steps far too close to Kaia. One moment, we're all practicing—fine, we're all watching Kaia practice—and the next, he's swooping in like some dashing hero, making comments that have her blushing.

I can't help but scoff internally. There wasn't even any real danger. Kaia's magic may have flared, but it's nothing we couldn't have handled. Yet here he is, playing the gallant savior, and Kaia's falling for it hook, line, and sinker. Her shadows—usually so perceptive—seem conflicted around him. They retreat, yet there's a curiosity in their movement that sets my teeth on edge.

I study him carefully, noting the easy grace of his movements, the charming smile that seems just a touch too perfect. There's something... off about him that makes the shadows around me writhe uneasily. I back away from Finn and Kaia... he can handle it.

"Aspen," I murmur, not taking my eyes off the newcomer as he continues to charm Kaia while Finn attempts to lighten the suddenly charged atmosphere. "A word?"

I don't wait for a response; I just turn and stride a few paces away, trusting that he'll follow. When he does, I keep my voice low and measured. "What do you make of our new friend?"

Aspen's icy blue eyes flick between me and the group. His expression is thoughtful as we watch Kaia laugh at something Finn says, while Darian maintains that calculated proximity to her. "He seems... convenient," Aspen says finally. "Do you know anything about him?"

I shake my head, frustration bubbling beneath my carefully composed exterior. "Nothing. And that's what worries me. In a place like Arcanum, secrets don't stay hidden for long. Yet I've never even heard his name before today."

"Worried about the competition?" Aspen's tone is light, teasing, but there's a knowing glint in his eyes that makes me want to squirm. Particularly as we watch Darian lean close to Kaia again, saying something that makes her cheeks flush.

I scoff, perhaps a touch too quickly. "Don't be ridiculous. I'm simply concerned about Kaia's safety. We don't know anything about this Darian character or his intentions."

"Uh-huh," Aspen drawls, a smirk tugging at his lips. "And I'm sure your concern has nothing to do with the way Kaia's looking at him right now. Or how well she and Finn seem to be getting along."

I refuse to turn and look, even as every fiber of my being screams to do just that. "I don't know what you're talking about," I say stiffly.

Aspen's laugh is soft and knowing. "Come on, Malrik. You're not fooling anyone. Well, maybe Kaia, but that's because she's oblivious to her own charms. The rest of us? We see right through you."

I open my mouth to argue, to deny everything, but the words stick in my throat. Because damn it all, he's right. I hate that he's right. I hate that I care this much, that Kaia has somehow wormed her way past all my carefully constructed defenses. And I especially hate how she looks at Finn with such easy affection, at Darian with such intrigue, while I... I stand here in the shadows, watching.

"Fine," I growl, running a hand through my hair in frustration. "Maybe I am... concerned. But that doesn't change the fact that we need to be careful. There's too much at stake here."

Aspen's expression softens. "I know. And we will be. But Malrik?" He waits until I meet his gaze. "Don't let your feelings for Kaia—or your jealousy of Finn, or your suspicion of Darian—blind you to potential allies. Or push away the ones you already have."

He pauses, his voice dropping even lower. "And Malrik? You need to tell her."

With that, he turns and heads back to the group, leaving me to stew in my own tangled emotions. I watch as he rejoins them, seamlessly inserting himself into the conversation.

Tell her.

The thought makes my insides squirm. She'll think I'm an idiot. Or that I'm trying to use her, manipulate her. She doesn't trust me, not enough yet. And I can't blame her. After all, I'm the one who stepped into her life uninvited, carrying shadows of my own. But it doesn't stop the pull I feel toward her—the way she fights to appear strong even when her shadows betray her vulnerability, the fierce determination in her eyes when she thinks no one's watching. There's something about her that draws me in, even as she keeps everyone at arm's length.

I'm about to rejoin them when Torric saunters up, his golden eyes narrowed as he takes in the scene. "Where the hell have you been?" I ask, unable to keep the edge from my voice.

Torric shrugs, a lazy roll of his broad shoulders that does nothing to hide the tension in his stance. "Blowing off steam. Thorne's little announcement had me itching for a fight." His gaze locks onto Darian. "Who's the new guy?"

I clench my jaw, watching as Darian leans in to whisper something in Kaia's ear, her shadows swirling uncertainly around her feet. "Calls himself Darian. Swooped in to 'save' Kaia when her magic flared up."

Torric snorts, crossing his arms over his chest. "Save her? Please. Our girl can handle herself." The possessive 'our' doesn't escape my notice, and for once, I don't bristle at it. Torric's certainty in her strength should reassure me. Instead, it leaves me uneasy. He doesn't see what I do—how easily Darian's charm could pull her into something dangerous.

"Exactly. But he's got her eating out of his hand now, like he knows exactly what she wants to hear. And what worries me most is that she seems to want to believe it."

"You think he's a threat?" Torric's voice drops, all traces of nonchalance vanishing as his eyes track Darian's every move.

I hesitate, weighing my words carefully. "I'm not sure. Something's off about him—the way he moves, so smooth it's almost rehearsed. Like he's not just charming Kaia; he's studying her. It feels calculated, as if every glance and smile serves a purpose I can't yet see. And I'm not sure I want to find out."

Torric grunts, his fingers flexing like he's itching to summon his blade or punch something. "Well, if he tries anything, I'll be more than happy to show him the door. Preferably from a great height." For once, I can't find it in me to disagree. The tension in the air crackles between us, unspoken but understood. Darian might not know it yet, but he's under heavy scrutiny.

The corner of my mouth twitches in what might almost be a smile. For all our differences, Torric and I are aligned in this—protecting Kaia. Even if she'd probably hex us both for thinking she needs protection.

Chapter 19
FINN

I keep my arm draped casually around Kaia's shoulders, but every muscle in my body is tense. Bob hovers anxiously nearby—good old Bob, always the first to sense trouble—while I watch this Darian character work his so-called charm.

"I'd be happy to help you explore other ways to... combust," Darian says, his voice dropping low enough to make the suggestion unmistakable. "Something tells me you burn hotter than you let on."

Oh, he did not just— Okay, maybe he's smoother than I gave him credit for. I feel Kaia's sharp intake of breath and see the way her shadows flicker and curl like smoke, responding to the heat in his words. Time to lighten the mood before this gets too intense.

"Careful there, Romeo," I quip, tightening my hold on Kaia ever so slightly. "Some of us are trying to keep the combustion metaphors strictly theoretical." I wiggle my eyebrows at her, trying to draw out that eye-roll I adore. "Though I have to admit, the light show would be spectacular."

Darian's smile doesn't waver, but something flashes in his eyes—recognition? He's watching the shadows too closely, tracking their movements with too much interest. Most people either ignore them completely or, like Thorne, stare in obvious fascination. But he's... studying them.

I catch Malrik's eye across the room, and for once, we're in perfect agreement. Whatever this guy's deal is, he's not just another student with a hero complex.

"So, Darian," I keep my tone light, playful. "That was some fancy shadow work. Don't think I've seen anything quite like it before. Where did you say you trained?"

He doesn't miss a beat. "Here and there. You pick things up when you travel."

Vague much? I'm about to press further when I feel Kaia's shadows twist anxiously. Even Finnick, usually up for any chaos, seems to be keeping his distance from our new friend. That's... not normal.

"Well, you'll have to teach me that trick sometime," I say, knowing full well he won't. "Always good to have another shadow specialist around. Right, Kaia?"

She looks up at me, and I see the confusion in her violet eyes. She's sensing something's off but can't quite put her finger on it. I want to tell her what I'm seeing, how her shadows are practically screaming their distrust, but now isn't the time.

Malrik finally materializes again at her other side, bringing with him that dangerous chill that usually makes me want to crack inappropriate jokes among other things. Right now, though, I'm grateful for it. Darian's smile dims just slightly—point for Team Broody.

"I should go," Darian says smoothly. "But I look forward to seeing more of your... talents, Kaia." The way he says it makes me want to set something on fire. Preferably his perfectly styled hair.

Darian inclines his head, his storm-gray eyes lingering on Kaia's for a moment too long. "Until next time," he says, his voice low and deliberate.

As he walks away, the air feels heavier, as if his presence had left a shadow of its own.

Kaia relaxes slightly against me, her shadows immediately creeping closer, with Bob taking up his usual protective stance.

Good boy, Bob.

"Well," I say, trying to dispel the lingering tension, "he's... intense."

Kaia snorts. "Says the guy who juggles fireballs for fun."

"Hey, my chaos is purely recreational. That guy?" I shake my head. "He's playing a different game entirely."

I catch Malrik's eye again, and this time there's a whole silent conversation in that glance. We're going to have to watch this one carefully.

"So," I grin down at Kaia, "about that combustion theory—"

She elbows me in the ribs, but the soft smile she tries to hide makes my chest ache. I'd make a thousand stupid jokes just to keep that smile there—and to keep anyone like Darian from taking it away.

"Shut up, Finn."

"Make me, Trouble." She has no idea how much I'd actually like her to try. And I don't miss the smirk that crosses Malrik's face. Looks like I'm not the only one.

The shadows dance around us, clearly relieved to return to our usual banter. But I don't miss how they keep reaching toward Malrik, or how intently Bob is watching the door Darian just left through, his unease mirroring my own.

Chapter 20
DARIAN

I arrive early to Professor Thorne's classroom, positioning myself where the shadows are deepest. Perfect vantage point to watch Kaia arrive—not that I should care about seeing her expression when she walks in. My fingers drum against my thigh as I wait, Thorne's earlier words echoing: "Get close to her. Gain her trust. Whatever it takes."

The problem is, after yesterday's encounter in the training arena, I'm starting to think it won't take much acting at all.

I can still feel the electricity that sparked through me when I stepped between her and her wild magic, the way her violet eyes had widened when she looked up at me. Her shadows had been everywhere, raw power unlike anything I'd seen in my years of training. Even after Thorne pulled me away for my "official introduction" to the academy, I'd found myself watching her from the shadows, unable to look away. There was something about her that drew me in—fierce and beautiful, even as she struggled to contain her magic.

When Kaia enters the classroom now, her presence fills the room like a storm rolling in. Her shadows coil around her feet, more alive than any I've ever seen. Even Thorne looks at them as if they're something that puzzles him. She carries herself with forced confidence, but I catch the tension in her shoulders, the way her eyes dart to the corners of the room as if expecting an attack.

"Ms. Draven," Thorne's voice carries that perfect blend of authority and warmth I've spent years learning to recognize as artificial. "I trust you've considered my offer?"

Her shadows ripple as she shifts her weight. "I have, but—"

"Excellent." Thorne doesn't let her finish. Classic. "Then allow me to introduce you to one of our most promising advanced students. Darian?"

I see her body tense, her eyes go wide and her shadows dance like anxiety now flows through them.

That's my cue. I step from the shadows, offering what I hope passes for a disarming smile. "Kaia. A pleasure to see you again." Thorne's eyebrow lifts slightly—I probably should have mentioned our earlier encounter. Too late now.

She startles, her shadows flaring before settling into defensive coils. The way they move is mesmerizing—nothing like the rigid, controlled shadows Thorne has taught me to manipulate. These are wild, responsive. Real.

"Darian will be assisting with your training," Thorne continues. "He has a particular talent for shadow manipulation that I believe will complement your... unique abilities."

I watch emotions flicker across her face: surprise, suspicion, reluctant interest. She's sharp—she knows there's more happening here than Thorne is saying. But I also see the loneliness etched in the corners of her eyes, the desperate need to understand her powers. To belong somewhere.

"And if I say no?" She lifts her chin, defiant.

Thorne's smile doesn't waver. "My dear, you've already demonstrated that your powers require guidance. The question isn't if you'll train, but how difficult you choose to make it."

Her shadows lash out briefly before she reins them in. The display sends an unexpected thrill through me—so much raw potential, so much power just waiting to be unleashed. I step forward, deliberately softening my voice.

"I know it seems overwhelming," I say, meaning it more than I should. "But you don't have to figure this out alone."

Our eyes meet, and something electric passes between us. Her shadows actually settle slightly, which catches us both off guard. I shouldn't feel this pull toward her. This wasn't part of the plan.

"Fine," she finally says, though her tone suggests she's far from happy about it. "When do we start?"

"Now," Thorne answers, but I barely hear him. I'm too focused on the way her shadows reach toward me curiously before she pulls them back. There's something pure about their response, something that makes my carefully constructed walls waver.

This is going to be more complicated than I thought.

"Let's start with something simple," I suggest, moving closer. "Show me how you typically call your shadows."

As Kaia begins to demonstrate, I catch Thorne's approving nod from the corner of my eye. He thinks everything is proceeding according to plan. He doesn't realize that the rapid beating of my heart, the way my breath catches when Kaia's shadows brush against mine—none of that is an act.

I'm supposed to be her downfall. But as I watch her struggle with a basic shadow manipulation, her frustration evident but her determination unwavering, I wonder if she might end up being mine instead.

Focus, I remind myself. Remember why you're here. Remember what Alekir promised.

But as her shadows dance around her, reflecting her every emotion with stunning clarity, I'm finding it harder to remember why those promises seemed so important in the first place.

"Here," I say, stepping behind her to adjust her stance. "Try it like this."

Her shadows curl around both of us, and for a moment, I forget everything else. Forget Thorne watching from his desk, forget Alekir's plans, forget my own carefully crafted facade. For just a moment, I let myself feel the truth of my attraction to her, the genuine desire to help her understand her power.

The lesson continues, and I can't help but marvel at her raw talent. Her shadows respond with an instinctive grace that puts years of technical training to shame. It's breathtaking. And dangerous.

"You're doing well," I say, carefully modulating my voice. "But I think you're only scratching the surface of what you're capable of."

Her violet eyes narrow, suspicion and curiosity warring in their depths. "What do you mean?"

I glance at Thorne, receiving his subtle nod. "Your power feels... constrained. As if you're holding back. Possibly out of fear?"

Her shadows curl tighter around her ankles. "Maybe I have good reason to be afraid," she says, her voice low.

"Or maybe," I step closer, ignoring the way her shadows shift between us, "you've just never had the right guidance."

Thorne moves from his desk, his presence a sharp reminder of reality. "Darian has a unique understanding of shadow magic," he says smoothly. "He can help you reach your full potential."

I watch conflict play across Kaia's face—the desperate desire to understand her powers warring with years of learned caution. If only she knew how right she was to be suspicious.

"Try reaching beyond what feels safe," I encourage, pushing aside my guilt. "Your power is waiting for you to embrace it fully."

Kaia closes her eyes, concentration furrowing her brow. The air thickens with potential energy. For a moment, nothing happens. Then, ever so slowly, her shadows begin to expand, reaching further than before.

I catch my breath, both thrilled and terrified by what I'm witnessing. Because in this moment, watching her begin to explore her true power, I realize just how much damage I'm about to do.

And how much I wish I didn't have to.

As the lesson ends, Kaia's shadows retreat to their usual restless dance around her feet. She looks drained but there's a new light in her eyes—pride, maybe, or the first glimpse of what she could become. It makes my chest ache.

"Same time tomorrow?" she asks, trying to sound casual, but there's an eagerness in her voice she can't quite hide.

I nod, not trusting myself to speak. Her shadows ripple around her, their edges less restless now, brushing against my ankle as she turns to leave. The touch feels deliberate, almost like recognition, and it sends a jolt through me.

Thorne's hand lands heavy on my shoulder. "Well done," he says, his voice low with satisfaction. "She's beginning to trust you."

"Yes," I reply, the word tasting like ash. Trust I don't deserve. Trust I'm tasked to betray.

I follow her out, and as Kaia disappears down the hallway, her shadows trailing her like an afterthought, the ache in my chest sharpens. Thorne's praise feels hollow against the memory of her power unfurling, raw and untamed. Watching her step closer to that potential was thrilling, yes—but terrifying in equal measure.

Because in that moment, I wasn't just watching the birth of a weapon.

I was watching the woman who might one day turn that weapon on me.

Chapter 21
KAIA

My shadows are in a mood this morning.

For the third time, they send my books flying off the desk, scattering notes across the floor like confetti. Mouse lounges on my bed, watching with undisguised amusement as I crawl around collecting pages.

"Really?" I mutter, snatching a sheet from under his paw. "Is this about yesterday's training with Darian? Because I thought we agreed to—"

A sharp knock cuts me off. "Having a heart-to-heart with your shadows again?" Finn's voice carries through the door, honey-sweet with mockery. "Bob's been extra dramatic this morning. Even Patricia's concerned."

I yank the door open to find him lounging against the frame, all messy auburn hair and knowing smirk. The words die in my throat as his expression shifts, playfulness bleeding into something harder as he takes in the chaos of my room.

"What?" I demand.

"Nothing." But his usual lightness has an edge, like a knife wrapped in silk. "Just making sure you're ready for group training. Torric's already threatened to set something on fire if you're late again."

"When is Torric not threatening to set something on fire?"

"Fair point." Finn pushes off the doorframe but doesn't step back. His closeness feels deliberate. "So... how was yesterday's special training session?"

Something in his tone makes my skin prickle. "Fine. Darian's actually quite helpful."

"Hmm." That single syllable holds volumes of doubt.

Before I can press him on it, my shadows surge between us like a living wall, shoving a book into his chest with enough force to make him stumble.

"Ow! Okay, okay, message received," he laughs, but his eyes stay serious. There's something almost protective in the way he watches me. "Come on, Trouble. The twins are waiting."

The training yard crackles with tension when we arrive. Aspen and Torric are sparring, their magic colliding in spectacular bursts—fire and ice meeting in violent hisses of steam. At the edges of the yard, Malrik lurks in the shadows of a stone column, pretending not to watch while I pretend not to know he's here. But it's Professor Thorne's presence that makes my stomach twist—he rarely observes group sessions from what I've been told.

"Ah, Ms. Draven." His voice slides across the yard like oil on water. "I thought we might demonstrate what you learned yesterday. Darian?"

As if conjured by his name, Darian emerges from the shadows. Something flickers across Malrik's face—recognition? Warning?—but it vanishes before I can read it.

"Let's show them your progress," Darian suggests. His smile is warm, but his eyes calculate.

"I don't think that's necessary." I try, pushing all the confidence I can muster into the words.

"Nonsense," Thorne chimes in, all but ignoring my request.

The twins halt their sparring, steam still coiling around them like restless spirits. Torric's expression darkens as Darian moves closer to me. Aspen's hand finds his brother's arm—a silent warning.

"Perhaps a practical demonstration?" Thorne's suggestion carries the weight of a command. "Mr. Agere, if you'd assist?"

Torric steps forward, eager as always for a fight, but Thorne gestures to Aspen instead. The calmer twin moves with fluid grace, though I catch the tension riding his shoulders.

"The objective is simple," Thorne continues, pacing the edge of our impromptu arena. "Kaia will attempt to breach Aspen's defenses using what she's learned. Darian will... guide her technique."

My shadows coil tight around my ankles as Darian steps behind me. His hands ghost over my shoulders, adjusting my stance. "Remember what we practiced," he murmurs, his breath warm against my neck. "Reach for the deeper shadows."

A shiver runs through me—from his touch or something else, I'm not sure. But the moment his hands settle, a subtle pulse runs through me, like my shadows are being pulled or stretched in ways they've never moved before. My skin prickles as a strange, unwelcome sensation crawls up my spine.

From the corner of my eye, I catch it—a fleeting nod from Thorne to Darian. My chest tightens.

Darian's voice remains soft, soothing. "You feel that? That connection to something deeper? Focus on it."

But it feels wrong. The shadows don't react like they normally do—they hesitate, jitter, as if uncertain. Even Bob, my steady presence, flickers uneasily near my ankle.

Aspen raises his hands, and a wall of crystalline water shimmers into existence. Behind it, his face distorts, but I read concern in the set of his jaw.

"Begin," Thorne commands.

I try to push my unease aside, reaching for the shadows like I always do. But instead of responding with their usual fluidity, they jerk and pull in strange, erratic movements. My heart pounds as Darian's hands press lightly against my back, guiding me, but it feels invasive, like someone reaching into a part of me they shouldn't.

"Let it flow," Darian murmurs, but his voice sounds distant now, layered with something sharper, darker. My shadows lash out, not at Aspen's barrier but in wild arcs that scrape across the ground, uncontrollable.

A gasp escapes me as the necklace against my skin grows warm—no, searing. The amethyst glows faintly, and my shadows snap back to me, tearing away from whatever influence they were under. Darian stumbles back slightly, his hand withdrawing as if burned.

"Enough!" Malrik's voice cuts through the air, sharp and commanding. He steps into the arena before Thorne can speak, his silver eyes blazing. My shadows rush to him, clinging like frightened children.

Aspen lowers his barrier, his gaze locked on Thorne. "What the hell was that?" he demands, his calm veneer cracking.

Thorne's expression is smooth, unreadable. "A momentary lapse in control, nothing more. Ms. Draven has much to learn."

But I know better. The crawling sensation, the tug on my magic—it wasn't mine. And the way Darian avoids meeting my gaze tells me he knows it too.

"That's enough." Thorne cuts through the tension with practiced ease, his voice carrying over the murmurs of the group. "This session is concluded. Kaia, remember what we discussed about control. The rest of you... I'm sure you have other matters to attend to."

As the group disperses, I feel the weight of unspoken words pressing in. Torric looks ready to argue, his hands twitching like they're itching for a fight, but Aspen steers him away with quiet murmurs, his calm demeanor masking something stormy beneath. Malrik vanishes into the shadows without a backward glance, but the chill he leaves behind lingers, settling uneasily in my chest.

Finn lingers, though. Of course he does.

"Hey." His hand catches my arm, his touch grounding me when I feel like I might float away on the tide of unease. His green eyes meet mine, searching. "Just... be careful, okay? Some shadows hide sharper teeth than others."

His voice is low, meant for me alone, but there's something in his tone—a warning, a plea—that makes my heart stutter. He's gone before I can ask what he means, vanishing in a blur of fire and mischief, leaving me with nothing but questions and the unsettling feeling that I'm missing something vital.

Darian appears at my side, smooth as ever, his smile soft, almost apologetic. "They're just protective. It's sweet, really."

"Yeah," I mutter, my gaze fixed on the space Finn just vacated. "Sweet."

But as I look down, my shadows twist restlessly around my ankles, their movements jagged, uneasy. Bob brushes against my calf, his form flickering with something like agitation. Even Patricia, usually preoccupied with her endless shadow tasks, hovers close, almost wary.

Darian notices, of course he does. "Your shadows have a life of their own," he says, his tone casual, but his eyes sharp, watching every flicker and curl. "It's fascinating, really. You don't see that level of instinctive magic very often."

I force a smile, but it feels thin. "I guess they like to keep things interesting."

"They certainly do," he agrees, his gaze lingering on the amethyst pendant at my throat. "You're full of surprises, Kaia."

There's something in the way he says my name that makes my shadows ripple—not in the usual playful way, but like they're bristling. I take a step back, creating just enough space to feel like I can breathe again.

"Well, I should get to class," I say, my tone clipped. "Thanks for the, uh... guidance."

Darian's smile doesn't falter, but there's a flicker of something in his expression—disappointment, maybe? Annoyance?—that I catch before he schools it into something more polite. "Of course. We'll continue tomorrow. Usual time."

I nod, but as I walk away, I can feel his eyes on my back, and I don't know what to make of it. My shadows tighten around me like a protective shield, and I clutch the amethyst pendant against my chest, its warmth a small comfort against the growing cold in my gut.

My insides feel at war with each other. My feelings a jumbled mess right up there with Finn's chaos. And don't even get me started on that mage. I've got too much to worry about without these men getting into my head.

133

Chapter 22
KAIA

The corridors of Arcanum whisper with secrets as I make my way to class. It's been a week since Darian's magic wrapped around mine, since his touch left me feeling both thrilled and wrong in ways I can't explain. My shadows have clung closer than usual, agitated and skittish, when a familiar voice cuts through my brooding.

"Kaia! Hold up!"

A flash of lavender hair bobs through the crowd like an exotic bird. Seren practically bounces to my side, her mismatched earrings—one a tiny dragon, the other a crescent moon—jangling merrily. The sight of her loosens something in my chest.

"Where have you been?" I ask, relief flooding through me. "I was starting to think one of your experimental portals had finally swallowed you whole."

"Family drama." Seren rolls her eyes, falling into step beside me. Her satchel clinks with what I'm sure are dubiously legal magical ingredients. "I've been gone for a week dealing with Gran's divination mirror. It cracked, and you know how she gets about omens. I had to talk her down from sealing the entire house in protective runes. Even the outhouse, Kaia. The outhouse."

I can't help but laugh, picturing Seren's eccentric grandmother frantically scrawling symbols on every available surface. "Please tell me you at least brought back some of her chaos cookies you've told me so much about."

"As if I'd dare return without them." She pats her bag, which emits a faint purring sound. "Though I'm starting to regret ever mentioning them, since now I have to share. But enough about my domestic disasters." Her eyes glitter with mischief. "How's your smorgasbord of sexy treating you?"

Heat creeps into my cheeks. "Is that what we're calling it now?"

"Well, what would you call it? Because from where I'm standing, you've got yourself quite the collection of drool-worthy specimens circling." She waggles her eyebrows suggestively. "Come on, spill. I want all the juicy details I missed."

"It's..." I hesitate as my shadows coil tighter. "Complicated. There's been some tension lately. And then there's Darian—"

Seren stops dead in her tracks, nearly causing a pile-up in the hallway. "Darian? As in Darian Luthar? Mr. Tall-Dark-and-Magically-Delicious himself?"

"You know him?"

"Know him?" Seren's laugh has an edge of hysteria. "Kaia, darling, everyone knows Darian Luthar. He's practically academy royalty. And have you seen the way he moves? It's like watching living shadow given form."

Damn. Breathe, girl.

My stomach twists. I'd known Darian was skilled, but hearing Seren gush about him makes me question my own misgivings. "He's been helping me with my shadow work," I admit.

Seren's squeal echoes off the stone walls, drawing curious stares from passing students. "Private lessons with Darian Luthar? Kaia, you lucky witch!" She grabs my arm, practically vibrating. "How have you not spontaneously combusted from the sheer hotness?"

"It's not like that," I protest, even as something warm and dangerous flutters in my chest. "It's just training."

"Uh-huh." Her skepticism could cut glass. "I've been back a day and already I'm seeing Malrik and Finn act like jealous watchdogs. What happened while I was gone?"

I stumble, nearly tripping over my own shadows. "What do you mean?"

Seren's expression sobers. "You really haven't noticed? In Magical Theory, when Professor Thorne mentioned your 'special sessions,' those two actually agreed on something. The looks they were exchanging..." She shivers. "Let's just say I've seen less intense planning sessions before actual battles."

"Perfect," I groan, rubbing my temples. "Just what I need. More drama."

"Hey," Seren's hand finds mine, squeezing gently. Her usual playfulness gives way to genuine concern. "You okay? I know I joke, but seriously – if any of this is too much..."

I force a smile. "I'm fine. Really. It's just..."

"A lot?" She nods. "Well, if you ever need a break from all the testosterone and brooding, you know where to find me. We can stuff our faces with chaos cookies and practice hexing the patriarchy."

That pulls a genuine laugh from me. "Thanks, Ser. I might take you up on that sooner rather than later."

As we round the corner to our next class, a familiar figure materializes from the shadows. Malrik steps into our path, silver eyes locked on mine with an intensity that makes the air feel thick. The rest of the world seems to fade away, sounds muffling as though underwater.

"Kaia," he says softly. "A word?"

Seren's eyebrows shoot up, and she gives me a not-so-subtle thumbs up. "I'll save you a seat," she whispers, practically skipping into the classroom. "Try not to get devoured by the sexy shadow man!"

Heat floods my cheeks as I turn back to Malrik. He's closer now, having moved with that liquid grace that makes him seem more shadow than man. My own shadows curl around us both, as if trying to draw us even nearer. The air between us feels charged, dangerous.

"What's up?" I ask, aiming for casual and missing by miles.

Malrik studies me for a moment, something unreadable flickering across his face. "Be careful with Darian," he says, voice pitched low enough that I have to lean in to hear him. "He's not what he seems."

"What are you talking about?" The warmth in my chest curdles into defensiveness. "Darian's been nothing but helpful."

Malrik's jaw clenches, a muscle ticking beneath his pale skin. "There are things you don't know about him. About his past—"

"Stop." I cut him off, frustration bubbling up inside me. "Is this what all of that was about in class last week? You all think I can't take care of myself? That I need protection from the big, bad shadow mage?"

My shadows flare in response to my anger, coiling around my arms like dark vines. But Malrik doesn't back away. If anything, he moves closer, until I can see the faint violet flecks in his silver eyes.

"This isn't about protection," he says, each word carefully measured. "It's about power. And the price it demands." His hand lifts, almost touching my cheek before dropping away. "Just... watch how your shadows react when he's near. They see what you're choosing to ignore."

The warning bell rings, sharp and intrusive. Malrik steps back, his usual mask of cool indifference sliding into place.

"Ask yourself why Thorne chose him to train you," he adds quietly. "Of all people."

I scoff, glaring at him.

That's ridiculous, right?

Before I can respond, he melts into the shadows, leaving me with the ghost of his almost-touch on my skin and questions burning in my throat. My shadows twist restlessly around my ankles, and for the first time, I wonder if they're trying to tell me something I've been too stubborn to hear.

Mouse appears at my feet, violet eyes gleaming with unusual intensity. He headbutts my leg gently, as if in warning or comfort—I'm not sure which.

What terrifies me most is the growing certainty that Malrik might be right. And if he is, what exactly have I gotten myself into?

Chapter 23
KAIA

I slip into Professor Idorath's classroom, Malrik's warning still echoing in my mind. My shadows haven't settled since our conversation, twisting and writhing like agitated snakes around my ankles. I catch Seren watching me with concerned eyes, but I shake my head slightly. I'm not ready to discuss whatever that was with Malrik—not when I'm still trying to convince myself he's wrong about Darian.

The familiar routine of class should be comforting, but all I can focus on is the weight of different gazes on me: Seren's worry, Malrik's intensity from across the room, and Darian's warm smile that suddenly feels calculated. He sits across the room where Alenya is practically drooling over him, but his attention is fixed on me. His smile is warm and inviting, designed to put me at ease—but my shadows pull back slightly, and I can't ignore their warning this time. I also can't help but snicker as Alenya notices the silent conversation Darian and I seem to be having. The look of annoyance on her face brings me joy.

"Today we'll be working with binding runes," Professor Idorath announces, his chalk scratching precise symbols onto the board. "Partner up. And try not to blow anything up this time." He looks pointedly at Finn, who merely grins and waggles his eyebrows.

Before anyone else can move, Torric drops into the seat beside me, his presence radiating heat like a furnace. "You look like you're having a fantastic morning," he says dryly.

"That obvious?"

"You're doing that twitchy thing with your hands. Dead giveaway." He starts setting up the rune materials with surprising care. "Want to talk about it?"

"Not particularly."

Torric shrugs, but I catch the concern beneath his casual demeanor. "Fair enough. Just remember—" he pauses, his usual brashness softening for a moment, "—you don't have to prove anything to anyone here. Especially not to people who think they know what's best for you."

I glance at him sharply, but he's focused on arranging the crystals for our rune work, his expression purposefully neutral. Across the room, I notice Aspen watching us with that quiet intensity he gets sometimes. When our eyes meet, he gives me a subtle nod.

The twins might drive me crazy, but there's something steadying about their presence. No hidden agendas, no cryptic warnings. Just solid, reliable support.

"Now," Torric says, a familiar glint of mischief in his eyes, "want to help me create the most explosively awesome binding rune this class has ever seen?"

Despite everything, I feel my lips twitching. "I thought we weren't supposed to blow anything up?"

His answering grin is positively wicked. "Rules are more like guidelines, really. Besides," he nods toward where Darian sits with Alenya, who is now destroying his perfectly controlled rune work, "some people could use a little chaos in their lives."

As if to emphasize his point, my shadows give an enthusiastic little wiggle. I hear Finn snicker from somewhere behind us, followed by what sounds suspiciously like "Team Chaos for the win!"

The crystals Torric sets up catch the light, throwing tiny rainbows across our shared desk. His hands move with surprising precision for someone who usually solves problems by setting them on fire.

"See, the trick is," he explains, sketching the first line of the binding rune with perfect form, "you have to make it look like you're following the rules before you break them."

I raise an eyebrow. "And how often does that actually work for you?"

"About as often as your sarcasm works as a defense mechanism." He doesn't look up from his work, but I catch the slight curl of his lips. "Now pay attention, Sunshine. I need you to draw the shadow aspect while I handle the fire element."

The shiver that washes though me when he calls me that catches me off guard. I'm not used to Torric like this, fun, almost kind and dare I say, charming?

"Because that combination has historically worked out so well?" But I'm already reaching for my chalk, my shadows swirling with anticipation.

"Trust me. Shadow and Fire can be great together."

He pauses his work, his gaze now focused entirely on me and I'm more than grateful right now that we're in the middle of class and there's a crowd of people because otherwise... yeah.

I clear my throat, trying to bring us back to the present. "Famous last words."

I start sketching my half of the rune, trying to focus despite being acutely aware of Darian watching. The chalk feels warm under my fingers, responding to my magic in a way that's both familiar and unsettling.

"Careful with that line," Torric murmurs, his shoulder brushing mine as he leans closer. "You want it to curve just... there." His hand hovers near mine, not quite touching but close enough that I can feel the heat radiating from his skin.

My shadows flicker, and the chalk skids slightly. Behind us, Finn's poorly disguised laugh turns into an unconvincing cough.

"Something amusing, Mr. Veylan?" Professor Idorath calls out.

"Just admiring everyone's technique," Finn replies with sugary innocence. "The level of... concentration is inspiring."

I force myself to focus on the rune. Shadow and fire. Opposing forces that shouldn't work together, and yet...

"Ready?" Torric asks, his own chalk poised to complete the final line of his half.

I nod, acutely aware of how the air feels suddenly charged with more than just magic. We draw the last lines simultaneously, our chalk meeting in the middle of the desk.

The rune flares to life.

And several things happen at once.

The fire element surges, more responsive than either of us expected. My shadows leap to meet it instinctively, and instead of canceling each other out, they merge. The resulting burst of energy sends our papers flying and makes the crystals hum at a frequency that sets my teeth on edge.

Bob, Patricia and Finnick have all taken on an ember like quality that doesn't seem real.

"Oh shit," Torric breathes, but he's grinning like a kid on Winter Solstice morning.

Professor Idorath whirls around. "What did you—"

But it's too late. The rune glows once, twice, and then the classroom erupts into controlled chaos. Shadow-flames dance across the ceiling, casting everyone in flickering violet light. They don't burn—they're not real fire—but they move with a life of their own, spinning and twirling like they're putting on a show.

"That's... not supposed to happen, right?" I manage, watching as one particular shadow-flame does what I swear is a pirouette.

"No," Torric agrees, sounding entirely too pleased. "It's better."

From somewhere behind us, Finn starts slow clapping. Several other students join in, while Professor Idorath looks torn between impressed and exasperated.

Only two people aren't watching the aerial display. Malrik's eyes are fixed on me, his expression unreadable but intense. And Darian... Darian is staring at the shadow-flames with an intensity that sends a shiver down my spine. I don't miss the slight twitch of his lips, as if he's pleased with what he sees. Malrik's warning echoes in my mind: *Watch how your shadows react when he's near.*

"Well," Professor Idorath says dryly, "I suppose that's one way to demonstrate the binding of opposing forces." He waves his hand, and the shadow-flames dissipate with a sound like wind chimes. "You both are lucky the forces decided to work together against the odds. Otherwise, the backlash could have destabilized the entire rune matrix, or worse," he says, his tone clipped. "And less theatrics next time Mr. Agere."

"No promises," Torric mutters, and I have to bite my lip to keep from laughing.

As the class returns to normal, I catch Aspen watching his twin with that mix of fondness and exasperation only siblings can master. When he glances at me, there's warmth in his eyes, and something else—something that looks almost like pride.

Mouse, who had been curled up in my bag this whole time, pokes his head out and chirps approvingly at the lingering wisps of shadow-flame. At least someone appreciates our artwork.

Chapter 24
KAIA

Another week into our lessons, and I still can't decide if Darian is the best or worst thing to happen to my training.

"You're thinking too hard again," he says, his voice soft but sure. We're in one of the smaller practice rooms, where Professor Thorne has been having us work on precision control. "Shadow magic isn't about perfect form—it's about instinct."

My brow furrows, trying to make sense of Darian's words. They clash with everything Professor Thorne has drilled into us since I got here. The shadows around us pulse and flicker, responding to my conflicted emotions.

"But Professor Thorne always says there's no room for improvisation in Shadow manipulation," I argue, my voice barely above a whisper. The dim light of the practice room casts Darian's face in stark relief, his high cheekbones and sharp jawline emphasized by the interplay of light and shadow.

Darian's lips curl into a knowing smirk. "Ah, but that's where the true mastery lies, Kaia. Thorne teaches the basics, the rigid structure. But once you understand the rules..." He pauses, lifting his hand. The shadows in the room coalesce around his fingers, dancing and swirling in mesmerizing show that I can't look away from.

My shadows coil restlessly at my feet, and Mouse watches from his perch on a nearby shelf, his violet eyes narrowed with clear disapproval. I try to ignore both of them.

Darian steps closer, his movements smooth and deliberate. Unlike Malrik's predatory grace or Finn's chaotic energy, Darian moves like someone who's never questioned his right to occupy space. He adjusts my stance with light touches: a nudge to my elbow, a hand settling on my shoulder. Each contact sends a jolt through me, and my shadows twitch in response.

"Let's try again," he says with more calm than he could possibly feel.

"Easy for you to say," I mutter, trying to focus on the task and not the way his proximity makes my pulse race. "Your magic actually behaves."

He chuckles, the sound low and warm. "Who says behaving is the goal?"

Before I can respond, he moves behind me, close enough that his chest brushes my back. I stiffen automatically, my shadows coiling tighter.

"Relax," he murmurs, his hands settling on my arms. "You're holding too much tension. Your shadows feel that—they'll reflect it back at you."

It's impossible to relax with him this close, but I try anyway, letting my shoulders drop. His breath stirs the hair at my neck, and my shadows ripple uneasily.

"Better," he says, his voice softening. His hands trail down my arms, barely skimming the surface. "Now, stop trying to control them. Shadows don't like being forced—they want to move with you, not for you. Let them show you what they want."

I close my eyes and take a slow breath. For once, I let go of the tight grip I've been keeping on my power. To my surprise, my shadows respond, pulling together into the barrier I've been struggling to form all morning. It's simple but steady.

"See?" Darian says, his hands sliding back to my shoulders. "You're stronger than you think."

Mouse growls softly from his perch, but the sound is lost under Darian's next words.

"You're too focused on getting it perfect," he murmurs against my ear. "Perfection isn't the goal. Feeling is."

My shadows pull away from him sharply, but I pay them no mind, too caught up in the moment. His hands skim down my arms again, lingering at my wrists.

"Let's try it again," he says, pressing closer. "This time, don't overthink. Trust yourself."

The barrier begins to take shape, but every brush of his fingers sends another shiver through me. My shadows writhe uneasily, trying to put space between us.

"Good," he whispers. His thumbs brush the insides of my wrists. "You're getting it."

"Darian—" My voice comes out breathless, uncertain.

"Hmm?" His hum vibrates against me, his lips grazing my neck, and the barrier collapses completely.

"Touching display."

Malrik's voice cuts through the room like winter wind. My shadows scatter as I spin toward the door, where he leans against the frame with deceptive casualness. His silver eyes are sharp, taking in every detail of the scene.

"We have the room reserved," Darian says pleasantly, though something darker edges his tone. "For training."

"Is that what you're calling it?" Malrik steps forward with liquid grace, power rolling off him in waves. "Fascinating technique."

Heat floods my face. "It's not—we weren't—"

"Working on control," Darian finishes smoothly, his hand returning to the small of my back like a brand. "Something you might consider studying yourself, Duskbane."

Malrik's eyes narrow dangerously, and the shadows in the corners of the room seem to deepen.

Before either can escalate, Finn bursts in with his usual chaotic energy, though his smile feels forced.

"Kaia! There you are! I've been looking everywhere—" He stops short, his grin faltering as he reads the room. "Oh. Sorry. Didn't realize you were... busy."

"We're not," I say quickly, stepping away from Darian. My shadows dart toward Finn like they're seeking refuge, brushing his boots before curling back around my feet.

"Actually," Darian catches my wrist, his grip light but insistent, "we should run through that one more time. Professor Thorne wants to see improvement by tomorrow's class."

He's not wrong—Thorne has been watching me like a hawk lately, his dark eyes always weighing and measuring. But something in Malrik and Finn's matched stares makes my skin crawl.

"I can help with that," Malrik says, his voice deceptively soft. "Since you seem so concerned with her progress."

Darian's smile doesn't waver, but tension radiates from him. "That's kind of you. But Professor Thorne assigned me as her partner for a reason."

"Did he?" Finn sprawls into a nearby chair with calculated carelessness. "And what reason would that be?"

The air thickens with power as Mouse bristles on his shelf, violet eyes fixed on Darian.

"I should go," I snap, yanking my wrist free. "It's almost dinner anyway."

"I'll walk you," three voices say at once.

The silence that follows makes my chest tight, like the walls are closing in. My shadows swirl frantically, pulling toward both Finn and Malrik while shrinking from Darian.

"I'm capable of walking myself," I say, grabbing my bag. Mouse leaps down to my side as I head for the door. "Thanks for the help, Darian. I'll... I'll see you tomorrow."

I escape before anyone can argue, but not before catching Darian's amused murmur and Malrik's answering growl.

In the corridor, I press against the cool stone wall and exhale slowly. My heart races, though I can't tell if it's from the tension or from Darian's lingering touch. Mouse bumps against my leg while my shadows coil close, as if trying to shield me from my own choices.

"I'm fine," I tell them, unconvincing even to myself. "Everything's fine."

Mouse's unimpressed stare says otherwise.

I push off the wall and head for the dining hall, but the weight of the moment follows me: Darian's possessive touch, Malrik's controlled fury, Finn's faltering smile. Something's shifting between all of us. I'm just not sure what it is yet.

Chapter 25
KAIA

The dining hall is half-empty when I arrive, dinner hours nearly over. Perfect—quiet enough to avoid questions but noisy enough to drown out my thoughts. I claim a corner table, Mouse settling underneath while my shadows drift around the legs.

Bob starts arranging my silverware with military precision.

Fantastic.

"Stop that," I mutter, deliberately shifting my fork crooked just to see what he'll do. The shadow twitches, then firmly corrects it. "I'm trying to eat, not prepare for a royal inspection."

"Talking to yourself again? Or are the shadows keeping you company?"

Seren drops into the seat across from me, her lavender hair catching the torchlight. She dumps a stack of books beside her plate, the top one glowing with what I'm certain are illegal runes.

"What happened to you?" she asks, grinning. "You look like you've seen a ghost. Or worse—Professor Idorath's attempt at dancing."

A laugh escapes before I can stop it. "Nothing happened. Just... an intense training session."

"With your sexy new tutor?" She steals one of my rolls, ignoring my protest. "The one with the cheekbones and the brooding?"

"Darian doesn't brood," I say, stabbing my potatoes. "He's actually really helpful. And nice. And—"

"And totally not why you're sitting here looking like you want to disappear into the shadows." She raises an eyebrow. "I mean, more than usual."

My shadows swirl faster, and I swear one of them nods in agreement.

"It's complicated," I say finally.

"Isn't it always?" Seren shrugs, opening her notebook. "But you know what's not complicated? This ridiculous enchantment I found in the restricted section. Want to see something explode?"

I blink. "Should I be worried that's your solution to everything?"

"Hey, if it works..." Her grin widens as she sketches something in the margin. "Besides, it's better than brooding about boys. Some of us have more important things to focus on."

"I'm not brooding about boys," I say flatly.

"Sure you're not." Her expression softens slightly. "Just... be careful, okay? Some kinds of attention aren't as nice as they seem."

Before I can ask what she means, her notebook starts smoking.

"Oh void," she yelps, slamming it shut. "That wasn't supposed to happen for at least three more components!"

Mouse chuffs in amusement as Seren grabs her books and bolts. I follow close behind, trying not to laugh as we dodge angry glares from the kitchen staff.

We burst into the hallway at full speed, Seren clutching her smoldering notebook like a bomb.

"Explain to me again how this was supposed to work?" I ask, trying not to trip over Mouse, who thinks this is a fantastic game.

"It's basic runic transference," she huffs, dodging a startled first-year. "I amplify the power source through a stabilization matrix, then channel it into—"

"Into an unholy firebomb?" I point at our smoking trail.

"Details," she mutters, clearly annoyed that I'm ruining her fun with facts.

Behind us, someone yells about "damage to academy property" and "repeat offenses." My shadows dart ahead, guiding us around corners, though Bob lingers just long enough to topple a particularly tall stack of scrolls.

"Was that necessary?" I hiss.

Bob doesn't answer, but his smug ripple says everything.

Seren yanks me into a side passage, and we flatten against the wall as heavy footsteps pass by. That's when I notice Finnick jumping excitedly trying to get the attention of whoever is out there.

Damn traitor.

"Well," she says, clutching her notebook triumphantly, "that was invigorating."

I glare at her, then at her singed notes. "You're going to get us expelled."

"Please." She waves dismissively. "They wouldn't dare expel me. I'm too brilliant. And you..." Her grin sharpens. "You've got Thorne's dark little eye on you, so you're basically untouchable."

"Lucky me," I mutter. My shadows twist uneasily at Thorne's name. "Next time you decide to play with forbidden runes, leave me out of it."

"You say that now," she teases, tucking away her notebook, "but we both know you'll come running the second I mention explosions again."

I start to argue, but Mouse's laughing huff makes me glare at him instead.

All of you! Traitors!

We step back into the main corridor, and Seren heads toward the library, still muttering about calculations. I hesitate, suddenly drained. Between Darian's training and Seren's chaos, my nerves feel raw.

"Coming?" she calls over her shoulder.

I shake my head. "I need some air. I'll see you later."

Even as Seren vanishes down the hall, her laughter trailing behind her, the unease remains. My shadows twist tighter around me, their restlessness matching the knot in my chest.

Chapter 26
KAIA

The courtyard beckons, its open archways promising escape from the academy's suffocating halls. As I step into the cool night air, Mouse pads silently beside me, his form rippling with barely contained energy. My shadows stretch in the moonlight, but their movement is agitated, defensive.

"You're paranoid," I tell Mouse as we pass an empty fountain. The sound of water would be soothing if the basin wasn't dry. Everything here feels half-alive, caught between what it should be and what it is. "Nobody's following us."

Mouse's muscles tense, and he grows slightly larger—a warning sign I've learned to heed. His ears flatten as he stares at the edge of the courtyard. Following his gaze, my stomach flips. Darian leans casually against one of the archways, his arms crossed and a faint smile playing on his lips. He looks like he's been waiting—like he knew exactly where I'd go.

"Couldn't sleep?" he asks, pushing off the wall with an effortless grace that makes my pulse quicken despite myself.

Bob positions himself between us like a barrier. The other shadows follow his lead, creating a subtle but distinct wall. My stomach churns as Darian steps through them as if they're nothing but smoke.

"Stalking me now?" I try to keep my voice light, but there's an edge to it. "That's not a great look for you."

He chuckles softly, closing the distance between us with measured steps. "I was worried about you. You seemed... overwhelmed earlier."

Overwhelmed? Oh, you know, just caught between three arguing guys with more simmering hostility than a poorly written tavern brawl.

"I'm fine," I say, crossing my arms. "I'm always fine."

"You don't have to pretend with me," he says, his voice dropping to that hypnotic tone that seems to bypass all my defenses. "I see you, Kaia. All of you."

The words hit somewhere deep, somewhere I've tried to keep locked away. My shadows surge forward, their edges sharp with warning. Bob tries to pull me back, his form stretching protectively around my ankles. Mouse grows larger still, his growl vibrating through the stone beneath our feet.

But Darian's magic pulses gently, creating a bubble of calm that makes their warnings feel distant, unimportant. "Your shadows are remarkable," he murmurs, reaching out to brush his fingers against one. "But they're just the beginning. There's so much more power inside you, waiting to be unleashed."

His words wrap around me like warm honey, and I feel myself swaying toward him. The courtyard fades until all I can see is Darian—the intensity in his eyes, the curve of his smile, the way his magic seems to resonate with something deep inside me.

"I can help you," he continues, voice low and compelling. "Together, we could be unstoppable."

He reaches for me, and despite my shadows' frantic attempts to intervene, I let him. His hand cups my cheek, the touch sending electricity through my veins. Mouse's growl turns desperate, and he lunges forward, but Darian's magic pushes him back with casual ease.

"Tell me to stop," he whispers, leaning closer.

I should. Every instinct screams at me to step back, to listen to the shadows' violent protest. Instead, I find myself frozen, caught between desire and dread.

His lips brush mine, gentle at first, then deeper, more insistent. His magic wraps around us like a cocoon, amplifying every sensation until I'm dizzy with it. My shadows' movement grows frenzied, but their panic feels muffled, distant.

When we break apart, my head spins. Through my dazed state, I catch a flicker of triumph in Darian's eyes that sends a chill down my spine.

"You see?" he breathes against my lips. "This is just the beginning."

Mouse suddenly crashes into my legs, breaking Darian's magical hold. He's fully grown now, his shadowy form rippling with protective fury. The shock clears my head enough to step back, my heart pounding.

Darian's eyes widen as he takes in Mouse's massive form, a flicker of uncertainty crossing his face before it's replaced by a smirk that sends shivers down my spine. "Impressive," he murmurs, his gaze roving over Mouse's rippling shadows. "I didn't realize your little pet had such... potential."

Mouse's growl deepens, the sound vibrating through the stones beneath our feet. His form seems to absorb the moonlight, growing darker and more substantial with each passing second. The air around us grows heavy, charged with an energy that makes my skin prickle.

"He's not a pet," I manage to say, my voice shakier than I'd like. I take another step back, grateful for Mouse's presence against my legs. My shadows swirl around us, agitated and defensive, but they feel weak compared to the raw power emanating from Mouse.

"I should go," I manage, my voice unsteady.

Darian doesn't try to stop me, but his smile holds an edge that makes my shadows coil tighter. "Sweet dreams, Kaia," he says softly. "Think about what I said."

I flee before I can do anything else stupid, Mouse herding me forward like he's orchestrating an escape. By the time I reach my building, the night air has cooled the heat in my cheeks, but my mind won't stop spinning.

Mouse returns to his smaller form but stays alert, watching me with obvious concern as my shadows curl around me like a protective cocoon. Bob hovers near my face, his form shifting in what feels like worry.

I burst through the doors of the Shadow faction's common room, my heart still pounding and my mind a whirlwind of confusion. The familiar scent of old books and smoldering incense hits me, but even the comforting atmosphere can't calm the storm inside me.

As I enter, four heads snap up in unison. Malrik, Finn, Torric, and Aspen are sprawled across the room, their expressions morphing from relaxed to concerned in an instant.

"Kaia! What happened?" Malrik's deep voice cuts through the others, his dark eyes searching my face.

Finn leaps up from his perch on the windowsill, his lithe form moving with feline grace. "Are you alright? You look like you've seen a ghost."

Torric's hulking form rises from an armchair that suddenly seems too small for him. His brow furrows with concern, and I can see the shadows around him stirring restlessly. "Who do I need to punch?"

Aspen, ever the quiet observer, simply tilts his head, his silver eyes gleaming in the firelight as he studies me intently.

Their concern washes over me like a wave, threatening to drown me. I shake my head frantically, unable to form words. My shadows swirl around me, agitated and defensive, reflecting the turmoil inside me.

"I... I can't," I manage to choke out, my voice barely above a whisper. "I just need... I need to be alone."

Before they can protest or ask more questions, I bolt for the stairs. My feet barely touch the steps as I race upwards, my shadows propelling me forward. I can hear their voices calling after me, a mixture of confusion and worry, but I don't slow down.

The winding staircase seems endless, the stone walls closing in around me. Portraits of past Shadow faction members watch me with painted eyes that seem too knowing. Their whispers follow me, a susurrus of judgment and curiosity that makes my skin crawl.

Finally, I reach my room, slamming the door behind me and leaning against it, breathing heavily. The familiar space should be comforting, but tonight it feels like a cage. Moonlight streams through the stained-glass window, casting colorful shadows across the floor. My bed, with its mountain of pillows and thick comforter, beckons invitingly, but sleep feels impossible.

Mouse materializes beside me, his form still larger than usual, radiating protective energy. He nudges my hand, a low whine escaping him.

"I'm fine," I tell them, collapsing onto my bed. But even as I say it, I can feel the lie taking root, threatening to grow into something I can't control.

In the darkness, my shadows whisper their warnings, and for the first time, I wonder if I've been listening to the wrong voice all along.

Chapter 27
Kaia

The knock on my door this morning isn't so much a knock as it is a battering ram of impatience wrapped in noise.

"Kaia!" Finn's voice booms through the wood, too loud for this hour. "Open up! I know you're in there!"

I groan and bury my face deeper into my pillow. If I ignore him, maybe he'll evaporate into the ether.

"Don't make me break down the door," Finn threatens, though he sounds more amused than serious. "Because I will. And then Malrik will lecture me, and I don't think either of us wants that."

Mouse growls softly from his perch near the window, and my shadows twist protectively around the bed. Bob hovers near the door like he's sizing it up for barricade duty.

"Fine!" Finn's voice grows dramatically tragic. "If this is how it ends, so be it. Alone, abandoned—left to wallow in ignorance. Oh, the humanity!"

The door bursts open.

"What the—?" I sit up, blinking as Finn practically dances into the room, his energy exploding into the space like a rogue spell.

"Where were you last night?" he demands, dropping onto the foot of my bed with all the grace of a sandbag. My shadows scatter in irritation, and Bob ripples indignantly as Finn's sock-clad foot nearly lands on him.

"Sleeping?" I reply, still groggy.

"Liar," Finn snorts, bouncing slightly on the mattress. His hair's a mess, his shirt half-tucked, and his socks don't match.

Quick footsteps in the hallway cut through his interrogation, and Aspen appears in the doorway, breathing a little harder than usual.

"Finn, you can't just—" Aspen takes in the scene and sighs. "Of course you already broke in."

"I knocked!" Finn says, throwing himself backward across my feet like an indignant cat.

"That wasn't knocking," a deeper voice chimes from behind Aspen. Torric fills the doorway like an impenetrable wall, still glistening from morning training. "That was an assault on architecture."

"What are you doing here?" I ask Torric, pulling my legs away from Finn.

"Following him," Torric answers with a jerk of his thumb. "Besides, we all saw you when you came in last night."

"I told you I'm fine!"

"Then why were upset when you came in last night?" Finn asks, propping himself up on his elbows.

"I wasn't—"

"She was with Darian," another voice cuts in. Malrik steps into view, his silver eyes pinning me like a spotlight. Unlike the others, he looks composed, which somehow makes the accusation worse.

Silence falls. Even Finn stills.

"How do you know that?" I ask, my voice sharper than intended.

Malrik doesn't flinch. "I know a lot of things. Like how Darian isn't who he pretends to be."

"What's that supposed to mean?" Torric demands, his presence heating the room like a spark ready to ignite.

"It means," Malrik says, voice calm but dangerous, "our new transfer has an agenda. One that involves Kaia."

Finn sits up straight, all playfulness gone. "Okay, cryptic shadow man, maybe try being clear for once?"

"I am being clear," Malrik replies, finally stepping fully into the room. Each deliberate step makes my shadows shiver. "Darian is working with someone who wants to use Kaia's power."

My shadows twist uneasily at his words. Bob stretches toward Malrik, seeking confirmation, while Mouse flattens his ears.

"That's ridiculous," I say, but my voice wavers. "He's helping me train. Professor Thorne assigned—"

"Thorne?" Aspen interrupts, his usual calm cracking. "The same professor who's been pushing you harder than anyone? The one who specifically requested Darian as your training partner?"

"You're all paranoid," I snap, throwing off my blanket and standing. "I can take care of myself."

"Can you?" Malrik asks quietly, his gaze shifting but unreadable. "We're just worried about you."

I glance down. My shadows coil tightly around my legs, their patterns jagged and unfamiliar. Even Bob looks agitated.

"This is insane," I mutter, running a hand through my hair. "Since when does what I do concern you?"

"It matters." He states, ignoring my objections. "Some of us pay attention," Malrik says, his gaze flicking briefly to Finn, who straightens defensively.

Torric grunts, "If Darian's a threat—"

"We don't know that," I cut in.

"If he's a threat," Torric continues, ignoring me too, "we need to do something."

"Like what?" Finn asks, standing. "Challenge him to a duel? That went great last time."

"Last time?" I look between them. "What last time?"

The silence thickens. Finn and Malrik exchange a look, and dread twists in my gut.

"What aren't you telling me?" I demand.

Before anyone can answer, the bell for first period tolls, its low chime breaking the tension.

"We'll be late," Aspen says, though he doesn't move.

"Then we'll be late," Malrik replies, his eyes still on me. "This is more important."

"More important than what?"

A new voice answers. "Training, of course."

I whirl to find Darian standing in the doorway, as polished and unreadable as ever. His pleasant smile feels more like a mask, and my shadows recoil beneath the bed. The guys tense around me, how he managed to sneak up on them is beyond me.

Darian's gaze sweeps the room before settling on me, heat growing in them as he takes me in, still in my pajamas. "Professor Thorne is waiting for us."

"She's not going," Malrik says.

"I wasn't aware you made her decisions," Darian replies smoothly.

"He doesn't," I say sharply, grabbing my bag. "And I don't need anyone to."

"Kaia—" Aspen starts, but I cut him off. "No. Next time you want a group meeting about me, try inviting me first." I glare at them. "Now, get out!"

I'm probably acting like a toddler not getting their way but I need them out and I need to get moving if we're going to make it to training anytime soon.

Finn's voice cuts through the tension as he stands in front of me. "Your shadows are screaming," he says softly. "But you're not listening."

Something in his tone makes me pause. My shadows twist beneath me, sharp and anxious.

Darian breaks the moment. "We should go," he says. "Thorne doesn't like to wait."

I glance at the others. Malrik's expression is unreadable, but his eyes burn with worry. Finn's usual grin is gone, replaced by something deadly serious. The twins stand close, Aspen calm, Torric bristling.

"Fine," I say. "But this isn't over."

"No," Malrik replies, his gaze locked on Darian. "It isn't."

The close the door behind them and I quickly dress for the day. Sometimes uniforms are a godsend, I don't have to think about what to wear from the few crappy pieces in my wardrobe.

I make my way down to the common room where they're all waiting, talking in hushed tones but you can still feel the tension radiating through the room. Darian's hand lands on the small of my back as leads me from the room, and I swear I hear Finn mutter something about Bob being right all along. But that's ridiculous. Isn't it?

Chapter 28
KAIA

The walk to the training room is silent, weighted with unspoken tension. My shadows stick close, their usual fluidity replaced by something tighter, more wary. Even Mouse, padding along beside me, seems to move with unusual caution, his violet eyes scanning every corner.

"Your friends are very protective," Darian says finally, breaking the silence. His voice is smooth, neutral, but I hear an undercurrent of something else—amusement, maybe.

"They're not my—" I start, then hesitate. What are they? Friends? Allies? Protectors? The word feels too small for whatever bond has tangled us together.

Darian glances at me, his expression inscrutable, but there's a flicker of something in his eyes—curiosity? Concern? "You know I only want to help you, right?" His words sound sincere, like always. But doubt creeps in, prickling at the edges of my thoughts.

We reach the training room door, and he gestures for me to enter first. As I pass him, my shadows bunch together, forming a barrier between us. The movement feels intentional, as if they're trying to tell me something. Maybe it's time I started listening.

The training room is darker than usual, the sconces along the walls flickering weakly. The air feels heavy, thickened by shadows that seem to pulse in time with my heartbeat. Professor Thorne stands in the center, his tall frame casting long, jagged shapes across the floor.

"You're late," he says, not bothering to turn around.

"My fault," Darian replies smoothly, his voice slipping into its usual practiced charm. "I had trouble finding her." He locks the door behind him and joins me in the center of the room.

Something about the way he says it makes my skin crawl. My shadows press closer, wrapping around my legs like frightened children, and for once, I let them.

"No matter," Thorne says, finally turning. His dark eyes meet mine, and the intensity of his gaze makes my chest tighten. "Today's lesson is about control. Real control."

He raises a hand, and the sconces dim further, plunging the room into near-total darkness. The shadows on the floor twist and writhe like living things, reaching toward the center of the room where Thorne begins to circle slowly.

"Your shadows respond to emotion," he says, his voice a low, even hum. "To instinct. But true power requires discipline."

His gaze shifts to Darian. "Demonstrate."

Before I can react, Darian's magic surges outward. It hits like a cold wind, sharp and unnatural. My shadows rear up, a reflexive barrier, but his power cuts through them like they're smoke.

"Stop fighting," he murmurs, stepping closer. His tone is soft, coaxing. "Let me show you how to use them." And I swear for just a moment I see a hint of regret in his eyes.

His magic wraps around my shadows, pulling at them, trying to bend them to his will. The sensation is wrong—cold and invasive, like claws scraping over raw nerves. My shadows writhe in protest, their panic feeding into mine. Like they're remembering the same feeling I do, how we've felt this before that day at training when Darian put his hands on me.

"I said stop fighting," Darian snaps, the warmth in his voice fracturing.

Pain lances through me as his magic digs deeper, and I cry out. My shadows scream—a high, keening sound I didn't know they could make.

Mouse launches himself at Darian, a streak of fury and claws, but he collides with an invisible barrier and falls back with a yelp. The world tilts, spinning wildly. My legs buckle, but before I can hit the floor, Darian catches me. His grip is gentle, but it feels like a trap.

"Shh," he whispers, his magic shifting, softening. The chill fades, replaced by something warm and heavy, like a blanket pressing down on my mind. "You're just overwhelmed. The shadows are too strong today."

"You—" I try to speak, but the words slip away, scattered and foggy.

"You pushed yourself too hard," he says, his tone soothing now. "Rest. Everything's fine."

The last thing I see before the darkness claims me is Mouse, his fur bristling as he struggles against unseen forces, and Bob rippled frantically, his form breaking apart like ink dissolving in water.

When I open my eyes, I'm sitting on a bench in the courtyard. The sunlight is too bright, making my head pound. Darian is beside me, his face creased with concern.

"You fainted during training," he says, brushing a strand of hair from my face. His touch is light, calculated, and it sets my nerves on edge.

"The shadow magic was too intense," he continues. "Professor Thorne thinks you need rest."

"I..." My voice is weak, and my thoughts feel distant, blurred around the edges. My shadows curl weakly around me, mirroring the heaviness in my limbs and the fog in my thoughts.

"What happened?"

"Nothing to worry about," Darian says, his smile warm and reassuring. Too reassuring. "You're just learning your limits. Let me help you back to your room."

He stands and offers his hand. Reluctantly, I take it, letting him pull me to my feet. My body feels heavy, uncooperative, like I'm moving through water.

As we walk, Mouse follows silently, his tail low, while Bob hovers close to my shoulder like a protective specter. Their behavior feels off, but my thoughts are too hazy to unravel why.

Maybe Finn and the others were wrong about Darian.

Or maybe I'm just too tired to face the truth.

Chapter 29
MALRIK

The library is silent except for Finn's restless pacing. He hasn't cracked a single joke since Kaia left—a sure sign of how serious things have become.

"We should have stopped her," Torric growls, his fingers tapping an agitated rhythm against the table.

"How?" Aspen asks, calm and deliberate as always. "She's right—we can't make decisions for her."

"We can when she's walking into a trap," Torric snaps, the heat in his voice sharp enough to burn.

I stay silent, watching Finn wear a path into the carpet. There's something he isn't saying—something important. And now, he can't keep it to himself any longer.

"Finn," I say quietly. "Tell them."

He freezes mid-step, running a hand through his already messy hair. "Tell them what?"

"About the shadows." I hold his gaze, steady and unyielding. "About what we've seen."

The twins exchange confused glances. Aspen is the first to break the silence. "What about the shadows?"

Finn laughs sharply, but it lacks his usual humor. "They've been warning us about Darian from the start. And yeah, I should've said something.

But it's not like you'd have listened." He takes a ragged breath, "That Bob practically has an aneurysm every time he's near? That they physically push Kaia away from him?"

"Bob?" Torric asks, his golden brows knitting together.

"The big one," Finn and I say in unison.

"You can see them?" Aspen's eyes widen in surprise. "Both of you?"

"Yes," I admit. "For different reasons. But that's not what matters. What matters is that her shadows know something's wrong. They've known all along."

"And you didn't think to tell us earlier?" Torric stands, heat rolling off him in waves.

"Would you have believed us?" I reply coolly.

Before he can answer, the library doors burst open. Kaia stumbles in, pale and shaken, her shadows more wild and erratic than I've ever seen them. Bob writhes like a storm cloud ready to burst, his edges jagged and flickering. Mouse's fur bristles, his low growl vibrating through the air.

The argument dies instantly.

"Kaia," Aspen says, desperate worry in his voice.

The moment Kaia stumbles, Torric is there, catching her before she hits the ground. His usual bravado vanishes, replaced by genuine concern as he scoops her into his arms. Her head lolls against his chest, and my stomach twists at how small and vulnerable she looks.

"We need to get her to her room," I say, already moving towards the door. The others follow without question, our earlier disagreements forgotten in the face of this new crisis.

As we hurry through the corridors, I can't help but notice how Kaia's shadows cling to her, more agitated than I've ever seen them. Bob, usually so playful, now writhes like a mass of angry snakes. Mouse, typically aloof, presses close to Torric's legs, his violet eyes wide with fear.

We reach Kaia's room, and Aspen rushes ahead to open the door. Torric lays her gently on the bed, his hands lingering for a moment as if reluctant to let go. Finn paces at the foot of the bed, his usual energy turned frantic and sharp.

"This isn't right," he mutters, running a hand through his hair. "This isn't normal training."

"No," I agree, moving closer to examine Kaia. "It's not."

That's when I see it. A flicker of darkness blooms under her skin, branching like jagged lightning through fragile glass. Then, as quickly as it appeared, it fades.

"Did you see that?" I ask, my voice tighter than I'd like.

The others crowd around, and we watch in horrified fascination as the process repeats. Black veins spider across Kaia's skin, reaching towards her heart before retreating again.

"What is that?" Aspen whispers, his usual calm shattered.

"Nothing good," Torric growls, heat radiating from his clenched fists like a simmering blaze, while Aspen's calm facade cracks, his eyes betraying a flicker of panic.

Finn leans in, his face uncharacteristically serious. "It's like... it's fighting something. Look."

He's right. Each time the darkness spreads, Kaia's shadows lash out in desperate waves, clawing at the encroaching darkness as though fighting for their own survival. But with each cycle, the darkness reaches a little further, lingers a little longer.

"We need to do something," Aspen says, looking to me with desperate eyes. "Can you... I don't know, use your magic to help?"

I shake my head, frustration burning in my chest. "My magic doesn't work that way. I can see shadows, influence them, but this..." I gesture helplessly at Kaia's prone form. "This is beyond me. This isn't shadow."

"Then what do we do?" Torric demands, his voice rising with each word. "We can't just stand here and watch!"

"We need to find out what Darian and Thorne did," I say, forcing my eyes away from her to meet the other's gaze.

Torric and Aspen nod nearly in unison, they're rune marks flaring with power. And Finn looks angrier than I've ever seen him. They won't get away with this," Finn says, his voice low and lethal, the sharp edge of his anger slicing through the room. The heat of it lingers, palpable, alive.

I can't help but watch him—really watch him. The way his energy coils, barely restrained, how his green eyes burn with a fierce determination that draws shadows toward him like moths to flame. Something about it is unsettling. Or maybe it's the way it stirs something in me, something I'm not ready to think about.

My shadows twist, echoing the chaos in my chest, but Finn doesn't notice. His focus is all Kaia. Maybe that's what keeps me from stepping closer. Maybe that's why I stay silent.

Chapter 30
KAIA

I wake with a start, my head pounding and mouth dry. Sunlight streams through unfamiliar curtains, and for a moment, panic grips me.

Where am I? What happened?

My shadows writhe anxiously around me, reflecting my disorientation.

As my vision clears, I realize I'm in my room at the academy. But something's off. The air feels thick with tension, and there's a lingering scent of lavender and... smoke?

I try to sit up, but a wave of dizziness forces me back down. That's when I notice them—Torric, Aspen, Finn, and Malrik, scattered around my room like sentinels. Torric slumps in a chair by the window, his golden hair mussed. Aspen lies on the floor, fingers twitching as a small puddle shimmers and vanishes beneath him. At the foot of my bed, Finn sprawls, his fingers nearly brushing my restless shadows. And Malrik... Malrik's leaning against the wall, silver eyes already fixed on me, alert despite the exhaustion evident in the set of his shoulders.

"What—" I croak, my voice barely a whisper.

The sound is enough to rouse the others. Torric jerks awake, nearly falling out of his chair. Aspen blinks sleepily, the puddle beneath him evaporating instantly. Finn rolls over with a groan, narrowly avoiding tumbling off the bed.

"Kaia!" Aspen's the first to reach me, cool fingers brushing my forehead. "How are you feeling?"

I open my mouth to answer, but no words come out. How am I feeling? I'm not even sure. Everything's a blur.

"Here," Finn says, pressing a glass of water into my hand. His usual smirk is absent, replaced by a worried frown that makes my stomach churn.

I sip the water gratefully, my shadows curling around the glass as if to help steady my shaking hand. "What happened?" I finally manage.

The four of them exchange glances, a silent conversation passing between them. It's Malrik who finally speaks, his voice low and carefully controlled. "We were hoping you could tell us. You collapsed last night after... training."

The way he says "training" sends a shiver down my spine. My shadows react instantly, lashing out defensively before retreating to coil tightly around my ankles. Patricia's not even scribbling notes, she looks like she's reduced herself to finger painting on the floor.

"I... I don't remember," I admit, frustration building. "Just training with Darian, and then..." I trail off, the memories slipping away like smoke.

Torric growls, the air rippling with heat as a nearby potted plant shrivels under the intensity. "That bastard. I'll kill him."

"Get in line," Finn mutters, his usually playful tone edged with steel.

I blink, trying to piece together the fragments of memory floating just out of reach. There's a hazy image of Darian's face, his enigmatic smile, but nothing concrete. No matter how hard I concentrate, the details slip away like water through my fingers.

"I... I really can't remember," I say, frustration coloring my voice. My shadows twist around me, mirroring my inner turmoil. "It's all just... blank."

The others exchange worried glances, but I hurry to reassure them. "I don't feel like anything bad happened, though. Just... tired, I guess?" I'm not entirely sure if I believe my own words, but I need to calm them down. Their concern is palpable, filling the room like a thick fog.

Aspen's cool hand finds mine, squeezing gently. "It's okay, Kaia. We're just glad you're awake and that Lira was able to help."

My brow furrows, "Lira was here?"

"She helped stabilize you, but honestly I don't think we really understand what she did or what was going on with you. Just that you're whole body was freaking out."

A shiver runs through me, but none of that sounds possible. If I was that bad I would have known, I would remember, right?

But I offer them a small smile, grateful for their steady presence. My gaze drifts to each of them in turn - Torric's barely contained fury, Finn's uncharacteristic seriousness, Malrik's calculating stare. A warmth blooms in my chest, touched by their obvious concern. At the same time, a flicker of irritation sparks within me. Do they think I'm so helpless?

I push myself up, ignoring the slight dizziness that accompanies the movement. "I appreciate you all being here, but I'm feeling much better now. We should get ready for class."

"Class?" Torric scoffs, crossing his arms. "You need to rest, Kaia."

I shake my head, my resolve strengthening. "What I need is normalcy. Besides, I've missed enough classes already."

They start to protest, but I hold up a hand, silencing them. "I'm going to class," I say firmly, my shadows rising around me as if to emphasize my point. "End of discussion."

For a moment, tension crackles in the air. Then Finn breaks into a grin, some of his usual mischief returning. "Well, you heard the lady. Looks like our vigil is over, gents."

I roll my eyes, but I can't help the small smile that tugs at my lips. Finnick bounces like his big brother just made his day. "Alright, out. All of you. I need to get ready."

They file out reluctantly, each casting worried glances over their shoulders. As the door closes behind them, I let out a long breath, my shoulders sagging. My shadows curl around me, offering silent comfort.

I move to my wardrobe, fingers trailing over the familiar fabrics. As I dress, I catch sight of my reflection in the mirror. My skin is paler than usual, dark circles shadowing my eyes. The amethyst necklace gleams against my collarbone, pulsing gently. I touch it absently, a frown creasing my brow. Something about it feels... different, but I can't put my finger on what it is.

The group of us trudge across Arcanum's sprawling grounds, my boots sinking into dewy grass. The air crackles with anticipation—or maybe that's just my frayed nerves. My shadows are unusually subdued, clustering close to my feet instead of their usual playful swirling.

As we approach the outdoor training area, my breath catches. The field has become a labyrinth of writhing shadows, its inky tendrils forming impossible, gravity-defying structures. My shadows ripple with renewed excitement, clearly shaking off any remnants of the last twelve hours. It's as if recognizing a kindred spirit in this ethereal maze, though Bob remains conspicuously close to me.

"Ah, Miss Draven." Professor Thorne's silky voice snaps me from my awe. Mouse's hackles rise at the sound. "Welcome to your Shadow Maze."

I quirk an eyebrow, trying to ignore how my necklace seems to grow colder at his proximity. "Mine? Let me guess—another fun way to potentially get myself killed?"

Thorne's lips twitch, his eyes lingering on my shadows' defensive positioning. "Consider it a test of your instincts, your ability to harness your shadows under pressure."

I turn to the guys, my heart racing despite my attempts to appear calm. They gather around me, forming a protective circle that both comforts and irritates me.

Torric's golden eyes blaze with concern, his hand resting on my shoulder. The warmth of his touch seeps through my clothes, a stark contrast to the chill emanating from my necklace. "This is ridiculous," he growls, glaring at Thorne. "You can't expect her to do this so soon after... after whatever happened last night."

I feel a flicker of gratitude, but also a surge of defiance. "I can handle it, Torric," I insist, though my shadows betray my uncertainty, curling tighter around my ankles.

Finn steps forward, "You've got this, Kaia," he says, flashing a grin. "Show that maze who's boss—and break a record while you're at it."

His enthusiasm is infectious, and I find myself smiling despite my nerves. My shadows perk up, swirling with energy.

Aspen's cool presence is a balm to my frayed nerves. He doesn't say much, but his steady gaze speaks volumes. "We believe in you, Kaia," he says softly, "Trust your instincts."

I nod, grateful for his quiet support. My shadows reach out, brushing against Aspen in a silent thank you.

Then Malrik steps forward, his silver eyes intense. "Remember, Kaia," he begins, his voice low and serious, "the key to navigating shadow magic is to—"

"To what, Malrik?" I snap, irritation flaring. "To stay calm? To trust my instincts? To not get myself killed?" My shadows lash out, reflecting my sudden anger. "I think I've figured that out by now."

Malrik's eyes widen slightly, taken aback by my outburst. The others shift uncomfortably, and I immediately regret my harsh words. But before I can apologize, Thorne clears his throat.

"If you're quite finished with your pep talk," he drawls, "it's time to begin, Miss Draven."

I take a deep breath, squaring my shoulders. The maze looms before me, a writhing mass of darkness that seems to pulse with its own life. My shadows quiver with anticipation, eager to merge with this new, vast expanse of their kin.

"Good luck," Aspen murmurs.

"Kick some shadow ass!" Finn cheers.

Torric just nods, his jaw clenched tight.

Malrik says nothing, but I feel his eyes on me as I step forward.

With one last glance at my guys, *not my guys,* I go to step into the maze.

"Good luck, Kaia." Darian's voice, smooth as silk, drifts from behind me. Before I can react, his lips brush my cheek—too light to fight, too heavy to ignore. 'Show them what you're made of,' he murmurs.

The temperature spikes as Torric growls. Aspen's face hardens, and even Malrik's glare turns deadly.

I square my shoulders, pushing down the complicated tangle of emotions. "Right. Let's do this."

Chapter 31
KAIA

As I step into the maze, my anger from this morning resurfaces. The shadowy walls seem to dance, reacting to my mood. Great. An obstacle course with performance anxiety.

"Focus, Kaia," I mutter. My shadows swirl erratically, mirroring my inner turmoil.

I round a corner and find myself face-to-face with a writhing mass of darkness. It coalesces into a wall, blocking my path. I reach out, willing my shadows to merge with it, to carve a passage. Instead, they skitter away, refusing to obey.

"Seriously?" I hiss. "Now is not the time for a rebellion."

I take a deep breath, trying to center myself. The shadows on the walls waver, almost taunting me. Fine. If my shadows won't cooperate, I'll do this the old-fashioned way. I charge forward, shoulder first, and burst through the inky barrier.

I stumble out the other side, covered in shadow residue that clings like cobwebs. "Ugh, gross."

The maze shifts before me, and I choose a path at random. After becoming hopelessly lost, the maze finally presents a new challenge. A chasm opens before me, too wide to jump. My shadows nudge me, trying to form a bridge, but I resist. I don't need their help. I'm supposed to do this on my own, right?

"I've got this," I mutter, searching for another way across. But as I stand there, indecision gnawing at me, I can't help but wonder—am I being stubborn, or am I finally taking control?

The shadows go still around me, waiting for my next move.

Suddenly, my amethyst necklace glows against my skin, startling me. A warm, tingling sensation spreads from the stone, and for a split second, I swear I hear whispers—ancient, melodic voices just beyond my comprehension.

"What the hell?" I mutter, grasping the pendant. It throbs again, more insistent this time.

Before I can ponder this new mystery, a familiar voice calls out from behind me. "Kaia! Are you alright?"

I whirl around to find Darian striding toward me, concern etched on his unfairly handsome face. My heart does a little flip, even as my brain screams suspicious timing.

"Darian? How did you get in here?" I ask, torn between relief and wariness.

He flashes that disarming smile. "I convinced Thorne to let me observe. You looked like you could use a friendly face. Besides, you've been in here for hours."

I snort, gesturing at the chasm. "What I could use is a bridge."

Then it hits me. "Hours?" I say bewildered. I've been in here minutes.

Darian's expression turns serious. "Thorn's kept an eye on you. You've been walking in circles."

No freakin' way.

"But this?" He continues, gesturing toward the chasm, you have the power to cross, Kaia. Trust your instincts."

"My instincts are telling me to turn around and find another way," I grumble.

He steps closer, his gray eyes intense. "Your shadows want to help you. Why are you fighting them?"

I bite my lip, memories of the guys' warnings flashing through my mind. "I don't know who to trust anymore."

Darian's hand finds mine, his touch warm and reassuring. "Trust yourself, Kaia. That's all that matters."

As if on cue, my necklace hums. This time, instead of resisting, I close my eyes and let the sensation wash over me. My shadows respond, swirling around my feet with renewed purpose.

"You can do this," Darian murmurs.

I take a deep breath and step forward. My shadows surge, forming a solid bridge across the chasm. I cross swiftly, turning back to see Darian's approving smile.

"See?" he calls. "You don't need anyone controlling you. You're incredible on your own."

His words soothe the lingering doubts in my mind. Maybe the guys were wrong about him. Maybe Darian is the only one who truly believes in me.

"Thanks," I say, meaning it. "I guess I just needed a push in the right direction."

Darian's smile widens. "That's what I'm here for. Now, shall we tackle the next challenge together?"

As we move deeper into the maze, I can't help but feel grateful for his presence. My necklace continues to flare with a faint glow occasionally, but

I'm too focused on Darian's encouragement to give it much thought. For the first time since entering this maze, I feel like I might actually succeed.

I nod, a smirk tugging at my lips. "Together it is. Though I'm pretty sure I just proved I can handle myself."

Darian chuckles, his gray eyes twinkling. "That you did. I'm merely here to bask in your glory."

As we round another corner, I catch sight of my reflection in a shimmering wall. My shadows dance around me, agitated. Bob, in particular, seems to be throwing a full-on tantrum, stretching and contorting into bizarre shapes.

"Whoa there, buddy," I mutter. "What's got your darkness in a twist?"

Darian glances at me. "Everything alright?"

I hesitate, torn between confiding in him and brushing it off. The guys' warnings echo in my mind, clashing with Darian's recent helpfulness.

"Just my shadows being drama queens," I say finally, forcing a laugh. "You'd think I'd canceled shadow-palooza or something."

Darian's brow furrows. "Your shadows seem... distressed. Are you sure you're okay?"

I bite my lip, conflicted. On one hand, Darian's concern seems genuine. On the other, Bob's increasingly frantic movements are hard to ignore.

"I don't know," I admit. "It's like they're trying to tell me something, but I can't figure out what."

Darian steps closer, his voice low and soothing. "Maybe they're reacting to the stress of the maze. You've been through a lot today."

I nod slowly, wanting to believe him. But a nagging doubt persists. "Yeah, maybe. It's just... Finn and the others seemed pretty adamant about—"

"About me being untrustworthy?" Darian finishes, his tone carefully neutral.

I wince. "Well, yeah."

He sighs, running a hand through his dark hair. "Kaia, I know they mean well. But you have to ask yourself: who's actually been here, helping you?"

I swallow hard, the weight of the decision pressing down on me. Trust Darian, who's been nothing but supportive? Or listen to the warnings of guys who aren't even here?

Bob stretches impossibly long, forming what looks suspiciously like the word "NO" at my feet. My stomach tightens at the sight, a battle waging inside me. Is it paranoia, or are my shadows truly trying to warn me of something I'm refusing to see? Doubt gnaws at the edges of my thoughts, but I push it down, unwilling to confront what that "NO" might mean.

"Oh, shut up," I mutter, kicking at the shadow. To Darian, I say, "You're right. You've been here. You've helped me. I... I trust you," I say, though the words taste like ash on my tongue.

The moment the words leave my mouth, my shadows erupt in chaos. Finnick seems to be having a full-on meltdown, while the others twist and writhe like they're in pain.

Darian's smile, however, is radiant. "I'm honored, Kaia. Now, shall we show this maze what you're really capable of?"

I nod, pushing down the lingering unease. As we continue on, I can't shake the feeling that I've just made a monumental choice. I just hope it's the right one.

Another shadow wall looms before us, this one rippling with strange patterns. My shadows coil anxiously around my feet, but I ignore their protests.

"Ready?" Darian asks, his hand finding the small of my back.

I nod, gathering my power. This time, when I reach for the shadows, they respond—reluctantly, like children being dragged to bed. The wall parts beneath my touch, revealing the maze's exit.

"Impressive," Darian murmurs as we step through. "You're getting stronger every day."

My necklace flickers once, sharply, sending a cold shiver through my chest. A small part of me wonders why it's choosing now to act up.

This is the moment I need to focus on the victory, not the unease creeping in the background of my mind. "Thanks to you," I say. "I couldn't have done this without—"

"Kaia!" Finn's voice carries across the field. He's running toward us, the others close behind.

Darian's hand tightens slightly on my waist. "Speaking of interruptions," he says softly, then turns to face me fully. "Before they get here—would you do me the honor of being my date to the Equinox Dance this weekend?"

I blink, caught off guard. "The dance?" I didn't even know there was a dance. Although to be fair, I've had a few things going on. Somehow Darian was the first to ask me. None of my... nope, not going there.

His smile is warm, genuine. "Unless you'd rather go alone?"

"No! I mean, yes. Yes, I'll go with you." The words tumble out just as Finn reaches us, slightly out of breath.

"Kaia, are you okay? That maze looked intense and—"

"She's fine," Darian cuts in smoothly. "Better than fine, actually. We were just discussing the dance."

Finn's face falls slightly. Behind him, Malrik's expression darkens, and Torric looks like he might actually burst into flames.

"The dance," Aspen repeats carefully. "How... convenient."

I bristle at his tone. "Is there a problem?"

"No problem," Darian says, squeezing my hand. "They're just concerned, as always." He turns to me with another heart-stopping smile. "I'll pick you up on Saturday at eight?"

I nod, ignoring the way my shadows twist unhappily around our joined hands. As Darian walks away, I face my friends' worried expressions with a lifted chin.

"Don't," I say, the warning in my voice sharper than intended. "Just... don't."

Chapter 32
DARIAN

The corridor is dark when I reach Thorne's office, but I know he's waiting. He always is.

Thorne's shadows aren't like Kaia's. Hers pulse with life, reflecting her emotions. His are cold, oppressive—more guards than companions. They don't dance or play; they watch, unnervingly still.

"Well?" His voice emerges from the darkness.

I force a smile, though something in my chest twinges uncomfortably. "It's done. She trusts me completely now."

"And the dance?"

"She said yes. Just as you planned." I try not to think about how her shadows had recoiled when I asked her, their sharp, frantic movements striking like alarm bells in a silent room. Even that ridiculous one had twisted itself into warning shapes, spelling out desperate pleas she refused to see, as if they were fighting to save her from something only they could understand.

Thorne steps into the dim light, his satisfaction palpable, etched into the faint smirk curling his lips and the sharp gleam in his eyes. Every movement exudes a calculated confidence, as though the entire room bends to his will, shadows included. His shadow stretches behind him, too sharp and angular to be natural. "Excellent. And her... companions?"

"Suspicious, but powerless to stop it. The more they protest, the more she pulls away from them." The words taste bitter. I've seen how they look at her—especially that chaos mage, Finn, and the brooding prince, Malrik. They see her shadows for what they are. They understand.

"You've done well." Thorne's praise feels like ice down my spine. He pauses, studying me with those piercing eyes. "You're not... attached, are you?"

I think of Kaia's smile, bright and unguarded. Of her shadows, wild and playful, trying desperately to protect her. Of the way her friends looked at me, knowing but unable to prove anything. Of how the amethyst necklace reacts with warning whenever I'm near, a power that even Thorne doesn't fully comprehend. Its pulse isn't random; it's precise, almost deliberate, as if the relic itself recognizes my intent. I can't shake the feeling it's not just reacting—it's judging.

"Of course not," I lie smoothly, my years of training making the words flow easily. "She's just another piece in the game."

"See that it stays that way." Thorne's voice drops to a whisper, but the threat is clear. "We can't afford any... complications. Alekir has waited too long for this."

I nod and turn to leave, pushing down the guilt that threatens to rise. Behind me, I hear Thorne mutter an incantation, and the shadows around him writhe in ways that remind me too much of Kaia's—except these shadows scream.

As I walk away, I remember the warmth in Kaia's eyes when she agreed to the dance, the trust I'm about to shatter. But it's too late now.

For both of us.

At the end of the hall, Mouse watches me, his violet eyes burning with quiet judgment. He doesn't growl anymore. Somehow, the silence is worse—a condemnation I can't ignore.

I've made my choice. The price of betrayal is steep, but I'll pay it. The weight of it presses against my chest, suffocating, but I push it down. Kaia's trust, her unguarded smile—they've become everything I didn't know I needed. And yet, I'm the one unraveling it, tearing apart what little good I've found in myself. The cost isn't just hers to bear; it's mine, too, though I know she won't see it that way.

Even if it destroys everything I never knew I needed.

Chapter 33
ASPEN

The tension crackling through our group makes even Arcanum's enchanted staircases shift more erratically than usual. Kaia storms ahead, her shoulders rigid, the shadows on the walls seeming to recoil from her fury, their movements jagged and erratic as if mirroring the storm brewing inside her. It's not just her anger—they feel it too, feeding off the intensity and heightening the unease that grips the rest of us. I've never seen her like this—her usual warmth replaced by something cold enough to make even a water mage shiver.

We pass through the great hall, its enchanted ceiling a mass of roiling storm clouds. The few students lingering there avert their eyes, sensing the discord radiating from our group. Our reflections catch in the towering windows—four dark figures following Kaia's beacon of blonde hair, moving in tense silence.

The portraits in the Shadow wing huddle together, whispering as we approach the common room. The massive obsidian door, etched with ever-shifting runes, swings open at Kaia's touch. Inside, plush velvet couches in deep purples and midnight blues stand in pools of silvery light from floating orbs. Shadow vines creep up the walls, their delicate leaves seeming to absorb what little illumination remains.

The moment the door closes, Kaia whirls to face us. Her eyes, usually soft lavender, now blaze with an inner fire that makes me step back. Even her hair seems to move in a nonexistent breeze.

"What the hell is going on with you all?" Her voice could cut glass. The room itself reacts, shadows in the corners growing deeper, more menacing.

I open my mouth to speak, but Kaia barrels on, her frustration pouring out like a dam breaking. "First you try to sabotage me before the maze, then you have the audacity to look disappointed when I succeed?" She throws up her hands, and I swear sparks fly from her fingertips.

"Kaia, we weren't—" Finn starts, but she cuts him off with a glare that could freeze hellfire.

"Save it, Veylan. I'm not finished." Her burning gaze pins each of us in turn. "You were all so sure I couldn't handle myself. Well, guess what? I did. And none of you were there, but Darian was."

"We were just outside, Kaia. We came with to support you, remember?" Torric's tone strains for lightness.

"Do you hear yourself?" she snaps. Mouse paces between us, tail lashing anxiously, his ears pinned back as if he can sense the storm brewing between us. His movements are sharp and restless, a clear reflection of the unease gripping the room, as though he's bracing for something to snap. "You've been 'here for me' since day one, and suddenly he shows up and—"

"And what?" Torric snaps, heat radiating from him. "Supports you? Believes in you? Doesn't treat you like glass?"

"That's not fair," I keep my voice steady despite the tension crackling through the room. "We're trying to protect you because we care."

"Protect me?" Her laugh holds no humor. "From what, exactly? From succeeding? From proving I don't need a bunch of overprotective guys hovering over me?"

"From getting hurt," Malrik says quietly, his gaze flicking to something beside her. "There are things you don't know about Darian."

"Oh really?" Sarcasm drips from her words. "And I suppose you're all experts on him now?"

Finn steps forward, his usual playfulness replaced by urgency. "Kaia, please. Just listen for a minute. Your shad—"

"Don't." She cuts him off. "I don't want to hear about what my shadows are doing, or what you think they're trying to tell you. I'm sick of everyone thinking they know what's best for me."

Mouse lets out a low growl, but for once, I can't tell if it's directed at us or at Kaia. The floating lights dim slightly, as if responding to the mounting tension.

"The dance," Torric says suddenly, golden eyes flashing. "That's what this is really about, isn't it? Him asking you to the dance?"

Something flickers across Kaia's face—uncertainty?—but vanishes before I can be sure.

"The dance is just a dance," she says, defensive edge creeping into her voice.

"Is it?" Malrik's tone stays carefully neutral, but I hear the concern beneath. "Or is it another way for him to isolate you?"

"Isolate me?" She throws her hands up. "I'm literally surrounded by people trying to control my life right now!"

"We're not—" I start, but Torric cuts me off.

"Fine," he snaps, golden eyes blazing. "Go to the dance with him. Trust him instead of us. But don't come crying to us when it all falls apart."

"Torric," I warn, but the damage is done. Kaia's expression hardens to steel.

"Don't worry," she says, voice cold enough to freeze flame. "I won't."

She turns on her heel and strides toward her room, Mouse trailing behind. Her door slams hard enough to rattle the shadow vines, their trembling mirroring the unease she leaves behind. Silence descends, heavy and suffocating. Finn slumps onto a couch, running a hand through his disheveled hair. Malrik's expression remains unreadable, but his knuckles whiten where he grips a chair back.

I turn to my twin, still radiating enough heat to make the air shimmer. "That could have gone better."

No one answers. We don't need to. The empty common room says enough.

"So," Finn breaks the heavy silence, "anyone else feel like we just made things way worse?"

Something dawns on me, dread pooling in my stomach. "Did anyone ask her?" My question hangs in the air, met with stunned silence.

Torric scoffs, "Ask her what?"

"To the dance," I say, the weight of our failure settling over us as their expressions shift—shock, remorse, guilt.

Finn laughs but there's no humor in it. "We're all idiots."

Right now I couldn't agree more.

Torric's only response is a growl as he stalks toward the exit, leaving the scent of smoke in his wake.

For a long moment, none of us move. The common room feels emptier somehow, colder, despite the lingering heat from Torric's anger.

"I should go after him," I say finally, though I make no move toward the door. We all know how Torric gets when he's like this—he needs space to burn off his temper, literally sometimes.

"Let him go," Malrik says, his voice tight. He's watching the spiral staircase leading to the upper levels, his silver eyes distant. "He's not the one we need to worry about right now."

Finn makes a sound that might be a laugh, if laughs could bleed. "No, we just pushed Kaia straight into Darian's arms. But hey, at least we proved her point about being controlling."

"What choice did we have?" I ask, sinking into an armchair. The velvet feels cool against my skin. "You both can see her shadows. You know something's wrong."

"Yeah, and fat lot of good that did us," Finn mutters. He glances up toward Kaia's room on the second floor. "Bob's having a complete meltdown, by the way. Never seen him this agitated. It's like he knows something we don't, and he's trying to scream it at us in the only way he can."

I still haven't gotten used to them talking about the shadows like they're people. But after everything I've seen, everything they've told us, I'm starting to wonder if maybe they are.

"Something happened in that maze," Malrik says quietly. "The way her shadows responded to him... it wasn't natural."

"They were terrified," Finn adds, his voice uncharacteristically serious. "They kept trying to pull her away from him, but it was like she couldn't even feel it anymore."

A chill runs down my spine, despite the lingering warmth from Torric's outburst. "Could he be manipulating them somehow?"

Malrik's expression darkens. "It's possible. There's old magic that can interfere with shadow bonds, but it's dangerous. Unstable."

"Like everything else about this situation," Finn mutters. He's sprawled on the couch but his usual easy demeanor is gone, replaced by something tighter, more worried. "Bob's been trying to warn us for weeks. I thought if I could just make her laugh about it, make her see..."

"We all tried," I say quietly. Above us, the vaulted ceiling seems to absorb our words, the enchanted shadows there shifting restlessly. "Each in our own way."

"And failed spectacularly," Finn adds with a bitter laugh.

Malrik moves to the window, his reflection fragmenting in the glass. His silver eyes are distant, unfocused, as if searching for answers in the jagged pieces of his image. The tension in his shoulders speaks volumes, the weight of unspoken fears pressing heavily on him. Whatever plan he's formulating, it's clear he knows time is running out. "The question is: what's his endgame? The dance is too public for anything obvious."

"Unless that's the point," I say slowly, an idea forming. "What if the dance isn't the plan? What if it's just meant to isolate her from us, to cut her off when she's most vulnerable? If he can sever her ties to us, she'll have no one left to turn to but him."

"Make her choose him publicly," Finn catches on, sitting up straighter. "Prove he has her trust completely."

"While discrediting any warnings we might try to give," Malrik finishes, turning back to face us. His silver eyes gleam in the dim light. "It's clever."

"It's manipulation," I correct him. "And Kaia's walking right into it."

"While we sit here discussing it like some sort of shadow council," Finn groans, flopping back down. "She'd hate this, you know. All of us plotting about her life."

He's right, and we all know it. The silence that follows feels heavy with that knowledge.

"I should find Torric," I say finally, standing. "Before he burns down half the training grounds."

"I'll keep an eye on things here," Finn says, waving vaguely at the upper levels. "Someone should monitor the shadow situation, even if she won't listen to us about it."

Malrik straightens, shedding the weight of his concern like a cloak. The intensity in his silver eyes sharpens to steel. "It's time I had a chat with Professor Thorne about his star pupil."

"Be careful," I warn. "If Darian's as dangerous as we think..."

"Then we're already in trouble," Malrik finishes smoothly. "Might as well make it count."

"Oh, and Aspen?" Finn calls as I reach the door. "When you find your hot-headed twin, maybe remind him that setting things on fire won't actually solve this?"

Despite everything, my lips twitch. "I'll try. But you know Torric."

"Yeah," Finn sighs, his voice heavy with unspoken fears. "That's what worries me." And for once, I agree completely

Chapter 34
ASPEN

I find Torric exactly where I expect him – methodically destroying practice dummies in the outdoor arena. Heat shimmers around him, his rune glowing like molten gold, pulsing with his barely-contained storm. It's not just power—it's a glimpse into the chaos inside. My brother has never been subtle about his emotions, but this display seems excessive even for him.

"That's the fourth dummy this week," I say, leaning against the wall as my rune cools the stone. "At this rate, they'll bill you for replacements"

Torric doesn't turn, but his shoulders tense. "Not now, Aspen."

"Our trials start in an hour." I keep my voice steady, watching steam rise where his sweat hits the ground. "And you're out here trying to burn down the academy."

He whirls to face me, golden eyes literally blazing. "What do you want me to say? That you were right about Darian? That we should have seen this coming?"

"I want you to breathe," I say calmly. "Before you set the entire arena on fire. Again."

A growl rumbles from his chest, but I see him struggling to control his breathing. After a moment, the temperature drops slightly. Progress.

"Kaia's walking into a trap," he growls, his voice raw. "We all know it, but we're doing nothing." Flames lick at his clenched fists, and for a moment, I think he might ignite. "Every instinct I have is screaming at me to stop this before it's too late, but we just keep standing here like there's nothing we can do."

"Probably," I agree. "But we'll be there this time."

The temperature spikes again as another dummy bursts into flames. "Will we? Or will we just stand by like we did with—" His voice breaks off, but I don't need him to finish. Elena. The sister we couldn't save, the shadow haunting his rage.

I let out a slow breath, frost crystallizing in the air. "This is different."

"Is it?" His laugh is harsh. "Because from where I'm standing, we're about to watch someone else we care about walk straight into danger while we do nothing."

The words sting, but I maintain my composure. "And your solution is what, exactly? To burn everything in sight?"

For a moment, I think he might actually attack me. His rune flares brighter, and I feel my own power rise in response. But then his shoulders slump, the fight draining out of him.

"I can't lose anyone else," he says quietly. "Not like that. Not again."

And there it is – the real reason behind his rage. Not just Kaia, but everything we couldn't prevent before. Everyone we couldn't save.

"I know," I say softly. "But this time is different. We're stronger now. All of us."

I watch my brother pace, his footsteps leaving scorch marks on the stone, each mark a reminder of the fire he's holding back. It's as if his emotions are too fierce to be contained, spilling out in small, destructive bursts that mirror the turmoil inside him. Around us, the academy is in full swing, an undercurrent of tension spreading as students prepare for the trials. But here in our bubble of steam and frost, time seems suspended.

"Your rune only flares like that when you're trying to ignore something else," I say carefully. "Or someone."

Torric stills. "Don't."

"The way you look at her during training—"

"And you?" he presses, cutting me off. "Always calm, always steady—the one she can lean on. At least I'm honest about how I feel. You? You're all control and no courage."

Now I want to set something on fire. "We're not having this conversation."

"Aren't we?" His voice softens. "You're falling for her too."

The accusation hangs in the air between us. I could deny it, maintain that careful distance I've cultivated. But we've never lied to each other, not about anything that matters.

"Yes," I admit finally. "But it doesn't change anything. The trials come first. Her safety comes first."

Torric laughs, but it's gentler now. "Brother, when has anything about Kaia ever been simple?"

I can't help but smile at that. He's right, of course. From the moment she arrived with her shadows and her secrets, nothing has been straightforward.

"What are we going to do?" he asks, and for a moment he sounds young again, uncertain.

"What we've always done," I reply. "We protect her. Together."

Above us, storm clouds gather as the trial hour approaches. I feel the weight of what's coming settle around us like a shroud. But this time, we're ready. This time, we won't stand by and watch.

Torric extinguishes the last dummy, the flames snuffing out with a hiss. "Together," he says, his voice steadier now. As we head toward the arena, the storm clouds overhead seem to mirror my thoughts. I pray we're strong enough for what's coming—and that this time, we don't fail.

Chapter 35
MALRIK

The library's shadows welcome me like old friends as I move silently between the stacks. It's late—well past curfew—but sleep has been elusive lately. Particularly since... I pause, my hand hovering over an ancient text on shadow manipulation. It's been five days since she accepted his invitation, and the academy's shadows have been restless ever since.

I pull the tome from its shelf, its weight familiar in my hands. The leather binding is cool against my skin, a stark contrast to the warmth that floods my chest whenever I think of her.

Kaia.

Her name echoes in my mind, a bittersweet melody that refuses to fade.

Five days. It feels like an eternity.

I settle into my usual alcove, surrounded by flickering candlelight that barely keeps the encroaching darkness at bay. The shadows seem to whisper her name, a constant reminder of her absence. Of how Darian has managed to do what none of us thought possible – isolate her from those who care about her most. Not that she even knows how much we care, how much I care... but that's not the point.

My fingers trace the intricate patterns on the book's cover, but my mind is far from the arcane knowledge within. Instead, I see flashes of her – the way her eyes used to light up when she mastered a new technique, the sound of her laughter echoing through the training grounds. Now, those moments feel like relics from another life.

The few glimpses we've caught of her have been... unsettling. Her eyes, once so full of warmth and curiosity, now hold a distant, confused look. It's as if she's seeing through us, rather than truly seeing us at all. The easy camaraderie we once shared has been replaced by stilted conversations and awkward silences.

I clench my fist, feeling the shadows around me respond to the surge of emotion. This is exactly what Darian wanted, I realize. To drive a wedge between Kaia and those who would protect her. And we've let it happen, helpless to stop the slow unraveling of whatever this connection is that we share.

The worst part is how it's affecting me. I've always prided myself on my control, on keeping my emotions carefully in check. But now? Now I find myself lying awake at night, replaying every interaction, searching for some clue I might have missed. Some way I could have prevented this.

I close my eyes, letting out a slow breath as I try to center myself. The shadows respond, curling around me like a comforting embrace. But even they can't fill the void left by her absence.

It's more than just concern for a friend, I admit to myself in the safety of the darkness. The ache in my chest, the constant worry that gnaws at me – it speaks of deeper feelings, ones I've been reluctant to acknowledge. Feelings that make Kaia's distance all the more painful.

I open the book, hoping to lose myself in its pages, but the words blur before my eyes. Instead, I see her face, hear her voice. I remember the way she looked at me the last time we spoke – confused, and so so angry.

And yet, while she grows more distant, he seems to grow bolder. That thought draws my attention to the shadows shifting restlessly near the restricted section, and I follow their lead.

Movement catches my eye. Through a gap in the shelves, I spot Darian in the restricted section, hunched over a tome with an intensity that seems almost desperate. His usual smooth confidence is notably absent. Interesting.

As I drift closer, I let the shadows mask my presence. The page he's studying comes into focus—diagrams of soul-binding rituals. My blood runs cold.

"Research for Professor Thorne's class?" I ask quietly, stepping into view.

Darian startles—actually startles—before his mask slides back into place. But I catch the flicker of something raw in his eyes. Fear? Guilt? It vanishes too quickly to name, but the tension in his posture betrays him.

"Malrik. Bit late for a study session, isn't it?"

"I could ask you the same thing." I lean against the shelf, noting how his hand twitches toward the book. "Soul-binding is dangerous magic. Not typically covered in our curriculum."

"Just expanding my knowledge." His smile doesn't reach his eyes. "We can't all be born understanding the shadow realm like you."

The jab is meant to unsettle me, but I merely raise an eyebrow. "No, we can't. Just as we can't all be trusted with certain kinds of power."

Something dark flickers across his face before he can hide it. "Speaking of trust," he says, his tone deceptively light. I heard about your little group's falling out. Such a shame. Kaia seemed so close to all of you."

My shadows coil tightly, but I keep my voice neutral. "Concerned about our friendship, Darian? How thoughtful."

He shrugs, gathering his books. "Just making conversation. Though I suppose I should thank you all. If you hadn't pushed her away, she might never have agreed to be my date for the dance."

I want to freeze the smirk off his face, but I force myself to stay still. "Indeed. Funny how things work out."

"Well, I should go. Big day tomorrow." He pauses at the end of the aisle. "Don't worry, I'll take good care of her."

Only when his footsteps fade do I let my careful control slip. The shadows around me writhe in response to my anger, and I have to take several deep breaths before they settle.

"What are you planning?" I murmur, running my fingers over the spine of the book he left behind. The leather is cold to the touch, unnaturally so. When I open it, the pages fall to a detailed description of binding shadows to one's will.

"I know you're there," I say softly to the shadows in the corner. They've been watching me all evening, more agitated than usual. Bob shifts forward slightly. The others hover behind, waiting.

"Show me," I whisper. "Show me what you've seen."

The shadows coalesce into scenes that make my heart race: Darian and Thorne in hushed conversation, the professor's hand tight on his student's shoulder. The necklace pulses with violet light whenever Kaia's shadows draw near, as if sensing something more profound than proximity. It feels almost alive, its reaction a deliberate warning to anyone paying attention. Darian practices something in an empty classroom, his own shadows twisting in ways that seem... wrong.

But it's the final scene that makes my blood run cold. Darian at the edge of the academy grounds, kneeling before a figure cloaked in darkness. The air around them crackles with an oppressive energy, shadows swirling like a living storm. Though the figure's face remains hidden, its presence radiates a chilling authority, the kind that bends the world around it to its will. The shadows can't—or won't—show me the figure's face, but the aura of wrongness is unmistakable.

"When?" I ask sharply. The shadows ripple in response—last night.

Footsteps echo from the other end of the library. The shadows immediately scatter, returning to their usual patterns. Bob brushes against my hand, his edges rippling with agitation. It feels like urgency, a wordless plea to act before it's too late.

"Still lurking in dark corners, your highness?" Finn emerges from between the stacks, his usual grin in place, though it doesn't quite reach his eyes.

"Some of us actually study, chaos mage," I reply drily. But there's something off about his casual stance, a tension in his shoulders that betrays his light tone.

"You saw something," I say quietly.

Finn's smile fades. "Maybe. Or maybe I'm just spreading chaos and rumors like always." He picks up a book, flipping through it without really looking at the pages. "But hypothetically, if someone had seen our newest student practicing some very questionable magic in the east tower at midnight..."

"Hypothetically," I drawl, "that someone might want to share what they saw with someone else who's been having similar concerns."

Finn meets my eyes, all pretense of humor gone. "He's going to hurt her, isn't he?"

I think of the shadows' warning, of the dark figure and Darian's desperate research. "Yes. The question is: what are we going to do about it?"

A slow, decidedly wicked grin spreads across Finn's face. "Well, as it happens, I have a few ideas about that. How do you feel about crashing a dance?"

Despite myself, I feel my lips twitch. "I thought you'd never ask."

As we begin plotting, I notice Bob has returned, joined by the other shadows. They hover around us like eager conspirators, and I'm reminded that we're not the only ones who want to protect Kaia. Whatever Darian and Thorne are planning, they're about to learn a crucial lesson about the nature of shadows—they're not just extensions of darkness.

They're family.

And no one messes with our family.

Chapter 36
FINN

"All right, people," I announce, dramatically flicking open a scroll Bob insists is the latest tactical plan. "The shadows have their orders. Every exit covered, patrols rotating on the half-hour. If Darian so much as breathes wrong, we'll know."

Bob flickers proudly at the center of the room, while Patricia demonstrates what looks like a salute. Malrik watches with an expression I can only describe as begrudging respect.

"This is absurd," Torric mutters, leaning against the wall with his arms crossed. "They're shadows, not soldiers."

"Bob disagrees," I say, pointing to where Bob appears to be drafting a new set of patrol routes. "And personally, I think we should be a little worried about how good they're getting at this."

Malrik sighs, running a hand through his hair. "They're better organized than half the academy's guards."

"Thank you!" I exclaim. "Finally, some appreciation for Bob's hard work. Next, we're moving on to shadow merit badges—"

Torric growls. "We don't have time for this, Finn."

I snap the scroll shut with mock gravity. "Fine, fine. Let's get serious."

"About time," Aspen says, glancing up from where he's adjusting his cuffs. "What's the plan?"

"Step one," I begin, holding up a small pouch of enchanted marbles, "ensure the dance is suitably chaotic. Just in case we need to slip through unnoticed."

Torric glares. "Your big plan is 'chaos?'"

"Not just chaos," I correct. "Controlled chaos. The kind that distracts everyone from, oh, I don't know, Darian pulling some villainy in a dark corner."

Malrik pinches the bridge of his nose. "You're impossible."

"And yet," I say, grinning, "here you are, still listening."

Before Malrik can retort, footsteps echo in the hallway. Bob freezes mid-gesture, signaling the other shadows to hide. Malrik steps closer, his shoulder brushing mine as we all instinctively brace for something unexpected.

The door creaks open, and Seren steps in, her lavender hair escaping its updo in loose curls. She pauses, taking in the scene: four tuxedoed guys in a storage room, a scroll of patrol plans, and a suspiciously proud-looking shadow that she can't see, but that's besides the point.

"What are you all up to?" she asks, her tone a mix of curiosity and amusement.

"Us?" I say, feigning innocence. "Nothing suspicious at all. Just four totally normal dudes hanging out. In tuxedos. In a shadowed closet. Nothing weird about that."

"Right," she says, arching an eyebrow. "And I'm the Queen of Omnia."

Malrik shifts uncomfortably, muttering, "Not another one." But Seren doesn't miss a beat.

"Kaia told me what was going on," she says, stepping further into the room. "I didn't think it was this bad."

Aspen clears his throat. "We're not acting strange."

Her gaze sharpens, flicking to the patrol plans still clutched in my hand. "She said you were overbearing, overprotective and trying to pull her away from Darian." She looks around the room, her eyes softening. "You're worried about her."

It's not a question, but none of us answer right away. The silence speaks for itself.

Finally, Malrik says, "You wouldn't understand."

"Try me," Seren replies, her voice softening. "I'm her friend too, you know. And I'm not blind."

The room falls quiet again, the weight of her words settling over us. Seren crosses her arms, looking directly at Malrik. "I know you all care about her more than she realizes. And honestly? I'm glad."

"You are?" Torric asks, skepticism thick in his tone.

"Of course," she says. "Kaia's strong, but she doesn't see how much she matters to people. She used to doing everything on her own and being alone. She isn't used to needing anyone else. And if you're doing all of this to keep her safe..." She gestures vaguely to Bob and the patrol routes. "Well, it's kind of sweet. In a weird but adorable kind of way."

"She doesn't like to admit it, but she's scared of getting hurt. I've seen it since the first day we met. She pretends she's fine on her own, but deep down, she doesn't believe anyone will stay." Seren breathes deep like she knows she shouldn't be saying this but needs to anyway.

Malrik exhales slowly, his tension easing just a fraction and I don't miss the pink tinge to his cheeks. "She's walking into danger tonight, Seren. We can't stand by and let her get hurt."

"Then don't," Seren says simply. "But you might want to make sure she knows you're there for her when it counts. Not just in the shadows."

Her words hit harder than I expect, and I glance at the others. Aspen's jaw tightens, Torric looks away, and even Malrik seems to be considering what she said.

Before anyone can respond, I catch movement outside the window. Darian, his stride as calculated as always, heads toward the Shadow Faction wing. My stomach twists.

"Showtime," I mutter, nodding toward the courtyard.

Malrik straightens, his expression hardening. "Let's go."

Seren steps aside, but as we pass, she puts a hand on my arm. "Finn," she says quietly. "Be careful. And take care of her."

"Always," I promise, and for once, there's no joke in my voice.

The moment we step outside, the shadows fall into formation. Bob straightens, his earlier playfulness gone as the shadows snap into formation. Their fluid edges sharpen, radiating purpose. The change is so sudden it sends a shiver down my spine. Whatever Darian's planning, we won't let him win. Not tonight.

As we move toward the dance, I glance at Malrik, Aspen, and Torric. Seren's words echo in my mind: *Make sure she knows you're there when it counts.*

Now is when it counts.

Chapter 37
Kaia

"Ow!" I yelp as Seren attacks another tangle with her enchanted hairbrush. "Are you trying to scalp me?"

"Beauty is pain, darling," she says cheerfully, wielding the brush like a weapon. "Now hold still. I'm almost done with this section."

My shadows writhe sympathetically around my feet, and I swear one of them is mimicking Seren's enthusiastic brushing motions. Another keeps trying to steal the brush when she's not looking, probably to save me from further torture.

"I don't see why I can't just wear it down," I mutter, wincing as she starts on another section.

"Because," Seren says with exaggerated patience, "this is your first Equinox Ball. Everyone who matters will be there. Including all those brooding boys who keep following you around like lost puppies."

"They don't—" I start to protest, but she cuts me off with a wave of her brush.

"Please. I've seen the way they look at you. Especially when they think no one's watching." She pauses, studying my reflection. "Although lately, it seems like Darian's the only one you're noticing."

Something in her tone makes me shift uncomfortably. "He's... different. Easy to talk to."

"Mm-hmm." Seren's reflection raises an eyebrow. "And the fact that he's gorgeous has nothing to do with it?"

"They're all gorgeous." I retort before I can stop myself.

My face reddens, "Can we just focus on the hair torture?" I ask, desperate to change the subject. My shadows flicker restlessly, and I force them to still.

Hours later, I barely recognize the girl in the mirror. My usual mess of blonde waves has been transformed into an intricate updo, with delicate wisps framing my face. Tiny crystals catch the light with every movement, making it look like I'm wearing a crown of stars.

The midnight blue gown Seren loaned me flows like liquid starlight, hugging my curves before cascading into a full skirt with a daring slit up one side. My eyes, usually a stormy violet, shimmer with flecks of silver thanks to her careful application of some kind of magical cosmetics.

"Holy shit," I whisper.

Seren beams. "I know, right? You're welcome."

I stand, fighting the urge to hide under the bed. Part of me—the part that's spent years trying to be invisible—wants to change into my regular clothes and forget this whole thing.

But a larger part is tired of hiding.

"Ready?" Seren asks, practically vibrating with excitement.

I take a deep breath, squaring my shoulders. "As I'll ever be."

"Good. You look fantastic. Now, I have a few last minute touches to make. I'll see you down there in a bit." Seren pauses at the door, glancing back at me with a hesitant smile. "You'll be amazing tonight, Kaia. Just... don't let anyone dim your light." Then she's gone, her lavender hair disappearing down the corridor like a comet.

The room suddenly feels too quiet without her bubbly energy, and I'm left alone with my reflection and my thoughts.

I turn back to the mirror, studying the stranger staring back at me. The girl in the glass is ethereal, otherworldly—a far cry from the scruffy, shadow-wielding outcast I've been for so long. My fingers trace the delicate curve of my cheek, the arch of my brow, as if touching my face might shatter the illusion.

Who am I now? The question echoes in my mind, persistent and unsettling.

I used to be so sure of myself, of my place in the world. Looking out for myself, taking care of myself. I was Kaia, a girl who tried to blend in, and just get through the day and knowing full well that I had no one else but myself.

Okay and Mouse.

But now? Everything's blurred, like looking through frosted glass and I don't know what to do about it. There's no more time to dwell about it now, I'm sure Darian is already waiting.

I make my way down to the shadow faction common room and just as I suspected. Darian is already there.

At the base of the stairs, Darian waits in a perfectly tailored black tuxedo that makes his gray eyes gleam like polished silver. When he looks up, his expression shifts into something almost reverent.

"You're breathtaking," he says, offering his hand. "I don't know whether to call you a star or a storm."

I manage a smile, though my shadows twitch uneasily. "You might be laying it on a little thick."

"Can you blame me?" He steps closer, his hand warm as it settles on my waist. "Shall we?"

The walk to the ballroom is quick, we make casual conversation but I don't really remember it. The beat of my heart pounding in my ears, my anxiety, it's all about to boil over.

The ballroom takes my breath away. Enchanted constellations swirl overhead, casting ever-changing patterns across the crowd. Floating candles drift like stars, their light reflecting off the polished marble floor. The air tastes like magic—sharp and sweet and slightly dangerous.

Darian guides me through the crowd with perfect grace, but I can't shake the feeling that something's off. My shadows brush against my ankles insistently, like they're trying to pull me back.

"You're tense," Darian murmurs, his voice low and intimate.

"Just not used to this," I say, forcing another smile.

His hand tightens slightly at my waist. "You should let yourself enjoy it. After all, you deserve to shine, Kaia."

A shiver runs down my spine at his words, though I'm not sure why. Before I can respond, the music changes to a slower melody. Darian pulls me closer, and I catch a glimpse of Finn watching us from across the room. His usual grin is nowhere to be seen.

"They don't understand you," Darian says suddenly, his voice soft but weighted.

I blink, startled. "What?"

"Your friends," he clarifies. "They care about you, yes. But they don't see your true potential. Not like I do."

"That's not—" I start to protest, but he continues smoothly.

"They mean well. But they're afraid of what you might become. They want to keep you safe, controlled." His thumb traces small circles on my back. "But what if you don't need protecting? What if you need freedom?"

His words sink deep, finding purchase in doubts I've tried to ignore. My shadows twist sharply, and Darian glances down with the briefest frown before his expression smooths.

"Trust me," he whispers, leaning closer. "I can help you become everything you're meant to be."

The way he says it makes something cold settle in my chest, but before I can dwell on it, the music shifts and another voice cuts through the tension.

"Mind if I cut in?"

I turn to find Finn standing beside us, his usual mischievous grin firmly in place. But there's something different in his eyes—something almost fierce.

"Actually," Darian starts, but I'm already stepping away from him.

"Sure," I say, ignoring the way Darian's fingers tighten briefly before letting go. My shadows seem to sigh with relief, curling happily around Finn's ankles.

Finn's grin softens into something warmer as he pulls me into the dance. "You look incredible, by the way. Like some kind of shadow goddess."

I laugh despite myself. "Now who's laying it on thick?"

"Hey, I'm always honest about the important stuff." His hand is warm on my waist, steadying rather than controlling. "Like how Bob's been trying to trip Darian all night. He's currently doing a victory dance around my feet."

I glance down and can't help smiling at the way my shadows seem to preen under his attention. "You're ridiculous."

"You like it," he says confidently, then spins me in a surprisingly graceful turn.

"When did you learn to dance?" I ask, momentarily forgetting my unease.

His eyes sparkle with familiar mischief. "I contain multitudes of surprises. Also, Malrik's been teaching me. Don't tell him I told you—he'll deny everything."

The mention of Malrik makes me glance around, finally spotting him near one of the massive windows. He's watching us with an unreadable expression, but something about his intensity makes my heart skip.

"He's worried about you, you know," Finn says softly, following my gaze. "We all are."

I stiffen slightly. "I can take care of myself."

"Oh, we know that." Finn's tone is light but his eyes are serious. "Doesn't mean you have to, though."

Before I can respond, he dips me dramatically, making me yelp in surprise. When he pulls me back up, we're much closer than before. His breath catches slightly, and I realize I'm staring at his lips.

"Kaia," he starts, his voice rougher than usual.

The music swells, and something in the enchanted constellations above shifts. The moment breaks as Finn glances up, his expression sharpening.

"What is it?" I ask, but he's already straightening, though his hand stays warm on my waist.

"Nothing good," he mutters, then flashes me a quick grin that doesn't quite reach his eyes. "Rain check on that dance?"

I watch Finn weave through the crowd, his shoulders tense, and a part of me wants to follow. But my feet stay rooted, my shadows coiling around my legs like chains. Across the room, I feel Thorne's gaze settle on me, sharp and deliberate. It makes my skin crawl, but when I blink, he's gone.

The enchanted constellations continue to swirl overhead, but their light seems colder now, my shadows twist anxiously around me.

Chapter 38
MALRIK

From my position near the window, I watch Finn spin Kaia across the dance floor. Her shadows trail after them like excited puppies—a sight that would be amusing if I wasn't so focused on the way Thorne keeps glancing at the enchanted constellations overhead.

"You're brooding again," Aspen says quietly, appearing beside me with two glasses of something that sparkles suspiciously. "Here. You look like you need this."

I accept the drink but don't take my eyes off the dance floor. "The alignment's wrong."

"What?"

"The constellations." I gesture upward with my glass. "They're not just decorative. Someone's using them to channel energy."

Aspen's expression sharpens. "Thorne?"

"Him and someone else. The patterns are too complex for one person." Across the room, Darian's movements are deliberate, his every step calculated. He's weaving through the crowd like he's part of the dance, but his focus never strays far from Kaia. My jaw tightens as I catch the faintest smirk playing on his lips. "We need to—"

"Already on it," Aspen cuts in smoothly, nodding to where Torric has intercepted Darian's path. My lip twitches despite myself. The twins might be opposites in temperament, but their coordination is impressive.

Across the room, Finn finally releases Kaia. Her shadows seem reluctant to let him go, and I catch myself almost smiling at their antics.

"You could ask her to dance, you know," Aspen suggests mildly.

I shoot him a look. "That's not—"

"Part of the plan?" His tone is dry. "When are you going to admit this is about more than just protecting her?"

Before I can respond, a shift in the magical current makes my skin prickle. Above us, the constellations pulse with an unnatural light. Kaia's shadows react instantly, coiling around her legs like agitated snakes.

"Time to move," I mutter, already striding toward her.

Kaia

I'm still trying to process what happened with Finn when a familiar voice cuts through my thoughts.

"May I?"

I turn to find Malrik standing beside me, his hand extended with casual grace. His silver eyes seem to glow in the shifting light, and something about his intensity makes my heart skip.

"I don't really—" I start to protest, but my shadows are already reaching for him, rippling eagerly around his polished shoes.

His face serious, "Please, Kaia."

"Fine," I say reluctantly. I want to be mad at him, but the look in his eyes, the vulnerability in his voice, makes me reconsider.

Malrik moves with fluid precision, each step perfectly timed to the haunting melody. Unlike Darian's practiced charm or Finn's playful energy, Malrik's touch feels... grounding. Like gravity given form.

"Are you okay?" he observes quietly.

I tense. "I'm fine."

"Are you?" His gaze is too knowing. "Can you feel something is wrong?"

"What are you talking about?" I challenge, even as unease crawls up my spine because I can feel something's wrong. I'm just not sure what.

Instead of answering, he spins me into a turn that brings us closer together. "Look up," he murmurs, his breath warm against my ear. "But don't make it obvious."

I glance at the enchanted constellations, trying to see what has him concerned. At first, they look normal—just swirling patterns of magical light. But then I notice how they're shifting, forming intricate geometries that seem to pulse in time with...

"My necklace," I breathe, The constellations aren't just moving—they're building something. The lines pulse, sharper with each beat, and I feel it echo in my chest, like a spell tightening its grip around me.

Malrik's hand tightens slightly at my waist. "Someone's channeling power through the alignment. Using the ball as cover."

"Thorne?"

"Among others I believe." His tone is grim.

A chill runs down my spine as I remember Darian's words about freedom and potential. "What do they want?"

"You tell me." Malrik's silver eyes lock with mine. "What has Darian been promising you?"

I start to pull away, but he keeps us moving smoothly through the dance. "He's just been helping me train. He understands what it's like to—"

"To feel different?" Malrik's voice is soft but intent. "To have power others fear?"

"You don't know what it's like," I snap, even as my shadows curl around his ankles almost apologetically.

"Don't I?" For a moment, his careful control slips, and I catch a glimpse of something ancient and dark in his eyes. Then he blinks, and his mask is back in place. "Just... be careful who you trust with your shadows, Kaia. Not everyone sees them for what they are. Some would twist them into something unrecognizable. Something dangerous."

Before I can process that cryptic warning, the music changes and Torric appears beside us.

"Time to switch," he says gruffly, though his eyes are alert. "Assuming little miss sunshine doesn't mind dancing with someone less broody?"

Malrik releases me with a slight bow that somehow manages to look both elegant and sarcastic. As Torric pulls me into the new dance, I glance back, but Malrik has already melted into the crowd.

Chapter 39
KAIA

"You look like you're trying to solve a puzzle with half the pieces missing," Torric observes, his usual bluntness oddly comforting.

I snort. "That obvious?"

"Only to those of us paying attention." His rune pulses faintly as we turn, and I realize he's using it to track something—or someone—through the crowd. "Which, by the way, is more people than you think."

"What's that supposed to mean?"

He spins me, and I catch a glimpse of Finn and Malrik having what looks like an intense discussion near one of the giant windows. Aspen stands between them and the rest of the crowd, his casual pose not quite hiding his defensive stance.

"It means," Torric says as he pulls me back, "that some of us actually give a damn about what happens to you. Whether you want us to or not."

"I never asked for—"

"Protection?" He raises an eyebrow. "Good thing we're not asking permission then." He keeps his tone light, but the flicker of worry in his golden eyes betrays him. For all his bravado, Torric's concern feels as solid as the rune pulsing faintly on his chest.

I open my mouth to argue, but movement near the edges of the room catches my eye. Thorne is walking purposefully toward a side door, and Darian is nowhere to be seen.

My shadows ripple with sudden urgency, and my necklace pulses warm against my skin.

Something's coming. I feel it in my bones, in the thickening magic that clings to every breath.

Finn

Everything goes to hell when the constellations start bleeding silver.

"That's not good," I mutter, watching droplets of starlight fall like rain. The other students seem mesmerized by the display, oohing and ahhing at what they probably think is part of the show.

They don't notice how the drops sizzle when they hit the ground. Or how they're forming a pattern around—

"Kaia," Malrik breathes, already moving. I grab his arm.

"Wait. Look."

Torric has maneuvered Kaia to the edge of the room, keeping her away from the worst of the magical discharge. Smart guy, even if he looks like he's about to murder someone. Probably Darian, who's watching the whole thing with poorly concealed interest.

"I think someone's trying to trigger her necklace," Malrik says quietly. "The alignment is amplifying its power."

"Yeah, I got that part. Question is: what do we do about it?"

A shadow—Bob, definitely Bob—tugs at my pant leg urgently.

"I know, buddy. We're working on it."

Kaia

The world has gone slightly silver at the edges, and my skin feels too tight. My amethyst necklace pulses against my chest in time with the falling starlight, each beat sending ripples of warmth through my body.

"Don't look up," Torric murmurs, his hand firm on my waist as he guides me through another turn. "Just keep dancing."

"What's happening?" I try to glance at the constellations again, but he smoothly blocks my view.

"Nothing good. But we've got it handled."

"We?"

His rune flares briefly. "I told you, I'm not the only one who's been paying attention."

Before I can demand clarification, the temperature around us drops sharply. My shadows coil tighter, and I swear I can feel them trembling.

Across the room, Thorne raises his hand in what looks like a casual gesture. But I recognize the pattern his fingers trace in the air—it's the same one he taught me for binding shadows.

Except this is bigger. Much bigger.

The falling starlight begins to spiral, forming intricate patterns that remind me of—

"Interesting, isn't it?"

I jump at Darian's voice. He's suddenly beside us, smile pleasant but eyes sharp.

"The way magic responds to emotion. To power." He holds out his hand. "One more dance?"

My shadows practically hiss, pressing against Torric's legs like they're seeking shelter.

"She's good here," Torric growls, his rune pulsing brighter.

Darian's smile doesn't waver. "I wasn't actually asking."

Chapter 40
MALRIK

The moment Darian approaches them, I feel the shift in magical current. He's trying something. Something that makes my blood run cold.

"Finn," I snap.

"On it."

He moves through the crowd like quicksilver, and I follow in his wake. Aspen appears on my left, water rune gleaming.

We're not going to make it in time.

Darian raises his hand, silver light gathering at his fingertips, and I see the exact moment Kaia realizes what's happening. Her eyes go wide, violet darkening to storm-cloud gray.

But before anyone can move, before Darian can complete whatever spell he's attempting, something unexpected happens.

Mouse appears at Kaia's feet and grows. Not just bigger, but massive. The size of a real panther, with eyes that burn like violet flames.

The magical display sputters. Darian stumbles back, his perfect composure cracking.

And then the lights go out.

Kaia

In the sudden darkness, I feel my shadows surge. Not with fear or anger, but with... purpose.

They curl around me like armor, responding to something in the air. To the way my necklace seems to sing against my skin.

When the emergency lights flicker on, I'm standing alone. Mouse has returned to normal size, looking smug. My shadows ripple with satisfaction.

Darian is nowhere to be seen.

"Well," Finn says, appearing beside me with a grin that's only slightly forced. "That was exciting. Also, remind me never to piss off your cat."

"Mouse isn't—" I start automatically, then pause. "What just happened?"

"Would you believe me if I said temporary magical blackout?" He offers his arm with an exaggerated bow. "Totally normal. Happens all the time at fancy parties."

I know he's deflecting. I know there's more going on than anyone's telling me.

But my shadows are calm now, almost pleased. Mouse purrs at my feet. And when I glance around, I catch glimpses of the others—Malrik melting into the shadows, the twins moving to cover the exits, Aspen speaking quietly with some of the faculty.

All of them watching out for me, in their own ways.

"Fine," I say, taking Finn's arm. "But this conversation isn't over."

His grin softens into something more genuine. "Wouldn't dream of it, trouble." He glances at Mouse. "Though maybe we should let Bob explain. He's been dying to tell you everything."

Despite everything, I laugh. And if I lean into him a little more than necessary as we head for the exit, well... my shadows aren't telling.

The night isn't over. Questions still buzz under my skin, and my necklace still pulses around my neck.

But for now, surrounded by people who apparently "give a damn" whether I want them to or not, I let myself breathe.

Tomorrow will bring answers. Or at least better questions.

237

Chapter 41
KAIA

The air carries a bitter chill, but I barely notice as I pace the length of my room. My shadows trail after me restlessly, their agitation matching the storm in my head. Mouse watches from my bed, his violet eyes tracking every movement, still tense from earlier. I needed some time to clear my head but I honestly think I'm just making it worse at this point. Like talking myself off a ledge that's five miles down the road.

"He was right there," I mutter, running my fingers over my necklace. It hums against my throat, warmer than usual after tonight's chaos. "Thorne was pulling some shit all along, and I never really saw it."

I'm so stupid.

A soft knock interrupts my brooding and self loathing. Before I can decide whether to ignore it, Finn's voice filters through the door.

"I come bearing peace offerings. And snacks. Mostly snacks."

My shadows ripple toward the door eagerly, still keyed up from the chaos of the ball and Thorne's betrayal. Even Mouse perks up, though he seems more alert than usual.

"Go away, Finn."

"See, I would, but Bob's already letting me in."

Sure enough, he's slipped under the door and is now tugging at the handle from the other side. I throw my hands up in exasperation as the door swings open.

Finn stands there grinning, arms full of what looks like half the kitchen's worth of food. His easy demeanor, complete with that familiar sparkle of mischief in his eyes, is at odds with the faint bruise darkening his jaw—a mark from tonight's chaos. It's as though he's determined to brush off the tension with charm and a tray of sugar. "I figured we could all use a midnight feast after... you know, the whole 'evil professor' thing."

"We?" I ask, just as more footsteps echo down the hall.

Aspen appears first, carrying drinks and wearing an expression that manages to be both apologetic and determined. His water rune still shimmers faintly from earlier. Torric follows, his fire rune flickering with residual energy, and finally, Malrik materializes from the shadows themselves, because apparently near-death experiences haven't taught him to use doors like a normal person.

"No," I say firmly. "Absolutely not. I don't need an intervention."

"Good, because this isn't one," Finn says cheerfully, already spreading snacks across my desk. "This is just friends making sure you don't brood yourself into oblivion. While eating sugar."

"You're not going to let this go, are you?"

"Nope!" He pops the 'p' sound, tossing me a package of my favorite cookies. "Besides, your shadows are already setting up a snack fort."

He's right. My traitorous shadows are arranging cushions in a loose circle, creating a cozy gathering space. Even Finnick is helping, though he seems to be mostly stealing cookies.

"Fine," I sigh, dropping onto a cushion. "Start talking."

Chapter 42
KAIA

The others settle in, forming a careful semicircle. Aspen's expression is a blend of quiet determination and unease, his shoulders tense as he sets the drinks down. Torric's brows are furrowed, and his fire rune flickers faintly like it's mirroring his agitation. Malrik's silver eyes remain unreadable, but his deliberate movements and the way he takes a seat with precision suggest he's bracing for something. Even Finn, usually relaxed, settles in with a slight edge to his grin, his hands quick as he passes out snacks, like he's trying to fill the silence. Close enough to talk, but giving me space.

"We should have told you sooner," Aspen says quietly, breaking the tension. "About our suspicions."

"You think?" The words come out sharper than I intend, but I can't quite help it. "How long have you all been... what? Coordinating? Spying?"

"Since the training accident," Torric admits, his rune flickering faintly. "When Darian conveniently showed up and was suddenly inserted into your life."

"He was helping me," I protest, but it sounds weak even to my ears.

"Was he?" Malrik's voice is soft but intent. "Or was he studying you?"

I open my mouth to argue, then close it as memories surface. The way Darian always seemed to know when my shadows were acting up. His carefully worded questions about their behavior. The calculating look in his eyes when he thought I wasn't watching.

"Start from the beginning," I say finally. "I want to know everything."

They exchange glances, having one of those silent conversations that should irritate me but instead makes something in my chest ache. It's the kind of ache that comes from watching people care—because that's what this is. And from realizing, despite all my efforts to push everyone away, they've stayed. It's unfamiliar and raw, a strange mix of gratitude and fear.

Finally, Finn speaks up.

"It started with Bob, actually," he says, grinning when Malrik rolls his eyes at the name. "Your shadows have been trying to warn you for weeks. But only a few of us could see them."

"What do you mean, see them?" I look between him and Malrik.

"Most can see the effects," Malrik corrects. "The way they move things or create patterns with actual shadows. But the shadows themselves?" He gestures to where Bob is currently trying to steal another cookie. "Most people just see disturbances in the light."

"But you can see them clearly," I say slowly. "Both of you."

Finn nods. "In living color. Or, well, living darkness. Whatever. Point is, they've been putting on quite a show trying to get your attention."

"They were especially dramatic around Darian," Malrik adds dryly. "Though subtlety isn't exactly their strong suit."

As if to prove his point, my shadows start reenacting what looks like an interpretive dance of their dislike for Darian. Mouse watches with what I swear is amusement.

"Okay, but that doesn't explain why you were all at the ball tonight," I press. "Or what happened with the constellations."

"That was my fault," Malrik says, surprising me. "I caught Darian researching soul bonds in the library. He didn't want me to know what he was looking at and seemed a little too calm for it to just be nothing." He takes a breath, like this is hard for him to admit. "The things he was researching... it wasn't just soul bonds, but honestly I'm not sure what to make of it yet."

"Which is why we were watching tonight," Finn adds. "Though I still say my chaos distraction plan would have worked better."

"Your plan involved releasing enchanted origami birds into the punch bowl," Malrik reminds him.

"Exactly! Pure genius."

Despite everything, I feel my lips twitch. "You're all ridiculous," I mutter, but there's no heat in it. "So let me get this straight," I say, picking at a cookie. "You've all been secretly coordinating to protect me because my shadows told you Darian was suspicious?"

"Well, when you say it like that, it sounds ridiculous," Finn grins, then yelps as Bob swats him with a shadowy tendril. "But you have to admit, they've been acting weird."

I look down, a little ashamed because I know he's right and I chose to ignore it.

"It wasn't just the shadows," Malrik says quietly. His silver eyes catch mine, and something in his gaze makes my heart stutter. "There are... patterns, in shadow magic. Rules. The way Darian watched you—studied you—it felt wrong."

"And the way Thorne kept pushing you in training," Aspen adds. "Always testing your limits, but never explaining why."

Torric's rune flares briefly. "Plus, Darian's a creepy bastard."

"Very diplomatic, brother," Aspen sighs.

"What? Am I wrong?"

I almost smile, but then another thought hits me. "Wait. Is this why you've all been... you know..."

"Charming? Devastatingly handsome? Excellent dance partners?" Finn suggests innocently.

"Around," I finish, ignoring the way my cheeks heat. "Always showing up when I'm training or studying or—"

"No," Malrik cuts in, his tone leaving no room for doubt. "That was..." he pauses, looking almost uncomfortable.

"That was just us wanting to be around you," Finn finishes simply. "The protective stuff came later."

"Oh." I look down, watching my shadows swirl gently around everyone's feet. They seem completely at ease, especially with Finn and Malrik. Even Mouse has abandoned his usual alertness to sprawl across Finn's lap.

"We should have told you sooner," Aspen says again. "But we were worried—"

"That I wouldn't believe you?"

"That you'd pull away," Malrik corrects softly. "You've spent so long trying to handle everything alone."

"Yeah, well, look how well that turned out," I mutter, but there's less bitterness in it now.

"Hey." Finn leans forward, his usual playful demeanor gone serious. "You handled yourself pretty well tonight. Mouse going full battle-panther? That was badass."

"Indeed," Malrik agrees, his lip twitching. "Though perhaps next time we could avoid the dramatic blackout."

"That wasn't me," I protest. Then pause. "Was it?"

"Your shadows," Malrik explains. "They were protecting you. From whatever Darian and Thorne were trying to do with the alignment."

"Which was what, exactly?"

The others exchange glances again. Finally, Aspen speaks. "We're not entirely sure. But it had something to do with your necklace. The way it reacted to the magical convergence..."

"It's not just a normal piece of jewelry, is it?" I touch the stone again, feeling its steady warmth.

"No," Malrik says quietly. "I don't think it is."

A comfortable silence falls as we all process that. My shadows continue their lazy patterns, occasionally stealing snacks or nudging someone affectionately. It should feel strange, sitting here with them like this. Instead, it feels... right.

"So what now?" I ask finally.

"Now," Finn says, reaching for more cookies, "we figure it out together. No more secrets."

"Except for Bob's secret cookie stash," Torric adds dryly. "That's sacred."

I laugh despite myself, and the last of the tension drains away. My shadows settle contentedly, and Mouse starts purring.

"Together," I repeat softly. Testing how the word feels.

My necklace pulses once, warm and sure, like an answer to a question I wasn't sure how to ask.

"Speaking of secrets," Finn says, sprawling back against a cushion, "can we talk about how Malrik has apparently been holding out on us? Mr. 'I understand shadow magic' better than anyone over here."

Malrik stiffens slightly. "I never claimed—"

"No, you just casually read magical alignments and speak fluent shad-ow-ese." Finn grins. "Very mysterious. Very broody prince."

I sit up straighter. "Wait, prince?"

"Former prince," Malrik corrects sharply, shooting Finn a look that could freeze fire. "Of a realm that no longer really exists. It's not relevant."

"Seems pretty relevant to me," I counter. "Especially if it helps explain what's happening with my shadows."

Malrik is quiet for a long moment, his shoulders stiff and his gaze fixed on the floor as though weighing his words. When he speaks, his voice is carefully controlled, each word deliberate, as if he fears the weight of what he's about to reveal. "Absentia—my realm—was once a bridge between worlds. Between light and shadow, life and death. The magic there... it was different. Deeper."

"Like my shadows," I say softly.

He meets my eyes. "Similar, yes. But yours are..." he pauses, searching for words. "Purer, somehow. Less corrupted."

"Corrupted by what?"

Another loaded glance passes between the others.

"There are stories," Aspen says carefully, "about an ancient power that tried to harness shadow magic. To control death itself."

"Alekir," Malrik says, the name falling like stone. "The Soulbinder."

My necklace flares sharply, and my shadows coil tight. Even Mouse lifts his head, suddenly alert.

"Easy," Finn murmurs, reaching out to steady me as the room seems to tilt. His hand finds mine, warm and grounding. "Maybe we should save the spooky history lesson for tomorrow."

"No," I manage. "I need to know. Everything you know about this Alekir, about my shadows, about the necklace—all of it."

"Not everything tonight," Malrik says firmly. "Some knowledge needs... context."

"Then give me context," I challenge. "Because right now, all I know is that my magic attracts dangerous attention, my necklace reacts to weird alignments, and apparently there's some ancient shadow-binding guy who might be relevant to all this."

"Don't forget your grumpy shadow army," Finn adds helpfully. "And their cookie addiction."

As if on cue, Bob swipes another treat. Finnick is buried in a pile of them and Patricia is daintily nibbling on one.

"The point is," Torric cuts in, "you're not facing this alone anymore. Whatever's coming—whether it's Darian, Thorne, or something bigger—we've got your back."

"Whether you want us or not," Aspen adds with a faint smile.

"Very reassuring," I mutter, but I'm fighting a smile too.

"Oh please, you love us," Finn declares. "Even Bob agrees. Look at him nodding."

"Bob is eating another cookie."

"Multitasking!"

I laugh, and some of the heaviness lifts.

"We'll figure it out," Malrik says quietly. When I look at him, his expression is intent. "All of it. Just... trust us?"

The question hangs in the air, weighted with more than just tonight's revelations.

"I do," I realize, surprising myself with how true it is. "I trust you. All of you. Even if you're terrible at sharing important information."

"In our defense," Finn says, "we were going to tell you everything tonight. You know, after the ball. Preferably over snacks and with less magical drama."

"Since when do our plans ever work out that smoothly?" Aspen asks dryly.

"Fair point. New plan: expect chaos, bring snacks."

"That's your plan for everything," Malrik points out.

"And has it ever failed?"

"Constantly."

"But entertainingly!"

As they bicker, I lean back against my cushions, letting their familiar voices wash over me. My shadows have settled into comfortable patterns: one draped across Finn's shoulders, another curled near Malrik's feet, the rest scattered among the twins like lazy cats.

Mouse, still in Finn's lap, catches my eye and lets out a quiet chirp that somehow manages to sound smug. It's a sound that seems to say, "See? Trust isn't so hard." For a moment, I let myself wonder if Mouse understands more than he lets on—a tiny, furry reminder that letting others in might not be the worst thing.

"Yeah, yeah," I whisper. "You were right."

The necklace glows warmly, like a gentle laugh, as if it's offering comfort in its own mysterious way. It feels almost alive, a steady presence grounding me in the midst of all the chaos. For a fleeting moment, I wonder if it's telling me I'm not alone. And for the first time in a long time, I believe it. I've spent so long convincing myself that I don't need anyone, that it's safer to keep people at arm's length. But tonight, with all their ridiculousness and chaos, they didn't leave. They stayed, even when I pushed them away. Maybe... maybe they're not like the others.

Even if my allies are ridiculous, shadow-seeing, snack-stealing idiots.

My idiots.

Chapter 43

FINN

I can't help but grin as I watch Kaia's shadows play with the snack wrappers. They're like mischievous kittens, if kittens were made of living darkness and had a concerning fondness for sugar. Bob—and I'm still pretty proud of that name—is currently trying to fashion some kind of wrapper crown. His antics are a small, welcome reminder of the lightness we all need right now, weaving a thread of camaraderie into the heavy air. The little showoff.

"So," I say, popping another cookie into my mouth, "now that we've had our dramatic revelation hour, who wants to place bets on what fresh chaos tomorrow brings? My money's on Darian sprouting horns. It would explain the hair."

Malrik gives me a look that's half exasperation, half amusement. It's a familiar expression. "Perhaps we should focus on more pressing matters. Like how to keep Kaia safe while we figure out what Darian and Thorne are planning."

"Ooh, good point. I vote we stuff her in a closet until graduation. A nice, cozy closet. With snacks."

Aspen rolls his eyes. "Be serious, Finn."

"I am being serious! Have you seen what happens when Kaia gets hangry? Way scarier than Darian."

I'm about to launch into my very well-thought-out closet protection plan when I notice something. Kaia hasn't made a snarky comment about my brilliant ideas in at least five minutes. Which is approximately four minutes and fifty-nine seconds longer than usual.

I glance over and—yep, there it is. Sometime in the last few minutes, exhaustion seems to have finally caught up with her. Kaia's curled up on her cushions, fast asleep, her arms loosely wrapped around one of the pillows. Her shadows have cocooned her in a way that feels both protective and tender, their soft, swirling movements a quiet testament to the trust she's placed in us tonight.

"Uh, guys?" I whisper, nodding towards our sleeping friend. "I think we broke her."

The others follow my gaze, and I swear I see Malrik's expression soften. It's a good look on him. Less broody prince, more... well, still broody. But in a softer way.

"Should we wake her?" Torric asks, his voice uncharacteristically gentle.

Aspen shakes his head. "Let her rest. After everything that's happened, she needs it."

I nod in agreement, carefully extracting myself from the snack circle. Mouse, who had been using my lap as a bed, gives me a disgruntled look before hopping over to curl up next to Kaia. His choice feels deliberate, like he's declaring her part of the group's inner circle—someone worth protecting and comforting, even in sleep.

"Well," I say quietly, stretching, "I guess that's our cue to leave. Unless we're having a slumber party. In which case, I call dibs on braiding Malrik's hair."

Malrik shoots me a glare that could probably turn lesser men to stone. Luckily, I'm made of sterner stuff. And have great hair-braiding skills.

"We should go," Aspen whispers, already gathering up the remnants of our snack feast. "Let her rest."

I nod, but can't help lingering as I watch Kaia sleep. Her face is relaxed in a way I've rarely seen, the constant furrow between her brows smoothed out. Even her shadows seem calmer, like they can relax now that she has.

"She looks..." I trail off, searching for the right words.

"Peaceful," Malrik finishes softly. When I glance at him, his silver eyes are fixed on Kaia, his expression uncharacteristically tender. "Like the weight of the world isn't on her shoulders for once."

"Yeah," I agree, feeling a lump form in my throat. "It's nice."

We stand there for a moment, all of us watching Kaia. It's weird how something as simple as seeing her sleep can make my chest ache like this. Like I'm seeing the person she could be—should be—without all the fear and secrets weighing her down.

"Do you think..." Torric starts, then pauses. When he continues, his voice is uncharacteristically hesitant. "Do you think she's really forgiven us? For keeping things from her?"

I want to make a joke, to lighten the mood like I always do. But the worry in Torric's voice strikes a chord in me. Because yeah, I've been wondering the same thing.

"I hope so," Aspen says quietly. "But even if she hasn't fully forgiven us yet, I think... I think we're on the right track."

"She trusted us enough to fall asleep," Malrik points out. "That's not nothing."

He's right. I've seen how guarded Kaia is, how she always seems to have one eye on the exits. The fact that she felt safe enough to let her guard down completely around us? It's huge.

"Plus," I add, unable to resist lightening the mood just a little, "Bob seems to have forgiven us. And we all know he's the real power behind the throne."

As if to prove my point, the shadow in question detaches itself from Kaia's cocoon and does what I swear is a little victory dance. Show-off.

"We should go," Malrik says again, but there's a hint of amusement in his voice. "Before we wake her up."

We start to tiptoe towards the door, but I can't resist one last look back. The sight of Kaia, curled up and peaceful, hits me like a punch to the gut. It's not just that she looks vulnerable—though she does, her usual sharp edges softened by sleep. I'd do anything for her. The thought hits me like a sucker punch, unexpected but undeniable. I'm not the guy who gets attached, who sticks around. But with Kaia... it's different. She's different. She's like a storm—messy, unpredictable, and impossible to ignore. But she's also the calm after it, the part that makes you want to stay, even when you're used to running. And for the first time, I don't want to run from it.

But as I watch the gentle rise and fall of her chest, the way her shadows curl protectively around her like a living blanket, I can't bring myself to be scared. Instead, I'm filled with a warmth that spreads from my chest to my fingertips, leaving me feeling both grounded and lighter than air.

I think about how far we've come since that first day, when Kaia stormed into our lives like a hurricane of sarcasm and poorly concealed pain. I remember the walls she put up, the way she'd flinch at unexpected touches or kind words. She's not the same person now, and I hope I had something to do with that.

I sigh, a bit lost in my thoughts. I'm about to turn away when I notice something odd. The amethyst necklace, usually hidden beneath Kaia's clothes, has slipped free. The glow pulses softly, sending ripples through the shadows like a stone dropped into a still pond. As the light spreads, the patterns shift—stars blooming into constellations, their edges shimmering with a faint violet glow that feels almost alive.

"Uh, guys?" I whisper, nudging Malrik. "Is it just me, or is her necklace doing the magical nightlight thing again?"

Malrik turns, his eyes narrowing as he takes in the scene. "It's reacting to her shadows," he murmurs, a note of fascination in his voice. "Look how they're moving."

He's right. The shadows aren't just swirling randomly anymore. The patterns shift and reform, their lines weaving together like an ancient map. For a moment, they seem to pulse in time with Kaia's breathing, as though tied to her heartbeat.

"Constellations," Aspen breathes, coming to stand beside us. "They look like the star charts from the ball."

"Okay, that's officially weird," I declare. "Cool, but weird. Should we wake her up?"

Malrik shakes his head. "No. Let her rest. We'll ask her about it in the morning."

"If she remembers," Torric points out. "You know how dreams can be."

I nod reluctantly, but I can't shake the feeling that we're witnessing something important—a quiet but powerful moment that ties Kaia's magic, her shadows, and that mysterious necklace together. It's as if the pieces of a puzzle are shifting into place, promising answers just out of reach. Something that could be a key to understanding all of this.

As we watch, one of the shadow-constellations seems to detach itself from the others. The shadow bobs hesitantly toward me, its movements jerky, like it's still figuring out how to exist on its own. Its edges flicker like a faint flame, struggling to hold its shape.

"Hello, little star buddy," I whisper, holding out my hand. The shadow pauses, then gently brushes against my fingers. It feels... warm. Alive. Like touching starlight, if starlight was made of shadows. It sparks a flicker of awe in me, a reminder of how uniquely Kaia's magic threads the extraordinary into the everyday—a mystery I can't help but want to unravel.

"Finn," Malrik warns, but I can hear the curiosity in his voice.

"It's okay," I assure him, though I'm not entirely sure why I feel so certain. "They're just saying hello."

The shadow constellation twirls around my hand once more before drifting back to rejoin its fellows. As it settles back into place, I swear I hear a faint melody. Like windchimes made of stardust.

"Did you guys hear that?" I ask, but the others are already shaking their heads.

"We should go," Aspen says again, tugging gently at my sleeve. "Before we wake her."

I let Aspen pull me toward the door, but the shadow's warmth lingers on my hand. Things are about to get interesting—I can feel it.

Chapter 44
Darian

Dawn bleeds through the classroom windows, casting long shadows that seem to shift unnaturally, like they know what I've done—or failed to do. The weight of last night's failure settles heavily on my shoulders. I keep my hands clasped behind my back, hiding the slight tremor as I meet Thorne's unrelenting gaze. His silence feels sharper than words.

"You've embarrassed me," Thorne finally says, his tone deceptively calm. "You were entrusted with a task, and you failed spectacularly."

"I tried—" I start, but he slashes a hand through the air, silencing me.

"You failed," he repeats coldly. "Worse, you've wasted the power I gave you. The *gift of shadow* within you wasn't for you to squander. Use it, Darian."

The words cut deeper than they should. I clench my fists at my sides, the familiar burn of resentment flickering to life in my chest. "Her shadows overwhelmed mine," I admit, forcing myself to remain steady. "They're... different. Stronger. I couldn't hold them back."

"Excuses," Thorne snaps, the word cracking like a whip. "Do you think I gave you the shadows for their strength alone? They are a tool. You've allowed them to become a crutch."

A leash is what he truly means and I flinch at the rebuke, even as I feel the corrupted magic within me stir, an almost sentient force that I've never fully understood. It coils uneasily, more restless than usual after last night's failure.

"I'll fix it," I say, though the words sound hollow. "I can still—"

"What you *can* do," Thorne interrupts, leaning closer until the faint scent of ozone prickles my senses, "is stop making excuses and reclaim control. Or I will."

"And if you do?" I ask, my voice quieter, my pulse hammering against my ribs.

"Then she becomes expendable," he says simply, as if he's discussing the weather. "And so do you."

The words are a reminder of how little I matter in the grand scheme of his plans. A part of me wants to fight back, to push against the chains he's wrapped around me. But the shadows inside me stir, coiling tighter, as if warning me to stay silent. I can't tell whether the cold fear curling in my chest is from Thorne's words or the magic he forced into me all those years ago—magic that twists in ways I barely understand, that sometimes feels like it's trying to consume me.

Thorne straightens, his calm mask slipping back into place. "You have one chance to set this right. Do not waste it."

I nod stiffly, my hands still trembling as I turn for the door. Just before I reach it, his voice cuts through the room like a knife.

"Remember, Darian," he says, his tone deadly soft. "Those shadows may live within you, but they are not yours. They are mine. Don't make me take them back."

The memory rises unbidden: the searing pain as light twisted into shadow, the way Thorne's magic dug into my soul like claws. Even now, the phantom ache lingers, a constant reminder of what I owe him—and what he could take from me.

The door shuts behind me, the finality of the sound ringing in my ears. I press my palms against the cool stone wall outside, trying to calm my racing heart. Inside me, the shadows churn, a restless tide of power that has never truly felt like my own.

I hate them. And yet, without them, what would I be?

Chapter 45
KAIA

This morning I woke on a pile of cushions, still in my dress from the ball and an ache in my chest that I can't seem to shake. The air hums with residual energy, each breath thick with the weight of magic—an electric, thrumming force that tingles against my skin and pulls at the edges of my awareness, as if trying to whisper secrets I can't hear. My shadows coil restlessly at my feet as I pace the length of the common room, their movements reflecting the chaos in my mind. Finn's usual flippant remarks have been conspicuously absent, and even Mouse seems subdued, perched on the arm of a chair with his violet eyes tracking my every move.

"They're trying to tell us something," I say aloud, more to myself than to the others. "But I can't make sense of it."

"You're not supposed to yet," Malrik replies, his voice low but steady. He's leaning against the far wall, arms crossed, his silver eyes fixed on me with an intensity that makes my skin prickle. There's a flicker of something unreadable in his gaze—unease, or perhaps a knowledge he's not ready to share. "It's not a message for your mind; it's for your magic."

"Great," I mutter, running my fingers over the necklace at my throat. Its warmth pulses in time with my heartbeat, a steady reminder of its presence—and its secrets.

"What did you see in the dreams?" Aspen asks from his spot near the window. His voice is calm, but there's a sharpness in his gaze as he watches me.

I hesitate, the fragmented images still swirling in my mind like smoke. "Wings," I finally say. "Massive wings made of shadow and starlight. They kept forming patterns—constellations, I guess—but I couldn't read them. It was like trying to remember something I've forgotten."

Finn, sprawled across the couch, sits up straighter. "So, your shadows are trying to enroll you in celestial cartography? Sounds fun." His grin fades slightly as he glances at Malrik's glare, the humor a thin shield against the palpable tension in the room. "Not that anyone here appreciates my stellar wit," he adds, softer now.

"It's not a joke," Malrik snaps, his tone cutting. "Those constellations appeared at the ball. Her shadows created them when—"

"When Darian touched me," I finish quietly, the memory sending a shiver down my spine. "And now they're in my dreams."

"But what if they're not dreams," Aspen says. "What if they're memories?"

The room goes silent, the weight of his words settling heavily over us. My fingers tighten around the necklace as my shadows ripple in agitation, their movements erratic and sharp.

"Memories of what?" I ask, my voice barely above a whisper.

"Of who you are," Malrik replies. "And what you're meant to become."

The door bursts open, breaking the tense stillness. Torric strides in with his usual aggressive energy, his fire rune faintly glowing. "What's with the secret meeting? And why does it feel like the air's about to explode?"

Aspen rolls his eyes at the way his brother barges in. "The magical energy in here is... unusual," he says, his gaze sweeping settling on me once again. "Something's shifting."

"Yeah," Finn quips, "Kaia's shadows are doing interpretive dance again."

"Focus," Malrik snaps, his irritation bubbling to the surface. "Aspen, did you find anything in the texts?"

Aspen nods, pulling a worn leather-bound book from his bag. The edges are frayed, and the leather is cracked with age, its surface etched with faint, arcane symbols. "I found references to stellar magic being used as a form of communication." Like a language written in light and shadow. But the details—how it worked, who used it—those were in the missing pages."

"Torn out," Torric growls. "Let me guess, recently?"

Aspen nods. "And if I had to bet, I'd say Thorne or Darian had something to do with it. Whatever was on those pages, it was important enough to hide. If they've been studying this for years, they might already know more than we realize. We're playing catch-up."

The necklace at my throat flares hot, sending a wave of searing warmth through my chest. My shadows respond instantly, surging upward like a living tide, their movements fluid yet deliberate. They spiral and weave through the air, forming intricate patterns that pulse with energy, each twist and ripple resonating with the heavy hum of magic that thickens the room. Patterns form in the air—wings, stars, and something else—something that feels important but stays just out of reach. The energy makes my skin tingle, the air thick with potential.

"Kaia?" Aspen asks cautiously, clearly sensing the shift in the room even if he can't see it. "Your necklace is glowing."

"You're doing that thing again," Torric adds, stepping closer. "Where the air gets all weird."

"It's not me," I whisper. "It's them."

My shadows ripple and twist, their movements deliberate and purposeful. Finn stands, his usual humor replaced by a rare seriousness. "Looks like they're trying to tell us something now."

Bob detaches from the rest and moves toward the center of the room. The others follow, forming a swirling mass that grows brighter as the necklace pulses. The light and shadows merge, creating a shape so vivid it takes my breath away.

Wings. Starlit and massive, filling the room with their ethereal glow. A gasp escapes me, unbidden, as the sheer power of the sight presses against my chest. Finn mutters, "Now that's a statement," while Malrik watches in silent awe, his usual composure faltering for just a moment.

"That's what I saw in my dreams," I say, my voice trembling. "But now... it feels different. Like they're mine, but not."

A strange mix of awe and fear rushes through me. They feel familiar, like a long-lost memory, but there's a weight to them—a power that doesn't just belong to me. It's overwhelming, but also... right. Like they've always been there, waiting for me to see them.

"They're not just yours," Malrik says, stepping closer. "They're part of something bigger."

The wings shift, their patterns changing until they resemble constellations. Aspen moves closer. "The texts mentioned artifacts of power responding to their wielders. But they're supposed to be long gone."

"Clearly not," Finn says, gesturing at the wings. "And I'm guessing that's why everyone's so interested in Kaia."

"Good luck to them," Torric mutters, his hand finding my shoulder. "She's got us now."

The room falls silent again as the wings dissolve into faint starlight, leaving behind an almost tangible stillness. My shadows return to their usual restless state, but something feels different. They're not just mine anymore—they're something more.

"We need to be ready," Malrik says quietly. "Whatever's coming, it's bigger than Thorne. Someone doesn't want Kaia to discover what she really is."

"Let them try," Torric says with a sharp grin. "We'll be ready."

I clutch the necklace, its steady warmth grounding me as the room buzzes with quiet determination. Whatever's coming, I'll be ready. And for the first time, I know I won't face it alone.

Chapter 46
FINN

The corridors of the academy stretch ahead, dimly lit and eerily quiet for this hour. The faint drip of water echoes somewhere unseen, and the air carries a chill that raises goosebumps along my arms. My footsteps echo against the stone floor, a rhythm that usually settles my nerves but tonight only amplifies them.

"This is a terrible idea," I mutter, even as I keep moving. "Why did I let Malrik talk me into this?" The truth is, I hate feeling useless. Kaia's shadows, the wings, the necklace—it's all connected to something bigger, something I can't joke away. I've spent too long being the guy who lightens the mood with a well-timed quip, safe behind my humor. But when Kaia looks at me, she sees past the wisecracks. Like she's glimpsing someone worth counting on. And that terrifies me almost as much as it thrills me.

I pause at an intersection, trying to remember Malrik's hastily sketched map. The restricted section should be just ahead. As I turn the corner, a flicker of movement catches my eye—just a tapestry stirring in a draft, but enough to make my heart jump.

The door to the restricted section looms ahead, its heavy iron handle gleaming faintly. "Don't think about the wards," I tell myself. "They're probably deactivated at this hour. Probably."

Taking a deep breath, I push the door open. The air inside carries the scent of old parchment and dust. Shelves stretch toward the high ceiling, crammed with books that practically vibrate with forbidden knowledge. Their spines shimmer faintly, some embossed with symbols that seem to shift when viewed too long.

I scan the shelves quickly, searching for anything related to stellar magic or artifacts of power. Most titles are written in languages I can't read, their faded lettering making me squint. Then I spot it—a thin, leather-bound volume tucked between larger tomes. Its cover bears no title, only a faint, embossed design that looks like a constellation.

I run my fingers over the design, feeling the grooves warm under my touch, almost alive. The air grows heavy with possibility. I pull the book free, its pages crackling as I open it. Diagrams of constellations fill the first few pages, accompanied by notes in a spidery hand. One sketch catches my eye—a swirling cluster of stars arranged in the shape of a phoenix, its wings outstretched. Beneath it, the notes describe the "Rebirth Constellation," linked to cycles of destruction and renewal, though the text grows fragmented, hinting at something intentionally erased.

My heart jumps when I spot a passage describing "living constellations" and their connection to wielders of ancient power. But before I can read further, footsteps echo down the corridor outside. I clutch the book to my chest, scanning for cover. The shelves are too narrow, the tables too exposed. Finally, I spot a shadowy alcove near the far wall and dart toward it.

A figure steps inside—Professor Thorne, his sharp features made sharper by the dim light. He moves with the precision of someone who knows exactly where they're going, selecting a book from a shelf near the center of the room. Its dark cover bears an intricate silver design.

"Not yet," he mutters, barely audible. "But soon."

I press deeper into the shadows as he turns, his gaze sweeping the room one last time before departing. The door closes with a soft click that seems to echo in my bones.

I wait a full minute, my legs trembling slightly as I step out. Thorne's presence here can't be coincidence, not with everything happening with Kaia. Whatever secrets this book holds just became far more dangerous—and far more vital.

The academy feels different as I make my way back, as though the walls themselves are holding secrets. One thing's certain: we're not ready for what's coming. But maybe what I found tonight will help us survive it.

Chapter 47
ASPEN

The training field stretches before me, a canvas of trampled grass and well-worn equipment. My footsteps echo in the early morning stillness as I make my way across the dew-dampened ground. The air is crisp with autumn's bite, charged like the moment before a storm breaks.

Kaia's presence lingers behind my eyelids every time I blink—an aura of power that I can't fully comprehend. Yesterday's training session haunts me: the way she seemed more alive, more confident than she has been. Over these last few weeks since the dance, it almost seems as if she's accepted we've got her back. I'm grateful for it, but the way Finn and Malrik talk about her shadows still troubles me.

"Come on, Aspen," I mutter, watching my breath mist in the air. "There's something you're missing. Something important."

The harder I try to grasp at the fleeting wisps of memory—of my mother's stories about shadow warriors, of ancient tales whispered around fires—the further they slip away. It's maddening, like trying to catch smoke with my bare hands. I know there's a connection that should mean something to me, but it's just out of reach.

I approach the weighted bags, stripping off my shirt and tossing it aside. The morning air sharpens my focus, a physical reminder that I'm here, that

I'm fighting. My water rune pulses faintly, responding to the moisture in the air.

"You should have done more," I berate myself, clenching my fists. "Should have seen the signs with Darian sooner."

The first punch lands with a satisfying thud. Impact travels up my arm, grounding me in the moment. Each strike punctuates my determination to do better. Sweat beads on my forehead as my water rune pulses in rhythm with my movements, its blue light flickering brighter with every hit.

"Stupid, useless memory," I growl. "What good is being empathic if I can't even figure out how to help her?"

I pause, breathing heavily, hands braced against the bag. Something in the old stories nags at me—I can almost hear my mother's voice, recounting tales of shadow warriors who wielded magic as vast as the stars. But the details blur, like ink smeared on wet parchment.

"I won't let you down again, Kaia." The words carry the weight of an oath. "Whatever it takes, I'll figure this out. I'll keep you safe."

The sun climbs higher in the sky as I throw myself back into the workout, my muscles burning with the effort. The rhythmic thud of my fists against the bag is suddenly interrupted by a cheerful voice.

"Wow, what did that poor bag ever do to you?"

I whirl around to find Seren standing a few feet away. Her lavender hair shimmers in the sunlight, and her mismatched clothes are adorned with crystals and runes that catch the light.

These days, it's hard to know who to trust.

"Seren," I say, my voice guarded. "What brings you out here?"

She shrugs, her hazel eyes filled with genuine concern. "Just checking on you. You look like you're trying to punch your way through to another realm." She pauses, then adds softly, "How's Kaia doing? I haven't seen her since the dance. Not since... well, you know."

I study her face, searching for any hint of deception. The empath in me reaches out, testing the emotional waters. All I sense is sincere worry and a touch of protective anger—directed not at Kaia, but at those who might harm her.

"She's... managing. It's been a lot to process."

Seren nods, her expression somber. One of her runic charms flares briefly, its glow humming with an energy that feels both familiar and otherworldly.

"I can imagine. Those shadows of hers... they're something else, aren't they?"

My heart rate picks up. "You can see them?"

"No," she says, fidgeting with a crystal. "But sometimes, when the light hits just right, I swear I can feel them. Like they're watching. Protecting her." Her hazel eyes fix on mine. "Why? Can you?"

I hesitate, then trust my instincts—and my empathic senses. "No, unfortunately. But I know they're there. Always."

Her eyes widen, gold flecks catching the morning light. "Maybe knowing she's not alone would help more than hurt." She pulls out a crystal. "But that's not why I'm here. I saw Darian last week, being sketchy."

My jaw tightens. "How so?"

"He was throwing away ancient book pages—ones with runes that pulse when Kaia's nearby. It's almost like they're connected to her magic. Why would he discard them? It's as if he was trying to hide something—or worse, destroy it before we could figure it out." She leans closer, voice dropping. "And I saw him with another girl. But here's the weird part—when I tried to look at her, my eyes kept sliding away. Like she wasn't quite real."

An unsettling chill races down my spine. Who else could Darian be working with? And why did the thought of someone 'not quite real' feel so disturbingly familiar?

"The pages are warded in my room," Seren adds. "They kept trying to move on their own. I'll bring them when I get a chance—we can investigate together."

I can't help but chuckle at her enthusiasm, though the thought of self-moving pages unsettles me. "Sounds like a plan. And Seren? Thanks for looking out for Kaia. It means a lot."

Her expression softens. "She's stronger than she realizes, you know. But even the strongest people need someone in their corner." With a mock salute, she turns to leave, her charms tinkling softly in the breeze.

As her footsteps fade, I face the weighted bag with renewed purpose. Her unwavering confidence in Kaia has cut through my doubt, leaving behind focused determination. Each strike carries a promise now. The morning sun stretches across the field, and hope pierces through the darkness. I have a lead—and this time, Darian won't see us coming.

Chapter 48
DARIAN

The sunlight filtering through the stained-glass windows of my private quarters casts kaleidoscope patterns across the floor, but does nothing to warm the chill that's settled in my bones. It's not just the cold of the room—it's the icy weight of doubt and duty pressing down on me, seeping into my very core. Every step I take feels heavier, as though my body is fighting against the inevitability of what I must do. I pace restlessly, my perfectly polished shoes clicking against the stone floor. Each step leaves a faint trace of shadow, a reminder of power that isn't truly mine—power borrowed from a source I barely understand, one that feels more like a curse than a gift. It clings to me, insidious and cold, as though waiting for the perfect moment to claim something I haven't yet realized I've lost.

"Pull yourself together," I mutter, running a hand through my immaculate hair. The mirror shows my reflection—perfect, controlled, everything a proper agent should be. Yet it feels like a mask I can barely hold together, a fragile shell hiding the cracks beneath. The perfection I see doesn't comfort me; it suffocates, reminding me of the expectations I can never truly escape. But my eyes betray me, haunted by what I have to do. "You have a job to do. Alekir's counting on you."

But the memory of Kaia's smile, the way her eyes light up when she laughs, keeps intruding on my carefully constructed plans. The way her shadows dance when she's happy, so different from the corrupted darkness Alekir commands. I grab a nearby vase, hurling it against the wall with a satisfying crash. The shadows in the room ripple at the violence, hungry and eager.

"Damn it all!" I shout to the empty room. "Why did she have to be... her?"

A memory surfaces unbidden—her laughter echoing in the training grounds, her shadows curling around her like a protective shroud. I'd watched from a distance, telling myself it was part of the mission, but the ache in my chest had been real. And that's the problem: it still is.

I sink into a plush armchair, my head in my hands. The weight of my mission, of Alekir's expectations, presses down on me like a physical force. The shadow mark on my chest burns coldly, a constant reminder of my oath. But for the first time in years, I'm questioning everything.

A knock at the door startles me from my brooding. "What?" I snap, quickly composing my features into their usual mask of cool indifference. The shadows retreat to their corners, well-trained.

A trembling first-year pokes his head in. His eyes dart around the room, clearly sensing something off but unable to identify what. "M-Mr. Luthar? You're needed in the headmaster's office."

I nod curtly, dismissing the boy with a wave. As I straighten my tie and head for the door, I can't shake the feeling that I'm balancing on a knife's edge. One wrong move, and everything could come crashing down.

But which move is the right one? That's the question that haunts me with every step.

I spot her across the courtyard, her golden hair catching the late afternoon sun like a beacon. The amethyst necklace at her throat pulses faintly, its rhythm seeming to mock my own heartbeat. My shadow mark burns beneath my shirt, responding to its power.

Kaia.

I hesitate for a split second before striding towards her, my face a carefully composed mask of casual charm.

"Kaia," I call out, my voice smooth as silk despite the turmoil inside. "Can we talk?" She whirls to face me, those mesmerizing violet eyes narrowing with suspicion. Her shadows—so much more alive, more real than Alekir's corrupted versions—coil protectively around her feet. I spot the one Finn calls "Bob" shifting into a defensive position. The others follow suit, creating a subtle barrier between us. One shadow darts forward, almost touching the edge of mine before recoiling sharply, like it's tasted something bitter. The others ripple in response, their movements sharper now, more deliberate.

They know.

"What do you want, Darian?" The sharp edge in her voice cuts deeper than I care to admit. Mouse lets out a low growl from his perch on a nearby bench.

I hold up my hands in a placating gesture, noting how her shadows track every movement. "Just to talk. I know things have been... tense between us lately."

Kaia's shadows ripple, their edges sharpening like blades with a faint hiss, as if the very air protests their movements. The shimmer along their forms catches the waning sunlight, giving them an almost metallic gleam, poised and deadly. Another one seems to be taking notes on my every gesture.

"Tense? That's putting it mildly, don't you think?"

I swallow hard, torn between the mission pounding in my head and the unexpected ache in my chest. My shadows pulse faintly under my skin, restless and uneasy. When hers shift, mine recoil slightly, their corrupted edges no match for the pure, fluid power radiating from her. It's like they're afraid—of her or of what they can never be.

"Look, I know I've made mistakes. But there's so much you don't understand about what's really going on here."

"Oh? And I suppose you're going to enlighten me?" Her sarcasm is biting, but I catch a flicker of curiosity in her eyes. The chaotic shadow swirls around her ankles, mirroring her conflicted emotions.

I take a step closer, lowering my voice. The shadows in the courtyard lengthen as the sun dips lower, and I feel my power strengthening with the approaching darkness. "I could, if you'd let me. There are forces at work here bigger than either of us, Kaia. Dangers you can't even imagine."

For a moment, I see uncertainty cross her face. Her shadows waver, their aggressive edges softening slightly. It's all I can do not to reach out and touch her, to pull her close and forget about everything else.

The weight of my duty coils around my throat, tightening with every breath. The shadow mark flares again, a cold reminder that hesitation isn't an option.

Chapter 49
KAIA

My emotions war inside me—anger, confusion, and that damned lingering attraction I can't quite squash. His gray eyes are intense, almost pleading, but I've learned the hard way how practiced his performances can be.

In the weeks since the dance, I've tried to find my footing. My shadows have grown stronger, more coordinated, but so have the questions. And Darian... he's been both a ghost and a constant presence in my thoughts.

Bob presses against my legs protectively, his shadowy tendrils curling around my ankles with a faint, soothing pulse. Patricia hovers nearby, her form flickering like a quill mid-sentence as she meticulously documents every micro-expression that crosses Darian's face. Her shadow-notes dart and swirl with purpose, an almost palpable reminder of her sharp focus. My necklace pulses with warmth against my skin—a warning or encouragement, I'm not sure which.

I cross my arms. "Right," I drawl, "because you've been so forthcoming and trustworthy up until now."

He flinches, and I hate the tiny part of me that wants to comfort him. Mouse is at my side now, growing slightly larger than his usual form, violet eyes fixed unblinkingly on Darian.

"I deserve that," he admits softly. "But Kaia, please. Just hear me out."

I bite my lip, warring with myself. Part of me wants to tell him exactly where he can shove his explanations. But another part remembers genuine moments—his pride when my shadows formed their first perfect shield, the warmth in his smile during early training sessions. Was any of it real?

"Fine," I say finally, my tone clipped. "You've got two minutes. Make them count."

As Darian begins to speak, I can't shake the feeling that whatever he's about to say is going to change everything. Again.

I have no idea if this will work, but I mentally nudge Bob, hoping he can hear my thoughts.

Hey buddy, can you let Finn or Malrik know where I am? Just in case.

The shadow gives me a subtle salute before detaching a small part of himself to slip away beneath the courtyard stones.

Patricia redoubles her note-taking efforts, while another odd shadow swirls restlessly around my feet, clearly unhappy with the situation. The remaining shadows form a loose circle around us, not quite threatening but definitely alert.

Darian's words wash over me, and I find myself begrudgingly drawn in. "The factions, the prejudice against shadow magic – it's all based on fear and misinformation," he says, his voice low and urgent. His own shadows seem to ripple beneath his skin, nothing like my living companions but somehow familiar—a resemblance that tugs at something in my memory, as though I've encountered their essence before. "There's so much potential in what you can do, Kaia. Potential to bridge worlds, to heal rifts that have existed for centuries."

I arch an eyebrow, though my heart races at his words. My necklace warms against my skin, responding to something in his speech. "And let me guess, you just happened to stumble upon this groundbreaking information?"

He has the decency to look sheepish. Something flickers across his face—pain? Regret? It's gone too quickly to read. "I've... done research. A lot of it. Trying to find history that was hidden, the true nature of shadow magic – it's all been twisted over time."

As much as I hate to admit it, his words strike a chord. I've felt it, haven't I? The way my shadows respond to emotion, to life itself. The way they protect and nurture, not just defend. They're not just darkness and danger—they're family. Mouse presses against my legs, as if agreeing with my thoughts.

"So what, you've been playing both sides this whole time?" I ask, hating how my voice wavers. Patricia's shadow-notes flutter more urgently.

Darian steps closer, and my traitorous heart skips a beat. I hate the way his presence stirs something unbidden—an infuriating mix of vulnerability and longing that clashes with my simmering anger. Part of me wants to lash out, to remind him of the trust he's shattered, while another part aches to believe that there's still truth in his words. There's something in his eyes—a desperation, a longing that feels too real to be fake. "I didn't know what to believe at first," he admits. "But the more I learned about you, about your power..." He trails off, his gaze intense. His hand twitches, as if he wants to reach for me.

I'm about to respond when a familiar arm drapes across my shoulders, bringing with it the scent of pine and mischief. Finn. My shadows practically purr, surging toward him with obvious joy. Bob's messenger portion reforms, mission accomplished.

"Hey there, troublemakers," Finn says, his tone light but his eyes sharp. The Finnick immediately swirls around his feet in greeting, while Patricia shows him her notes with obvious pride. "Having a nice chat?"

Darian's expression flickers for just a moment, his shadows retreating slightly before smoothing over. "Actually," he says, "I was just telling Kaia about some information I've uncovered. Information that could help keep her safe."

Finn's arm tightens almost imperceptibly around me. His usual playful demeanor is there, but there's steel underneath—a quiet, unyielding strength that radiates through his touch. It's a reminder that while he thrives on jokes and mischief, his loyalty and protectiveness are unshakable when it matters most. "Oh?" he says, all faux casualness. "Do tell. I'm always up for a good story."

As Darian launches into an explanation about ancient wards and protective spells, I can't help but notice how different his shadow energy feels from mine. His is contained, controlled—almost artificial. Like a perfectly tailored suit that doesn't quite fit. Mouse's ears perk up at certain words, and I make mental notes of what catches his attention.

"The key is understanding that shadow magic isn't inherently dark," Darian explains, his hands moving eloquently as he speaks. "It's about balance. Light and dark, life and death—it's all connected. Your necklace there? It's more than just a piece of jewelry. It's a key."

The pendant pulses warmly at his words, and my shadows ripple in response. Finn's hand finds mine, squeezing gently. I'm grateful for his grounding presence as Darian continues.

"A key to what?" I ask, unable to help myself. Even my skepticism can't completely squash my curiosity.

Darian's eyes light up with an intensity that's either genuine passion or incredibly good acting. "To understanding your true heritage. To unlocking powers that could restore balance to all the realms. It was protected for centuries as far as I can tell. Your necklace is depicted in a few ancient texts."

I feel Finn tense beside me at the mention of my necklace in ancient texts. My shadows cluster closer, responding to the shift in atmosphere. The sun dips lower on the horizon, casting long shadows across the courtyard. In the growing darkness, I swear I can see something shifting beneath Darian's skin—a glint of metallic tension coiling and uncoiling, like chains straining against an unseen force. The sight sends a chill skittering down my spine, the unnatural movement a silent warning that whatever binds him is more than just shadows.

"That's fascinating," Finn says, his voice deceptively light. "Really. But you'll forgive us if we're a bit skeptical about your sudden desire to share all this information." His free hand absently strokes Bob's tendrils, earning a shadow-purr. "Especially given recent events."

Darian's perfect composure cracks, just for a second. Something like real pain flashes across his face. "I know I have no right to ask for your trust," he says softly. "But Kaia... there are things coming. Things that—"

He's cut off by a sudden commotion near the main hall. Students pour out of the doors, chattering excitedly about dinner. The moment breaks, reality rushing back in.

"We should go," I say firmly, though my mind is racing with questions. "Thanks for the history lesson."

As Finn steers me away, I glance back once. Darian stands alone in the growing darkness, his shadows writhing beneath his shirt like restless snakes. For a moment, he looks lost, almost vulnerable. Then his mask slips back into place, and he turns sharply on his heel, striding away.

"Well, that was interesting," Finn murmurs as we head toward the dining hall. "Bob's been trying to tell me something about him for weeks, you know."

I lean into his warmth, grateful for his steady presence. "Yeah? What's Bob's theory?"

"That there's more to this than just Darian being an ass." Finn's voice grows serious. "Your shadows... they don't hate him, exactly. They pity him. And that worries me more than anything else."

My shadows ripple faintly, their movements softer now, less defensive. One of them brushes against Darian's retreating figure before curling back to me like an apology. I don't know what they're trying to tell me, but the ache in my chest deepens.

My necklace pulses once, strong and clear, as if in agreement. I wrap my arms around Finn before I can stop myself. I'm suddenly cold despite the lingering warmth of the day.

"Come on," Finn says, his usual cheeky grin returning. "Let's get some food. I hear they're serving those pastries you like—you know, the ones Finnick keeps trying to steal?"

That gets a laugh out of me before I can stop it.

Chapter 50
KAIA

The training arena pulses with magical energy, a thrumming current that crackles in the air and makes my shadows twitch restlessly at my feet. It feels alive, charged with a tension that hums through my veins and sets my nerves on edge. Seren's presence beside me is a welcome anchor, her lavender hair catching the light from the enchanted sconces above.

"Your fan club's getting bigger," she murmurs, nudging me with her elbow. "Even Malrik's lurking closer than usual today."

Heat creeps up my neck as I follow her gaze. She's right—they're all here. Torric and Aspen stand near the weapon racks, heads bent in conversation. Finn lounges against a pillar, his usual grin in place as he juggles small orbs of chaos magic. And Malrik... Malrik watches from the shadows, his silver eyes catching mine for just a moment before sliding away.

"They're not my fan club," I mutter, but my shadows betray me, curling almost happily at the sight of them.

"Sure, sure." Seren's knowing smirk is insufferable. "And I'm the Queen of Light."

Before I can retort, Professor Thorne sweeps into the arena, his dark robes billowing dramatically. An immediate hush falls over the room, accompanied by a chill that makes my skin prickle.

"Today's exercise," he announces, his voice like silk over steel, "will test your adaptability. You'll rotate partners every fifteen minutes. The goal is simple: survive."

My stomach drops at his tone. Beside me, Seren whispers, "Well, that's not ominous at all."

"First pairing," Thorne continues, his violet-flecked eyes finding mine with unsettling precision. "Kaia Draven and Torric Agere."

Torric's grin is immediate and predatory as he pushes off from the weapon rack. Even from here, I can see the fire rune on his chest beginning to glow beneath his shirt.

"Try not to swoon," Seren whispers, giving me a gentle shove forward. "Though I wouldn't blame you if you did."

"I don't swoon," I hiss back, but my heart's already racing as Torric approaches, all six-foot-five of him radiating dangerous charm.

"Ready to dance, Sunshine?" he asks, golden eyes gleaming with challenge.

I force my expression into something resembling confidence. "Only if you can keep up, flame boy."

The smirk on his lips is the only warning I get.

The first clash of our magic sends sparks flying—literally. Torric's flames dance and weave around my shadows, their fiery arcs casting sharp contrasts against the twisting tendrils of darkness. Each collision sparks with energy, sending shimmering embers and faint wisps of smoke curling into the air. The heat brushes against my skin, a stark counterpoint to the cool, fluid movements of my shadows as they push back, neither side willing to yield. We move in a deadly dance, testing defenses, looking for openings.

"Your form's improved," he notes, sending another burst of flame my way. "But your stance is still off."

Before I can process his words, he's behind me, one hand on my waist, the other adjusting my shoulder. The sudden heat of his touch sends a jolt through me, scattering my thoughts. My shadows stutter in their movements, caught between defensiveness and intrigue, mirroring the conflict in my chest.

"Like this," he murmurs, his breath hot against my ear. "Feel the difference?"

My shadows flicker erratically, betraying my flustered state. "I—"

But Torric is already moving again. Everything intensifies as we find our rhythm. He's showing off now, each burst of flame more elaborate than the last, his golden eyes alight with challenge.

"Come on, Sunshine," he taunts, sending a spiral of fire my way. "Show me what you've got."

My shadows surge forward, meeting his flames in a hiss of magic. The collision sends more sparks raining around us, and I can't help but grin at the display.

"That all you've got?"

His answering laugh is rich and deep. He moves like a predator, all coiled grace and barely contained power. When he catches my wrist to adjust my form again, his touch burns in the best way.

"Your magic responds to your emotions," he says, voice dropping low. "So stop holding back."

"I'm not—" I start to protest, but he's already moving, his fire racing toward me in a wave.

My shadows react instinctively, rising up to meet the flames. For a moment, we're locked in perfect balance, fire and shadow dancing together. I feel alive, electric, powerful.

Then Torric grins, and suddenly he's behind me again, one arm around my waist. "Better," he murmurs. "But your balance is still off."

This time when he adjusts my stance, his hands linger. One slides down my arm, guiding my movement, while the other stays firm at my hip. I'm hyper-aware of every point of contact, of the heat radiating from his chest against my back.

"Breathe," he reminds me, and I realize I've been holding my breath. When I inhale, I catch his scent—smoke and spice and something uniquely him.

My shadows flicker and swirl around us both, seemingly drawn to his warmth. One curls around his wrist where he holds me, and I swear I feel him shiver.

"Interesting," he murmurs, but before I can ask what he means, Thorne calls for the switch.

Chapter 51
KAIA

Training with Aspen is like stepping from fire into cool water. His movements are deliberate, every strike and parry executed with an almost meditative precision. Where Torric's energy is overwhelming, Aspen's is steady, his presence radiating calm assurance that makes it easier to focus and breathe. He moves with fluid grace, each strike precise and measured. When he corrects my form, his touch is gentle but sure.

"You're still tense from sparring with my brother," he observes, demonstrating a defensive move. "Here, like this."

He guides me through the sequence slowly, his chest barely brushing my back as he shows me the proper stance. Where Torric burns, Aspen soothes. His presence is calming, grounding.

"Better," he says softly, and his approval sends an unexpected warmth through me. "Now try it again, but trust your instincts this time."

We fall into a smooth rhythm, blades dancing between us. Aspen moves like he's reading my intentions before I make them, always exactly where he needs to be. When our blades lock, bringing us face to face, I notice flecks of darker blue in his eyes.

"You're holding back," he says quietly, his gaze searching mine. "Why?"

The question catches me off guard. "I'm not—"

"You are." His free hand touches my chin briefly, tilting my face up. "You're afraid of your own power."

His voice drops lower, rougher, sending a shiver down my spine that has nothing to do with magic. Before I can respond, he steps back, twirling his blade in a defensive pattern. "Again," he says. "But this time, trust yourself."

"Next!" Thorne's voice hammers through the noise of the students sparring.

When Finn becomes my partner, the energy shifts completely. He bounces on his feet, grinning that infectious grin that always makes me want to smile back.

"Ready to see some real magic, Trouble?" he asks, summoning his chaos magic in swirling patterns.

"Is that what you're calling it now?" I tease, but I'm already moving, shadows ready.

Training with Finn is unpredictable and exhilarating. His chaos magic keeps me on my toes, never knowing what to expect. One moment he's creating miniature fireworks, the next he's conjuring random objects to throw in my path.

"That's cheating!" I laugh as I dodge a suddenly appearing rubber duck.

"Creative problem solving," he corrects, green eyes sparkling. "Duck!"

"Very funny—" I start, but then realize he means it literally as one of his spells goes wild. He tackles me out of the way, and we hit the ground rolling.

We end up with him hovering over me, both breathing hard. The weight of him above me is grounding, yet electric, sending a rush of awareness through my body. The air feels charged, like something unspoken lingers between us, waiting to be acknowledged. His freckles stand out against his flushed skin, and there's something in his eyes I've never seen be-fore—something that makes my breath catch.

"You okay?" he asks, voice uncharacteristically soft.

"Yeah," I manage, very aware of everywhere our bodies touch. "Thanks for the save."

His thumb brushes my cheek. "Anytime, Kaia," he says, using my actual name for once. The moment stretches, charged with possibility. His gaze flickers between my lips and meeting my eyes and I'm not sure I've ever wanted anything more than for Finn to close the distance between us.

But I see something on the edge of my vision. When I turn my head, Finn does too only to notice Malrik watching us, his silver eyes intense. Something passes between him and Finn—a look I can't quite interpret. My shadows ripple in response, sensing undercurrents I don't understand.

The rest of training passes in a blur of magic and motion. The warmth of Torric's hands, the steady assurance of Aspen's guidance, and the way Finn's eyes lingered on me stay with me, an intoxicating mix of comfort and disarray that I can't quite shake.

And through it all, Malrik watches from the shadows, his gaze heavy with secrets that ripple like an invitation to uncover something hidden and dangerous. The weight of his stare feels like a challenge—daring me to understand the depths he keeps concealed, even as I'm not sure I want to know. His eyes hold a quiet intensity, an unyielding question that tugs at something deep inside me—truths about the shadows, about him, and perhaps even about myself. I fear what they'll reveal, but honestly I need to know, and I need to know yesterday.

Chapter 52
KAIA

My next rotation pairs me with Darian, and my shadows coil tight and defensive, their playful mood evaporating. Mouse, who's been watching from the sidelines, lets out a low warning growl.

"Shall we begin?" Darian asks smoothly, but something feels off about his smile today. His eyes are too sharp, too calculating.

We circle each other warily. His shadow magic mirrors mine, but where my shadows feel alive and responsive, his seem... wrong somehow. Hollow.

"Your control is improving," he notes, sending a tendril of darkness toward me. "Though I notice your shadows react quite... differently to each partner."

I block his attack, trying to ignore the way his words make my skin crawl. "What's that supposed to mean?"

"Oh, nothing really." His smile doesn't reach his eyes. "Just interesting to observe their behavior. Particularly around Finn and Malrik."

Speaking of them—I can't help glancing over to where they're paired together. Their usual antagonism has transformed into something else entirely. Finn's chaos magic spirals wild and bright, while Malrik's shadows dance in response. They move together with surprising grace, like they've forgotten anyone else is watching.

When one of Finn's spells goes astray, Malrik pulls him out of harm's way. They collide, Malrik's hands steadying Finn's waist, and for a moment, they just stare at each other. They freeze in that position, Malrik's hands still gripping Finn's waist, their breath mingling in the space between them. The magic crackles around them like static before a storm.

"Fascinating," Darian murmurs, following my gaze. "Quite the complicated dynamic you all have here."

My shadows lash out before I can stop them, leaving a thin black line across his sleeve. "Sorry," I say, not feeling sorry at all.

"No need to apologize." His smile turns predatory. "Your shadows merely prove my point. They're quite... protective of certain people, aren't they?"

Before I can respond, Thorne calls an end to training. I retreat quickly, gathering my things while trying to sort through the confusing tangle of emotions the session has left me with.

Seren appears at my side, eyes dancing with amusement. "Well, that was enlightening."

"Shut up," I mutter, but there's no heat in it.

"I mean it," she says, more seriously. "You might want to figure out what you're feeling here babe. Because from where I'm standing, things are getting interesting."

I watch as Torric argues with Aspen about proper defensive stances, his golden eyes still flickering to me occasionally. As Finn teases Malrik about "getting handsy" during their practice, making the normally composed shadow prince actually flush. Mouse circles my feet protectively, clearly still unsettled by Darian's presence.

My shadows swirl restlessly, reaching out toward each of them in turn—drawn to Torric's heat, Aspen's calm, Finn's chaos, even Malrik's darkness. It doesn't escape my notice that a small tendril reaches for Darian after hesitating a beat.

"I have no idea what I'm feeling," I admit quietly.

Seren squeezes my shoulder. "That's okay too. Just... be careful, yeah? Not everyone here has your best interests at heart."

Her gaze drifts to where Darian stands with Thorne, their heads bent in quiet conversation. Something about their posture sets off warning bells, but before I can analyze it further, Finn bounds over.

"Survival achieved!" he announces cheerfully, throwing an arm around my shoulders. "Though I think Bob is traumatized by Malrik's footwork."

"Bob?" Seren asks, bewildered.

"Don't ask," I groan, but I can't help leaning slightly into Finn's warmth.

"Bob is a perfectly respectable name for a shadow," Finn insists, and I swear I see Malrik roll his eyes from across the room.

"I hadn't realized you named them." Seren snickers and I barely hold back another groan.

She looks around the floor even though I know she can't see them. "So do I get to name one now? That one—" she points randomly to a spot where there are absolutely no shadows. "That's Chloe! Isn't she cute?"

"No way. Absolutely not. Naming shadows is my job. No one else's," Finn declares, flailing his arms dramatically like a conductor in the middle of a symphony.

"It's not a shadow naming convention," I murmur, but Finn's too busy gesturing wildly at my shadows to notice.

My shadows curl happily around Finn's ankles. The simple comfort of his presence helps settle the chaos in my mind.

"Come on," Seren says, tugging me toward the door. "Let's get you fed before you have to process any more feelings."

"I'm not—" I start to protest, but her knowing looks stop me. "Fine. Food first. Emotional crisis later."

As we leave, I feel their eyes on me—gold, gray, blue, green, and silver—each gaze carrying its own weight of unspoken possibility. Mouse bumps against my leg supportively, but I swear he's laughing at me too.

I'm definitely in trouble.

Chapter 53
KAIA

The dining hall is packed when we arrive, the air thick with magic and chatter. Seren leads me to our usual table, but before we can sit, Alenya's voice cuts through the noise.

"Well, if it isn't the shadow witch and her pet chaos mage." She stands with Rynessa at her side, both of them radiating disdain. "Quite the show in training today. Though I noticed you needed quite a bit of... hands-on instruction."

Heat creeps up my neck, but before I can respond, a warm presence appears behind me.

"Jealous, Alenya?" Torric's voice rumbles, deep and dangerous. "I don't see anyone lining up to help with your form."

Alenya's perfect features twist into a scowl. "As if I'd want—"

"Is there a problem here?" Aspen appears at my other side, his tone deceptively mild. But I feel the subtle shift in temperature as his water magic responds to his mood.

"No problem," Rynessa says quickly, tugging at Alenya's arm. "We were just leaving."

As they retreat, Finn materializes with a dramatic sigh. "Aw, and here I was hoping to show them my new trick. Finnick's been practicing his interpretive dance."

Finnick swirls dramatically at our feet.

"Would you stop encouraging them?" I groan, but I'm fighting a smile.

"Never," Finn declares, dropping into the seat beside me. "They're artists, Kaia. Artists!"

Torric and Aspen take seats across from us, and I try not to think about how natural this feels—being surrounded by them, their presence both comforting and confusing.

Aspen leans forward slightly, his blue eyes thoughtful as they meet mine. "You seemed more confident today," he says. "Your magic—it's different now, isn't it?"

Torric nods, biting into a roll. "Yeah, like it's more in sync with you. Less... reactive and more deliberate."

I blink, startled by their observations. I know they can't see my shadows the way Finn or Malrik can, but they've noticed the shift in how I wield them. It's subtle, but it means something—that even without seeing the shadows, they can sense the changes in me.

"Maybe I'm just getting better at it," I say, trying to downplay the significance.

"Or maybe," Torric smirks, "you've been holding back until now."

Aspen glances at me, a flicker of curiosity in his expression. "Whatever the reason, it's clear you're finding your footing." He smiles faintly. "It's good to see."

The warmth in his tone catches me off guard. Before I can respond, Torric leans forward, the mischievous glint in his golden eyes impossible to ignore.

"Though if it's Finn inspiring this new confidence, I don't think I want to know how."

His gaze darts meaningfully to Finn, who waggles his eyebrows in response. I groan, covering my face with one hand.

"Please stop," I mutter. "This is not a group therapy session."

"What can I say?" Finn interjects, grinning. "Bob and I have been bonding."

"Bob is not—" a smooth voice cuts in, making us all turn. Malrik stands at the end of our table, looking somehow both annoyed and amused. "Never mind. I'm not encouraging this madness."

But he sits down anyway, deliberately not looking at Finn, though I notice his shadows reach out to brush against Finn's sleeve when he thinks no one's watching.

Mouse, curled under the table, lets out a huff that sounds suspiciously like laughter.

"Traitor," I mutter to him, but he just blinks innocently up at me.

The conversation flows easily after that, but I'm acutely aware of every interaction—the way Torric's knee presses against mine under the table, how Aspen's hand brushes mine when he passes the salt, Finn's constant commentary that makes even Malrik's lips twitch with suppressed smiles.

"You know," Seren whispers in my ear, "for someone who claims not to have a fan club, you're doing a pretty good impression of holding court right now."

I elbow her sharply, but I can't deny the warm feeling in my chest as I look around at these impossible, infuriating, wonderful people who have somehow become mine.

Even if I'm not quite ready to examine exactly what that means.

The peaceful moment shatters when Darian sweeps into the dining hall, his presence sending an immediate chill through me. Mouse tenses under the table, a low growl rumbling in his chest.

"Kaia." He stops beside our table, that perfect smile in place. "Professor Thorne would like to see you. About your... performance today."

My stomach drops. Across the table, Torric half-rises, but Aspen's hand on his arm stops him.

"I'll walk with you," Malrik says suddenly, his silver eyes fixed on Darian. "I need to discuss something with Thorne anyway."

"That won't be necessary," Darian says smoothly. "The Professor was quite specific—"

"Wasn't asking permission," Malrik cuts in, his tone leaving no room for argument. For a moment, something dark flashes across Darian's perfect features.

Finn stands too, his usual playful demeanor gone. "Actually, I think we could all use a walk. Work off lunch and all that."

"Guys, I can handle—" I start, but Seren kicks me under the table.

"Let them come," she mutters. "There's strength in numbers Kaia."

As we leave the dining hall, I find myself surrounded—Malrik and Finn on either side, Torric and Aspen following close behind. My shadows seem to draw strength from their presence, swirling more confidently around us all, as if feeding on the unspoken bond we share. Each tendril moves with purpose, reflecting the steady reassurance their company brings, wrapping me in a tangible sense of unity and resolve.

At my feet, Mouse pads silently, his violet eyes fixed on Darian's back. Even Finnick, usually the most dramatic of my shadows, moves with purpose, his tendrils gliding with an almost solemn precision. He darts ahead briefly, scanning the path as if ensuring our safety, then loops back, his movements steady and deliberate, a stark contrast to his usual flair for theatrics.

"Your shadows are awfully coordinated today," Darian observes, glancing back. "Almost as if they're responding to something. Or someone."

I feel Finn and Malrik exchange a look over my head, some silent communication passing between them.

"Maybe they just don't like your cologne," Finn quips, but there's an edge to his voice I've never heard before.

We reach Thorne's office too quickly. Before Darian can protest, Malrik steps forward.

"We'll wait," he says simply. It's not a request.

Darian's smile tightens. "Suit yourself."

Inside, Thorne's office is dark and cold, the air thick with the faint metallic tang of old magic. Shadows cling to the corners like living things, their shapes shifting just enough to make my heart race. The faint creak of the wooden floor beneath my feet and the oppressive silence amplify the unease that crawls up my spine. He looks up from his desk, eyes gleaming.

"Miss Draven," he says smoothly. "Let's discuss your control issues, shall we?"

My shadows coil closer, responding to the threat I can't quite name. Outside, I know they're waiting—my impossible, unexpected protectors. The thought gives me strength. The oppressive weight of his gaze bears down on me, daring me to falter. But I'm done playing the game by his rules. Done being the frightened girl who gets pushed around.

Fuck this.

"Actually, Professor," I say, straightening my spine, "I'd love to discuss your teaching methods first."

Something dangerous flashes in his eyes, but I stand my ground. I'm done being afraid of my own power.

Let him try his worst. The fear that once gripped me is gone, replaced by a steady resolve. I'm not alone anymore, and the strength of my shadows mirrors the confidence building inside me. For the first time, I feel ready to face whatever comes.

Chapter 54
MALRIK

I lean against the wall outside Thorne's office, every shadow in the hallway twisting and rippling in rhythm with my agitation, their movements sharp and restless, mirroring the tension I keep buried beneath my calm facade. Finn paces restlessly, his usual humor replaced by barely contained energy that makes my shadows want to reach for him.

"She shouldn't be in there alone," Torric growls, flames flickering beneath his skin.

"She's not alone," I say quietly, watching Bob—and damn Finn for making me use that ridiculous name—slip under the door after her. "Her shadows are stronger than Thorne realizes."

Finn pauses his pacing to shoot me a knowing look. His chaos magic crackles in the air, bright and erratic, sending shimmering arcs of energy that make my shadows writhe as if caught in an unseen current. "They're different today. More focused."

"I noticed," I murmur, remembering how naturally our magic intertwined during training. How right it felt.

"Around certain people, you mean," Aspen says softly. Always the observant one.

Before I can respond, a pulse of power emanates from Thorne's office. Kaia's shadows, but different—stronger, more controlled, their movements sharper and more purposeful, as though responding to an inner rhythm that wasn't there before. They radiate a quiet power, undeniable and deeply rooted. My own shadows react instinctively, reaching for the door as if drawn by the surge of power radiating from within, their movements urgent and almost protective.

Finn's hand finds my arm, steadying me. The touch sends an unwelcome spark through my chest. "Easy there, Your Broodiness. She's got this."

He's right, though I'd rather swallow broken glass than admit it. Through my connection to the shadows, I can feel Kaia's power growing, a steady pulse of strength that resonates through the magic like a drumbeat. Her presence is sharper now, more defined, as if she's finally beginning to embrace the enormity of her potential. The shadows carry her defiance, standing firm against whatever game Thorne is playing, and the sensation is both grounding and electric.

"You feel it too, don't you?" Finn asks suddenly, his voice low enough that only I can hear. "How strong she's becoming."

I stay silent, but my shadows betray me, curling toward him like they've been doing more and more lately.

"That's what I thought." His fingers squeeze my arm gently before letting go. "We need to help her understand what she's capable of."

"Not yet," I murmur, watching the shadows dance between us. "She has enough to deal with, and we need to figure out everything first.."

When the door creaks open, Kaia steps out, her chin held high despite the faint tremor in her hands. Her shadows ripple like banners in a silent victory parade, their sharp, fluid movements echoing her defiance.

"Everything okay?" Aspen asks, while Torric practically vibrates with the need to check her for injuries.

"Fine," she says, but her shadows reach for us all—seeking Torric's warmth, Aspen's calm, Finn's chaos, and my darkness. "Just another lesson in control."

I catch Darian watching this interaction with calculated interest, and my shadows coil defensively. He knows something we don't—about Kaia, about her shadows, maybe even about all of us. Darian's gaze lingers too long, his expression unreadable but far too interested. It's not just Kaia he's studying—it's all of us. The way we move, the way our powers intersect. Like he's already planned how to tear us apart.

"Well," Finn announces, throwing an arm around Kaia's shoulders, "I don't know about you, but I could use a drink." He adds quickly with a grin at Aspen's look, "Maybe two."

As we walk away, I notice how naturally we fall into formation around her—not just protecting, but belonging. My shadows tangle with Finn's chaos magic and her shadows, while Torric and Aspen flank us like golden guardians.

And if my shadows linger a bit too long around Finn, drawn to his wild energy and inconvenient charm, stirring a mix of frustration, curiosity, and something more dangerous? That's a problem for another day.

Right now, we have a shadow girl to protect. Even if she's becoming more than any of us bargained for.

Especially for me.

Chapter 55
KAIA

I pace the empty classroom, my footsteps echoing against the cold stone walls. Shadows curl and twist anxiously around my ankles, their agitation mirroring the turmoil in my chest. Mouse prowls nearby, his tail lashing as if he, too, can sense my unease.

"You're going to wear a hole in the floor," Finn calls from his perch on a desk. "Though Bob could patch it up. He's getting pretty handy with construction work."

Bob puffs up dramatically at the mention of his name, but I don't laugh. My thoughts are a tangled mess, and even Finn's humor can't untangle them.

Something's wrong. The shadows won't stop moving, and the weight of Thorne's watchful gaze from earlier still lingers like a phantom.

"You need to breathe," Malrik's low voice cuts through the room, grounding in its quiet intensity. He leans against the far wall, his silver eyes tracking my restless movement.

"I can't," I admit, pressing my hands to my temples as my shadows writhe like living echoes of my turmoil. "They won't settle. It's like they're trying to tell me something, but I don't know how to listen."

Mouse growls low, pacing circles around my feet. The shadows respond by curling tighter, their sharp edges brushing against my skin.

Malrik straightens, pushing away from the wall with slow, deliberate movements. "Then let me help." He doesn't wait for my reply, stepping closer until the chaotic shadows flicker, uncertain.

"What are you—" My question dies in my throat as he extends a hand, palm up, and lets one of my shadows brush against his fingers. They tremble, retreating slightly, before cautiously curling toward him again.

"Shadows reflect their master's state of mind," he murmurs, his voice as steady as the tide. "They're connected to you, and right now, they're feeding on your stress."

I close my eyes, taking a shaky breath. "I don't know how to stop it."

"You don't need to stop it." His voice is closer now, and when I open my eyes, he's standing directly in front of me. His presence is grounding, his silver gaze impossibly calm. "You need to meet them where they are. Let them feel what you're feeling, and they'll quiet."

I shake my head. "What if I can't?"

"You can." His fingers brush mine, sending a spark through my skin. His shadows stir faintly around his feet, a dark mirror of my own. "You're stronger than you think, Kaia."

His words settle over me like a balm, and I focus on the warmth of his touch, the steadiness in his presence. Slowly, my shadows begin to calm, their movements softening, no longer jagged and sharp.

"There," he says, his voice almost a whisper. "See? They trust you. You just have to trust yourself."

The room feels quieter, the suffocating weight in my chest lifting. I meet his gaze, gratitude swelling in my throat. "Thank you."

Malrik's lips quirk into the faintest smile. "Anytime."

Behind us, Finn's exaggerated sigh breaks the moment. "Well, this has been thoroughly heartwarming. But if Bob starts writing poetry about you two, I'm blaming Malrik."

I exhale slowly, letting the tension drain from my body as my shadows soften further, their once-frantic movements now gentle, almost soothing. They ripple around Malrik's fingers before curling back toward me, their presence no longer a weight but a quiet reminder that I'm not alone.

"They've always known what I needed before I did," I say softly, more to myself than anyone else. "But I've been so focused on keeping them controlled, I didn't stop to listen."

Malrik's hand lingers near mine, his expression unreadable but steady. "Then listen now. They're on your side, Kaia. Always have been."

The truth in his words settles over me like a warm blanket, and for the first time in days, I feel a flicker of clarity. My shadows twine together at my feet, almost shyly, like they're waiting for approval.

Finn, of course, can't leave the moment alone.

"That's all very touching," he interrupts, hopping off the desk and clapping his hands together. "But can we talk about how Bob's been shipping you two since day one?"

I blink at him, caught off guard by the abrupt shift. "What?"

"Bob," Finn repeats, gesturing toward the shadow in question, who promptly puffs into a perfect heart shape between me and Malrik. "See? Matchmaker extraordinaire."

Malrik's expression tightens, his jaw working as he levels a glare at the shadow. "I will end you," he mutters darkly.

The sudden absurdity of it all—Malrik's death glare at a shadow, Bob's unapologetic showmanship, and Finn's unrelenting grin—snaps the last of the tension in the room. A laugh bubbles out of me, unbidden and unstoppable, and for the first time in a long while, it feels like I can breathe again.

Bob responds by pushing me forward, sending me stumbling against Malrik's chest. Heat blooms under my skin where his hands steady me, and the closeness sends my heart racing. For a moment, I freeze, caught between the surge of embarrassment and the unspoken tension crackling between us. His gaze holds mine, unreadable yet magnetic, and I feel the weight of everything unsaid pressing down on me.

"Subtle, Bob," Finn comments, but his voice has dropped to a register I've never heard before.

"I hate you all," I mutter, but I don't move away from Malrik's grip.

"No, you don't," Finn says softly, sliding off the desk to approach us. "That's kind of the problem, isn't it?"

The air in the room feels charged, electric with unspoken words. Malrik's hands are still on my arms, his warmth seeping through my skin like a salve. Finn stands close, his usual mischief replaced by an intensity that makes my breath catch. We're frozen in this moment, the three of us, and I can feel the weight of our shared history pressing down on us like a physical thing.

My shadows curl around our feet, intertwining with Malrik's darker ones, creating intricate patterns on the stone floor. The classroom feels both too small and infinitely vast, as if the rest of the world has fallen away, leaving just us and this crackling tension.

Finn's eyes flick between Malrik and me, something unreadable flickering in their depths. His usual smirk is gone, replaced by a softness I rarely see. Malrik's grip tightens almost imperceptibly, and I find myself leaning into him, drawn by some invisible force.

The silence stretches, filled with the sound of our breathing and the faint whisper of shadows moving against stone. I open my mouth, though I'm not sure what I'm about to say, when a deep, amused voice cuts through the tension like a knife.

"Well, don't let me interrupt. Though if this is turning into some kind of group hug, I'd like to be included."

We all startle, breaking apart as if burned. Torric stands in the doorway, his massive frame filling the space, a wry smile playing at the corners of his mouth. It's so uncharacteristic of him to joke—especially about something like this—that for a moment, I can only stare.

The spell broken, Finn recovers first, his trademark grin sliding back into place. "Torric, my man! Didn't know you had it in you. Come on in, the water's fine."

Malrik mutters something under his breath that sounds suspiciously like a curse, his hands falling away from my arms. The loss of contact leaves me feeling strangely bereft, and I wrap my arms around myself, trying to recapture some of that warmth.

As if on cue, Seren bursts into the room, her lavender hair wild and her arms full of crumpled papers. Her wide eyes and quick movements radiate a frantic energy. "Found something," she announces, dropping the papers onto a nearby desk. "You're not going to believe what our dear friend Darian's been throwing away."

Aspen follows close behind as Seren spreads out torn pages that look like they've been rescued from trash bins. Objects start sliding into place seemingly on their own—Patricia helping, though only Finn, Malrik, and I can see her doing it.

Torric's eyes widen at the moving papers. "Okay, that's creepy. I know your shadows are doing that, but seeing things float around..."

"You get used to it," Aspen says calmly, though he keeps glancing at the spaces where he thinks the shadows might be. He's not quite right—Bob is actually three feet to his left, looking amused.

"Look at this," Seren says, smoothing out a particularly worn page. "These are notes about some kind of ritual. And this symbol keeps showing up." She points to a mark that makes my shadows violently recoil—Bob abandoning his post to surge protectively in front of me, Patricia's usually neat form fragmenting with distress, while Finnick's playful energy turns sharp and defensive. The newer shadows dart behind the older ones, like frightened children seeking shelter.

The temperature in the room plummets as they all press closer to me, their usual fluid movements turned jerky and panicked.

And I just calmed them down. Fantastic.

Malrik and Finn both tense, seeing their violent reaction. The others only notice when several books go flying off the shelves.

"Sorry," I mutter, trying to calm my shadows. "They don't like that symbol."

"They're terrified of it," Malrik says quietly, his eyes tracking their agitated movements. "I've never seen them react like this."

"Maybe because it looks like this," Seren says grimly, flipping through an ancient text she's pulled from her bag. The same symbol appears on a page about binding shadows—trapping them, controlling them. "Looks like our new friend's been studying up on shadow imprisonment."

My shadows cluster around me protectively. Mouse growls, the sound echoing in the suddenly silent room.

"We need a plan," Aspen says, ever practical. "If Darian's researching this kind of magic..."

"We spring his trap," Malrik says immediately, his eyes meeting mine. Without thinking, he reaches out to steady one of my more panicked shadows—something that makes Torric and Aspen exchange confused looks, since to them he's just reaching into empty air.

"While protecting you," Finn adds, dropping his usual humor for fierce determination. Bob moves to stand between us, and Finn absently pats what appears to be empty space to the others.

"Are they doing the shadow thing again?" Torric asks, squinting at the space between us. "Because I swear I just felt something cold move past me."

"That's Bob," Finn says cheerfully. "He's saying hi."

"I don't know why you've named shadows we can't even see," Torric mutters.

"Bob's a perfectly respectable name," Finn protests, while Malrik pinches the bridge of his nose in exasperation.

I look around at my unlikely group—the twins with their steady strength despite not fully understanding what they can't see, Seren with her brilliant chaos and acceptance of everything weird, and Finn and Malrik, who see all of me, even the parts I tried to hide. My shadows dance between them all, finally free to show their true nature, at least to those who can see them.

"Okay," I say finally. "But we do this together. No more secrets, right?"

"No more secrets," Malrik agrees, his fingers brushing my wrist where one of my shadows has coiled like a bracelet.

"Except Bob's secret handshake," Finn adds. "That's sacred."

The tension breaks as everyone laughs, even Malrik cracking a smile that takes my breath away. My shadows celebrate by creating increasingly ridiculous shapes that only half the room can see, leading to some very confused looks from Torric when his papers suddenly arrange themselves into what I'm pretty sure is meant to be a rude gesture.

"Did you just?" Finn's eyes light up at Malrik actually giving an order to one of the shadows. "You're giving them orders now?"

"Shut up."

"You love us."

"I will end you."

"Bob, back me up here—"

Their bickering fades into the background as I watch my shadows play between them. Something in my chest loosens, a knot of loneliness finally beginning to unravel.

These men have given me so much already, and they're willing to stick by me. How did I get so lucky?

Mouse bumps my hand, purring loudly, while Bob creates a triumphant arch over my head that makes Seren squint and mutter something about feeling a cold breeze. I can practically hear Finn naming the newer shadows in the background while Malrik pretends not to care.

We have a professor to confront and a conspiracy to unravel. But for now, in this moment, I let myself feel the warmth of belonging.

Even if that belonging comes with incredibly nosy shadows and two men who are going to drive me crazy.

"Bob, no encouragement," I mutter as the shadow tries to push me toward them again.

But I'm smiling as I say it.

Chapter 56
KAIA

We're in the Shadow common room, where twilight wraps around us like a comfort. My shadows, sensing the shift from tension to sanctuary, become more animated. Finnick immediately demonstrates this newfound energy by attempting to redecorate, knocking over no fewer than three candlesticks in rapid succession.

"Finnick, no," Malrik and I say in unison, while Finn beams with pride.

"He gets it from my side of the family," Finn declares, sprawling across a plush armchair. My shadows—not just Bob, Patricia, and Finnick now, but several newer ones I haven't seen before—swirl around him affectionately.

"When did..." I trail off, watching two unfamiliar shadows in particular interact with my usual ones. One seems to be attempting increasingly dramatic acrobatics while the other keeps trying to catch it before it can knock anything over. Bob appears to be organizing them all, like a general with new recruits.

"They started showing up a few days ago," Malrik says quietly, his eyes tracking their movements. "Bob's been... training them, for lack of a better word."

"That enthusiastic one is Steve," Finn adds helpfully, pointing to the shadow currently attempting a backflip. "And the responsible one trying to stop him from breaking everything is Linda. She's shy but she's got spirit. They showed up together, actually. Linda basically adopted Steve on the spot."

"Like a shadow mom," I observe, watching Linda successfully redirect Steve away from a precariously balanced stack of books.

"Exactly!" Finn beams. "See? The naming system makes perfect sense."

Malrik pinches the bridge of his nose. "We are not naming every shadow that manifests."

"Try and stop me, princeling. Besides, Bob and Patricia approve. Look at them nodding."

Sure enough, both shadows are nodding emphatically while Finnick eggs Steve on in the background.

I sink onto the couch, trying to process this new development. "So they're just... appearing? And joining up with mine?"

"They're responding to your magic evolving," Malrik explains, his gaze tracking Steve's latest backflip attempt. "But it's more than that. Shadows gravitate toward what protects them. You're... building something here, Kaia. Whether you realize it or not."

"Like a tiny shadow army," Finn says cheerfully. "Bob's their commander. Patricia handles intelligence. Finnick's in charge of chaos—"

"That's your influence," Malrik mutters, but there's something soft in his voice when he looks at Finn.

"You love it," Finn shoots back, his grin sharp but his eyes warm.

The air between them crackles with tension. My shadows—all of them, even the new ones—go suddenly still and watchful. Even Finnick stops causing havoc to pay attention.

"You two are ridiculous," I say, but my voice comes out breathier than intended. "We're supposed to be planning—"

"Oh, Bob's got plans," Finn assures me, his gaze flickering between Malrik and me. "Detailed ones. Patricia's taking notes."

Sure enough, the scholarly shadow appears to be transcribing something in the air, while Bob directs the newer shadows into what looks suspiciously like battle formations.

"Should we be concerned that your shadows are plotting strategy without us?" Malrik asks, moving to sit beside me on the couch. The proximity sends a jolt through me, and my shadows ripple in response.

"Probably," I manage. "But I'm more concerned about why Finnick is teaching the new ones to pick locks."

"That's my boy," Finn says proudly, just as Finnick successfully opens a cabinet across the room. Three new shadows immediately dive in to explore its contents.

"We're doomed," Malrik declares, but he's fighting a smile.

"Admit it," Finn says, sliding off his chair to join us on the couch, effectively bracketing me between them. "You love our little shadow family."

"I tolerate you both," Malrik corrects, but his hand brushes mine where it rests between us.

"Both of us?" Finn's voice drops lower, and suddenly the room feels too warm. "Just tolerate?"

Bob, ever helpful, dims the remaining candles. Patricia hustles the newer shadows out of view, like a chaperone clearing the room. Even Finnick goes suspiciously quiet.

"I hate everyone in this room," I announce to no one in particular. "Including the shadows."

"No, you don't," Finn and Malrik say together, and the synchronization sends a shiver down my spine.

My heart pounds as Finn and Malrik crowd closer on either side. The air feels thick, charged with possibility. The pull I feel toward them both is undeniable, but it's terrifying too—letting them in, letting anyone in, feels like a risk I don't know how to take. And yet, I can't seem to pull away.

"You two are impossible," I mutter, but I don't move away.

"Impossibly charming," Finn quips, his breath warm against my ear.

"Impossibly frustrating," Malrik counters, his fingers tracing patterns on my wrist.

A shiver runs through me. My shadows dance excitedly, swirling around us in dizzying patterns. Even Bob seems to have abandoned his usual decorum, creating heart shapes that pulse in time with my racing pulse.

"Traitors," I tell them, but there's no heat in it.

Finn chuckles, the sound vibrating through me. "They're just being honest. Unlike some people."

"I'm always honest," I protest weakly.

"Oh really?" Malrik's voice is a low purr that makes my toes curl. "Then tell us honestly, Kaia. What do you want?"

The question hangs in the air, heavy with promise. My shadows go utterly still, waiting.

"I..." My voice falters as Finn's hand comes to rest on my knee, Malrik's on my waist. "This is a terrible idea."

"The best ones usually are," Finn murmurs, nuzzling against my neck.

Malrik's thumb traces my bottom lip. "Answer the question, little nightshade."

My breath catches as Malrik's thumb traces my lip. "I want..." The words stick in my throat, overwhelming me with sensation. Finn's lips brush my neck, sending sparks dancing across my skin. Malrik's silver eyes hold mine, intense and hungry.

"Yes?" Finn prompts, his voice a low rumble against my skin.

A new shadow—possibly Steve—chooses that moment to drop a book on the table with a loud thud, scattering the tension like shattering glass. Its leather cover is etched with intricate designs, but one symbol stands out—a mark identical to the one Seren had shown us. My stomach churns as the room's lightness evaporates, replaced by the oppressive weight of the unknown.

"What the hell is that?" Finn mutters, already leaning forward.

Malrik's hand tightens around mine. "Something we need to figure out. Quickly."

"Back to work then," Finn says, his usual cheer dimmed. "But this conversation isn't over."

"Focus," Malrik orders, but his hand doesn't move from where it's resting against mine.

"Always am," Finn replies cheerfully, but his thigh presses warmly against my other side as he leans in to read.

I try to concentrate on the text, but all I can think about is the heat of them on either side of me, the way my shadows keep trying to wrap around all three of us, and the growing certainty that I'm in serious trouble. And judging by Bob's smug expression, my shadows agree.

Chapter 57
Kaia

The shadows take me as I drift into sleep, dragging me into a world that isn't mine. They writhe and twist, their edges jagged and wrong, trying to pull me under. Above me, a symbol pulses in the dark—the same one from Darian's notes. Unlike the gentle darkness of my own shadows, these feel corrupted, bitter.

My shadows try to fight back, but they're being torn away one by one. Bob goes first, his usually steady form dissolving into nothing as he tries to maintain his protective stance. Then Patricia, her last gesture an attempt to shield the others. Finnick doesn't even get a chance for a final joke before he scatters like smoke. Even Steve and Linda, still so new, are ripped apart like paper in a storm.

"They were never truly yours," Thorne's voice echoes through the void. "Just borrowed power, waiting to be claimed."

I try to scream, but shadows pour into my mouth, choking me—bitter and sharp, like swallowing glass. Mouse's panicked yowl seems to come from very far away, followed by the sound of claws scrabbling against stone.

"Kaia!"

Hands grip my shoulders, shaking me awake. I lash out instinctively, my shadows surging up—

"Easy," Aspen says softly. "You're safe. It's just us."

My eyes snap open to find Aspen and Torric in my room. Aspen sits on the edge of my bed, his hands still steady on my shoulders, while Torric hovers near the door, practically vibrating with barely-contained energy. The air around him seems to shimmer with heat, though his expression is caught between concern and awkward uncertainty.

"You were screaming," Torric explains gruffly. "The whole wing probably heard. Mouse was raising hell at our door until we followed him."

I try to slow my breathing, checking frantically for my shadows. They're all there, clustering around me protectively. Bob does a quick head count, moving with military precision as he organizes the others into a defensive formation. Patricia fusses, trying to straighten my sweat-soaked hair while weaving gentle, swirling patterns in the air around me that somehow make it easier to breathe. Even Finnick is subdued, pressing close like a concerned puppy, though he can't seem to help making little shadow-rabbits hop across my blanket in an attempt to cheer me up.

"Sorry," I manage. "Just a dream."

"Must have been some dream," Aspen says quietly. Though he can't see them, he seems to sense my shadows' agitation. The temperature in the room has dropped several degrees from their distress, and frost patterns crystallize on my water glass. "Want to talk about it?"

I shake my head, then immediately change my mind, panic clawing at my throat as Aspen starts to get up. "Actually... could you stay? Just for a bit?"

The twins exchange a look I can't quite read. Something passes between them—some silent communication born of years together.

"Both of you," I add quickly. "I just... I don't want to be alone."

Torric shifts uncomfortably, running a hand through his disheveled hair. "You sure? We could get Seren, or—"

"Please?"

Something in my voice must convince them. Aspen squeezes my shoulder once before moving to grab the chair from my desk. His movements are deliberately calm, like someone approaching a spooked animal. Torric, after a moment's hesitation, sits at the foot of my bed, his back against the wall. The mattress dips under his weight, and I notice his hands are clenched into fists, like he's fighting the urge to punch something.

"The mighty shadow girl, afraid of bad dreams?" he teases, but his voice is gentle, and his hands slowly unclench.

"Shut up," I mutter, pulling my knees up. Mouse settles in my lap, purring so loudly it vibrates through my bones. Bob positions himself by the door while Patricia creates a gossamer-thin curtain of shadows across the window.

"I think it's time for one of Torric's legendary jokes," Aspen says, his tone all mock-seriousness.

Torric groans. "Legendary for what? Being terrible?"

"Exactly," Aspen deadpans. "But they always work."

"Fine," Torric mutters, throwing me a mock-glare. "But I'm charging you for emotional damages after this."

"Tell me," I say, feeling my lips twitch despite everything. My shadows seem to perk up too, especially Finnick, who drifts closer in anticipation. Even Bob turns slightly from his guard position, trying to pretend he's not interested.

"Why did the mage try to charm a water bucket?" Torric begins, his tone mock-serious.

Finnick is already miming a bucket spilling over dramatically.

"No," I gasp through a half-laugh, "please tell me he didn't—"

"Oh, he did," Torric says with a grin, the punchline drowned out by Finnick's exaggerated reaction.

I don't remember falling asleep again, but I wake briefly to find Aspen still in the chair, reading by magelight, while Torric snores softly from his spot against the wall. My shadows stretch upward, weaving together into a shimmering canopy that filters the room's dim light into soft, shifting patterns. It feels like being cocooned in safety, their presence wrapping around us like a silent promise. Patricia has woven a delicate shadow-blanket around Torric, its patterns matching his steady breathing. Finnick, for once peaceful, curls near Aspen's feet like a contented cat.

"Sleep," Aspen murmurs, not looking up from his book. "We're not going anywhere."

As I drift back into sleep, I'm struck by how much they've given me without asking for anything in return.

Chapter 58
KAIA

The dining hall is oddly quiet when we arrive for breakfast, probably because it's far earlier than most students typically emerge. The twins flank me automatically—a gesture I'm trying not to read too much into—as we make our way to our usual table.

Finn's already there, sprawled dramatically across two chairs while gesturing with a half-eaten muffin. His eyes widen comically when he spots us, and he sits up so fast he nearly falls.

"Well, well, well," he drawls, waggling his eyebrows. "What do we have here? A walk of shame from the mighty Agere twins?"

Torric chokes on air while Aspen suddenly becomes very interested in the ceiling.

"It's not—" I start, but Finn holds up a hand.

"Don't try to explain. Bob told me everything." A wave of betrayal washes over me as I glance at my shadow.

Really, Bob? I thought we were on the same side.

My traitorous shadow nods solemnly from his post near my shoulder. Patricia, meanwhile, is pretending to take detailed notes.

"Bob," Malrik's dry voice cuts in as he approaches our table, "is a terrible gossip."

Bob straightens indignantly, puffing up as if to say *How dare you?!* while Finnick dissolves into silent shadow-giggles.

"You weren't there," Finn says, pointing his muffin at Malrik accusingly. "Our sweet, innocent Kaia, corrupting not one but TWO noble warriors—"

"I had a nightmare," I interrupt, dropping into a chair. "They helped. That's all."

"A likely story." Finn turns to Mouse, who's looking entirely too pleased with himself. "And you, sir, are supposed to be her chaperone. I expected better."

Mouse yawns widely, showing all his teeth.

"Speaking of expectations," Seren announces, appearing with perfect dramatic timing, "I expect details. Immediately."

"Nothing happened!" Torric protests, his face nearly as red as his fire rune.

"Oh honey." Seren pats his arm. "Your hair says otherwise."

His hands fly to his head, trying to smooth down his unruly locks. "What's wrong with my hair?"

"Everything," Finn and Seren say in unison.

I drop my head onto the table with a thunk. My shadows pat my back consolingly, though I'm pretty sure Finnick is still laughing.

"If you're quite finished," Malrik says, somehow making the words sound both bored and amused, "perhaps we could discuss why Kaia had a nightmare bad enough to warrant a twin intervention?"

The humor fades as I describe the dream—the wrong-feeling shadows, the symbol, Thorne's voice. Even Finn stops fidgeting, his expression growing serious.

"A symbol from Darian's notes?" Aspen asks, frowning. "What kind of symbol?"

I grab a napkin and start sketching with a borrowed pencil. It takes a few tries to get it right—my hand keeps shaking—but finally I have a rough approximation of what I saw. Three curved lines intersect with what looks like a twisted tree.

The moment I finish, Mouse hisses. Malrik goes very still.

"What?" I look between them. "What is it?"

"That's..." Malrik's voice is carefully neutral. "That's not just any symbol. It's the mark of Absentia—my realm."

"Why would your realm be in my dream?" I hated how my voice trembled, betraying the unease crawling under my skin.

But before he can answer, Alenya's voice rings out across the dining hall, sharp with malice.

"Well, isn't this cozy? Playing breakfast club this morning are we? Although I don't remember monsters in that movie."

Finn's eyes narrow. "Speaking of monsters—"

"Don't," Aspen warns quietly.

I straighten in my chair, fighting the urge to let my shadows lash out at her smug face. "Did you need something, Alenya? Besides attention?"

Her smile turns cruel. "Oh, I just thought you should know—Professor Thorne's looking for you. Something about... special training."

The way she says it makes my skin crawl. Or maybe it's the memory of his voice from my dream: *They were never truly yours.*

"Tell him I'm busy," I say, but Alenya's already sauntering away, clearly pleased with herself. My shadows starting to chase after her like a small militant group, but I reign them in.

"I don't like it," Torric growls. The air around him feels warmer than usual.

"You don't like anything," Finn points out, but he's watching Alenya's retreating form with unusual focus. "Though in this case, I agree. Something's off."

"The symbol," Malrik says, tapping the napkin. "We need to research this. Now."

"What, all of us?" I ask.

"Safety in numbers," Aspen says firmly. "Besides, if Thorne's looking for you..."

"We make sure he doesn't find you alone," Torric finishes.

Mouse growls his approval while Bob snaps into what can only be described as a tactical formation. Even Finnick manages to look serious for once.

"Fine," I sigh. "To the library we go. But Finn?"

"Hmm?"

"If you make one more comment about the twins in my room, I'm letting Bob eat your lunch."

Bob perks up hopefully.

"So cruel," Finn sighs, pressing a hand to his heart. "I love it."

I shake my head and try to cover the smile on my face but it's really useless at this point. "Alright, Let's go."

The weight of the napkin in my hands feels heavier than it should. If Malrik's realm is tied to this, the answers can't wait. And neither can we.

Chapter 59
KAIA

The library is mercifully empty this early, though I suspect Finn's theatrical warnings to other students about "highly contagious shadow plague" on our way here might have something to do with that.

"Was that really necessary?" Malrik asks as we claim a secluded table near the restricted section.

"Absolutely," Finn says cheerfully. "Bob agreed with my tactical decision."

Bob, who's currently arranging other shadows into a perimeter guard, gives what might be a thumbs up.

"Focus," Aspen says, already spreading out several ancient texts. "Malrik, what exactly is Absentia? You've been a little vague on the details."

"A realm between realms," Malrik says, his voice dropping lower. "Think of it as a bridge—not just between places, but between life and death itself. But it was never meant to exist that way," Malrik adds, his voice growing heavier. "Absentia was... designed. A construct with a purpose long forgotten by most."

"Was?" I catch his use of past tense.

"Before its corruption." His finger traces the symbol slowly. "Before Alekir began working to shatter its purpose."

"They say his goal was not just power but freedom—freedom for something locked within Absentia itself." Aspen adds, and the room seems to grow colder. Malrik's expression darkens further, his jaw tightening. Even Finn, normally quick with a joke, is uncharacteristically silent, his gaze fixed on the table as if trying to process the weight of what we've just heard. Malrik nods grimly. "A sorcerer who tried to claim dominion over death itself. The stories say he nearly succeeded, but the Valkyries stopped him."

My heart skips. "The Valkyries?"

"Ancient warriors who maintained the balance between realms." His silver eyes meet mine. "They were wiped out many generations ago."

"By this sorcerer?"

"By Alekir," Malrik says quietly. "The Soulbinder."

A chill runs through me every time I hear the name. My shadows press closer, and Mouse's fur stands on end.

"Okay, creepy history lesson aside," Finn interrupts, "what does this have to do with Thorne?"

"Here." Aspen turns one of the books around. "Look at this illustration."

We crowd around the page. It shows the same symbol, but with annotations in a spidery script.

"Can anyone read that?" I ask.

"It's Ancient Shadowtongue," Malrik says. "It describes the ritual Alekir used to try to bind souls to his will. He needed three things: a corrupted shadow realm, a powerful artifact, and—" He breaks off, staring at the page.

"And what?"

"A Valkyrie's heart."

The silence that follows feels like ice in my lungs. My hand goes instinctively to the amethyst necklace I always wear—the one I've had since before I can remember.

Patricia suddenly starts frantically pointing at something on the next page. It's another illustration, this one showing a familiar-looking pendant.

"The Heart of Eternity," Malrik breathes, his voice laced with reverence and unease. His silver eyes darken, lingering on the pendant as if drawn to it by some unseen force. "The Valkyries' most powerful artifact. It was lost when they fell," he continues, his fingers brushing the edge of the illustration with a mix of awe and trepidation.

"Lost," Torric says slowly, "or hidden?"

Everyone looks at my necklace.

"No," I say, backing away. My heart pounds painfully in my chest, and my fingers curl into fists as if I can physically hold onto the denial. "No, that's not—it can't be—" My voice cracks under the weight of the truth threatening to swallow me whole, my shadows shifting erratically around me like they share my panic.

Malrik's expression tightens, and I see the conflict etched into every line of his face. He's hesitating—something I'm not used to seeing from him.

"Malrik," Aspen says softly, breaking the silence. "You need to tell her. She deserves to know."

My breath hitches, Aspen's words pulling at the loose threads in my mind. "Tell me what?"

Malrik exhales slowly, his silver eyes meeting mine with an intensity that makes it hard to look away. "I've suspected for a while," he admits. "Your necklace... it's more than a trinket. I didn't know for sure until now, but..." He gestures toward the illustration in the book. "It matches. Perfectly."

"You suspected?" My voice is a mix of disbelief and hurt. "And you didn't think to tell me?"

"I wasn't sure," Malrik says, his tone steady but edged with regret. "And I didn't want to add to your burdens without proof. You've had enough to deal with, Kaia. But seeing this... it confirms what I hoped wasn't true."

My stomach churns as I try to reconcile his words. He'd suspected all along? And kept it from me? Part of me wants to lash out, to demand why he thought it wasn't my right to know. But another part—the part that knows he's right—makes the words stick in my throat. I could hold onto the hurt, let it fester—but what good would that do? There was too much at stake, and we didn't have the luxury of indulging in my pride. Not now.

The weight of everything is too much, threatening to crack the fragile equilibrium I've found. Then Finn's voice cut through the silence, unexpectedly gentle.

"Kaia." His tone carried no humor, just quiet sincerity. "Your shadows. They've always been different. Special."

"And Thorne's been obsessed with training you specifically," Aspen adds.

"But that would mean..." I can't finish the thought.

"It would mean," Malrik says grimly, "that Thorne isn't just training you. He's preparing you for something."

A sound from deeper in the stacks makes us freeze. Bob and Finnick move in perfect sync toward the noise, while Patricia's notes dissolve into defensive shadows.

"We need somewhere secure," Malrik says, already gathering the most crucial texts. "Somewhere warded."

"Your room?" Finn suggests, then adds quickly at our looks: "What? Everyone knows he's paranoid about security. Probably has more protective spells than the treasury."

"He's not wrong," Malrik admits reluctantly. "And I have resources we can't access here."

"Fine," I sigh. "Let's move before we attract more attention."

As we hurry from the library, I notice my shadows are unusually coordinated, moving with purpose rather than their usual chaos. Even Finnick seems to understand the gravity of the situation.

"Hey." Finn bumps my shoulder gently. "Whatever this is, we'll figure it out. Together."

"Besides," Torric adds with a grim smile, "if anyone tries to take your heart, they'll have to go through us first."

"Technically," Malrik drawls, "they'd have to go through Bob first. And he takes his job very seriously."

Bob straightens proudly while Patricia nods in emphatic agreement.

"Yes!" Finn whispers not so quietly, pumping a fist in the air. "Bob's MVP material. I've been saying it for weeks," Finn adds, winking at the shadow, who nods solemnly.

I want to believe it's that simple. But deep down, I know this is something far darker than I want to imagine.

Chapter 60
KAIA

"Huh," Finn says as we enter Malrik's room. "I was right about the black silk sheets. Classic brooding vibe. Do you practice brooding in here, or is it just natural?"

"Finn." Malrik's voice carries a warning, but there's a flush creeping up his neck.

"What? I'm just appreciating the aesthetic. Very broody prince of darkness. Very you."

I try not to look at the bed at all, but my shadows apparently have no such restraint. Patricia is literally taking notes on the decor while Finnick bounces experimentally on the mattress.

"If we could focus," Aspen says, though his lips twitch. "Preferably before Kaia spontaneously combusts." My cheeks burn as I glance around, avoiding their eyes. Why does everyone insist on making this more embarrassing than it already is? Even my shadows seem to mock me, their flickering shapes hinting at silent laughter. Traitors.

I snap my gaze away from where Malrik is shrugging off his outer robe, revealing a criminally well-fitted shirt underneath. "I'm not—I mean, I'm fine."

"Sure you are, sunshine." Torric drops into a plush armchair, grinning. "That's why you're drooling."

I am not drooling. Okay, maybe I am, just a little.

"Can we please," I say through gritted teeth, "focus on the potentially life-threatening situation?"

"Right." Finn sprawls across the foot of Malrik's bed like he owns it. "The whole 'Thorne might be working with an evil soul binding madman thing. Much less interesting than—ow!"

A book has mysteriously flown off the shelf and hit him in the head. Malrik looks far too innocent.

"The ritual Alekir attempted," Malrik continues smoothly, ignoring Finn's dramatic pouting, "required specific circumstances. A convergence of power that only happens—"

"During the new moon," Aspen finishes, studying one of the texts. "Which is..."

"Three weeks away," I realize, my fingers brushing against my necklace without thinking. The subtle weight of the pendant feels heavier as Malrik's expression darkens.

"Well that's not ominous at all," Finn mutters, now using Malrik's expensive pillows to build some kind of fort. "Hey, anyone else notice how Thorne always wears high collars? Maybe he's hiding evil ritual tattoos. Or a hickey from Alenya's mom."

"Finn!"

"What? I'm processing through humor. It's very healthy."

"Nothing about you is healthy," Malrik says, but there's a fondness in his voice that makes Finn beam.

"Your shadows agree with me," Finn points out. "Look, they're already planning battle strategies."

He's not wrong. Bob has gathered the others for what appears to be a tactical briefing, complete with Patricia's detailed shadow diagrams and Finnick's enthusiastic but questionable suggestions.

Aspen sighs, pinching the bridge of his nose as Torric squints at the shadows' activity. "I hate that I can feel the chaos even if I can't see it."

"You get used to it," I say absently, my gaze lingering on Malrik. His demeanor is steady, but there's a tension to his movements that sets my nerves on edge. My shadows shift closer to him, as if trying to anchor us both.

"They grow on you," Malrik murmurs, then freezes as if he didn't mean to say it aloud.

His tone softened at that and I can't help but think of what it means to me that he's accepting of them.

An awkward silence falls, broken only by Mouse's amused purring.

I clear my throat but pause as movement catches my eye. A new shadow materializes near the others, its edges wavering uncertainly, as if testing its welcome. Linda immediately abandons her diagrams, drifting over with an air of fascination, while Steve bounces toward the newcomer, his exaggerated movements inviting chaos.

The shadow tilts slightly, observing them, before darting under Malrik's desk.

"Well, hello there," Finn coos, crouching to peer beneath the desk. "Who's this sneaky little void?"

"He's already in the restricted section of Malrik's collection," Aspen says dryly, clearly unaware of the shadows' movements.

"Restricted section?" Torric raises an eyebrow. "What are you talking about? There's nothing there."

Finn waves a hand dismissively. "You wouldn't understand. It's shadow business."

Torric groans. "Of course it is."

As if on cue, a faint scraping sound echoes from behind the desk. Moments later, the shadow emerges triumphantly, dragging something behind him.

"What's that noise?" Aspen asks, frowning as he glances toward the desk.

"Carl's doing his thing," Finn says, entirely too pleased.

"Carl?" I echo, raising an eyebrow.

"Yeah, Carl." Finn gestures dramatically at the shadow. "He looks like a Carl. You can't tell me he doesn't."

Torric glances at Aspen, then back at Finn. "You're naming him Carl, just like that?"

"Obviously." Finn gestures dramatically at the floor, where the shadows are engaged in a full-fledged tug-of-war over the object Carl has unearthed.

To everyone except Finn, Malrik, and me, it looks like the item has mysteriously appeared from nowhere.

"What is that?" Aspen asks, his tone suspicious.

Carl finally drags his prize into the middle of the group and lets it drop with a flourish.

A long, sleek object gleams faintly in the candlelight.

"Is that a—" Torric starts, before abruptly choking on his words.

"Malrik!" Finn exclaims, his eyes widening with unholy glee. "Is that what I think it is?"

"It's not—" Malrik's voice rises, uncharacteristically flustered. He snatches the object, his face a perfect storm of annoyance and mortification. "It's a weapon!"

"Sure it is, Your Darkness." Finn collapses into laughter, clutching his stomach. "A very... personal weapon?"

Aspen, ever the diplomat, tries (and fails) to suppress a smirk. "I suppose that's one way to disarm someone."

Linda and Steve watch with what can only be described as rapt fascination, while Carl bounces happily on the spot, clearly proud of himself.

"Carl's either going to save us all or kill us from secondhand embarrassment," Torric mutters.

"Carl's my new favorite," Finn announces. "He's an agent of chaos after my own heart."

Malrik groans, his composure in tatters. "I'm banning all shadows from my room."

"You'd miss them," Finn says, grinning wickedly. "Especially Carl."

Malrik looks like he's debating whether the effort of arguing is worth it. "Get back to work."

"Whatever you say, Prince of Pleasure," Finn retorts, dodging a book Malrik hurls in his direction.

The group dissolves into laughter, the earlier tension forgotten—at least for the moment.

"So, evil ritual. New moon. Final trial. What do we do?"

"We could just not participate," Finn suggests from his pillow fort. "Call in dead. Take a romantic vacation. I hear Absentia is lovely this time of year."

Malrik pinches the bridge of his nose. "For the last time, Finn, Absentia is not a vacation spot. It's a corrupted realm of eternal darkness."

"So... perfect for you then. Moody, dark, and dramatic—just like your soul.?"

Before Malrik can retort, Aspen holds up a hand. "There's something else. The ritual needs more than just the Heart and a Valkyrie's power. It needs... consent."

"What do you mean?" I ask.

"The bearer has to willingly give up their power," Aspen explains. "It can't be taken by force."

"Which explains why Thorne's been so invested in controlling you," Malrik says, his expression darkening. "He doesn't need trust. He needs submission."

A chill runs down my spine, my fingers curling protectively around my necklace. *Submission.* The word echoes in my mind, heavy with implications I'm not ready to confront. But like hell I'm submitting to anyone, let alone him.

"That's why he's been keeping you in line," Finn says, unusually serious. "He's playing the long game."

"Then we'll break it," Torric growls, the glow of his fire rune faintly visible beneath his shirt. "Whatever Thorne thinks he's building, it's not happening."

"Agreed." Aspen flips another page of the tome in front of him, his tone brisk. "But the ritual still needs a specific place—the nexus—and a very specific moment."

"The arena," Malrik says, his voice low. "It's not just a trial ground. It's built where the veils between realms are thinnest."

"Of course it is," Finn groans. "Because where else would an evil ritual go down?"

Finn somehow managed to migrate from his pillow fort to sprawl across both the bed and Malrik's lap. Malrik doesn't move him, which seems significant. Or maybe I'm just overthinking it, like always.

"Maybe that's why he's been here, waiting for the right student to come along. It couldn't have been anywhere else." Aspen replies thoughtfully.

"Because we couldn't have our dramatic showdown somewhere sensible, like a coffee shop."

"Yes, Finn," I drawl. "Let's invite the evil soul binding madman for scones."

"See? Kaia gets it."

"Kaia needs sleep," Torric mutters without opening his eyes. "She's starting to sound like you."

He's not entirely wrong. The words on the page are starting to blur, and my shadows are getting punchy. Bob's usual military precision has devolved into something more like interpretive dance, and Patricia appears to be doodling little hearts in her shadow notes.

"We should rest," Aspen says, ever practical. "Take shifts watching—Kaia, that wasn't a suggestion." He adds quickly, arching an eyebrow in challenge at me.

I open my mouth to argue, but the weight pressing down on me is undeniable. My limbs feel leaden, and even my shadows are slowing, their usual liveliness dimming. I sigh, the protest dying in my throat, and nod reluctantly. "Fine," I mutter, leaning back and letting exhaustion win.

I realize I'm swaying slightly where I sit cross-legged on the floor. "I'm fine."

"You're exhausted," Malrik says softly. "We all are."

"But—"

"No buts," Finn interrupts, finally extracting himself from Malrik's lap. "Except yours, going to sleep. I'll take first watch."

"Not alone," Malrik says immediately.

Their eyes meet, and something unspoken passes between them. My shadows flutter with interest while Mouse makes a sound suspiciously like a snicker.

"I'll stay too," I say quickly, not sure why my heart is suddenly racing. "Three sets of eyes are better than two."

"Technically, more like twenty," Finn says, grinning. "If we count your shadow squad."

Bob paces a precise perimeter, while Patricia's shadow notes now include detailed diagrams of defensive formations. Finnick, refusing to be completely serious even now, keeps adding artistic flourishes to her work - though even his usual chaos seems more focused and purposeful. Mouse watches them all with ancient eyes, his form seeming to grow more solid as the stakes rise.

"We'll get more books from the library," Aspen decides, hauling a grumbling Torric to his feet. "Meet back here in a few hours."

As the twins leave, I find myself hyper-aware of the room's new dynamic. Malrik still sits against his headboard, all dangerous grace and sharp edges. Finn has migrated to the window seat, his usual manic energy softened by fatigue. I'm caught between them, my shadows swirling with an agitation I don't want to examine too closely.

"You should rest," Malrik says into the silence. "We'll wake you if anything happens."

"I told you, I'm—" A yawn betrays me. "Fine."

"Sure you are, Trouble." Finn pats the space beside him. "Come on, this window seat is surprisingly comfy."

"I don't—"

"Kaia." Malrik's voice is quiet but firm. "Let us help."

Something in his tone makes me shiver. Or maybe it's the way Finn's watching me, his usual humor replaced by something deeper. My shadows practically shove me toward the window seat.

"Traitors," I mutter, but I go.

The window seat is comfy, and Finn is warm when I settle beside him. Through half-closed eyes, I watch Malrik pretending not to watch us while he reads. My shadows drift between them like lazy cats, equally content in either's presence.

"Sleep," Finn murmurs, and his fingers brush my hair with surprising gentleness. "We've got you." His touch is light, but it anchors me in a way I can't explain. A warmth blooms in my chest, easing the tension I didn't realize I was holding. For once, the chaotic swirl of my shadows settles, matching the steady calm they seem to draw from Finn and Malrik. Trusting them feels natural, even if it terrifies me.

The last thing I register is Malrik moving closer, his voice a low murmur as he and Finn discuss watch rotations. Their quiet conversation is intimate, but I'm too tired to overthink it. I fall asleep to the sound of their voices, feeling safer than I have any right to be.

Chapter 61
KAIA

I wake to warmth and whispers.

"—can't just tell her," Malrik's voice, unusually soft.

"Why not?" Finn. "Bob agrees with me."

"Bob is not a relationship counselor." My lips twitch despite myself. Of course Finn would drag my shadow into his matchmaking schemes. I can't decide whether to laugh or roll my eyes.

"Have you met Bob? He's very wise."

I keep my eyes closed, partly to gather my thoughts and partly because I'm suddenly aware of my position. Somehow in my sleep, I've ended up with my head in Finn's lap while my legs stretch across Malrik's. I can feel my shadows draped around all of us like a contented blanket, and Mouse is purring somewhere above my head.

"She needs to focus on surviving," Malrik continues. His hand rests lightly on my ankle, thumb tracing absent patterns that send shivers up my spine. The touch is gentle, almost thoughtless, but it sets every nerve alight. I can't tell if the warmth pooling in my chest is from his touch or the realization that even subconsciously, he can't seem to stop protecting me.

"Pretty sure that's easier with people you trust at your back." Finn's fingers card through my hair. "People who care about you."

"It's not that simple."

"It could be." Finn's voice turns serious. "We could make it simple."

The air feels charged, like the moment before lightning strikes. I should move. Should let them know I'm awake. Instead, I lie perfectly still, my heart thundering.

"Finn..." Malrik's voice carries a warning, but something else too.

"Tell me you haven't thought about it," Finn challenges. "Both of us. All of us." The words hang in the air, heavy with unspoken possibilities. I feel my shadows ripple with tension, their movements mirroring the nervous flutter in my chest. It feels like the world is holding its breath, waiting for an answer no one is ready to give.

A sharp intake of breath. "That's not—"

The door bursts open with a bang. I bolt upright, nearly cracking my head against Finn's chin as Torric stumbles in, out of breath and wild-eyed.

"We have a problem," he gasps. "A big one."

"We found something else in the restricted archives," Aspen says, holding up what looks like a student record book, old and covered in dust. "Remember those records Seren found about Thorne? We kept digging."

"What did you find?" Malrik demands, on his feet in an instant.

"Look at this faculty photo," Aspen says, opening to a yellowed page. "It's from twenty years ago."

We crowd around as he reveals the image. My blood runs cold.

There, in the old, fading photo, standing among much younger versions of our professors, is Thorne.

Looking exactly the same as he does now.

"That's impossible," I breathe.

"It gets worse," Torric says grimly. "The name listed isn't Thorne. It's Mikhael Aldrich."

Malrik goes very still. "Are you sure?"

"Look at the signature."

The spidery script matches the annotations in the book about Alekir perfectly.

"I don't understand," I say. "Who is Mikhael Aldrich?"

"Alekir's right hand," Malrik says quietly. "His most loyal follower. He disappeared after Alekir's defeat and was presumed dead."

"That's why he's been teaching here," Aspen says, flipping through more pages of the dusty book. "Waiting for the right moment. The right person."

"Kaia," Torric mutters. His hands clench into fists, his usual calm replaced by a simmering anger. "He's been playing the long game, hasn't he?"

Malrik nods grimly. "Decades of patience for one shot at fulfilling Alekir's goal. The trials were always about control, about finding the right Valkyrie to wield the Heart."

"But if Thorne—or Aldrich—is running this show, where does that leave Darian?" Finn asks, his voice sharper than usual. "He's the one who's been all over Kaia, playing the charming villain. What's his angle?"

Malrik's jaw tightens. "Aldrich doesn't share power. If Darian thinks he's an equal in this, he's a fool. He's being used, whether he realizes it or not."

"But that doesn't add up," I say, the weight of my necklace heavy against my chest. "Darian's not stupid. He must know something's off."

"Maybe not everything," Aspen says, thoughtful. "If he knew the full plan, he'd already be a liability. Aldrich keeps him in line by letting him think he's in control. But he's just a pawn."

"And his shadows," I add, my voice faltering as I recall both the unnatural tension I felt in the courtyard and that binding symbol from Seren's research. "There's something wrong with them. They don't feel... alive. They're rigid, like they're being forced into place. It's like they're more chains than companions—just like that imprisonment ritual we found."

Malrik's jaw tightens. "That would fit. The symbol in those pages Seren found, the binding magic—Aldrich doesn't share power willingly, but he does bind it. If Darian's shadows are controlled like that, it's another leash Aldrich has on him."

"And what happens when he realizes that?" Torric's voice is low, dangerous. "If Thorne—or Aldrich—has been keeping him in the dark, that's going to blow up in all our faces."

"Or it could turn him against Thorne," Finn suggests. "If Darian's not completely on board, we might have an edge."

"That's a risky gamble," Malrik says, his silver eyes narrowing. "Darian's not trustworthy. Even if he turns on Aldrich, it doesn't mean he'll side with us."

I bite my lip, my mind racing. "Wait," I say, the memory of that day in the courtyard suddenly vivid. "When Finn found me with Darian, something was... off."

All eyes turn to me, and I feel a flush creep up my neck. But this is important. I push on.

"Darian was... different. Softer, almost. He gave me information about the shadow faction, warned me about things to come. And he apologized." I shake my head, still confused by the memory. "It wasn't like him at all."

Finn's brow furrows. "I remember. He looked... conflicted when I showed up."

"Maybe he's not as on board with Thorne—Aldrich—as we thought," I muse, the pieces slowly clicking into place. "What if he's starting to have doubts?"

Malrik's expression is skeptical, but there's a glimmer of consideration in his eyes. "It's possible," he admits reluctantly. "Darian seems ambitious, but I don't think he's cruel for cruelty's sake. If he's realized the full extent of Aldrich's plans..."

"You're forgetting he one thousand percent has all the feels for Kaia." Finn smirks, but he doesn't actually seem happy about it. "Maybe she's got him questioning things."

Trying to change the subject "There is definitely something wrong with his shadows. I don't know what but they're not normal, but in a bad way."

"Right now, we don't have the time," Aspen interjects. "If Darian's a wildcard, we need to figure out how to use him—or neutralize him—before Aldrich does."

"Well," Finn says with forced lightness, "guess we know what he's been doing for the last twenty years. Teaching shadow magic to teenagers. Totally normal career change for an evil cultist."

My shadows coil anxiously while Mouse growls low in his throat. Bob attempts to herd everyone away from the door while Patricia frantically updates her notes.

"The trial," I realize. "He's been planning this for decades. Waiting for..."

"For you," Aspen finishes. "For someone with the right power. The right connection to the Heart."

"We have to tell someone," Torric insists.

"Who?" Malrik's laugh is bitter. "The Headmaster, who hired him? The other professors, who've worked with him for years? We have no proof beyond an old photo and a signature."

"Then we run," Finn says. "Get Kaia far from here before the new moon."

"He'd find me," I say, certainty settling cold in my chest. "He's been three steps ahead this whole time. Running would just put everyone else in danger."

"So we what?" Torric demands. "Just let you face him alone?"

"No," Malrik says with quiet steel. "We prepare. We train. And we make sure that when he makes his move, he finds out exactly how dangerous shadow magic can be."

Finn's hand finds mine, squeezing. "Well, when you put it that way, it almost sounds fun."

"This isn't a joke—"

"I know." Finn's eyes are fierce. "But if we're going up against an immortal death cultist, I'm doing it with style."

Despite everything, I feel my lips twitch. My shadows seem to rally, straightening their posture as Bob starts organizing what appears to be a tactical briefing.

"We need more information," Aspen says. "About Aldrich, the Heart, and the ritual. If there's anything we've missed, we have to find it now."

"Split up," Malrik orders, his tone sharp with resolve. "Twins, back to the archives. Finn and I will take the shadow wing's restricted section. Kaia—"

"Should stay here," Finn interrupts, glancing at me. "We can't risk Aldrich getting to her."

"I'll stay with her," Mouse's voice echoes in our heads, cutting through the tension.

The room goes dead silent. Even my shadows freeze mid-motion, Bob dropping the tactical map he was creating while Patricia's notes scatter like startled birds. The new, smaller shadows seem to reanimate, quickly getting into a formation "WTF?" spelled out with their bodies.

Slowly, as one, we all turn to stare at Mouse, who sits calmly grooming his paw on Malrik's desk.

I don't know whether to laugh or cry. My heart soars and shatters at the same time as his voice echoes in my head. My entire body starts to shake.

"What," Torric says faintly, "the actual hell."

"Did everyone else hear..." Finn waves vaguely at his head. "Or am I finally cracking?"

"If you're cracking, we all are," Aspen says, looking as rattled as I've ever seen him.

Malrik's eyes narrow. "You've been able to speak this entire time?"

Mouse fixes him with a violet stare. "Obviously."

"Obviously," Finn repeats in a slightly hysterical voice. "Right. Obviously the shadow panther talks. Why not? Makes perfect sense. Bob, buddy, you got anything to add? A sonnet maybe? A dramatic monologue?"

Bob shakes his head emphatically while Finnick mimes zipping his lips.

"Mouse?" I manage, finding my voice at last. "How... why now?"

He leaps down from the desk, padding over to wind around my legs. "Because now you need to hear me. "Things are worse than you know, little one." Mouse's voice is grave. "That binding symbol you found? It's just the beginning. There are older, darker things than Mikhael Aldrich, and they're all watching you, Kaia. Waiting."

"Worse than our professor being an immortal death cultist?" Finn asks. "Because that feels pretty peak worse."

"There are older, darker things than Mikhael Aldrich," Mouse says, his voice low and almost reverent, like the weight of the knowledge itself presses on him. "And they're all watching you, Kaia. Waiting." The words seep into the air, heavy and inescapable, leaving a chill that makes my shadows tighten protectively around me.

"Right," Torric says after a long moment. "So the cat talks. And knows things. Great. Fantastic. I'm going to need a drink."

"Drinking is not the answer," Aspen reminds him automatically, still staring at Mouse.

"The cat. Is. TALKING."

"Mouse," Malrik says with forced calm, "what exactly are you?"

Those violet eyes meet his. "A guardian. A guide. A piece of the puzzle you're all trying to solve." He pauses, his gaze turning distant. "I've seen this cycle before, in shadows cast long before Kaia's time. Those who reach too far always forget how far shadows stretch. It's a lesson Aldrich will learn too late."

The cryptic weight of his words settles heavily over the room, leaving a chill that makes my shadows tighten protectively around me.

Finn opens his mouth, probably to ask more questions, but Mouse cuts him off.

"Time is short. Go. I'll explain more when you return."

"He's right," I say, though my head is spinning. "We need those answers."

"We're coming back," Finn says again, squeezing my hand. His eyes flick to Malrik, something heated in his gaze. "And then we're finishing that conversation too."

My shadows flutter despite the tension while Mouse radiates smug approval.

"Go," I manage. "Before I change my mind about letting you all play hero."

I glance at each of them—Finn, with his easy grin masking an unrelenting loyalty; Malrik, with his constant vigilance and quiet strength; Torric, burning with righteous anger; Aspen, always steady, his mind working ten steps ahead. My shadows weave around me, drawn to their resolve like moths to flame.

I might have dragged them into this, but I won't let them fall for my mistakes. We'll come through this together. We have to.

Chapter 62

Kaia

The door closes behind them with a soft click that feels deafening in the sudden silence. I sink into Malrik's desk chair, my shadows coiling restlessly around my ankles, more agitated than I've ever seen them. Even Bob, usually so stoic, ripples with obvious tension.

"You could speak this whole time." The words scrape my throat. Mouse meets my gaze steadily, those familiar violet eyes now holding centuries of unspoken knowledge.

"Only when absolutely necessary," he says, voice deep and resonant in a way that makes my shadows stir. "Your mother's magic gave me form, but you gave me purpose. I was bound to guide you when the time was right—not before."

"My mother?" The word feels foreign on my tongue.

"Solveig."

The name hits like a physical blow. Linda wraps protectively around my shoulders while Patricia's frantic note-taking becomes almost desperate, as if trying to capture every detail of this moment. I grip the arms of the chair, seeking any anchor I can find.

"That's impossible. The Valkyries were ancient warriors. They vanished centuries ago."

Mouse's gaze never wavers. "Think deeper, Kaia. The dreams that wake you. The way shadows move as extensions of your will. The Heart of Eternity—why do you think it chose you?"

My hand flies to the necklace, its warmth pulsing against my palm like a second heartbeat. "If my mother was a Valkyrie... if I was there when they fell..." The implications crash over me in waves.

"Look at your shadows," Mouse says softly. "Really look at them."

I force myself to focus, truly seeing them for the first time. Bob's movements become precise, almost military. Patricia's note-taking transforms into something purposeful, archival. Even Finnick's chaos feels directed, intentional. They aren't just shadows. They never were.

"They're them," I whisper, understanding shattering everything I thought I knew. "The Valkyries who fell that night. They bound themselves to me."

I barely make it to the waste bin before I'm sick. Bob steadies me with an awkward pat while Finnick fetches water, their familiar personalities now carrying the weight of lost warriors. Mouse waits as I try to process this impossible truth that rewrites my entire existence.

"The others," I manage, wiping my mouth. "They can't know about this."

Mouse's violet eyes narrow. "They're already involved."

"Then I'll uninvolve them." I push to my feet, my shadows—the fallen Valkyries—rippling with shared agitation. "If Alekir's hunted me across centuries, I won't paint targets on their backs."

"Your mother and father tried to face him alone," Mouse says, his tone gentle but firm. "That's why she had to send you away. Why the Valkyries fell one by one. Don't repeat her mistake."

The words hit like a blade between my ribs. "That's not fair."

"Neither is taking away their choice to stand with you." Mouse's tail wraps around my wrist, the touch grounding me like it has countless times before. "They'll be hunted either way now. The only question is whether you face what's coming together or alone."

I close my eyes, feeling the weight of centuries pressing down. The warmth of my shadows—my mother's fallen sisters—wraps around me like an embrace, their strength flowing into mine.

"Tell me everything," I whisper. "What really happened that night?"

Mouse settles more comfortably, his violet eyes distant with memory. "Your mother was different from the other Valkyries. While most saw their duty as simply guiding souls between realms, Solveig and your father, Idris, believed in something more. But you—" his gaze sharpens "—you changed everything. A child born with both Valkyrie and shadow magic. The first of your kind."

The shadows draw closer as Mouse continues, his voice thick with old grief. "Alekir doesn't want to destroy you, Kaia. He wants to claim you, to make your magic his own. He sees you as the key to reshaping the realms in his image."

"The sanctuary fell quickly that night. Your father fought with his light-blade while Solveig carried you to safety. Their sisters followed, shielding your escape with their lives. But your mother knew what had to be done."

Mouse's voice softens to barely more than a whisper. "The Heart of Eternity wasn't just power—it was a key. Your mother used it to tear through time itself, but such magic demands a price. The Valkyries gave not just their lives but their very souls, binding themselves to you through the Heart. The soul-wisps that once sang to you became shadows, ensuring you'd never truly be alone."

The truth settles over me, heavy and inexorable. Tears fall before I can stop them, not just for their sacrifice, but for the depth of love that would make warriors bind their souls to protect a child. My shadows press closer, their movements gentle now, comforting. Bob stands at attention like the warrior he must have been, while Patricia's note-taking becomes a sacred record of their sacrifice.

"Your mother's magic protected you not just by sending you through time, but by veiling your memories. The forgetting wasn't just trauma—it was a shield."

Footsteps echo in the hallway, drawing closer.

"They're coming," Mouse says, his tail flicking toward the door. "And they deserve to know. Eventually." The violet in his eyes gleams with ancient wisdom. "But that choice, little shadow-walker, is yours."

I look down at my hands, where shadow magic dances like restless waves across my skin. My mother's gift, my father's legacy, my inheritance. The thought of losing any of them—Finn's irreverent humor, Malrik's steady strength, the twins' unwavering loyalty—cuts deeper than any blade.

The door creaks open before I can decide. Finn's voice, light and teasing, floats in first, followed by the familiar cadence of Malrik's footsteps. Aspen and Torric aren't far behind, their presence filling the room like the promise of a storm.

Chapter 63
MALRIK

Something's wrong.

I notice it the moment we return to my bedroom. Kaia sits too straight in my chair, her shoulders stiff and her hands gripping the armrests like they're the only things holding her together. Her shadows coil unnaturally tight around her, pulsing faintly with a tension that seems to echo her heartbeat. Her breathing is shallow like she's trying not to crack under some invisible weight. Even Bob, usually so militant in his posture, seems to vibrate with barely contained emotion. Mouse perches on my desk like a sentinel, his violet eyes holding centuries more weight than they did an hour ago.

But it's the tear tracks on Kaia's cheeks that truly catch my attention. She's tried to wipe them away, but I know her beautiful face too well by now. Know the way she holds herself when she's carrying something too heavy to share.

"Well," Finn announces, dropping dramatically into the nearest chair, "Thorne's definitely evil. Like, cartoonishly evil. Who knew?" He pauses, finally noticing the tension in the room. "What'd we miss?"

Kaia's shadows flicker—not their usual playful movement, but something deeper, almost reverent. Their edges shimmer faintly, like the remnants of an aura trying to break through. They move with a quiet purpose, coiling and shifting as though performing a silent ritual. The air around them feels charged, a hum of something sacred and untouchable, making the room seem smaller, more fragile. She meets my gaze for a fraction of a second before looking away, but it's enough. Something fundamental has shifted in those violet eyes.

"Kaia." I keep my voice carefully neutral, though my own shadows stir restlessly. "What happened?"

"I—" She stops, glancing at Mouse. Some silent communication passes between them, heavy with meaning I can't quite grasp. The shadows press closer to her, and for the first time, I notice they're moving with purpose rather than chaos. Almost like they're trying to shield her from us.

"You don't have to tell us," Aspen says quietly from his position by the door. Always the steady one.

Torric, predictably, disagrees. "Like hell she doesn't. What's going on?"

"It's complicated," Kaia says, and her voice carries new weight. "And if I tell you... if you know..." She swallows hard. "It puts you all in more danger."

"We're already in danger," I point out, moving closer despite the way her shadows bristle. "Thorne made sure of that."

"This is different." She looks down at her hands, where shadow magic dances across her skin in patterns I've never seen before. "This is..." Her voice cracks.

Finn stands, his usual humor gone. "Whatever it is, we're not going anywhere. Right?" He glances at me, and for once we're in perfect agreement.

I watch Kaia wage some internal battle, her shadows reflecting her turmoil. Mouse sits unnaturally still, waiting. Finally, she takes a deep breath.

"What do you know," she asks quietly, "about the fall of the Valkyries?"

Her question hits like a lightning strike. My breath catches as the pieces start aligning, a puzzle I hadn't known I was solving until now. The weight in her voice is palpable, each word steeped in an ancient grief there's no way I can comprehend. My own shadows stir restlessly, mirroring the sudden tension in my chest. I don't have answers, but something tells me this moment will change everything.

The words seem to draw all the air from the room. Even Torric goes still.

"The Valkyries?" Torric scoffs, but I catch the way his hand tightens on his sword hilt. "What do ancient myths have to do with—"

"They weren't myths." My voice comes out sharper than intended. The pieces are falling into place—her unique shadow magic, the Heart of Eternity, the way her shadows sometimes move like they have centuries of purpose behind them.

Kaia's eyes meet mine again, and this time I see it: the weight of ages, of a truth too vast to fully comprehend. "No," she says softly. "They weren't."

"But they vanished centuries ago," Aspen says, his analytical mind working through the implications. "The records say they were betrayed by someone named... Oh shit."

"Alekir," Kaia finishes, her shadows writhing at the name. Bob moves into what I now recognize as a defensive formation, while Patricia's note-taking becomes almost frantic. "He didn't just betray them. He destroyed them. Turned their own souls into Nightwraiths. And he did it because..." She falters.

"Because of you," I finish quietly. The room goes deadly quiet.

Finn drops back into his chair with uncharacteristic grace. "Okay, I'm going to need someone to explain why that's not as impossible as it sounds.

Because unless you're secretly several centuries old—" He stops, looking at her. "Holy shit."

"The Heart of Eternity." I take a step closer, my movements slow, deliberate, as if approaching something fragile and sacred. My voice lowers, almost reverent, ignoring the way her shadows bristle like an instinctive barrier. "It's not just a necklace, is it? It's a key. A way to move through—"

"Time itself," Kaia whispers. "My mother used it to save me. To send me forward, beyond Alekir's reach. But the magic... it required a price."

The shadows around her feet press closer, their movements heavy with a weight I can't fully grasp. I watch them ripple, deliberate and protective, and realize something is on the edge of revelation—but it's not mine to claim. Kaia's voice trembles as she finally speaks.

"The Valkyries who fell that night," she says, looking down at the small shadow army surrounding her. "They're not just shadows. They're my mother's sisters-in-arms. Their souls bound themselves to me through the Heart of Eternity."

Mouse's voice cuts through the silence, deliberate and steady. "And in doing so, they bound themselves to the only weapon Alekir could never corrupt. You." He meets each of us with that unyielding violet gaze. "Alekir sees her not just as a threat but as a key. The key to what he couldn't finish centuries ago."

Kaia glances at him, her expression unreadable but heavy with gratitude—or perhaps burden.

"I don't know if I'll ever feel worthy of their sacrifice," she continues, her voice breaking. "But knowing they're here—that they chose to stay—it's my reminder that I have to be. For them."

Tears glisten in her eyes, but she blinks them away quickly, as if allowing herself to cry would shatter the fragile composure she's clinging to. In that moment, my heart breaks for her and all she's truly lost. Centuries of grief and guilt have been woven into the foundation of who she is, and yet, somehow, she's still standing. Still fighting.

Her shadows tighten around her, and for the first time, I notice the subtle grace in their movements—the way they shift closer like an unspoken vow, bound by love and loyalty that transcends death. It isn't just magic; it's devotion. And Kaia, despite the weight of that devotion, carries it like a shield. Not for herself, but for us.

I can't stop the surge of instinct that runs through me—a need to close the space between us, to say or do something to lift even a fraction of the weight she carries. I step forward, reaching out before I fully think it through.

"Don't." Kaia's voice cracks, sharp enough to halt me mid-step. She doesn't look up, her hands clenched into fists against her lap. "Please. It's hard enough just..." Her breath shudders, and for a moment, it seems like she might break apart entirely. "I'm telling you this because Mouse thinks you deserve to know. Because you're already involved, and it's too late to protect you. But the fewer details you have, the safer you'll be."

"Like hell," Finn says, standing again. "You don't get to drop 'actually I'm a time-traveling Valkyrie' on us and then hold back the good stuff."

A ghost of a smile touches Kaia's lips, but her eyes remain haunted. "Finn..."

"No, he's right." Torric pushes off from the wall he's been leaning against. "We're already marked for death by your psychotic professor. Might as well know why."

"You don't understand." Kaia stands, her shadows swirling around her like a cloak. For a moment, I swear I see the ghost of wings in their movement. "Alekir spent centuries hunting Valkyries. He corrupted their souls, twisted them into monsters, all because he wanted..." She touches the Heart of Eternity. "He wanted what I can do. What I am. And if he finds out I'm here, that I survived..."

"Then we'll kill him," I say simply. The words come out steady, but beneath them I feel a surge of unshakable resolve. This isn't bravado; it's a promise. My shadows stir in agreement, mirroring the certainty hardening in my chest. Failure isn't an option—not this time.

She stares at me, those violet eyes wide with surprise. Behind her, I notice Mouse's approving nod.

"Just like that?"

"Just like that," Finn agrees, moving to stand beside me. His shoulder brushes mine, a casual touch that carries surprising weight. "We're kind of invested now. In case you hadn't noticed."

"Also," Torric adds with a feral grin, "I've been looking for someone worth fighting. An immortal soul-stealing psychopath sounds perfect."

"Idiots." Kaia's voice shakes, but there's something like desperate hope beneath the fear. "All of you. Complete idiots."

"Yet here we are," Aspen says quietly. He hasn't moved from his post by the door, but his calm voice carries through the room. "Though I have to ask—if Alekir's truly immortal, how exactly are we planning to stop him?"

A fair question. One that makes Kaia's shadows coil tighter.

Mouse's voice cuts through the tension, low and deliberate. "Alekir is no god," he says, his tone sharper than I've ever heard it. "He is a parasite. Sustained by the souls he has corrupted and twisted into fuel for his own power. Every life he has stolen keeps him tethered to existence, clinging to strength that isn't his." Kaia glances at Mouse, her expression caught between gratitude and something closer to fear. "The Valkyries he destroyed," she adds quietly, her hand moving almost unconsciously to where her shadows gather. "Their strength is part of him now. But the Heart of Eternity—" She hesitates, swallowing hard. "It was the one thing he could never touch."

"You're holding back," I say, watching her carefully. The shadows shift, and I catch Bob making what looks suspiciously like a shushing motion at the others. "There's more."

"There's always more," she says with a bitter laugh. "But trust me, the less you know about exactly what Alekir can do, the better chance you have of—"

"If you say 'surviving' one more time, I'm going to scream," Finn interrupts. He steps closer to Kaia, ignoring the way her shadows ripple warningly. "We get it. You're trying to protect us. Very noble. Very tragic. But has it occurred to you that maybe, just maybe, we want to protect you too?"

Something flickers in Kaia's eyes—pain or memory, I'm not sure which. "The last people who tried to protect me ended up—" She gestures at her shadows, and the weight of centuries hangs in that simple movement.

"Bound to you forever?" I ask quietly. "Standing guard over the thing they died protecting? That doesn't sound like failure to me."

Kaia's breath catches. Even Mouse looks surprised, his violet eyes narrowing thoughtfully.

"They're right," Aspen says, finally moving away from the door. "Whatever's coming, we face it together. All of us." He glances at his brother. "Right?"

Torric rolls his eyes. "Obviously. Though I still want to know how exactly a baby Valkyrie ended up with an army of shadow warriors for babysitters."

Mouse lets out a low rumble, his tail flicking with deliberate precision. "They were warriors once. And if they choose, they will be again."

"They're not—" Kaia starts, then stops as one of her shadows—Patricia, I believe, makes an unmistakably rude gesture at Torric. Despite everything, a reluctant smile tugs at her lips. "Okay, maybe they are a little bit like that."

"See?" Finn grins. "Even Bob agrees with us. And Bob is never wrong."

The shadow in question straightens proudly while Mouse makes a sound suspiciously like a snort.

I watch it all—the way Kaia's tension slowly eases, how her shadows remain protective but less frantically so, the careful way Mouse observes our reactions. There's still more she isn't telling us. Much more, if the weight in her eyes is any indication.

But for now, maybe this is enough. This careful balance between truth and protection, between past and present. Whatever truths Kaia hasn't yet shared, I'll wait for them. Because right now, the only thing that matters is showing her she isn't alone in carrying this weight."

Finn grins. "But seriously, if those shadows can fly, I'm calling dibs on the first aerial shadow ride.

Chapter 64
MALRIK

Hours of planning and questions have taken their toll. I watch as Kaia's responses grow slower, her words dragging like they're weighted down. Her shoulders sag, and her head tilts slightly to the side, as though even holding it upright takes too much effort. Her shadows droop with exhaustion, their once-fluid movements now sluggish and uneven, pooling at her feet. Even Bob's militant posture has softened, though he still maintains his guard near the door with Carl and Steve at his side.

"Enough," I say finally, cutting off Finn's fifteenth question about time travel logistics. "She needs rest."

"I'm fine," Kaia protests, but the way she's curled deeper into my armchair betrays her.

"You're barely conscious," I point out. "And my bed's right there."

She blinks owlishly at the bed in the adjacent chamber, as if just noticing it. "I can't take your—"

"You can and you will," I say, my tone firm but not unkind. I gesture to the others, meeting each of their eyes briefly to drive home the importance of rest. "We'll finish discussing theories of temporal magic and immortal soul-stealers tomorrow." Beneath the decisiveness in my words is a quiet resolve, a silent promise that ensuring Kaia's safety is more important than any unanswered questions.

Aspen, ever practical, nods. "He's right. We all need clear heads for this."

"But—" Finn starts, then catches my look. "Right. Sleep. Good plan. Excellent plan, even. Though I still want to know about the wings—"

"Tomorrow," I say firmly.

They file out, though not without protest—Finn's theatrical, Torric's gruff, Aspen's concerned. Mouse watches it all with patience in his violet eyes, then hops down from my desk.

"I'll stand guard," he says, and I'm still not used to hearing that voice in my head. He pads to the doorway, tail swishing. "The shadows will wake us if anything approaches."

Kaia doesn't protest as I help her to her feet, which tells me more about her exhaustion than anything else. Her shadows follow sluggishly as I guide her to my bed.

"I really can't—" she starts, but I silence her with a look.

"You can barely stand. Sleep."

She sinks onto the bed, immediately curling into the sheets and something in my chest tightens at how small she looks suddenly. The weight of centuries seems to press down on her shoulders, and I find myself wanting to shield her from it, however impossible that might be.

I turn to leave, but her hand shoots out, catching my wrist. "Wait." Her voice is barely a whisper, fragile as glass. "Please... don't go?" The vulnerability in her tone slices through me. My chest tightens, and for a moment, the weight of her trust feels overwhelming. Her shadows curl around both our hands, their warmth almost pleading, and I feel an unspoken promise settle deep within me: I will not fail her.

"I'll stay," I say softly, and sink down to sit on the edge of the bed. "Sleep, Kaia. I'm not going anywhere."

She tugs weakly at my arm until I give in, hesitating for only a moment before stretching out beside her. The warmth of her shadows brushes against me as she turns, curling into my side, and I feel the steady rise and fall of her breath against my chest. The intimacy of the moment is startling, but I let it settle over me like her shadows—gentle, protective, and binding. Mouse settles at the foot of the bed, his violet eyes gleaming in the darkness.

"I'm sorry," she mumbles against my shoulder. "For not telling you sooner. For trying to—"

"Sleep," I say again, gentler this time. "We have time."

She makes a sound that might be a laugh or a sob. "Time. Right."

But her breathing evens out quickly, exhaustion finally winning. I lie there in the darkness, watching her shadows—the fallen Valkyries—maintain their silent vigil. Bob takes up a guard position by the window while Patricia continues taking notes, though more drowsily now. Even Finnick has settled, curled protectively near Kaia's feet with Linda. The rest of her shadows curled protectively around her, their once-tense movements now softened into something almost tender. They seemed to hold her together in ways she couldn't yet voice.

I should be processing what we've learned. Planning our next move. Considering the implications of a time-traveling Valkyrie with an army of shadow-bound souls in my arms.

Instead, I find myself memorizing the way she fits against me—the gentle weight of her body, the way her warmth seeps through my shirt, grounding me. Her breath is steady now, soft against my chest, and I marvel at the trust it takes to let go so completely. The shadows cocooning us add a quiet hum of energy, a living testament to the bond we've only just begun to understand. Her hand still grips my shirt, as if afraid I'll disappear.

"I'm not going anywhere," I whisper again, though I know she can't hear me. "Any of us."

Mouse's approval rumbles softly through my mind as the shadows settle around us, keeping watch while their Valkyrie finally rests.

Chapter 65
MALRIK

I wake to the soft glow of dawn filtering through the curtains, painting the room in hues of gold and rose. The air feels warmer than usual, the faint scent of lavender lingering. For a moment, I'm disoriented, unused to the warm weight pressed against me. Then I remember.

Kaia.

She's still curled into my side, her face nestled against my chest. One of her hands is fisted in my shirt, as if even in sleep she's afraid I'll leave. Her golden hair spills across the pillow, catching the early morning light and turning it to liquid fire. I allow myself the luxury of simply watching her, memorizing every detail of this stolen moment.

Her lashes flutter against her cheeks, impossibly long and delicate, casting faint shadows on her skin. The usual furrow between her brows has smoothed out, leaving her features untroubled. The Heart of Eternity rests at her throat, its amethyst glow softly pulsing in harmony with the dawn's gentle light.

I trace the curve of her cheekbone with my gaze, marveling at the softness of her skin. A light dusting of freckles crosses the bridge of her nose—I've never noticed them before. They're utterly charming, a small thing that only makes her more beautiful.

Kaia stirs, her lashes fluttering like wings against her cheeks. I hold my breath, desperate to freeze this fragile moment in time. But it slips away as her violet eyes blink open, hazy with the remnants of sleep, then widening with realization as her gaze meets mine.

"Malrik?" Her voice is husky, confused. She starts to pull away, but I tighten my arm around her waist.

"It's alright," I murmur. "You're safe."

She relaxes incrementally, though I can feel the tension thrumming through her body. Her shadows coil closer, protective.

"I didn't mean to fall asleep on you," she says, a blush staining her cheeks. "You should have woken me."

I arch an eyebrow. "And miss the chance to be your personal pillow? Never."

That earns me a reluctant smile, though it fades quickly. Reality seeps back in like an unwelcome tide, and I see the centuries resettle on her shoulders, dimming the light in her eyes.

I don't want that for her. I want to keep the weight of everything she's carrying off her shoulders for just a little while longer. To preserve this fragile moment where she's just Kaia, warm and soft in my arms, not a time-traveling Valkyrie with the fate of realms on her shoulders.

Before I can second-guess myself, I lean in, my heart hammering in my chest, and press my lips to hers.

For a heartbeat, she goes utterly still. Then as if she's won some internal battle, she melts against me, her lips parting on a soft gasp. I cup her face gently, my thumb tracing the curve of her cheekbone as I deepen the kiss. She tastes of starlight and hidden magic, of secrets whispered in shadow.

Her hands slide up my chest, tangling in my hair, anchoring me closer. The Heart of Eternity pulses warmly between us, its amethyst glow an unspoken witness.

I pour everything I can't say into the kiss. My awe at her strength. My admiration for her fierce protectiveness. The way her smile makes my heart stutter. How seeing her in pain makes me want to tear the world apart.

When we finally break apart, we're both breathing hard. Kaia's eyes are wide, pupils blown dark with desire. A pretty flush stains her cheeks, and her lips are swollen from our kiss.

She's never looked more beautiful.

I'm lost in the violet depths of Kaia's eyes when she suddenly surges forward, capturing my lips in a searing kiss. All thoughts flee my mind as she presses against me, her body molding to mine like she was made to fit there. Her fingers find my hair again, nails scraping lightly against my scalp in a way that sends shivers down my spine.

I respond with equal fervor, one hand cupping the back of her head while the other splays across her lower back, drawing her impossibly closer.

She nips at my bottom lip, and I groan, the sound swallowed by her mouth. I trace the seam of her lips with my tongue, savoring her gasp as she grants me entry. I could drown in this kiss and die happy.

Kaia shifts, pushing me onto my back and straddling my hips in one fluid motion. The new position brings our bodies flush together, and I have to break the kiss, panting as desire courses through me. She looks down at me, hair tousled and the growing flush of her skin only makes me want to see more of her.

"Kaia," I breathe, reverent. My hands smooth up her thighs as she rocks against me, drawing a low groan from my throat. I'm so hard for her, and I don't think she knows half of what she does to me. She looks like a goddess above me as she leans down to capture my lips again.

I lose myself in the taste of her, the feel of her soft skin under my palms. My fingers trace the curve of her waist, dipping under the hem of her shirt to caress bare skin. Kaia shivers at my touch, pressing closer. Her shadows swirl around us, their excitement palpable in the air.

She breaks the kiss to trail her lips along my jaw, nipping lightly at my earlobe. I tilt my head back with a gasp, exposing my throat to her exploring mouth. Her teeth graze my pulse point and I grip her hips tightly, fighting the urge to flip us over and pin her to the bed.

"Kaia," I say as she rocks against me again. The friction is exquisite torture. "We should slow down..."

She silences me with another kiss. "I don't want to slow down," she murmurs against my lips. Her fingers make quick work of the buttons on my shirt, pushing it open to run her hands over my bare chest.

Just as my hands slide to the small of her back, a subtle movement at the edge of my vision catches my attention. But it's too late.

The door bursts open...

"Rise and shine, lovebirds! We've got evil professors to—

I freeze, my hands still gripping Kaia's hips as Finn steps into the room. Kaia lets out a startled yelp, trying to roll off me but getting tangled in the sheets. She ends up sprawled across my chest, her face blazing red as she buries it against my neck.

"Well, well, well," Finn drawls, leaning casually against the doorframe. His green eyes gleam with mischief as he takes in the scene. "Looks like I interrupted something... delicious."

I half-expect Kaia to scramble away, stammering apologies or excuses. Instead, she lifts her head slowly, fixing Finn with a glare sharp enough to cut steel. Her shadows coil protectively around us both, their movements deliberate yet tinged with amusement. Her shadows sharpen for a moment at the intrusion and then slowly start reaching out for Finn. Drawn to him as much as she's pulled to me.

"Finn," Kaia says, her voice dangerously low. "Get. Out."

But Finn, being Finn, only grins wider. He steps further into the room, shutting the door and dropping into my desk chair with exaggerated nonchalance. His boots hit the desk as he props his feet up, radiating defiance. "Why would I leave," he muses, "when the view in here is so much better?"

I should be annoyed at the interruption. I should be embarrassed to be caught like this. Yet all I can focus on is the way Kaia's flushed skin glows, her tousled hair framing her face like a halo. Even disheveled and glaring, she's breathtaking. But then there's Finn, sitting there with that infuriating grin. My thoughts flicker to him and the way his confidence electrifies the air. I bite the inside of my cheek to rein in the surge of something I'm not sure if I'm ready for.

"Finn," I growl, sitting up and pulling Kaia protectively against my chest. "This isn't the time for your games."

Finn's grin widens, his green eyes sparkling with wicked delight. "Oh, but I think it's the perfect time," he counters, resting his hands behind his head. "You two were about to make some... fascinating decisions. As your dear friend, I feel it's my duty to ensure you're thinking clearly."

"Void help me," I growl, but even as I hint for Finn to leave, part of me can't tear my gaze from the way his green eyes gleaming with unrelenting mischief. The current between the three of us is undeniable, crackling with possibilities.

Chapter 66
KAIA

I'm caught between mortification and lingering desire, my body still thrumming with heat even as embarrassment floods my cheeks. Malrik's arms tighten protectively around me, the tension in his muscles unmistakable. But there's something else—a spark crackling in the air, growing sharper under Finn's watchful gaze.

"Thinking clearly?" I manage to sputter, my voice higher than usual. "What are you even talking about?"

Finn's grin softens, his mischief giving way to something rawer, more vulnerable. As he moves closer, my breath catches at the intensity in his emerald eyes. "I'm talking about us, Kaia. All of us."

My heart pounds so loudly I'm certain they can both hear it. Shadows coil around us, reflecting the atmosphere. Even Bob seems unusually alert, his inky form rippling like the surface of a storm-touched lake.

"Finn..." Malrik's voice is low and warning, though I can feel the subtle shift in his posture. He angles slightly toward Finn at the same time I do. The current between the three of us crackling like fire on dry leaves.

Finn takes a steadying breath, running a hand through his tousled copper hair. "I mean it. I have feelings for both of you. And I'm pretty sure you both feel the same way about me." His gaze flicks between us. "Just like I know you're crazy about each other."

The silence thickens, heavy with possibilities I hadn't dared to consider. Malrik's arm tightens around my waist again as Finn steps closer, his usual confidence softened by something vulnerable.

"You can't just burst in here and say things like that," I manage, though my voice lacks conviction. The Heart of Eternity seems to hum against my throat, in sync with my racing heart.

"Why not?" Finn challenges, standing just close enough that I can see the flecks of gold in his green eyes. "Because it's complicated? Because we're in the middle of a crisis? Or because you're afraid I'm right?"

Malrik's fingers twitch against my side, his voice gruff. "Finn…"

"No," Finn says firmly. "I'm done pretending. Bob's been trying to tell us for weeks—haven't you, Bob?"

To my utter disbelief, Bob nods solemnly. Patricia and Finnick bob in agreement behind him, their shadowy forms almost smug. A laugh bubbles up in my throat despite the tension.

"You're taking relationship advice from shadows?" I ask, but the words don't carry the bite I intend. They're too close to the truth, and my shadows have always known me better than I know myself.

"They see everything," Finn says, his voice softer now. "The way Malrik watches me when he thinks no one's looking. The way you light up when I make you laugh. They see how we all orbit each other like stars caught in the same gravitational pull."

I swallow hard as Finn kneels beside the bed, bringing himself level with us. His proximity sends my pulse racing again. "Tell me I'm wrong," he says, his voice gentle but unrelenting. "Tell me you don't feel this too."

Malrik exhales sharply, his voice rough. "Of course we feel it." He glances at me, his silver eyes searching. For a moment, I think he might stop, but something in my expression—maybe the way my breath hitches—seems to give him the answer he needs. "But that doesn't make it simple."

"When has anything about us ever been simple?" Finn counters, brushing a strand of hair from my face. His fingers tremble slightly—a crack in his facade that twists something in my chest. "We live in a world of shadow magic and time-traveling Valkyries. Maybe it's time we stopped expecting things to make conventional sense."

I lean into his touch before I can stop myself, and Malrik's sharp intake of breath sends a thrill down my spine. The air hums with tension, and my shadows tighten their protective cocoon around us.

"What exactly are you proposing?" I whisper, though I think I already know the answer.

Finn's smile is softer now, his usual bravado tempered by sincerity. "I'm proposing we stop pretending. Stop fighting this." His gaze flicks to Malrik. "All of this."

Mouse chirps softly from the foot of the bed, his violet eyes gleaming with what feels like approval. My shadows coil closer, their movements languid and content.

Wrapped between these two men, I finally let myself stop fighting the pull. I'm tired of resisting, tired of pretending not to feel the electricity that arcs between us. "Okay," I breathe, the word barely audible.

Finn's grin lights up the room, hope blazing in his emerald eyes. "Okay?"

I catch his shirt in my hand, pulling him closer. "Okay."

He moves closer, the mattress dips under his weight, and I find myself caught between him and Malrik—not trapped, but grounded. My shadows move with a contented hum around us, and I swear Bob looks smug.

"So," Finn says, his usual playful tone softened by something deeper, "do I get a good morning kiss too, or do I have to wait my turn?"

Malrik's chest rumbles behind me with what might be a laugh. "Subtle as ever."

"You love it," Finn counters, though there's a flicker of vulnerability in his green eyes that makes my chest ache.

Before doubt can creep in, I lean forward and press my lips to his. The kiss is gentle, exploratory—nothing like the heated exchanges with Malrik earlier. Finn's hand comes up to cup my cheek, his touch steady and warm. Behind me, Malrik's arms tighten around my waist, not pulling me away but anchoring me.

When I pull back, Finn's emerald eyes are wide, his trademark grin replaced with something softer. "Wow," he breathes, his voice hushed. "Bob was right about everything."

A laugh bubbles up, and my shadows dance joyfully around us. Even Patricia seems to be scribbling furiously, her shadowy form alive with motion.

"This is insane," I say, though I can't help smiling. "We're in the middle of a war basically. Thorne and Darian are plotting who knows what, the Heart of Eternity is doing... something, and we're—"

"Finding strength," Malrik interrupts, his voice firm. "Together."

Finn nods, his playful expression becoming heated as he reaches out to trace the line of Malrik's jaw. "The world's never going to stop being complicated. But maybe if we stop fighting this, we'll be stronger for it."

Finn leans in, his gaze locked with Malrik's. Time seems to slow as they close the distance, their lips meeting in a kiss that's both tender and charged with restrained passion. Caught between them, I feel the heat of their bodies and the rhythm of their breaths, the moment electric.

The sight makes heat pool low in my stomach. Unable to resist, I lean forward, brushing my lips along the column of Finn's throat. His skin is warm and slightly salty, and the groan that rumbles through him sends a shiver down my spine. My shadows seem to echo my emotions, swirling around us in lazy, approving spirals.

Malrik's hands begin to roam, his touch leaving trails of fire across my skin. His fingers slip under my shirt, grazing my ribs, and I arch into him with a gasp. The Heart of Eternity glows warmly at my throat, as if echoing the harmony in this moment. My shadows coil protectively around all three of us, possessive and affirming, and for the first time in what feels like forever, everything feels... right.

The knock at the door shatters our moment. "Kaia?" Aspen's voice carries through the wood, tight with urgency. "We have a problem."

Dammit.

I open the door to find his usually calm expression drawn with tension. His eyes flick briefly over the three of us, but he merely arches one pale eyebrow before focusing back on the matter at hand.

"Professor Lira sent me. The group's trial has been moved up. We're expected in the arena within the hour."

My heart drops. "What? But we're not supposed to trial until next week—"

"Darian's demanded an immediate trial," Aspen cuts in, his voice low. "As a transfer student, he has the right to challenge his placement. He's chosen our group specifically."

"Of course he has," Malrik mutters behind me.

Finn moves to lean against the doorframe. "Let me guess – there's more."

Aspen nods grimly. "The trial parameters have been altered. Darian's insisting on using shadow constructs for the challenges. Claims it's to test our true abilities." He glances at me meaningfully. "Professor Lira wants to see us immediately. She says there's something we need to know before we enter the arena."

My shadows coil tighter around us, responding to the tension in the room. Even Bob seems unusually agitated, his shadowy form rippling with unease.

"Shadow constructs?" I repeat, feeling the Heart of Eternity warm against my throat. "Those are restricted. Only advanced practitioners can—"

"Darian claims he has no choice," Aspen says, his expression troubled. "That he's being forced to prove himself this way."

Aspen's usual calm is gone, replaced with a sharp edge that I'm not used to seeing. "Lira thinks there's more to this," he says, glancing down the hallway as if expecting someone to appear. "But we can't wait to find out what."

I meet Malrik's silver eyes, then Finn's green ones. We all know what this means – what Darian's really saying between the lines.

"Thorne," I whisper, and my shadows shudder in agreement.

"We should get to Lira," Malrik says, already moving to gather his things. "If anyone knows how to handle corrupted shadow constructs, it's her."

Finn straightens, some of his usual humor bleeding away. "Nothing like a surprise death trial to start the morning. And here I thought catching you two was going to be the highlight of my day." He grins, but it doesn't quite reach his eyes. For a fleeting moment, I see the tension he's trying to mask—the weight of everything we were walking into. My shadows swirl around us protectively as we move to follow Aspen.

"Whatever happens in that arena," Malrik says quietly, his hand finding the small of my back, "we stay together."

"All of us," Finn adds, his shoulder brushing mine as we walk.

I nod, drawing strength from their presence. A trial we shouldn't be facing, shadow constructs that shouldn't exist, and forces we can't yet prove are working against us. But I'll take whatever they throw at me. I refuse to be pushed around any longer.

Chapter 67
KAIA

Professor Lira's office feels different in the early morning light—more shadows than substance, with ancient texts floating on invisible currents and strange artifacts pulsing with barely contained power. The dim light casts everything in an otherworldly glow, amplifying the tension in the room, as if the very walls are holding their breath, waiting for the trial's outcome. She looks up as we enter, her silver-streaked hair loose around her shoulders, as if she's been running her hands through it for hours.

"Close the door," she instructs, skipping pleasantries. My shadows spread out, slithering like ink across the edges of the doorframe, their movements fluid and deliberate, as if testing the space before settling into place. Her lips quirk. "Good instinct."

"Professor—" I start, but she holds up a hand.

"The trial begins in less than an hour." She moves to a shelf, pulling down a heavy tome that writhes under her touch. "Shadow constructs aren't just projections of darkness. They're semi-sentient manifestations, and in the wrong hands—"

"They can be corrupted," Malrik finishes, his voice tight.

Lira's sharp gaze fixes on him. "Yes. And corrupted shadows will seek out the strongest source of shadow magic nearby." Her eyes meet mine. "Like moths to a flame."

My hand drifts to the Heart of Eternity. "Darian's going to use them against me specifically."

Fantastic.

"I think," Lira says carefully, "that Darian may not be the one making these decisions." She opens the book, revealing diagrams of shadow constructs that move across the page like living things. "These constructs respond to whoever holds their binding. And given Darian's... situation, I suspect he's not the one holding the strings."

"Thorne," Finn says, moving closer. "But we can't prove it."

"No. Which is why you need to be prepared." She turns to me fully. "Your shadows, Kaia—they're not just extensions of your magic. They're part of you. True shadows will recognize that. Even corrupted ones will feel the pull of authentic shadow magic."

Bob straightens at this, and Patricia's shadow-notes flutter rapidly, the faint script shifting and twisting as though the shadows themselves are reacting to the conversation, capturing every vital detail.

"So what exactly are you saying?" I ask, watching a diagram show a shadow construct dissolving into mist.

"Trust your instincts in the arena. Trust your shadows." The words hang in the air like a command. I inhale deeply, feeling the weight of her trust settle into my chest, and for a brief moment, the shadows around me ripple with a silent acknowledgment. "Corrupted constructs will try to overwhelm you with force. But real shadow magic isn't about force—it's about harmony. Understanding." Her gaze flicks between all of us. "Connection."

The Heart of Eternity thrums warmly, and I feel Malrik and Finn shift closer.

"And remember this," Lira adds, closing the book with a snap. "Shadow constructs can only corrupt or consume. Your shadows?" She gestures to Bob, who stands taller. "They can create, protect, defend. That's the difference between true shadow magic and whatever twisted version you'll face."

"Just defeat corrupted shadow monsters while avoiding death and proving Darian's being manipulated?" Finn's attempt at lightness doesn't hide his tension. "Easy."

Lira's expression softens. "Watch each other's backs in there. All of you." Her knowing look lingers on the three of us. "Sometimes our greatest strength comes from unexpected connections."

As we turn to leave, she calls out once more. "Kaia?" When I look back, her expression is fierce. "Show them what real shadow magic can do."

We find Aspen and Torric waiting in the hallway. Torric paces like a caged animal while Aspen leans against the wall, his calm exterior betrayed by the tension in his shoulders.

"Well?" Torric demands. "How bad?"

"Corrupted shadow constructs," I reply, watching his expression darken. "Darian's using them for the trial."

"Using them?" Aspen pushes off from the wall. "Or being forced to?"

"Does it matter?" Torric growls, but his anger isn't directed at us. "Either way, we're walking into a trap."

Finn steps forward, his usual grin sharp with purpose. "Then we set a better one."

In an empty classroom, my shadows seal the door while the twins lay out the arena's structure. Aspen breaks down strategies while Torric points out vulnerabilities in the magical barriers.

"The viewing areas here and here," Aspen explains, marking points on his quick diagram. "If—when—something goes wrong, we'll spot it from these vantage points."

"They're warded against shadow magic," he adds quietly. "That's why we should be there. If these constructs are corrupted, they can't reach us."

"Which means we can get word to Lira if things go really wrong," Torric finishes.

My shadows swell with approval—Bob actually salutes the twins while Patricia incorporates their strategy into her endless notes.

"Watch for shadows moving against the current," Aspen tells me softly. "Corrupted constructs can't maintain a natural flow. They'll always move slightly wrong."

As we head for the arena, the Heart of Eternity pulses warmly. Whatever Thorne has planned, whatever trap Darian's been forced to set—we're as ready as we'll ever be.

"Ready?" I ask Malrik and Finn.

Finn's grin is pure mischief. "To face certain death? Always."

Malrik's hand finds mine, squeezing once. "Together."

I catch Aspen and Torric watching us, something unreadable in their expressions. The air feels charged with potential and things unsaid—like unspoken fears of failure, or the weight of truths we're all too afraid to voice. Aspen's blue eyes hold mine for a moment too long, while Torric's usual intensity seems to burn brighter.

"Be careful in there," Aspen says softly, his hand brushing my arm.

"Show them what you're made of," Torric adds, voice rough with emotion he's trying to hide.

My shadows swirl around all five of us for a moment, as if reluctant to break the connection. Then we separate—three to face the trial, two to guard our backs. But the energy between us lingers, full of possibility and unspoken promises.

Chapter 68
KAIA

The arena feels wrong the moment I step inside. The air hangs thick with a metallic tang, each sound echoing unnaturally in the eerie stillness. Shadows pool in the corners, shifting like living things, while my own shadows coil tight around my ankles. Mouse's low growl reverberates off the stone walls. Ahead, Darian stands with Professor Thorne, their practiced calm setting my nerves on edge.

"Our star pupil arrives," Thorne says, voice carrying across the empty space. "With such... interesting companions."

Finn shifts closer on my left, his usual grin hardened to something dangerous. On my right, Malrik's silver eyes narrow as he tracks my shadows' agitated movements.

"Where is everyone?" The emptiness of the arena makes my skin crawl.

"The final trial is more... intimate." Darian steps forward, smile cold and empty. "Just our dark little corner of the academy."

Mouse's growl deepens as Bob surges forward, his edges sharpening with quiet menace. Malrik's hand twitches at his side, the silver of his eyes flashing with cold intensity.

"Funny." Finn's voice lacks its usual warmth. "Don't remember that being in the rules."

"Rules change." Thorne raises his hand, dark energy crackling around his fingers. "Much like loyalties."

Magic thickens the air as my shadows writhe in response. When Darian's eyes track their movements with calculated precision, understanding cuts through me like a blade. "The training sessions," I whisper. "All those times you helped me 'control' them. You weren't teaching me. You were studying them."

His smile turns cruel. "They're fascinating, really. Each one so distinct. The way they respond to fear, to anger... to betrayal." He takes a step closer, and my shadows recoil with what I now recognize as grief. "Did you ever wonder why I pushed you to show me every defensive pattern?"

The Heart of Eternity burns against my chest. "You were documenting them. Learning their every move." I falter. "Their very soul."

"Smart girl." His voice drips with mock praise. "They never trusted me, you know. But you were so desperate to understand your power that you never stopped to really see them."

Bob surges forward, his form shaking with fury. Patricia's movements become sharp, militant, while Finnick's chaos takes on a deadly edge. They move not just to protect me, but with the coordinated precision of warriors.

"Your shadows were right about him." Malrik's certainty grounds me. "Now let's make him regret studying them so... thoroughly."

Finn's hand brushes mine. "Yeah, what Shadow Prince said. Though I vote we skip the inspirational speeches—"

Power explodes through the arena before he can finish. Dark energy crackles from Thorne's hands as my shadows snap up instinctively. The arena doors slam shut with an echoing boom.

"You've trained her well," Thorne says to Darian. "Every instinct, every pattern, documented and analyzed."

But something rises beyond the pain of betrayal—anger, hot and fierce. My shadows respond with something new, flowing together with a deadly grace that feels ancient and familiar.

"You studied their patterns," I say, my voice growing stronger. "But they're not just patterns to follow. They're alive. They choose."

Bob surges forward, splitting into three separate shadows with liquid grace—a move Darian has never seen. His composed facade cracks. "Impossible. The large one only divides under extreme duress—"

"Guess your notes need updating." Finn's grin turns sharp as he summons his chaos magic. "Bob's been practicing."

The other shadows follow Bob's lead, weaving through the air like smoke. Patricia creates false targets while Finnick moves with deadly precision instead of his usual chaos.

"Your research is outdated," Malrik says, his own shadow magic rising to join mine. "They've evolved beyond your calculations."

Darian snarls, his hands blazing with sickly purple light. Each attempt to counter them meets empty air as they flow around his attacks like water around stone.

"Control them!" Thorne shouts, his own dark magic crackling.

"He knew their patterns," I correct, feeling the Heart pulse in time with my shadows' movements. "But patterns can change."

Mouse launches forward, growing larger with each bound, fading in and out of reality. New shadows rise in his wake, drawn to the Heart's power. Darian's careful composure shatters as his documentation proves worthless against their fluid grace.

The shadows surge forward as one, not bound by his limitations. Bob orchestrates their movements like a general commanding legions. Patricia weaves a complex web of shadow-light while Finnick implements chaos with surgical precision. The newer shadows fill the spaces between with deadly grace.

"Your weakness," Darian spits, "was always your fear of their power—"

"No," I cut him off. "My weakness was believing they needed to be contained at all."

The shadows respond to this revelation, moving in a rhythm as old as shadow itself. I'm finally learning to dance with them rather than control them.

Thorne slams his hands together, and the ground trembles. The air shudders with magic so tainted it feels like oil against my skin. The runes on his robes ignite with sickly green light as he summons shadows twisted by corruption—jerking like puppets on invisible strings.

"Let me show you what happens to shadows that are properly broken."

My own shadows recoil from the corrupted ones, radiating distress. The Heart pulses with their agony. "What did you do to them?"

"I made them useful," Thorne snarls. "Unlike your undisciplined pets."

Anger flares in my chest, tempered like steel. "They're not meant to be obedient. They're meant to be free."

The Heart pulses stronger, and the corrupted shadows pause, caught between Thorne's commands and something older, something true.

"Bob," Finn calls out, voice unusually serious. "Show them what willing shadows can do."

Bob approaches the nearest corrupted shadow with an almost reverent touch. For a moment, nothing happens. Then the corrupted shadow shudders, its jagged edges softening.

"No!" Thorne's face contorts. "They belong to me!"

"Shadows don't belong to anyone," I say as understanding flows through me. "They choose. They always have."

One by one, the corrupted shadows break free. Patricia and Linda weave between them, easing their pain, while Finnick disrupts the last of Thorne's hold with Steve and Carl's help. Even the newest shadows join in, offering strength to their wounded kin.

The freed shadows gather around me, their gratitude and growing anger palpable. Each pulse of the Heart strengthens our connection. "Together?" I ask softly, feeling their unanimous response ripple through the air.

Every shadow moves at once, their combined power surging through the arena like a tide of liquid night. Thorne staggers back, his control shattered. Then his expression twists into something desperate and cruel.

"This little victory means nothing!" Dark energy crackles around him, tainted and wrong. "I think it's time you meet some very old friends."

The temperature plummets as darkness pools at his feet—not shadows, but something that fills me with dread. "You and your precious shadows," his voice sounds unnatural. "I wonder how they'll fare against creatures that feed on shadow itself."

Skeletal figures form in the writhing darkness, their hollow eyes burning with pale, hungry light. My shadows press closer, their movements uncertain. Even Bob ripples with unease.

"Kaia," Malrik's voice is tight with alarm. "He's drawing power from somewhere else. Something ancient."

The memories rise unbidden—of the night I first met Thorne, and that night so long ago, filled with shadows and screams and my parents' final sacrifice.

"Nightwraiths."

Chapter 69
KAIA

"Nightwraiths," I whisper, the word falling from my lips like a curse. Around me, my shadows tremble with remembered terror. These are the creatures that forced their sacrifice, that made them bind their souls to the Heart of Eternity to protect me. And now, they face that same threat again.

Mouse's growl deepens into something ancient and deadly, a sound that carries centuries of remembered battle.

"Those are—" Finn's voice cracks. "Those are the things that nearly killed us last time? The ones that literally feed on shadows?"

"Those ones," Malrik confirms grimly, his power coiling tighter around him like a shield of silver light. "But these aren't just shadow-eaters now. They're executioners, coming to finish what they started centuries ago."

The arena darkens as the torches along the walls sputter and die. But this isn't the comfortable darkness my shadows thrive in—this is something older, something wrong. The air grows and each breath becomes a struggle against invisible weight. A twisted chorus of whispers fills the space, like voices speaking in a language made of nightmares.

My shadows press closer, their movements carrying the weight of the ancient memory. Bob stands like a general preparing for a last stand. Patricia's methodical movements become sharp, precise—a warrior remembering her final battle. Even Finnick's chaos takes on a deadly purpose.

The Nightwraiths fully take shape in the corrupted darkness, their skeletal forms more solid than I remember. Hollow eyes burn with pale, hungry light as they encircle us, their movements liquid and predatory. Each one filled with Thorne's tainted magic, bound to his will in a way that makes my guardians recoil with grief and fury.

Thorne's laughter echoes unnaturally through the arena. "You thought freeing a few shadows made you powerful?" His voice drips with cruel delight. "This should be fun."

The words hit hard. My shadows move forward in protective fury, but the Nightwraiths are faster. Their claws tear through our defenses like paper, and each strike does more than drain power—it threatens to unravel the very bonds that hold their souls to mine.

"Finn!" I shout over the chaos, struggling to maintain the defensive barrier as they reform around me, refusing to yield. "We need a plan!"

"Working on it!" He hurls bursts of chaos magic at the advancing wraiths, the explosions of light creating brief gaps in their ranks. But more pour in to fill the spaces, their hunger insatiable. "But I'm pretty sure this isn't a fix-it-with-sparkles situation!"

Malrik snarls beside me, his own shadow magic surging forward to reinforce our faltering defenses. His silver eyes blaze with barely contained fury. "Focus, Kaia! They trust you—they chose you!"

"I'm trying!" Sweat beads on my forehead as I push harder, feeling the toll of each attack not just in my magic but in my soul. The Heart of Eternity hums weakly against my skin, its warmth flickering like a candle in a storm. Each time the wraiths' claws tear through my shadow's forms, I feel their pain, their determination not to fail me.

Mouse launches himself into the fray, his form growing larger with each bound. His claws tear through wraith-smoke, scattering their essence, but they reform almost instantly. Their hollow eyes fix on him with ancient malice, recognizing a guardian of shadow.

"Your shadows can't save you this time," Thorne calls, his voice thick with triumph."

The wraiths surge forward as one, a wave of hungry darkness that threatens to devour everything in its path. My shadows rise desperately to meet them, but they're overwhelmed in seconds. Bob tries to coordinate a defense while Patricia attempts to analyze their patterns, but the wraiths are too many, too strong.

I push harder, drawing deep on the Heart's power, but something's different. Instead of giving me strength, each pulse feels weaker, the wraiths are draining not just my magic but the very bonds that hold my shadows' souls.

"Kaia!" Finn's voice cracks with fear. His chaos magic flares brilliant and wild, but the wraiths absorb it like drops of water in an ocean. Malrik roars something in a language I don't understand, his silver eyes blazing as he hurls pure shadow magic into the fight.

But it's not enough. It will never be enough. Not if I keep trying to fight this alone.

The wraiths press closer, their hunger an almost physical force. My knees buckle as the last of my defenses shatter. Mouse's desperate roar fades into the background as darkness closes in.

"No!" Finn's scream feels distant, muffled by the wraiths' cold embrace. My vision darkens as they swarm me, their hunger all-consuming. I feel my shadows' desperation, their refusal to let go. But I also feel something else—their absolute faith in me, in what we could become together.

And then... silence.

Chapter 70
KAIA

Am I dying?

The thought floats through my mind, strangely peaceful. But this is not the silence of defeat, it's something deeper. A stillness settles over me like a warm blanket, lifting the weight of the wraiths' presence. The arena fades away, replaced by soft, golden light. In that light, I see them.

My mother stands before me, her golden hair shimmering like captured sunlight, and beside her, my father's tall figure radiates strength and warmth. But they're not alone. Behind them, I see other figures translucent but distinct. Warriors in ancient armor, their forms flickering between light and shadow. I recognize them, not from memory, but from soul-deep knowing. All of them, the sisters who chose to become my shadows.

"Kaia," my mother says, her voice like a melody my heart will never forget. She steps closer, and the warmth of her touch feels so real it threatens to break me. "You've been fighting so hard to protect them. To protect everyone."

"I can't—" My voice cracks. "They've already given everything for me. I can't ask for more."

"Oh, my darling." She cups my face in her hands. "They didn't bind their souls to be your burden. They chose to become part of something greater. Part of you."

My father moves closer, his presence steady and grounding. The Valkyries behind him shift, their forms becoming clearer. "They didn't sacrifice themselves to be your guardians, Kaia. They sacrificed themselves to become your strength."

"I don't understand." Tears sting my eyes as I look at the warriors—my shadows, my sisters. "How am I supposed to fight without losing more?"

"By accepting what they freely gave." My mother's own shadows float around her feet, but they move differently than mine—not as servants or even partners, but as part of her very essence. "By completing what they began."

"Watch," my father says softly. The Valkyries step forward, each one distinct now. I see Bob's fierce loyalty in the stance of a tall warrior with determined eyes. Patricia's wisdom shines in another's careful movements. Finnick's spark lives in a third's ready grin. Linda's gentle healing spirit glows in a fourth, while Carl and Steve's synchronized energy pulses from two warriors standing shoulder to shoulder. At the edge of the group stands another presence, barely visible, that sends a wave of tranquility through my chest.

"We chose this," they speak as one, their voices echoing with power and purpose. "We chose you."

My mother's hand presses against my chest, where the Heart of Eternity pulses with growing warmth. "This isn't just a source of power or a connection to the past. It's the promise they made—every one of them. Not to serve, but to become."

"The wings you feel stirring?" My father's voice deepens with emotion. "They carry the essence of every Valkyrie who chose to bind their soul to yours. Who chose to make their power yours."

Understanding floods through me like warm sunlight. All this time, I've been trying to protect them, to keep them separate, to treat them as guardians. But they didn't bind their souls to me to be protected. They did it to become part of something new—something that had never existed before.

"You're not just my shadows," I whisper, finally understanding. "You never were. You're..."

"We're your sisters," they say together, their forms beginning to fade into familiar shadow. "And we've been waiting centuries for you to truly join us."

The golden light grows brighter, but I'm not ready to let go. "Wait—there's so much more I need to know—"

"You know everything you need to." My father's voice begins to fade. "The rest, you'll learn together. All of you."

"We love you," my mother whispers. "We're so proud of who you've become. Of who you're becoming."

"Rise," they say together as the light becomes blinding. The Valkyries step forward, their forms melding back into shadow—but now I feel each one, know each one. "Rise, and remember exactly who you are."

My eyes snap open to find the wraiths still circling, their claws poised for the final strike. But something has changed. The Heart of Eternity burns against my chest, no longer weakly pulsing but blazing with ful-filled promise. My shadows—my sisters—pause in their defense, feeling the shift.

The wraiths hesitate, their hollow eyes flickering with something that might be fear. They can feel it too—the change in the air, the surge of power that feels both ancient and new.

I rise, but my feet don't touch the ground. Power courses through me, not as something to be controlled but as something shared between souls who chose each other. The Heart flares brighter, and suddenly I understand what it's been trying to tell me all along.

This isn't about borrowing power. It's about becoming what we were always meant to be.

The transformation hits like a thunderclap. Wings burst from my back in a rush of searing heat and blinding light. The pain is excruciating but pure, like breaking through a barrier that was never meant to hold. Every nerve ending screams as the wings unfurl—massive and glorious, glowing with a radiant blend of violet, gold and shadow. Their edges ripple with the essence of every Valkyrie who chose to bind their soul to mine.

But it's more than just wings. My sisters surge around me, no longer holding back. Bob's steadfast courage becomes my shield, his military precision guiding my stance. Patricia's ancient wisdom flows through my thoughts, while Finnick's undimmed spirit fuels my determination. Each one shares not just their power, but their very essence—everything they chose to become when they bound themselves to me.

The Heart of Eternity thrums in perfect time with our unified heartbeat, each pulse carrying the weight of a promise finally fulfilled. This is what it means to be a Valkyrie—not to command powers or souls, but to rise together.

The wraiths falter, their forms flickering as I spread my wings wide. The light that radiates from them isn't just light—it's truth. The perfect balance of shadow and radiance, of sacrifice and strength, of past and future.

"No," I say, my voice carrying the echo of every sister who chose this path. "We are Valkyrie." The word feels right, like coming home to a family that chose each other.

With a single, unified motion, we unleash not just power, but completion. Light and shadow intertwine, surging outward not as weapons but as proof of what willing sacrifice and chosen loyalty can become. The wraiths dissolve, their screeches fading into silence as they face something their hunger cannot comprehend—the very thing they failed to destroy centuries ago.

Perfect unity. Perfect trust. Perfect choice.

When my feet finally touch the ground, my wings fold naturally against my back, humming with the essence of my sisters. Mouse returns to his smaller form, but his violet eyes shine with pride. My shadows settle around me, no longer just guardians but family in the truest sense.

"So..." Finn breaks the weighted silence, his voice shaky but warm. "That was terrifying. And amazing. But mostly terrifying. Do the wings come with an instruction manual? Because Bob looks like he's about to start a religion."

He's not wrong—Bob hovers near him with an almost reverent air, while Patricia frantically documents everything in her swirling shadow script. They move differently now, each one's personality clearer, stronger, now that their true nature has been revealed.

"Not the time, Finn." But Malrik's silver eyes haven't left me since the transformation, and something in his gaze makes my heart skip. He sees it all—not just the power, but the understanding behind it. The way my sisters move with me now, as extensions of myself.

The Heart of Eternity glows gently against my chest, steady and sure. There's still so much I don't understand about my heritage, these wings, about what being a Valkyrie truly means. But for the first time since my shadows—my sisters—appeared, I'm not afraid of the unknown.

"This changes nothing." Thorne spits from where he lies defeated. His voice cracks with desperate fury. "You have no idea what's coming. What he has planned—"

"Save it." I cut him off, and my sisters ripple with shared conviction. Each one moves with new purpose—Bob taking a defensive stance, Patricia analyzing the scene, Finnick ready to strike. Not just shadows anymore, but warriors remembering who they are. "We'll be ready."

Thorne staggers to his feet, dark energy crackling weakly around his hands. "This isn't over," he snarls. "He's coming, and when he does—"

My sisters surge forward as one, moving with renewed purpose. But Thorne slams his staff into the ground, unleashing a final blast of corrupted magic. By the time the air clears, he's gone, leaving only a lingering trace of tainted power to mark where he stood.

"Should we go after him?" Finn asks, but Malrik shakes his head.

"He's using the old shadow paths," Malrik explains grimly. "We'd never catch him now."

A weak cough draws our attention. Darian lies crumpled against the far wall, his attempted betrayal of Thorne having cost him dearly. Blood trickles from his nose, his magic flickering erratically around him.

"Please," he whispers as we approach. "I didn't—I didn't know what he really wanted. What he was planning..."

My wings flare instinctively, casting dancing shadows across his face. But it's my sisters who make him flinch—not with their power, but with their unity, their ancient purpose. Everything he tried to document and control reduced to nothing in the face of true understanding.

"We're not going to kill you, Darian."

"No," Malrik agrees, his voice cold. "The academy has cells beneath the Archives. Ancient ones, warded against magic. The board can decide what to do with him."

Chapter 71
KAIA

When the academy guards arrive, summoned by the magical backlash of our battle, they take one look at my wings, at the visible shadows moving with clear purpose around me, and hesitate.

"Take him to the cells," Malrik commands, and something in his voice—something that sounds like generations of shadow realm authority—makes them snap to attention.

As they lead Darian away, his final whisper catches in the air: "I really did care, you know. That wasn't all a lie."

My wings draw close, not hiding me but supporting me. My sisters coil around me with gentle certainty, their touch cool and familiar. Bob pats my ankle with the awkward comfort of a warrior unused to gentleness. Patricia's frantic documentation now carries the weight of recording history. Even Finnick's chaotic movements have purpose—a soldier's readiness wrapped in levity.

"The board will want answers," Malrik says quietly. "About all of this."

"Let them ask." I watch Darian disappear into the depths of the academy. "I have nothing to hide anymore."

But as my wings settle against my back and my sisters swirl in perfect harmony, I can't help wondering: what else did Thorne take with him when he fled? And what plans was he so desperate to protect?

Looking at my shadows—at Bob's steady presence, Patricia's meticulous wisdom, at all of them who chose to become part of me—I know one thing for certain. Whatever comes next, we face it not as master and servants, not even as guardian and ward, but as what we truly are: family, bound by choice and sacrifice.

My wings might be new, but my real power has been here all along: in every sister who chose to bind their soul to mine, in every friend who chose to stand beside me. In all the different ways love becomes strength.

I am Valkyrie. And I am not alone.

I never was.

Everything feels different. The air buzzes against my skin like static, tiny sparks prickling along my arms and legs, and my shadows move with a fluid grace that feels almost alive, shifting around me like a second skin. The wings—my wings—a comforting warmth against my back, somehow both solid and ethereal, as if they exist between worlds, bound by light and shadow. They carry a weight of permanence yet feel weightless, every shift as effortless as a breeze moving through air. When I breathe, they shift with me, as natural as blinking and just as unconscious.

"You know," Finn says, his voice still shaky but trying for normal, "when I said you needed to spread your wings, this wasn't exactly what I meant."

I try to laugh, but it comes out strangled. My shadows curl around my ankles reassuringly. Bob actually pats my foot, which would be funny if I wasn't so overwhelmed.

Malrik hasn't stopped staring, his silver eyes following every movement of my wings as they shift and stretch behind me. There's something raw and unguarded in his gaze, a vulnerability I'm not used to seeing from him. He meets my eyes, his voice low and reverent. "Gods, you're beautiful."

Heat rises to my cheeks, and I fight the instinct to look away, unwilling to let the weight of his words undo me. Before I can respond, Malrik clears his throat, his composure snapping back into place. From behind us, I hear Finn's barely contained snicker, the sound breaking the tension just enough to ground me again.

Malrik's gaze flickers to the amethyst necklace glowing softly against my skin. "The Heart of Eternity," he says, his tone steadier now. "It wasn't just protecting you. It was preparing you."

"For what?" I ask, but before he can answer, an explosion rocks the arena. My wings flare instinctively, and I feel my feet leave the ground again. The sensation of hovering should terrify me, but it feels right, like remembering how to swim.

The arena doors burst inward. My heart stops when I see Aspen and Torric in the doorway, their expressions frozen in a mix of awe and disbelief. Torric's jaw tightens, his usual confidence faltering as his gaze sweeps over me and my wings, while Aspen's brows draw together, his hand gripping the doorway like it's the only thing keeping him steady. Haloed by the light from my wings, they look as shaken as I feel. I've faced down Nightwraiths, discovered my heritage, and grown actual wings, but somehow this—facing the twins with my new reality—makes my throat close with fear.

What if they see me differently now? What if this is too much, too strange, too—

"Holy shit," Torric breathes, and the raw awe in his voice makes my wings flutter nervously.

Aspen just stares, his expression making my heart skip. My shadows stay coiled tight around me, protective while Mouse brushes against my leg, a solid reminder that not everything has changed.

Torric steps forward, his usual confident stride slightly hesitant. "If you think this changes anything," he starts, and my heart clenches until he finishes, "you're right. Now I definitely can't let you out of my sight." He gives me a crooked grin, the edge of humor softening the intensity in his voice.

The laugh that bursts out of me is half relief, half hysteria. Then Aspen moves closer, and something in his careful approach makes my wings fold closer to my back, not in fear but in a strange sort of shyness.

"Still you?" he asks quietly, holding out his hand. His blue eyes search mine, steady and unflinching, like he's trying to anchor me to the moment.

I take it, and his fingers are warm and steady against mine. A tether to the ground when everything else feels like it might float away.

"Still me," I manage, my voice barely more than a whisper. "Just... with some upgrades."

Aspen squeezes my hand lightly, the smallest gesture, but it feels like he's saying, *I see you. I'm here.*

"Upgrades," Torric snorts beside me, but I catch the faintest smile tugging at the corner of his mouth. "That's what we're calling divine transformation now?"

My wings shift, catching the light like stained glass. My shadows—brilliant and vivid—move with deliberate purpose around me. Bob stands at attention like a tiny general, Patricia frantically records every detail in shadow script, while Finnick darts around with exaggerated energy, testing the new balance of the group. I can't help but smile at their antics, the way they seem to reflect the new harmony settling in my chest.

Chapter 72
KAIA

"Not to ruin the whole goddess glow thing," Finn says, his grin as bright as ever, "but does anyone else think Bob's about to start demanding a promotion?"

The laugh that escapes me is shaky but real, grounding me in the moment. He steps closer, and my wings flutter in response, casting fractured patterns of light and shadow across the stone floor.

A memory flashes through me—my mother's wings, golden and brilliant, sheltering me as she whispered ancient words. My own wings draw close instinctively, mirroring that long-ago protection. The force of the memory makes me stumble, the bittersweet ache in my chest almost too much to bear.

Finn's strong arms catch me before I can fall. The warmth of his touch anchors me to the present, reminding me that I'm not lost in memories of what was. I'm here, with them.

"Kaia?" Multiple voices call out in concern, but it's Aspen steady presence that calms me, his hand still anchoring mine. My shadows curl around both of them, as if trying to hold onto this moment.

"I remember," I whisper, my wings trembling with the weight of memory. "Not everything, but... pieces. My mother—she had wings like mine, but golden. She used to shield me with them when I was scared."

The Heart of Eternity radiates warmth against my chest, as if encouraging the memory. Mouse presses against my leg, and I feel his silent support. Bob attempts to comfort me by patting my head while Patricia records every detail of the memory in her shadow notes.

"The memories will come," Malrik says, stepping closer. "The Heart protected them, just like it protected you."

"Yeah, well, next time maybe a warning before the whole divine revelation thing?" Finn suggests, but his hand finds mine, completing a circuit between me, him, and Aspen that sends warmth flowing through my wings. "Some of us have weak hearts," Finn says, his grin returning as if to prove otherwise. "And by 'some,' I mean me—just in case you were wondering."

"Speak for yourself," Torric growls, but he hasn't moved from his protective stance near us. His energy hums in sync with my new power, like complementary notes in a song.

My wings stretch slightly, unconsciously trying to encompass all of them. The gesture feels instinctive, like my body remembers what my mind doesn't—that Valkyries were protectors, guardians. My shadows respond in kind, creating a loose circle around our group, with Bob taking point like a tiny commander.

"So," I say, aiming for casual despite the power thrumming through my veins and my shadows' obvious pride, "anyone want to help me figure out how to get through doorways with these things? Because I have a feeling the academy's architect didn't plan for wingspan."

A sharp knock at the entry makes us all turn. Professor Lira stands in the doorway, her usual calm demeanor tight with urgency.

"The board has convened an emergency session," Lira says, stepping inside. Her silver eyes take in my wings with a mix of awe and concern, her fingers gripping the edge of the doorway tightly, as if bracing herself. The tension in her posture matches the urgency in her voice, a rare crack in her usual calm demeanor. "They're demanding answers."

"Now?" My wings twitch nervously, and I feel my shadows coil closer. "Do they have any idea what just happened?"

Her eyes flick to the shadows swirling at my feet before meeting mine, her tone softening slightly. "They want answers, Kaia. And they won't wait. The magical backlash from your transformation triggered every ward in the academy," Lira explains. "The board is... unsettled."

"Unsettled?" Finn snorts. "Our friend here sprouts divine wings, kicks some serious wraith behind, and they're 'unsettled'?"

"Lady Virath is leading the session," Lira says grimly. "She's already calling for immediate action."

Alenya's mother. Of course. My shadows ripple with unease, and Mouse's tail puffs up. Even Bob seems to bristle.

"What kind of action?" Aspen asks quietly, moving closer to me.

"They're talking about binding your power," Lira says directly to me. "Possibly expulsion. They're afraid, and fear makes people dangerous."

Torric growls low in his throat. "Let them try."

"No," I say, surprising myself with how steady my voice sounds. "If they want answers, we'll give them answers. All of us."

"The board won't like that," Lira warns. "They prefer to interview subjects alone."

"Too bad," Torric says, moving to stand beside me. His berserker energy hums in sync with my new power. "We go together."

"Together." Aspen adds, quiet but firm.

Malrik's silver eyes narrow thoughtfully, but he says nothing. I catch something calculating in his expression - he's seeing pieces of a game I don't fully understand yet.

The walk to the Celestial Chamber feels like walking to judgment. Students press against the walls, their wide eyes filled with fear and curiosity. Whispers flow through the crowd, sharp and hurried, like leaves rustling in a storm. Some glance at my wings with awe; others avert their gaze entirely, as if afraid to meet my eyes. My wings cast shifting patterns of light and shadow across the stone floors.

The chamber lives up to its name. The circular room beneath the academy gleams with enchanted constellations that spiral across the domed ceiling, their luminous trails shifting in fluid, mesmerizing patterns. The acoustics amplify even the faintest sound, making each breath and footstep echo softly. The light from the constellations dances across the polished stone floor, casting ethereal reflections that seem to shift and shimmer as though alive. The stars twinkle faintly, casting a soft, ethereal glow that seems to change as if the constellations themselves were alive, watching. Seven ornate chairs face a single stone platform in the center. Six are occupied - the Shadow Faction's seat stands conspicuously empty.

Lady Virath rises first, her white robes pristine, her golden hair—so like Alenya's—pulled back severely. Her posture is rigid, shoulders squared as though bracing against a storm, and her sharp gaze sweeps the room, landing on my wings with barely concealed horror.

"This is highly irregular," she says, her voice sharp. "The accused should come alone."

I feel my wings spread slightly, responding to the tension in the room. My shadows stay close, protective but not threatening. When I step onto the platform, I make sure to meet each board member's eyes.

"You want to know what happened in the arena," I say clearly. "You want to know what I am. I'll tell you. But first, you need to understand what Thorne was really doing here. What he was preparing for."

Looks of disbelief and anger are shared among the council. An older man in blue robes speaks "Professor Thorne has been an outstanding member of faculty for many years. We do not appreciate accusations against him without proof."

The recording crystals floating around the chamber pulse with light, capturing everything. I take a deep breath and feel my friends' presence behind me, solid and unwavering.

"That is the proof." I state, pointing at one of the crystals. My voice carries with a power that surprises even me. I hear a scoff from the council but can't place who it came from.

Before I can get another word out, Lady Virath interrupts. "Enough. We will review the crystals and reconvene in three days time." Her tone brooking no argument.

Frustration bubbles up, and my shadows react instantly - Bob actually looks offended while Patricia's note-taking becomes distinctly aggressive. But when Aspen puts a calming hand on my shoulder, I keep my mouth shut. Mouse presses against my leg, a low growl building in his throat.

Lady Virath's dismissal is clear, but as we turn to leave, I catch Malrik's gaze lingers on the empty chair, a flicker of something sharp—calculation, or maybe recognition—crossing his silver eyes.

Chapter 73
KAIA

The Chamber's doors close behind us with an echoing finality. My wings shift restlessly, responding to my unease, while my shadows cluster close. Bob maintains what he probably thinks is a subtle defensive formation, his shadowy form darting between positions like surveying the battlefield.

"Well," Finn says, breaking the tense silence, "that could have gone worse."

"How exactly?" Torric growls.

"They could have tried to arrest us. Or exorcise us. Though honestly, I'd love to see them try to exorcise Bob. He'd probably organize their banishing circles more efficiently."

The shadow in question straightens importantly, and I have to bite back a laugh despite the situation. But before I can respond, a figure emerges from a shadowed alcove.

"Kaia." Lira's voice is quiet but urgent. "All of you. Come with me. Quickly."

Something in her tone makes my shadows tense. Even Finnick's usual chaos stills as we follow her down a narrow corridor I've never noticed before, away from the main halls.

The passage opens into a small circular chamber, its walls covered in softly glowing runes that pulse faintly in rhythmic patterns, as though alive. The symbols shimmer with hues of gold and silver, casting ethereal reflections that dance across the smooth stone floor. The air hums with quiet power, each rune exuding an aura of ancient purpose, amplifying the gravity of the moment. Lira touches one and the entrance seals behind us, the magic humming with ancient power.

"We don't have much time," she says, turning to face me. Her silver eyes fixed on where my wings pulse in that other plane. "The board will review the crystals, but Lady Virath... she's not looking for answers. She's looking for confirmation."

"Of what?" Malrik asks sharply.

"That Kaia is exactly what she fears. What Alekir has been waiting for."

The name sends a chill through me. The Heart of Eternity almost vibrates in response, and another memory surfaces—my mother's voice, low and melodic, singing ancient lullabies about warriors who walked between realms. Her tone was both soothing and powerful, each note wrapping around me like a warm embrace, filling me with a sense of safety and awe.

"The Heart," I whisper, my fingers finding the amethyst at my throat. "It's not just for my protection, is it?"

"No." Lira's expression softens with something like grief. "Your mother—Solveig—she knew this day would come. The Heart wasn't just protecting you, Kaia. It was preparing you."

Malrik hums quietly with the knowledge he was right.

Dammit.

A hand squeezes my shoulder in comfort. I'm not even sure who it is, but I know I can't dwell right now. I shake my head as if clearing my thoughts, looking back at Lira. "For what?" But even as I ask, I feel the truth settling into my bones.

"The Valkyrie weren't just warriors," Lira explains. "They were guardians of the gates between realms. Every door, every threshold where one world bleeds into another—they kept the balance."

"Until Alekir," Malrik says, his silver eyes sharp with understanding. There's something in his voice—a weight of knowledge that makes my shadows stir uneasily.

"Until Alekir," Lira confirms, and the name seems to darken the very air. "He didn't just want to cross between realms. He wanted to break down the walls completely. To let chaos reign."

Mouse growls softly, and my shadows coil tighter. Bob forms what looks like a battle plan in shadowy script, while Patricia's note-taking becomes almost frantic. The newest shadows, barely formed wisps of darkness, press closer to their more experienced siblings, seeking reassurance.

"My parents stopped him?" I ask, though it feels more like a statement.

Lira nods, her silver eyes glinting with a mix of sorrow and admiration. "Solveig and Idris. Your mother and father were chosen for what they represented, light and shadow. The Heart of Eternity bound them together, not by love at first, but by duty. Their union was the key to sealing the gates Alekir tried to shatter."

I frown, the weight of her words settling heavily in my chest. "So it cost them everything?"

"It cost them their choice," Lira corrects gently. "Their bond wasn't their decision, it was their burden. But over time, they found something deeper. They fell in love, not because of the Heart's will, but despite it. And from that love, you were born."

Her voice softens, carrying an ache that feels centuries old. "Your mother hoped for a different future for you. One where you could be free to follow your heart, make your own choices, and live freely in a way she never could."

My shadows twist tighter, and Mouse's purr rumbles softly as he brushes against my ankle. "So she died trying to protect that future. To give me the chance to choose."

"Yes," Lira says, her voice a whisper. "To save the realms, yes, but also to give you the freedom she was denied."

"She knew it wouldn't last forever," Lira continues softly. "That's why she chose me—to watch over you, to help prepare you for when the seals began to fail."

The weight of it threatens to overwhelm me, but Finn's hand finds mine, grounding me. "No pressure or anything," he says lightly. "Just multi-realm-saving destiny. Totally normal Tuesday."

A laugh bubbles up despite everything. My shadows relax slightly, and even Bob breaks his militant pose to what I swear is an eye roll. The moment feels almost normal—just us, together, facing the impossible.

Until the temperature plummets.

My wings shift with warning just as the sealed entrance shatters in a flash of searing white light. The sound is wrong—not just loud, but discordant, like reality itself protesting.

Lady Virath stands in the doorway, her pristine robes crackle with an aura that doesn't belong here, and her eyes—too deep and too empty—seem to devour the light, leaving only a hollow chill in their wake. When she smiles, the expression doesn't touch those empty eyes.

"I wondered where you'd slither off to," she says, her voice carrying an echo that doesn't belong in this realm. "Always interfering, Lira. Always trying to delay the inevitable."

"The only thing inevitable," Lira says steadily, "is that you'll fail. Just like he did."

Lady Virath's laugh scrapes against my skin like broken glass, jagged and sharp, leaving an almost tangible sting in its wake. It carries a chilling resonance, as though the sound itself were imbued with malice, twisting the air around us. "Failed? Oh, you fool. He never failed. He was waiting. And now..."

The air warps, rippling like a mirage, but colder—unnatural, as though the fabric of reality is unraveling at the seams.. Through every shadow in the room, I see it—glimpses of another plane where a figure of smoke and malice stands behind Lady Virath, his form shifting between shapes but his eyes burning with ancient hunger.

The Heart of Eternity flares with golden light, and suddenly I understand. "The board meeting," I breathe. "The crystals. You wanted proof that I could access the gates."

"Very good, little Valkyrie." Lady Virath's smile stretches too wide. "Your mother may have sealed them, but you... you're the key to unlocking them all."

My shadows surge up as one, and my wings burst open in a flash of violent light. Mouse grows larger, his violet eyes blazing, while Bob assembles the others into perfect formation.

But Lady Virath doesn't flinch. If anything, her smile widens. "Do you really think your parlor tricks can stop what's coming? The seals are already weakening. Even now, he bleeds through the cracks between worlds."

As if in response, the shadows around us shudder. Through them, I glimpse the other plane—a figure towering over all, wreathed in shifting smoke that seems to consume itself, his outline flickering like an unfinished nightmare. His presence feels vast and boundless, pressing against the edges of reality, a storm of chaos waiting to break free.

"We've prepared for this," Lady Virath continues, her voice distorting further. "For you. The final key."

She raises her hands, and reality ripples again. Through the walls, through every shadow and dark corner, I feel them coming. Nightwraiths. Dozens of them. Hundreds. An army of darkness pressing against the thin barriers between worlds.

"The gates will open," she says, her voice carrying His echo now. "The realms will bleed together. And you, Kaia Draven, will be the one to break the seals your mother and father put in place. Her choice, her death—it will have been for nothing."

Thank You

First things first—thank you.

If you made it all the way to the end of *Shadows of Change*, I'm ridiculously grateful. This book has been a journey. A messy, emotional, chaotic, magic-drenched journey—and I'm so glad you were here for it. Whether you laughed at Finn's ridiculous commentary, rolled your eyes at Malrik's brooding, or found yourself strangely invested in the shadow army (Bob appreciates your support), thank you for reading. It means more than you know.

But Kaia's story is just beginning.

Book Two, *Shadows Rising*, picks up right where we leave off—with higher stakes, deeper bonds, and yes... all the smut you didn't get in Book One. Because you deserve it. The shadows are growing restless, the pattern is shifting, and the Heart of Eternity has plans of its own. Buckle up.

If you're also reading my other series, *The Ether Chronicles*, you'll know that while these worlds are separate, they share some familiar themes: magic that bites back, characters who don't always make the right choices, and love that refuses to fit into neat little boxes. There's no ether in Kaia's world—but there are secrets buried deep, and a history that's ready to change everything.

If you want to stay in the loop on upcoming releases, bonuses, or exclusive chaos from Bob, you can find me at ZoraStone.com, or hang out with me on social media @ZoraStoneAuthor. I'm usually there avoiding deadlines.

Once again—thank you for reading, for believing, and for letting Kaia's world take up space in your imagination.

We're just getting started.

—Zora Stone

Acknowledgements

Mom, I did it!

ABOUT THE AUTHOR

Zora Stone writes steamy fantasy romance where magic has attitude, found family matters as much as found love, and humor is the secret ingredient in every spell. A lifelong dreamer with a wild imagination and a serious coffee addiction, she believes the best stories happen when magic collides with reality, and romance sneaks in through the cracks.

When she's not conjuring tales of magical mayhem and emotionally complicated relationships, you'll find her negotiating with her cats (who insist the keyboard is their throne), debating the wisdom of "just one more chapter," or reminding her family that ice cream counts as dinner.

Zora lives in the Midwest with her husband, two kids, three judgmental cats, and an ever-growing collection of half-empty coffee mugs.

ALSO BY ZORA STONE

The Ether Chronicles

Crown of the Mist
Into the Ether
Ashen Oath
Veil of Echoes
Shattering the Void
To the Final End

Arcanum Academy

Shadows of Change
Shadows Rising
Shadows Found
Shadows Revealed

www.ingramcontent.com/pod-product-compliance
Lightning Source LLC
Chambersburg PA
CBHW030909300726
48970CB00001B/76